NO KNIGHT

OTHER TITLES BY DONNA ALAM

My Kind of Hero

No Romeo

No Saint

The Whittingtons

The Interview

The Gamble

No Ordinary Men

No Ordinary Gentleman

Love + Other Lies

Before Him

One Night Forever

Liar Liar

Never Say Forever

Love in London

To Have and Hate
(Not) The One
The Stand Out

Phillips Brothers

In Like Flynn
Down Under
Rafferty's Rules

Great Scots

Hard
Easy
Hardly Easy

Hot Scots

One Hot Scot
One Wicked Scot

One Dirty Scot

Single Daddy Scot

Hot Scots Collection (boxed set)

Surprise Scot

Surprise Package

And More!

Soldier Boy

Playing His Games

Gentleman Player

NO KNIGHT

·MY KIND OF HERO·

DONNA ALAM

Montlake

This is a work of fiction. Names, characters, organizations, places, events, and incidents are either products of the author's imagination or are used fictitiously. Otherwise, any resemblance to actual persons, living or dead, is purely coincidental.

Text copyright © 2025 by Donna Alam
All rights reserved.

No part of this book may be reproduced, or stored in a retrieval system, or transmitted in any form or by any means, electronic, mechanical, photocopying, recording, or otherwise, without express written permission of the publisher.

Published by Montlake, Seattle

www.apub.com

Amazon, the Amazon logo, and Montlake are trademarks of Amazon.com, Inc., or its affiliates.

EU Product Safety contact:
Amazon Publishing, Amazon Media EU S.à r.l.
38, avenue John F. Kennedy, L-1855 Luxembourg
amazonpublishing-gpsr@amazon.com

ISBN-13: 9781662521065
eISBN-13: 9781662521072

Cover design by @blacksheep-uk.com
Cover photography by Michelle Lancaster

Printed in the United States of America

How often is happiness destroyed by preparation, foolish preparation!
—Jane Austen

Chapter 1
MATT

"I blame romance novels."

"They're not mine." I pause at the crosswalk and glance at the dusky sky as though seeking divine intervention. "I told you, my sister left them when she stayed over." It's not exactly a lie. Fat lot of use they've been, anyway.

"You're too nice for your own good," Fin continues, clearly on a roll. "And that is not a compliment."

From him, it's a bigger compliment than he realizes.

"Who in the hell goes to an ex's wedding and expects to have a good time?"

Me, obviously, I think as the light changes, and I step out among the tourists and native New Yorkers. My gaze connects with that of a striking blond coming the other way before her eyes drop admiringly over my tux. But I'm not in the mood. Not for women, and not for this conversation.

"I didn't realize she invited me to insult me," I insist. "I thought we'd parted on good terms."

"Was it an insult, though?"

"Well, I've been called a *ride* once or twice in my time," I say, leaning into my Irish accent. "But hearing I'm the boyfriend equivalent of training wheels isn't quite the same. Worse, she might be right."

"Huh?"

"Fin, the last three women I've dated *have* gone on to marry the fella after me."

"So you're like . . . a foster boyfriend. The one before they find their forever homes."

I pinch the bridge of my nose, beyond frustrated. *How the hell he has a wife, I'll never understand.* "Look," I grate out. "The day is done. Over with. All I want to do now is turn off my brain and have a drink."

"I like that plan. Saturday night, a hotel bar. May the odds be in your favor."

"I'm not going to the hotel bar." One hand sunk deep in my pocket, I scoot sideways between two teenagers engrossed in their phones.

"Pretty sure the saying is *Misery loves company* . . . not *Misery loves the minibar.*"

"I just want a drink," I mutter. "Not a lecture."

"Here's a revolutionary idea. Why not a drink and a little company?"

"You're a gobshite." I mutter the uncomplimentary epithet as I turn into a quieter side street, away from the hustle and bustle.

"You deserve to let off some steam. Treat yo'self, as the kids say."

"I'm not in the mood."

"You're definitely in *a* mood."

"Look, I'm over one-night stands."

"Said no man ever."

"I am who I am," I grumble, trying to keep a lid on my worsening mood.

"And like I said, you're *nice*."

Fuck it, maybe he's right. I have just spent the afternoon doing and saying all the right things. I pressed my lips to the cheek of a woman I once passionately kissed, shook hands with and congratulated the man she kisses now. I danced with mothers and grannies, toasted love and marriage, and fixed on a smile until my cheeks fuckin' hurt.

All because I'm a decent fella.

A nice guy all out of nice right now.

"What I feel like right now is getting *nice* and drunk in a place where the windows are dirty, the floors are scuffed, and there are pretzels on the bar that you wouldn't touch with a ten-foot barge pole."

"You do you, booboo. But it's more fun when you do someone else."

"Where the beer is cold," I say, talking over him, "and the people mind their own feckin' business."

"Oh, subtle, Matías."

"Subtle doesn't work on you."

"As the only married man between us, I really think you ought to pay more attention to the things I say. Maybe we should get you one of those cute bracelets with the beads and 'WWFD.'"

What Would Fin Do.

"So I can do the opposite?"

"Listen, if you want to settle down, you've gotta put yourself out there!"

Right now, I feel more like putting my fist in his face. It's just as well he's a couple of continents away.

"Besides, hotel bar, dive bar. Doesn't matter. You'll have to feign laryngitis because you know what that accent does to women, especially over there. Panties dropping left and right! Add in the James Bond getup, and they'll be like bees to a honey pot."

"There won't be a woman under sixty where I'm heading."

"Big panties, then." The bastard laughs. "Except it's Saturday night," he adds in an all-knowing and very fucking annoying tone. "Which means the ladies will come tottering out on their spiky heels in short, short dresses, looking for cheap pre-drinks before they hit the cocktail bars."

God give me strength . . .

"And who knows, maybe among that crowd is the girl for you, dreaming of a house in the burbs and a half dozen snot-nosed kids. It could all start tonight."

Reaching my destination, I put my hand to the door handle and pause as an image of just that flashes in my head. Love and family. It's what we were put on the earth for, surely. "Don't know what you're talking about." I yank on the door handle, my mood not improved.

The interior is dark and the place pretty quiet, just a few old fellas hunched over glasses at the bar or staring up at TVs playing a game I've no interest in. The bartender turns, acknowledging me with a nod. I was here yesterday. He knows what I'm drinking.

"Come on, Matías. There's beauty in the spontaneous. Even magic sometimes."

"How's this for magic," I say, already pulling the phone from my ear. "Watch as I make you disappear." And I do just that as I end the call.

I don't need this from him. I already have a sister and a mother hounding me about my love life.

Ma: *Why can't you find yourself a nice girl, Matías?*

Leticia: *How come you're the only one of your friends not married?*

Ma: *Such a handsome face* (while she squeezes the cheeks from my skull). *Why does no one else love it?*

"Jaysus," I mutter. Slotting away my phone, I rub my hand over my taut jaw. I think I must be really feckin' nice to put up with Fin's bullshit.

I wasn't lying. I am over casual relationships, one-night stands, and booty calls. I don't want to wake up next to some woman whose name I can't remember and hustle her out the door before she realizes, making us both feel like shit. And I can't admit to Fin that I'm envious of him. I mean, I'm happy for him, but I reckon I'm also allowed to feel a bit sorry for myself.

What I want is forever. *The fairy tale,* I think with a derisive snort.

I'm so lost in the bog of my thoughts that I don't immediately realize someone has stepped between me and the bar. At least, not until something hits me in the center of my chest.

"What the . . ."

My first thought is to offer an apology—*Sorry, I didn't see you there on account of you being the size of a flea.* But I don't get to do that, as she opens her mouth and declares loudly and very pointedly:

"You're late."

Chapter 2
MATT

"I'm sorry?"

My gaze slices up from the slender hand and perfectly manicured nails to find fierce blue eyes on mine. Typical man that I am, I take a quick but thorough inventory of the serious—and seriously pretty—woman currently accosting me. She's tiny and angry looking, like a bantam rooster. Striking like one too. Her hair is dark, glossy, and expertly styled. Jade-colored silk skims generous curves, her lips are painted plum, and her cheeks are highlighted by a subtle but shimmery hint. Sure, she's a tiny but pretty package. Though she's not happy about . . . something.

"We agreed to meet at seven, and even that was pushing it."

Pretty. Feisty. And confused.

My answer is a startled cough as she grabs my wrist and turns in the direction of the door, her wrap dress flaring to reveal a flash of toned, tan leg. Though her fingers and thumb don't meet, she's got some grip on her as she tries to tug me along. *Tries* being the operative word.

She makes a noise of frustration as her attention swings abruptly back. Something flickers in her expression, and I get the sense she changes her response a split second before the words leave her mouth.

"Glad to see the suit turned out okay." Her tone is almost begrudging as her gaze flicks over me. "The cuff links are a nice touch."

"Thanks?" I think?

"Tiffany knockoffs?"

"Graff, actually." And not knockoffs, thank you very much.

Her gaze lifts from the white gold knot, and as our eyes meet, something electric slides down my spine. It feels like recognition, not that we've met before and not that I have time to ponder the effect as she flicks the cuff link with her nail.

"Just don't expect me to cough up for them. I don't care if you did pick 'em up cheap on Canal Street."

"They were a gift," I find myself answering. As though I need to defend myself.

"Whatever."

I feel oddly bereft as she turns away again. Bereft and bewildered and wondering if I should put my free hand over my watch—it's worth more than my cuff links—but she's dressed too expensively to be a thief or scammer. And too tastefully to be touting for business in a dive bar, if you know what I mean.

"Come *on*, I don't have all night!" She tugs again, harder this time.

I catch the bartender watching our exchange. He looks more entertained than worried for my safety. I give a rueful shrug as though this sort of shit happens to me all the time.

"Listen, love," I say, ducking my head and keeping my voice low and soft. Kind, I suppose, though she doesn't look like she's escaped from the funny farm. "I think you're mistaking me for someone else." *Think* my arse, but it costs nothing to be polite.

"Is that an Irish accent?" Her lip curls in distaste, and it would seem discretion is not in her wheelhouse, given the lack of modulation in her tone. But at least she lets go of my wrist. Like it disgusts her.

"What of it?" My response wavers with amusement. I'd love to know why we're having this conversation and why this tiny, angry woman is trying to kidnap me from a pub. And so much for Fin's claim as to the knicker-dropping quality of my accent.

To give Fin his due, I've generally found women in the US to be more receptive when I open my mouth. I've lost count of the number of times I've heard "Oh, you're Irish? That's so cool! I have a little Irish in me too." *And as the old joke goes, they're often keen to have a little more in them before the end of the night.*

"You're supposed to be Spanish," the tiny bantam accuses, angrily tapping her beaded clutch against her thigh. "Why the hell put it in your bio if you're not?"

Well now, that's a coincidence, because I am Spanish. And Irish. Or a bit of a mutt, given I have one parent of each. But there's no need to say any of this. Not when she's obviously confused me for someone she's swiped right on. I'm not one for the dating apps, myself.

"Like I said, you've confused me—"

"Don't think you can back out now. Or screw any more money out of me."

"Money?" My brows jump almost to my hairline. There isn't usually an exchange of funds on a dating app. Unless it's some kind of fetish one, maybe? She is a tiny, bossy thing, and though that's kind of hot, I've no intention of spending the night having spiked heels applied to my ball sack. *Even if she has paid for the privilege.*

"I already paid for the suit. And your cab fare." She pierces me with the kind of look that might make a lesser man—or a less amused one—wither. "I knew I should've gone the professional route."

What the fuck? I become conscious of the bartender's straining ears as he sets my beer and whiskey chaser on the bar. So I take her wrist this time and move us a few steps away, ignoring how my hand looks giant sized on her.

"You mean, like, an escort?" I ask quietly.

"No, like a plumber," she snipes, still with the volume as she snatches her arm back. Though I will note the tiny contradiction in the pink flush across her chest.

I rub my hand across my mouth, mainly to hide my amusement. It's none of my business what she gets up to. But also, no fucking way! Why the hell would a woman as gorgeous as her need to hire a man for . . . whatever she's hired him for.

Even if it is a testicle stomping.

"You think that's funny?" she demands, placing her hand to the curve of her jutted hip, full of piss and vinegar and *don't fuck with me* attitude. "Of course you think it's funny. Because *you* don't live in the real world, bless your heart." She points an accusing finger over her tiny clutch. "You cuddle housewives for a living and pass it off as therapy!"

"I . . ." I didn't even know that was a thing.

"I should've listened to my gut, not Ava. 'It'll be cheaper,'" she adds in a breathy whine, presumably impersonating whoever Ava is. "'Carl says he'll give you a discount on the Cuddle Collective hourly rate. He's a decent guy.'" One dark, elegant brow lifts, full of derision. "But what Ava failed to mention is that Carl is unreliable, that he isn't really Spanish, that he lives in fucking Bushwick, and that he doesn't even own a suit!"

"This *is* my suit." Out of all the charges laid against me, I'm not sure why this is the one I choose to answer.

"Then why did I Venmo you money while you were standing in Abe's Formal Wear? You know what? I don't care. Carl from the Cuddle Collective might be cheaper, but if I'd hired an escort, at least I might get fucked at the end of the night, instead of just fucked over!"

"True story."

"Excuse me?" comes her combative retort.

"Always hire the right man for the job. That's my motto." I temper my amusement, entertained beyond belief. I can't remember a conversation I've found quite so . . . engaging. Or a woman I've found quite so fierce. Especially for one so small. After the day I've had, I'll take enjoyment where I can find it.

"Really?" she snipes.

"I can see the benefits, especially for a woman. Discretion springs to mind. Safety. Pleasure." And apparently, I have a motto now. "As for Carl . . ." My words trail off as I give my head a sorry shake. I am kinda sorry I'm not Carl right now.

Her eyes move to the bar behind, maybe noticing my drinks, her words turning hesitant. "You're really not Carl?"

"And this isn't a suit from Abe's Formal Wear."

Consternation knits her brow before her gaze moves over my tux. When her eyes eventually lift, I see the wind has been knocked from her blustery sails.

"My name's Matt."

"Shit," she says, bringing a hand to her forehead. Her eyes moisten, and she goes from angry to upset in a couple of blinks. "This cannot be happening. Not today."

"I'm sure Carl will be along," I offer, because here's the thing: I can't deal with tearful women. I don't mean that in the emotionally repressive, übermasculine bullshit way. Crying women just happen to be my kryptonite—being around them turns me inside out.

If a shrink ever got their hands on me, I'm sure they'd find the root cause is my three sisters and a horde of female cousins. That lot seemed to work out very early on that if they teared up in front of me, I'd give them anything they wanted. My Spider-Man figures to marry their Barbies, a live model to practice their makeup skills on, the last gingersnap in the jar, as well as the lifelong blame for smashing the TV screen with a hurley.

"Carl isn't coming," she says as her bottom lip sets to wobbling. "He's almost an hour late already. I can't believe I've been scammed by a jerk who cuddles housewives for a living!"

"I wonder if they've any vacancies."

"This is the worst," she says, appearing not to hear me. "All because I didn't want to hire a professional." Her watery eyes rise to mine. "It felt like a step too far. Too skeevy, maybe?"

"Right." I give a solemn nod and try to ignore the hollow sensation in my chest. No way anyone as lovely looking as her should need to hire a bloke for . . . whatever she was hiring him for. Not that I'm offering. As pretty as she is, all sad and interesting, and as hot and fiery as she was a few minutes ago, she might still be a few Cheerios short of a full fuckin' bowl!

"Oh, my God, what a mess. What an absolute disaster."

"I'm sure it's not as bad as all that," I find myself offering as a tear slides down her cheek.

Ah, now. Don't feckin' cry!

"It's worse. Worse than you could ever imagine," she answers pitifully.

"There now." I put my hands to her shoulders and maneuver us to a nearby table. "There's nothing in the world that can't be mended," I add, sounding like my granny as I press her down into a chair.

"How about trust? Or a person's soul?"

Fuck me, that was a bit dramatic. "Here." I quickly swipe up my whiskey from the bar and push the glass into her hands. "Drink this. It'll make you feel better."

She puts the glass to her lips, and—news flash—it does not make her feel better. It doesn't make me feel better either as she begins to cough and splutter, tears rolling freely down her face now.

"Oh, my God. That is the worst thing I've ever tasted." She stares at the glass in her hand with something like horror. "What the hell is it?"

"Irish whiskey." Who on this earth has never had a drop of the good stuff?

"Tastes like ass."

"It does not taste like ass. And I would know. I've tasted a lot of—"

"Ass?"

"Whiskey," I retort with a frown. "I've tasted enough whiskey to know what you have there is premium."

"If you say so."

"I do." I'm not normally so easily offended on behalf of my people. *Half* of my people. Whatever. I move to the bar and shove a fifty down in exchange for the shot and my pint before turning back to a pitiful sight.

"Ah, darlin'. Don't cry." I put my glass on the table as my stomach sinks.

"I'm not crying. It's the whiskey."

"That was fast. You've usually got to drink at least half a bottle before the tears start."

"I'm supposed to be at a wedding." Her shoulders rise and fall with a deep breath.

Pushing aside the coincidence, I down a good portion of my beer. She's not the only one in need of a drink, and that news doesn't exactly help. But because I'm not a complete dick, I crouch down in front of her and take her hands in mine. "Supposed to be?"

"My ex is getting married," she whispers. "*Will* be married by now."

"Ah."

"I'm not crying," she says, oblivious to the obvious as her shoulders begin to tremble again. "Not over him. I never cry. Unless—oh, my God. Maybe this is what happens when you have ten years of tears stored inside you. Why is this happening now? I'd rather store them as cankles than have this happen now!"

"Come on. There now." Jesus God, I sound like my sister soothing her little one. "I'm sure it's not as bad as all that."

"You wouldn't believe me if I told you," she retorts, shaking her head, her words all blubbery and wet. "Months of planning, for it to come to this."

Whoever said crying girls are attractive needs their head examined.

"Hush now," I say a little harsher, changing tack yet still borrowing my sister's parental tone. The one she uses when little Clodagh is overwrought. "No good can come from getting yourself in this state."

"What the fuck would you know?" she says, snatching away her hands.

"What do I know?" Not much, apparently. Because as my brain tries to formulate an answer, my mouth takes the opportunity to become an independent contractor. "Only that I'm exactly the kind of man to get you out of this."

Chapter 3
MATT

Maybe there is something about crying girls after all.

"Wait." She tilts her head, her pretty eyes so blue and so glossy. "What?"

"What?" Hang on—that wasn't the reaction I was expecting. I mentally play back my words, but before I can clarify—and by *clarify*, I mean backtrack the fuck away from this at a million miles an hour—her eyes widen and her expression morphs with understanding.

"You mean you're, like, a professional?"

Or *misunderstanding*, I should say.

"Well, I guess, but—"

"So that's what you meant when you said you'd tasted a lot of ass."

"Yes. Wait, no. I didn't say that."

"I'm not judging. Paid or not, you clearly *get* a lot of ass." Her eyes roam over me sort of speculatively.

"Thank you, I think." I feel my expression flicker. This is the most bizarre conversation ever. "But that's not—"

"Oh, my God." She grabs for my hands and holds them between us. "This is amazing!"

"Is it?"

"Divine intervention for sure! Thank you—thank you so much," she adds, her gaze tipping to the ceiling. "I mean, I'll obviously pay you. For your time. And only for your time. I mean, it's been a minute . . ."

A minute since she . . . had a ride?

Confirmation comes as her eyes drop to my crotch.

What in the name of all that is holy! She actually thinks I'm a male escort? I don't know if I should be flattered or horrified.

What Would Fin Do? I hear that bastard's voice in my ear like he's standing behind me, whispering over my shoulder—I hear it so clearly, in fact, that I glance at my wrist, half expecting to see a beaded bracelet there. I know exactly what Fin would do, the feckin' opportunist, because his emotional depths run as deep as a yogurt pot. Premarriage, anyway.

"Listen," I say, starting again. "I think we've got our wires crossed. When I said I'm the kind of man to get you out of this, I didn't mean physically." Not that I'm not tempted. Physically. What man wouldn't be? Feisty, fiery, and as hot as fuck, she's a regular pocket rocket, this one.

"'Always hire the right man for the job.' You said that was your motto. And the right man is you."

"That's not exactly what I said." Though it kind of is. "Look, I'm not . . ." Fuck, I can't even say it, the idea is so ridiculous. "What I meant was—what I *know is* you won't miss out on anything by not going to the wedding." My response sounds harsher than I mean it to, and because my knees are starting to ache, I take the seat next to hers.

"It's not like I want to go," she murmurs, dabbing her eyes with her fingertips.

"Then you don't have a problem. Don't go." I rest my arm on the table next to my pint.

15

"You don't understand. I've got to be there."

"Maybe you think you do, but take my advice—it's better you stay well away." I reach for my glass, maybe to prevent myself from spilling my own tale and tangling this knot tighter. Or maybe this is just really thirsty work.

"I don't have a choice." Her eyes meet mine, deep blue and solemn.

"Everyone has a choice. The truth is, he won't even miss you."

Her head snaps back like I've just slapped her across the chops with a wet kipper.

"What I mean is, he's moved on. You should too."

"I don't give a fuck about him," she says, her frown deepening. "Besides, it's not like he doesn't have to look me in the eye every day. In the office."

"Well, sure, working together is a complication."

"The complication is he's my boss. At least he is since he dumped me for the CEO's daughter."

"Oh."

"C.E. *Oh* . . ." She gives a deep shrug. "As an employee, I'm expected to go. As his ex, I damn well refuse to be a no-show." She grabs the remains of the whiskey and drains what's left, then sets the glass down with an air of finality.

Your funeral, I think to myself. There's no helping some people. "It looks like you've made up your mind."

"The day I got the invitation. And I knew I wouldn't be going alone."

She pierces me with a look that's a mixture of desperation and determination. I somehow know what's coming next.

"No." My tone is firm as I hold up a finger like I'm talking to my niece. "That's *not* happening."

"But you could do it." Her reflexes lightning quick, she grabs my wrist again. "You could totally do it!"

"I'm not sure that's a compliment."

"It is. Plus, you're here and you're available!"

"I'm not a taxi," I say, peeling away her hand. "And this is not happening."

"I'll pay you!"

"You couldn't pay me enough," I retort gruffly, patting the back of her hand to lessen the sting. There's no way I'm doing two weddings in one day. Not as a favor and definitely not as a paid date, no matter what Fin would do.

"I wasn't being cheap when I didn't hire a professional. I can afford to pay you well—really well."

Not as well as I'm usually paid, not that it matters. Fin might be right; I might be nice. But I'm not that nice. Or that fucking stupid.

"Please."

I find my hands in hers suddenly, her head bowed and a subtle floral scent rising between us. The pendant light overhead turns her hair shades of sable, copper, and mahogany. I curl the fingers of my right hand against the insane notion of running them through the silky strands.

"Looks like you've had a manicure." Her thumb slides over my thumbnail, my skin like fire reacting to the brush of her touch.

"It's not a crime to take care of yourself," I say gruffly. The hairs on my wrist stand like pins, but I know her game. I know exactly what she's doing.

"So you do okay for yourself. That doesn't mean you couldn't do with more money. Everyone likes money."

I've got more money than I could spend in a lifetime, but I'm not in the habit of telling people my business. I learned that lesson shortly after I made my first million, because next thing you know, they're googling your name, discovering your net worth, and eyeing you like you could be their new best friend. *Or their next ex-husband.*

"Maybe there's something else you want." She leans in, the action not at all accidental. *Cleavage for days.*

I cock a brow at the suggestion in her tone and spread my fingers wide on my thigh.

"No, I suppose not." Her tone dips, her shoulders with it. "Not that I was offering, exactly."

"Offering what, exactly?"

"*Not* offering." Her cheeks flush pink.

"Give it up, love. I've been to one too many exes' weddings today." Reinforcing my point, I flick my lapel. *Check out the tux. Savile Row, not Abe's Formal Wear.*

"Your ex?" Her expression flickers before she sits up straight. "But . . . but then you *know*."

"I know I'm not going to another one."

"Please, I'm desperate. You're exactly the type of man I should've hired. Compassionate and understanding—"

"And not the type you rent out for a few hours." I put my glass to my lips once more. She doesn't seem unstable, though I'm beginning to wonder if her ears are painted on under all that hair, because her listening skills leave a lot to be desired. "Regardless of what I do or don't do for a living, there's no way I'm suffering through two weddings in one day."

"Please? I'll return the favor—I'll come to your next one!"

Laughter bursts out of me. "Sounds like you've heard about me."

"You kind of have *heartbreaker* written all over you," she says, her voice lowered seductively.

"Insults one minute, flattery one minute." I give a mocking shake of my head as I ignore the stirring between my legs. "I'm just gonna finish my pint and be on my way."

Her eyes turn almost instantly glossy again. "I guess I can kiss my career goodbye," she whispers, putting her fingers to her trembling lips.

"Your employer can't dictate what you do in your spare time."

"I don't have any spare time, not with my job. It's my everything."

"That sounds less than healthy." *Kettle, meet pot. Though in my current assigned role, I expect that would cause a lot of chafing.*

"I love what I do. It's who I do it with that's the issue. I work in an office that's like a frat house. I spend ten-plus hours every day with a bunch of asshole finance bros."

"Banking?"

"Hedge fund."

"On the trading floor."

Surprise ripples across her brow. "Yeah, how did you . . ."

"The balls on you, for one thing." But talk about six degrees of separation. Well, six degrees plus the Atlantic.

"You think I'm ballsy?"

"You know you are. You've got more front than Bloomingdale's," I say, sounding like an old fart.

"Front. I like that." Her amusement fades once more to a flickering frown. "Know thyself, right?" She gives a tiny shrug. "People usually assume I work a back-office role."

"Then they aren't paying attention."

"It's because I'm a woman. Or maybe because the back office is where I started. Thank you for the compliment, but right now, you're confusing moxie with desperation." She rolls in her bottom lip, chewing it a little. "I'm the only woman on the floor. It was bad enough when I only had to listen to those assholes. Being central to it is a whole other experience."

I bite the end of my tongue to stop myself from asking. Not that she needs the invitation, apparently.

"When I was dating one of them, they left me alone. When he dumped my ass, it seemed all bets were off." She slides away a tiny lock of her hair, her gaze avoiding mine.

"Bets?" The word is out of my mouth before I can stop it, though she continues as though I haven't spoken.

"My ex proposed, and the CEO's daughter accepted. A wedding was planned, our presence requested, and by that, I mean *summoned*." Her frown is brief. "Good for the business, apparently. Today is an opportunity to show our clients how we're all one big family. Or so the story goes."

"We both know they can't really make you go."

"They can if I want a promotion. There or somewhere else. If I don't go, I isolate myself, and I've had to work twice as hard as anyone there to get where I am. I won't throw it all away."

"You're sure this is not about your ex?"

"Did you go to your ex's wedding today just to be sure she was done with you?"

I scratch the back of my neck. "It was nothing at all like that."

"Same. Like I said, I wouldn't give him the pleasure of not seeing my face today. You see, I still have feelings for him."

Well, that makes more sense. Though I've no clue why her words should feel like a fist to my face.

"I mean, those feelings are mostly loathing with a sprinkling of white-hot hate. But five days a week, and I've yet to give in to the compulsion to beat his brains into the carpet."

"I applaud your self-control," I say with a reluctant grin. "But if it's not about him, why hire Cuddle Carl?"

"In support of a lie." She gives a dramatic exhale, her bravado seeping out of her. "A lie I've been repeating for months."

"That you have a boyfriend," I guess.

"No. Kind of." She gives her head a tiny shake. "That one of them won't be taking me home at the end of tonight, no matter who has better odds."

"Odds? You can't mean . . ."

"That they've been running a book?" She nods. "It's open season on the new boss's ex since. I told them I had a boyfriend, not that it made one bit of difference. They don't believe that I'm gonna show up with someone, despite my talking my invisible boyfriend up at every opportunity."

"What?" *The fuck.*

"I know, right? I've sent myself flowers. Candies. Commissioned cute sketches and said they were from my artist boyfriend. What kind of a nutjob goes to all that amount of trouble? Well, I'll tell you what kind of nutjob. You're looking at her."

"Fuck that. You should drag their arses to HR."

"It's a family firm. Old-school mentalities where boys will be boys. Meanwhile, men . . ."

Men, on the other hand, do the right thing. They open doors. Offer seats. Put cloaks over puddles and . . . annihilate misogyny? Or at least I was raised to treat people well. To have respect. And wouldn't I have liked someone to rescue me from my ex's tirade earlier?

"Looks like they're right, anyway. I'll be there alone."

I almost groan with frustration. I'm no white knight, but that doesn't stop me from feeling like I ought to do something, my desire for a quiet drink and my integrity pulling me in opposite directions.

"Maybe I should just get drunk and pick one of them. Get it over with."

"You don't strike me as stupid," I reply, unsure why my internal organs hate the sound of that. Not my circus, not my clowns, right?

"Part of me wonders if it might put an end to their fascination."

"It won't."

In answer, she gives a careless shrug.

"Why hasn't he done anything about this—your ex—if he's the boss now?"

"The man who slept in my bed while professing his undying love to someone else? The same man who has wheedled his way into the CEO's family?" She gives a whiplash flick of her wrist. "You tell me."

I dip my head as I rub my hand over my mouth. Mainly to stop myself from calling a complete stranger a string of very offensive words. "You're better off without him." If my frown gets any deeper, I'll be able to offer her a seat on it. *An invitation I'll keep to myself.*

"Maybe I should beat all their brains into the industrial carpeting."

"Maybe you should."

"You don't think I'm too pretty for prison?"

I give in to a reluctant smile. I've heard it said that the crazy ones are crazy hot in bed. Not that I . . .

"I'm tired of repeating that I'm not interested. That I have a boyfriend. That I'm off limits. That their jokes are old and uncalled for."

"It's so fucking wrong," I put in, my tone low and angry on her behalf.

"But it's my experience. I just don't think that I can take things getting any worse."

I must be soft in the head. I don't know which is worse—that I'm contemplating giving in or the fact that I'll have to pretend to be a . . .

Gigolo?
Man whore?
Bro ho?
A male fucking escort.

Maybe worst of all, a two-time wedding guest in one day.

Chapter 4
MATT

Apparently, I am soft in the head.

Not only am I about to suffer through my second wedding reception of the day, but I'll also be pretending to be an escort who's pretending to be a boyfriend.

What a head fuck.

As I reluctantly capitulated, Ryan, according to her belated introduction—and spelled the boys' way, so she said—thrust her hand into mine and said she'd be eternally grateful for my help. It was strange how her tears seemed to almost evaporate.

After draining the last of my pint, I helped her into her coat, and we left the bar together. Much to the amusement of the barman, who seemed to think he'd just witnessed a lovers' tiff.

Meanwhile, I couldn't help but feel a little played, what with the flirting attempts and her tears. The tears were bad enough. *Those big solemn eyes.* And the flirting was cute, though a little desperate. But it was the genuine edge of her distress as she spoke of her ex and her so-called colleagues that changed my mind. No matter what my head told me, I couldn't ignore it. So I can make peace with what I'm doing and why I'm doing it. But what I can't get my head around is how I said yes to attending another feckin' wedding.

I'd almost rather she did want to stick the points of her heels in my ball sack.

At least her company will be more fun than what I had planned, which was probably introspection and an evening drinking myself morose. In fact, just walking down the street with her is more fun than what I'd planned. The waft of her floral perfume, the tap of her heels. The brush of her arm and the gentle sway of her hips.

The beauty in spontaneity.

It turns out, Fin might be right.

Fucking Fin, I think less charitably. He can shove the rest of his advice where the sun doesn't shine—shove it right up there along with his beaded bracelets, which, if I know him, he'd use as anal beads.

"Something funny?"

"Nothing." Nothing other than the fact I'm allowing a woman small enough to put in a mail sack to herd me down the street. Not that I have a mail sack on hand, but I could outrun her if I had half a mind. *The length of her legs . . . the height of her heels.*

Maybe that's why I'm still here. For those legs and those heels.

I examine the thought. It's a possibility.

"If I'd hired an escort, at least I might get fucked at the end of the night."

Her words pique my curiosity.

Not that I expect . . .

Not as though I'd say no either. I'm not *that* nice.

"Now you seem deep in thought," she says, her amused gaze darting my way.

"Deep?" I kind of scoff because my thoughts are very shallow.

"Wanna share with the class?"

"Not really." Fuck, she is lovely. I clear my throat and school my features. I said I'd help, so I will. Pot committed, in poker terms. This is a good decision, even if the situation is a bit fucked.

"I get it, Mr. Mysterious."

"No," I reply. I might not be her white knight, but I'm not a complete twat either. But that's not to say I can't have a little fun with this.

"No?" she repeats, her expression turning quizzical.

"No, you don't get it. Not for free, at least."

"Wow!" She gives an embarrassed-sounding chuckle as her gaze dips, her lashes like the dark sweep of an angel's wing. If I believed in angels, I reckon they'd look a bit like her. Petite, curvy, and with more than a bit of heaven in the sway of the arse.

"Where'd you say this wedding was?" I ask as we turn into the evening hustle of Lexington.

"It's at the Pierre."

So I'm pretty much backtracking to the Plaza. It'll be fun if I bump into anyone from that wedding. Maybe I'll just tell them I'm really into wedding cake.

"You can let go of my arm." I angle my attention her way. "I won't run off."

She gives a soft laugh as she glances at me from under her lashes. "Maybe I'm not willing to take that chance. Especially as it took so much persuasion to get you here."

"Some would say 'persuasion.'" *Others emotional blackmail.*

"Besides, these shoes are kind of high," she says, glancing down at the pointed toes of her green satin heels.

Like a fool, I do too. Dainty ankles and tiny feet. They'd look so fucking good resting against my—

"Vanity, thy name is woman." She releases a soft sigh. "And the devil, well, he must be Jimmy Choo."

I think the devil must be sitting in my brain if the image of those dainty ankles propped on my shoulders is any indication. "We could catch a cab, if you like," I offer, engaging a mental modesty shield. For her benefit.

"You're very sweet."

She wouldn't say that if she could see the images running through my head. Not that they mean anything. She's an attractive woman and I'm a straight, red-blooded male, that's all. A red-blooded male who has allowed her to think I sell sex for a living.

Fucking hell.

"It's all part of the service." How easily the words fall from my mouth. I should stick to them, stick to the story. Like I said to Fin earlier, nothing good comes out of a one-night stand. *Except the obvious, which is fun but short lived.* "Who's Ava?" I ask, thinking of earlier.

"My neighbor. I kind of ran my idea by her, mainly because she has a younger brother and—"

"Carl?"

She grimaces. "Turns out her brother is only a kid. In my defense, he looks way older than seventeen."

"Oh." I draw the sound out. "Corrupting youth?"

"Not if I can help it. Anyway, Ava suggested Carl. They work out of the same center."

"Do people actually cuddle for a living?" Sounds a bit far fetched.

"It's just a side gig for Ava. She teaches yoga mainly, but that doesn't mean she's not militant about the benefits of cuddling. Touch is a basic human need, according to her. Forgoing it is all kinds of bad for a person's physical, mental, and emotional health."

"Right." Sounds like money for old rope, if you ask me.

"I guess not everyone has someone to hold them," she continues, "but what I can't get my mind around is that the sessions are sixty minutes. Who wants to be held for an hour? I don't even want to have sex for an hour."

I laugh. At least until I realize she's not joking. *Someone hasn't been living up to their potential.*

"Don't tell me," she deadpans. "Your clients expect bang for their buck."

Literally, I would imagine. Not that I'm about to explain what the women I sleep with can expect from me, imaginary clients or otherwise.

I sense her studying me a second before she says, "Can I ask you a question?"

"Can't stop you." I can, however, opt not to answer. Or opt to stretch the truth a bit more. I haven't outright lied to her. It's more that she assumed. And that I haven't put her right.

This is so gonna come back to bite me in the arse.

"You said you'd been to your ex's wedding earlier. I suppose I've been wondering if she minded what you do for a living."

"I have a rule." I have a motto. Why not a rule? I scuff the soles of my shoes against the sidewalk for a step or two, stalling as I try to formulate said rule. "I don't talk about my private life. Not when I'm with a date." I sound like such a wanker. What woman would be interested in that level of bullshit?

"I could argue we're not on a date."

"And I would contend that, right now, you need me to be someone other than myself. So my private life remains just that."

"But if I met you in Starbucks tomorrow, say?"

"Then someone hit me on the head and dragged me in there. Starbucks is all that's wrong in the world."

"It's just coffee."

"Is that an invitation?"

"It's a hypothetical."

We fall quiet, though she turns her head, anticipating more, as I inhale.

"I will say we parted on good terms." Not a lie, because I thought we did.

"That must be nice. Not wanting to murder the person you used to love."

I make a noncommittal noise in lieu of an answer. I can't say I ever loved her, but I liked her enough to go to her wedding. *Liked,* past tense.

"You're a nice guy. For doing this, I mean. But I've still got to pay you."

I glance sharply her way.

"You just said this is a date, which I guess is a euphemism for a *booking*," she says, lowering her voice as a group of twentysomethings passes the other way.

"Are you saying you'd like to make a booking?" My tone is low and suggestive as the devil takes hold of my tongue.

"Yeah. Yes. I mean, not like *that*." Her cheeks turn so adorably pink. "I want to pay you, but not for—"

"Fringe benefits?" The horror on her face as I draw out that first sound. How I manage not to crack up with laughter, I have no feckin' idea.

"Exactly. Those. That." Her pitch climbs adorably with each word, making her sound Southern for some reason. "What I mean is, I should pay you for your time."

"Thanks, but this one's on me." *I wish,* I think absurdly. "On the house." *Instead of my fingers, my cock, and my face.*

"That's not right. I make good money. I paid Cuddle Carl—I can afford to pay you."

"Except I'm not the kind of man you can hire for a couple hours."

"Oh. Yeah. Right." She nods, embarrassed. And that makes me feel a little bit shit. "So how long is your—"

Wanna suck it and see? Thankfully, the '80s porn star voice and stupidity stay in my head.

"—usual appointment time?" she asks, oblivious to where my imagination has taken this. Taken us.

"That all depends on the circumstances. Not that it matters on this occasion."

"I'm not a charity case," she snaps. "Come on. How much is the boyfriend experience?"

The boyfriend experience, Jaysus. What alternative universe is this?

"Why, are you interested?" I ask smoothly instead. Which is better than asking if that's with or without socks littering the bedroom floor, I suppose.

"I guess I can see the attraction." With the deft sidestep, her gaze briefly slides over me.

"Aside from the obvious?" I find I quite like being objectified. By Ryan, at least.

"I mean, it's like you said earlier. All the benefits and none of the bullshit."

And there goes my ego, farting through the air like a burst balloon.

"His bullshit?" *The ex's?*

"Relationship bullshit. Infatuation. The rush. The relationship," she says, making an upward motion of her hand. "Big love," she adds as it levels out. Then a downward curve. "Rejection. Confusion. Breakup. Heartache."

"When you put it that way." Why do we bother—any of us? But then I think of Fin and Oliver and how love has completely turned their lives around. How their priorities have changed to include the happiness of another and how that seems to make them happier in turn. "But you missed some stuff."

She gives an adorable scrunch of her nose. "Sex? I don't miss having sex. Besides, I can meet my own needs. When necessary."

Now that is something *I'd* pay to see. Preferably sitting very close, breathing in the heat from her skin. "I meant laughter and fun. Respect. Good times. Mutual pleasures?"

"Not worth the risk," she says, her words barely audible.

"Right." *That fucker really did a number on her.* "You said I was nice," I say, rerouting the conversation. "So let me be exactly that tonight. Let me do this for you. Let me fawn all over you like Cupid shot me a good one."

"Why?" She sounds genuinely confused.

"For the narrative. In support of the lies you've had to tell. And on behalf of decent men everywhere. We're not all arseholes, you know."

"I know," she retorts unconvincingly.

"And maybe because I'm also in the mood to crack a few heads."

She laughs. I don't join in.

"It's just a pack-mentality thing," she says, her fingers shifting on my arm.

"Law of the jungle? You don't really believe that."

"Look, I just know what happens to the gazelle outside the pack. She gets looked on as lame."

"You must really like your job."

"Yeah, I do. Do you enjoy yours?" she demands.

"I'm having fun now."

"Well, that's good, but I don't need the macho kind of help. I've worked hard to get where I am, and I have plans. I want to make a name for myself, but not that kind of name. So bring on Cupid, but leave the tough stuff to me. Please." The latter seems like an afterthought.

"Fine." We fall quiet for a beat before I find myself saying, "I don't know how you can stand it. An afternoon in the company of my ex was enough for me."

"I thought you parted on good terms."

"Doesn't mean we were meant to be best friends."

She gives a heavy-sounding sigh. "I hear that. Why do we make life so complicated?"

Doesn't have to be, the devil suggests. *I could make it so easy. So easy.*

"Working with your ex must be a nightmare."

"It has its perks, especially as I'm his dirty little secret." She slides me a speaking glance. "And I don't hate seeing the fear on his face when I coast a little close to the C-suite offices."

"No?" I say with a chuckle.

"Oh, how his flat butt must pucker."

"There's a thought I'd like to bleach from my brain. Ex or not, he must be a massive fucknut if he's not doing anything to stop what's going on. It's harassment, plain and simple."

She makes a careless gesture before her grip tightens on my arm. "Next time, I'll find somewhere that isn't run by dinosaurs."

But her attitude is suspiciously blasé, I decide, as we fall quiet again.

A car honks at a set of lights, and a group of squealing girls piles out of an Uber as, across the street, a guy in hot pants and a sequined T-shirt belts out a song from *West Side Story*.

"He feels pretty, and I feel pretty awful for bringing you into this. But honestly, I don't need your protection," she repeats. "I fight my own battles."

"I don't doubt it," I say with a rueful chuckle. The way she accosted me, then hammered me, thinking I was Cuddle Carl. How she pivoted and hung on—come hell or high water, she wasn't giving up her plan. She's got buckets of pluck, and I like that about her.

Like not only that about her.

"Good, because it's true."

"Back in the pub," I begin, "when you found out I wasn't Cuddle Carl, I could've been anyone. I might *be* anyone—a murderer for all you know."

"Do you know what makes a good trader?"

"The ability to make money, I imagine."

"And how we do that is through instinct. I have excellent instincts." Twin flames of determination flare in her gaze. "So no, I didn't choose just anyone. In fact, the point that you are who you are—that you do what you do—kind of proves my point, don't you think?"

"Chosen," I repeat flatly. "I feel special."

"Oh so special?"

"Careful, or you'll have me borrowing that fella's sparkly T-shirt."

"You're already pretty."

"Thanks," I say with a gruff chuckle.

"But a murderer?" She makes a dismissive gesture. "I could see you as a hit man." Her amused gaze slides my way again, slides over me. Neck. Chest. But not quite brazen enough to dip lower. "An assassin, maybe."

"I'm more like the victim." I send her a pointed look, which she's careful to miss.

"A spy with that James Bond swag."

I give a soft snort, thinking back to what Fin said. "When you think about it, Bond can't be much of a spy when he introduces himself to the bad guys at every opportunity."

"You'd be like him."

"An idiot?"

"The kind of assassin who only kills bad guys."

"If you say so." She's so willfully oblivious, I'm impressed.

"You've got the look." Her next glance my way bears an edge of coquetry. "Tall, dark, and mysterious."

"Are you flirting with me?" It feels like she is as her heels clip-clip against the pavement to keep time with my regular strides. But she's in the driver's seat, and I'm just along for the ride. *I kind of like that too.*

"Just paying you a compliment. If we're judging books by covers, I'm saying you look like you're an expert of some kind. Dangerous. Confident. You might kill for a living. But you'd be a hit man with a heart. This is fate, Matt. You were meant to be by my side tonight."

I say nothing, mainly because I'm more like her pawn than her savior. But something tells me Ryan doesn't play damsel in distress very often, so maybe I should be flattered.

"You haven't asked what I think about you, aside from your balls of steel."

She pulls a face. "I'm almost afraid to hear more."

I give a low chuckle. "Now, that I don't believe."

"The hotel isn't very far," she says, changing the conversational direction.

"Yeah, I know where the Pierre is."

"Do you live in Manhattan?" There's an edge of discomfort in her question.

I fight a frown. "I'm only here for the wedding. For the weekend."

"Really?" *Was that surprise or gladness?* "All the way from Ireland?"

I give a noncommittal shrug.

"It's a long way to come for an ex's wedding."

"Yeah, I'm nice like that." Fuck. I'm even saying it about myself now.

"You're sure it wasn't a Hail Mary?"

"I object, you mean?" I pull a face. "Nah. What about you—you live here?"

"Lower East."

So much for being able to pay me well. I mean, all housing is expensive in Manhattan, but the Lower East Side is no view of the park.

We pause at the crosswalk, ignoring the waft of trash carried on the unseasonably warm breeze. Late October tends to be transitional, but the city is definitely resisting the change of season. The light changes, and we step out, then dodge a DoorDash cyclist who plows through the light. Ryan squeaks and clutches my arm, all awkward smiles and embarrassment a moment later.

She's fucking adorable in the moment. Not so adorable is the noise my stomach makes at the greasy scent of meat from a nearby food truck. I could go for a gyro. It's been hours since I've eaten.

"I hope there's food at this wedding. I'm so hungry I could eat the hind leg off the Lamb of God."

"What?" Her answer gurgles with amusement.

"I need food."

"There's food. Six hundred dollars a plate, so I heard." Her gaze dips to the slender watch on her wrist. "But I imagine the meal will be over by the time we get there."

"Great," I mutter. Not even a feed out of my good deed. *Supposed good deed.*

"If anyone asks, we should say your plane got in late. The timing might work in our favor." The latter she adds under her breath.

"Not for my stomach. I'm half starved."

"You don't look it."

Go ahead and call me a peacock, because I fucking preen under that verbal slip. "I'm a big lad," I say, not bothering to make that sound like anything other than what it is. "I'm not cheap to and kind of hard to satiate, once I get going."

"Is that so?" She's amused. And she's interested. She almost purrs.

I meant *to feed*, but that works too. If I was selling sex, I reckon I'd get paid pretty well. I've never had any complaints. Plenty of compliments. A few stunned looks. And several *You're the best I've ever had*s. I think that old adage *The quiet ones are always the worst* has a ring of truth to it.

What the hell am I thinking? This whole thing is like something out of one of my sister's romance books. The ones she keeps leaving like heavy hints around my house. *The ones I've read that have provided very little help.*

"Late works," Ryan announces suddenly, pulling me from my musing. "It means less time we need to be there."

"Right."

"Also, the band will be playing, so people won't notice your accent. Hopefully," she adds with a flicker of consternation.

"I have an accent?"

"Sorry to break it to you." Shielding her amusement, she glances at the window display of a boutique as we pass. "Maybe you should speak as little as possible, because it's an accent that doesn't work for the narrative."

"And what is that narrative?"

"Well, Nathaniel, Nate, my imaginary boyfriend, is Spanish."

"Like Carl from the Cuddle Collective."

"Like *Carlos* from the Cuddle Collective. Who I'm going to smother with a pillow," she adds quite happily.

"It's sounding more and more like you're the killer here."

Her brow furrows.

"Nate. It's not a very Spanish name," I continue, not sure what's made her frown. *Maybe she's vegan.*

"I know." Her shoulder lifts and falls carelessly. "The story kind of spun away from itself."

"Our backstory?"

"We met last summer in Florence." Her footsteps begin to slow until we're both stationary and facing each other. "And you're an artist, hence the sketches."

"The ones you sent to yourself."

"It was a good touch, right? Anyway," she adds when she finds confusion and not agreement on my face. "You were working on the banks of the river."

This is batshit crazy, right? "A Spanish artist? On the banks of the Arno?"

"Yeah, I guess."

"Why not an Italian artist?" Which would make way more sense.

"It just came out that way, okay?"

Touchy. "I can see that. Especially with a name like Nathaniel." Why not Matías? Or Sebastien or Hugo? On second thought, if she'd used my name or one of my brothers' names, this would be much weirder. "Was he—I—drawing or painting?"

"What does it matter?"

"I tell you what does matter. He'd fry in summer. Could be worse, I suppose. You could've picked the rainy season."

Her brow furrows again.

"Have you ever been to Florence?" I ask.

"Of course." Her shrug is pointed and prickly, though her answer is assured.

"It mustn't have rained. You would've noticed the smell."

"Florence smells?"

"All cities with ancient sewerage systems stink," I reply, outing myself as a bit of an engineering geek.

She wrinkles her nose, and it's fucking adorable. "I felt like shit in Florence. Does that count?"

"Don't tell me. You went to recover from a broken heart?"

"You know how it goes." She shoots me a quick look and a smile that doesn't meet her eyes.

"A bit."

I'm such a fucking liar. I've never had my heart broken, though I've had it bruised a few times. Or maybe that was just my pride, and the pain came from overuse—from putting myself out there too many times. The truth is, I'm a serial monogamist who's never truly been in love.

"Again, I truly appreciate your help. And again, I will pay you for your time."

"Help. Sure, let's go with that." I shoot her a look. "I would've gone with *coercion* myself." The rest I ignore. I've no intention of taking money from her. I'll have my payment in amusement, I reckon.

"You just said you wouldn't run away."

"That's not to say I haven't considered it. Along with putting you in a sack."

"Is that an Irish thing?" she asks, amused.

"Yep. It's what we do to women in pubs who won't take no for an answer."

"What about men who won't take no for an answer?"

"You might just find out when we get to this wedding. Anyway," I add before she can interject. Or argue again. "If we're not staying long, you can take me out for a feed as payment."

"A feed. Are you a horse?"

"It'll ease your conscience, I reckon. For hijacking my evening."

"My conscience?" she trills. "Now who's being bold?"

"I'm taking a leaf out of your book." How is it she's gotten prettier since we left the pub?

"I'd say your book gets enough action of its own."

Maybe. Maybe not. But I've never had an evening like this.

Chapter 5
RYAN

In the empty marble entryway, music resounds, glasses clink, the sounds of conviviality and happiness pouring from the room beyond. I blow out a breath, slow and steady, as I try to ignore my sweaty palms and rotating intestines. Despite what I've said, despite all the trouble I've gone to, I do *not* want to be here. But as with a dose of bad-tasting medicine, I just have to take it.

I pause at a glittering sign nestled in an ostentatious floral display, announcing the marriage of the happy couple. *Curse their lineage.* But not really. I've got nothing against the bride. I kind of feel for her, not that it makes any sense, considering all she has. But I guess she also has a cheating asshole of a husband now, so curse his ass because he deserves none of this.

"All good?"

I nod, resisting the urge to look at the man to my left. He is a whole lot of man. I'll admit I was a little shocked when I first set eyes on him. I almost swallowed my tongue. I thought Carl from the Cuddle Collective must've used some very unflattering photos on his business profile, because the man in front of me was plain gorgeous. I could even see that making sense in my head, the reasons for underplaying his attractiveness. *Don't want the ladies booking a platonic cuddle appointment thinking they'd get down (literally) to more than that.*

In short, Matt is a snack! He's fire. He's so freakin' hot that, in other, less dire circumstances, I'm not sure I could be so blasé about being on his arm. His hair is so dark it's almost black, and his eyes a deep forest green shot through with summer gold. He has the kind of chin that belongs to a comic book superhero, and I bet I could slice ham on those cheekbones. His shoulders are broad, and his thighs are thick. The man is country strong, yet he looks like he was born to wear a tuxedo. *Like a modern-day Cary Grant—thanks for introducing me to the archetype, TCM—so debonair, with oodles of charisma and kindness.* It's a reluctant brand of kindness, but it's there. Or else he wouldn't be here.

He's a good man. Maybe the last one in Manhattan.

Not that I recognized any of that as I stood in the run-down bar, coming to grips with the realization that he wasn't Cuddle Carl. Feeling my plans, feeling myself, unravel. It was blind panic and a sense of desperation that made me latch on to him. Despite my earlier bravado, I would've chosen just about anyone. He might've been eighteen or eighty, as bald as a billiard ball, or possessing the kind of face that only his mother could love. It didn't matter in that moment. I needed a man, and he was it.

I needed a man, and I was somehow blessed with a whole lot of one. A man whose job is kind of a mind fuck. And an actual fuck. A man who is a purveyor of pleasure, I suppose. At the thought, my stomach flips. *Not at all unpleasantly.*

I wonder what kind of money a night with him costs. No, I don't, not really. What I wonder about is what a night with him entails. *I bet he's worth every penny.*

I give myself an internal shake because it's not like he's doling out freebies. Besides, that's not why he's here. We have other fish to fry.

I turn to the table plan embedded in another ridiculously sized floral display. *You can find your seat here,* it reads, *but your place is on the dance floor.*

There's nothing quite like a cliché. And I should know.

So much for being bold, because I feel physically ill at the prospect of going in there. Not because *he's* there. The man whose gaslighting made me question my own sanity, the human facsimile whose ultimate betrayal left me in pieces. This apprehension is not about him, because no one gets to hurt me twice. It's more about the occasion. This wedding. The direction I thought, I imagined, our relationship was heading.

But I wasn't lying when I said I had to be here—that all employees of Dreyland Capital are expected to attend. I'm sure I could've feigned illness, gone on vacation, or claimed a clash of events. Maybe faked a broken leg. Except, I *had* to be here. I needed to see this for myself. As penance, if nothing else. Punishment for being taken in by a man.

Something I won't let happen again.

I also wasn't kidding or laying it on thick about my feelings toward my ex. I do see red every time I look at him. Like I could punch him in the face until it turns to Bolognese.

"Found us yet?"

I resist a tiny shiver as the puff of Matt's words brushes my neck. I realize I'm staring unseeing at the table plan. "Can't seem to find which circle of hell we've been put in."

"The wrathful one. That'd be circle nine."

I chuckle and add smart to the list of Matt's charms. Well read. Urbane. And I am so into the rhythmic rise and fall of his accent. Even if it isn't Spanish. And his voice? Yum. It's so deep and rumbling, it seems to hit a girl right where it counts.

Then I spot us—spot where we've been seated. *A table named Paris.*

That fucker.

"Found us!" I whip around with a second wind of determination. Paris was our first vacation. It was there he first declared his love.

Well, my place is wherever the hell I want it to be. And while I might not *want* to be here, some evils are just plain necessary. This is just another hurdle to jump. Something else I won't ever look back on. An experience that won't even get a second glance in the rearview mirror of my life. "Shall we?" I add brightly.

"Can't wait." His voice is low, and his tone is flat. But his eyes, they're dancing.

Boy, did I luck out when Cuddle Carl—a pox on *his* lineage—was a no-show.

"I think you're trying too hard." I poke him playfully in his chest. His broad, solid chest. "Tell the truth—you're a closet wedding fan." And don't get me started on the rest of him. Those long, elegant fingers on such capable hands. The kind of hands that might stop a girl from falling. *Maybe the side effect of Irish whiskey is becoming fanciful.*

"You got me." His chest moves with an amused-sounding huff. "That's exactly what I'm doing here."

"Knew it," I singsong.

"You've had me worked out all along."

His low tone causes a wash of goose bumps along my arms. And now I'm looking at his mouth, wondering what it would feel like to have those lips on mine. How it would move, the shapes it would make. How he'd taste. Whiskey laced, I'd bet, to match that dreamy (if unauthentic for tonight's purposes) accent.

"I guess we'd better get this shit show on the road." I turn to the oversize ballroom doors, and Matt follows.

"Ryan?"

In the doorway, I half pivot, my eyes flying wide as his hands slide around my waist. My body offers him no resistance as he pulls me close, the scent of his woody cologne hitting me so viscerally. My breath hitches as I find our lips are just a breath apart, and for one crazy moment, I think he might kiss me like we're in some classic movie.

"What are you doing?" My voice sounds kind of breathy, and I don't have the wits to be annoyed by that.

"Setting the tone. Strangers might walk in together, but lovers love."

"That doesn't even make sense." Maybe because my blood is pumping so hard, it's starving my brain. I feel tiny in his arms. I mean, I am physically small, but I rarely feel so.

"We're not late because my plane was." His voice is husky and pitched low. "We're lovers who've been separated by sea and by weeks. Everyone here—your colleagues, the people watching us right now, the people you like and the people you don't—they know the real reason we're late." His eyes seem lit from within. "They can sense what we've been up to."

Heat rises through me, like we've actually spent the afternoon fucking.

Wouldn't that have been something.

Oh, my God, am I blushing?

I think I must be in shock. Eighteen months, and not once have I felt that visceral pull of attraction. The whole time, I've been deadened from the neck down. Discounting the hate that still burns in my heart, of course. I haven't wanted sex at all—not with myself, not with anyone.

"No one's w-watching us," I stammer. Because why would they? *They better not be, or they might ask why steam is currently rising from my skin.* I give a tiny clearing of my throat and make to move away as though my knees aren't a little unsteady and my heart isn't jumping out of my skin. I'd better get a hold on this thing—a hold on myself, more like. "There really is no—"

His fingers tighten. I don't pull away because . . .

We're just playing a part. Even if I *really* want to dry hump him right now.

"Maybe you should've gone for an escort," he murmurs, sliding away a lock of my hair. "At least then you'd have control."

That heat coursing through me suddenly drops to my center, warming the space between my hips. "You think I'm not in control?" Damn the tiny waver in my voice.

He gives the kind of smile that causes me a jolt. Devilish? Rakish? I don't know what the word is, but there is something overtly sexual about it. I get the feeling that I've missed something. Missed something *in* him.

"It's cute that you think you are. But you see, when we step into this room, you're at the whim of a Latin lover. *Your* Latin lover," he says, exaggerating his accent with extravagant rolling *r*'s. Well, maybe not *his* accent, but someone's. Someone not at all Spanish and slightly comical.

"You'd better let me do the talking." The man sure is pretty, but his Spanish accent is anything but. But there's not a lot I can do about that now.

"I'm deeply offended," he says, looking the exact opposite.

"Seriously, I appreciate your help, but—"

His expression flickers. Annoyance, maybe?

"—for the love of God, please don't speak in here."

"You're dating a handsome mute. That's the story you're going with?"

"Better than Super Mario's hotter brother!"

"Super Mario is Italian."

"His Spanish cousin, then."

"Fine." His tone turns playfully flat. "I'll restrain myself."

"Good." But I'm still hanging on to him like a lover about to be kissed. "Want to tell me why we're still standing here like this?"

"A man without a voice. How else am I meant to get my point across?"

"I don't know. Mime? Interpretive dance? I was kidding," I tag on hastily when he moves a tiny inch. *He wouldn't, would he?*

"That's good, because I was thinking more along the lines of . . ."

My eyes fall closed as he draws closer, and his lips brush mine. It's barely a kiss—more a fleeting glance—but it's enough to register how soft his lips are. And how my body shimmers with the desire to curl into his embrace.

". . . that," he murmurs, pulling away.

Were his eyes so dark before? "That," I repeat, whisper soft.

"Couples kiss, Ryan. And they touch."

"Yes," I agree, not really sure what I'm saying. What I'm offering.

"Couples who've been separated by land and seas. Well, they just can't get enough. Do you think you can handle that?"

"Handle you?" Surely, I'd meant my retort to be full of derision, not want. Because despite his terrible Spanish accent, my fingers itch with his suggestion. Neurons fire, and my skin seems to tingle, every fiber of my being demanding more. More kissing, more touching . . . more everything.

But then I remember what Matt does for a living. It's like a drenching of cold water that extinguishes all that. "You're good at this. At pretending."

"Because I should be so lucky, right?"

"I should think you get lucky a lot." Even without the job.

"A compliment?"

"I do have eyes."

"Very pretty ones. But the thing is, I don't feel like taking directions tonight."

"You mean the accent?" I ask, slightly confused, slightly worried, and still feeling like I'm missing something.

"I can play the strong, silent type."

"Then I don't know what you're talking about."

"I know. And that's what makes this fun. For me, at least."

"Right. Fine." See also: whatever. "You can let go now."

"I don't think I will. Got to keep up those appearances."

"I told you. No one's watching us. Not when there's a bride and groom to moon over." I turn my head toward the room, my gaze connecting immediately with Heidi's. The accounts administrator looks thrilled, the two thumbs she holds up a pretty good indicator.

"Their moment's over." Matt's voice brings my attention back. "You're the big-ticket item now. The topic of next week's gossip. And who would prefer to watch some insipid bride over you?"

"She's beautiful."

"I bet she doesn't have a thing on you."

I make a noise. Disagreement. Annabelle has money. Privilege. A family who adores her. *And my ex, poor bitch.*

"You're a rare kind of beauty, Ryan. Your spirit is as captivating as your face."

"I don't need your flattery," I say, fighting the instinct to lean into that concept. That seduction. I can't remember the last time anyone said something so lovely to me.

Nice tits.

Your ass is the bomb.

You'd be prettier if you smiled a little more.

"But I do appreciate your diligence." I lift my hand to his chest, my fingers trailing upward. I touch the edge of his bow tie as though to straighten it, then ghost my thumb over his lips. A subtle thrill runs through me as his mouth parts and his eyes darken. "But I think I can handle a Latin lover for the night."

"Be careful what you promise, pretty girl."

But promises are only words. *As well I know.* "Let's get this over with."

Matt inclines his head, then straightens. Somehow, he ends up with his arm still around me. I'm not going to complain as we step into the room, him all poise and confidence and me on slightly shaky legs.

"Just what I need." As a server passes with a tray of champagne, I take two glasses without giving a hoot who they were for. I press one into Matt's hand and almost throw the other back.

"Thirsty?" he asks as I put the empty glass on a nearby table.

"Let's go with that." I'm not much of a drinker, but Lord knows I need all the help I can get.

"Champagne is the candy floss of booze," he says, examining his glass. "Satisfying for only as long as it touches the tongue." There's something sexual about his words, though not exactly overt. Story checks out about his career, I guess.

"You don't like champagne?"

"Let's just say there's nothing like a cold pint and a whiskey chaser to improve the mood. Or blacken it, I suppose."

Was he in that god-awful pub to drown his sorrows? The thought dies as he offers me his glass, and I take it.

"Come on," he says, sliding his arm around my waist. "I won't let you fall."

I try not to take too much comfort in his words. His touch, though? That I can handle. Even if it makes me realize I've missed this. Holding hands and hugging. Maybe Ava is right about touch being a basic need. Not that I'll be hiring Cuddle Carl anytime soon. *But hire Matt?* I roll my bottom lip to stifle a ridiculous smile.

I'm relieved to see I was right about the timing. The dance floor is packed and the tables surrounding it only half filled. When my gaze lands on Heidi's for a second time, she grins and fans her face theatrically from the other side of the room. *Agreed, Heidi, the man is hot as fuck.*

The music segues seamlessly to another song, and I almost laugh.

"What's funny?"

I give my head a tiny shake. Not the Supremes, that's for sure, as the unmistakable introduction to "You Can't Hurry Love" begins to flow from the speakers.

I'm sure my ex would disagree. Did disagree, in fact, after staring into Annabelle's doll-like eyes and seeing his future. Status, wealth, the Upper East Side town house. The guaranteed leapfrog effect to his career when he discarded me like one of his Twinkie wrappers. I should've known better than to trust someone whose favorite treat is so chemical filled it would survive an apocalypse. *And I thought I was supposed to be white trash.*

But being here, in the ballroom, at his wedding, makes me feel . . .

Nothing, surprisingly.

There's no flash of green envy as I take in the tables laden with white linens, gold accents, and flickering candlelight. I feel nothing for the floral displays as tall as I stand. The decor is elegant, refined, and timeless, and though it might be the kind of wedding I once dreamed of, it was never the kind of wedding I would ever have.

We were never destined for the Pierre. The most I could've hoped for was a quickie ceremony in Vegas. That way, there'd be no questions asked about my family's nonattendance. No gossip about little ole me.

I almost can't blame Pete for getting sucked into all this. But that doesn't mean I wouldn't happily crush him under the wheels of a bus. Then reverse over him.

Up ahead, a whirl of white catches my eye. The new Mrs. Peter. J. Langley in all her wedding finery. *Annabelle the perfect.* An alumna of Nightingale and Brown—hundreds of thousands of dollars of education for someone destined to be a nanny-overseeing UES mom.

That's not jealousy. Not *much* jealousy. I guess I feel sorry for her because she deserves better than a piece of shit like Pete. It's just not my place to tell her so. I doubt she'd even believe me. Not right now.

"It's this one here," I say over my shoulder as we weave through the tables. Not that we have far to go. Naturally, *the help* has been seated near the back. I'm relieved to find our table empty but for a graveyard of glasses filled with liquids to varying degrees.

Just what I need. Assholes only get worse when they're full of liquor. Ask me how I know.

"You're frowning at the table as though it's offended you." Bringing my attention back, Matt slides a lock of hair behind my ear, his expression one of soft indulgence.

"I'm not." I put my hand to the back of an empty chair and give a *'sup* nod of recognition as a couple of faces I vaguely recognize pass. *Analysts, I think.*

"Jesus," Matt mutters. "You really do work at a hedge fund."

"Did you think I made it up?" I drop my clutch to the table and, for the first time tonight, realize I haven't been glued to my phone. *In my job, if I'm not in contact, I'm not making money.*

He slides me a sardonic look. "Forgive me if I didn't believe everything you said."

"That's fair. So what convinced you?"

"The reek of Creed cologne and the glint of entry-level Rolexes," he says, hooking his thumb in the direction of the analysts.

Cuff links from Graff. His earlier words drop into my head. My eyes flick over a suit that's definitely made to measure, given his build and its fit. I glance at his wrist and the watch I can't see—that I haven't paid attention to. *Yet.*

"Patek Philippe," he says, lifting his wrist. "Wanna know which one?"

"No," I say quickly, uncomfortably caught out.

"My job pays well too."

"So I see." *Would that be thanks to generous sugar mama or a happily fulfilled client base?*

"Go on." He reaches for the gilt picture frame in the center of the table, surrounded by knickknacks oozing Frenchness. "Ask me. Whatever it is you're thinking."

Not in a million years would I utter the phrase *sugar mama* in his hearing. "And spoil your air of mystery?"

His mouth kicks up, and he reads the text accompanying the print in the frame, the reason for our cutesy designated table name.

"Peter proposed in Paris," he reads with an unimpressed twist of the lips. "Original."

Oh, you have no idea. "That's Pete."

"Pete?" He slides me a look.

"He prefers Peter. That's why I call him Pete," I say, acid sweet.

"Kill Stinky Pete," Matt murmurs as he puts it down.

"What did you just say?"

"I see you're unfamiliar with the villainous *Toy Story* character?"

"You have kids?" My heart plummets to my Jimmy Choos.

"Borrowed only. I'm an uncle," he says with an air of . . . something. "'Kill Stinky Pete' is what my niece would yell at the TV whenever the prospector in *Toy Story* popped up. When she was much younger, at least." He smiles, the memory causing something inside me to thaw. "She's more into Disney princesses these days."

"'Kill Stinky Pete.' I like it. Feels almost preordained."

"There's a reason he's at the top of your smother-with-a-pillow list."

My mouth curls lopsidedly. "Not painful enough. And the margin of error is too wide for my tastes."

"All right, killer," he says with a chuckle.

"Don't call me that." My words hit the air like bullets. "I just don't like it," I add, hoping to lessen my bite as I turn and make as if to pull out my chair. Until his hand engulfs mine and he squeezes it tenderly. Reassuringly.

"Hey, turn that frown upside down before people begin to think you don't fancy me."

As if, I almost answer, though I catch myself. Breath catches in my throat as I sense him closer. I feel the heat of his breath against my neck, the wisp of it making me shiver.

"And how could you not fancy me when I've spent the afternoon between your legs."

His words, that taunting tone. It feels like the thrust of two fingers deep inside me. As my body clenches emptily, I curl my toes in my shoes as a way to make sure I don't turn. Because if I turn, I might throw myself at him.

The last good man in Manhattan has game. *Of course he does. This is his stock-in-trade.*

"That was a little graphic," I murmur as I offer him my profile, chin slightly raised.

"What can I say? Your lover is a dirty talker. Don't pretend you don't like it."

"Because all the ladies like it?" I don't know why that came out so bitchy. *Am I jealous or something?*

"Haven't you heard that a gentleman never kisses and tells?" He pulls out my chair, waiting until I'm seated before positioning another to face me. "What's the plan?" He brushes his palm against his broad thigh as though to flatten any creases.

Damn. Those are some thick thighs.

Big deal, I school myself. *He also has big hands. And big feet. Are you gonna get all twisted up about those too? I bet he has big everything.*

"Ryan?"

"The plan?" My voice is crazy high, and my cheeks suddenly feel radioactive. I clear my throat and regulate my tone. "Honestly, I hadn't thought much beyond getting here." Because I've been so focused on the *getting here* and so worried something would go wrong. And it did. But also so right. "Maybe we just go with the flow?"

"I can do that." His doting boyfriend's gaze is for no one but me.

Lucky me. I wonder how many women he's bankrupted with his boyfriend experience.

"We can dance," he purrs, reaching out to trail the backs of his fingers along my jaw.

"We could."

"Maybe enjoy a couple of drinks."

"We could do that too." A couple of drinks is usually my limit, thanks to the chaos I was raised in. But my mother's vices are not my own, so I guess I can make an exception for today. *Come to think of it, I probably already have.* "We don't have to stay long."

"Because everyone can tell we're at the fucking-like-bunnies stage of our relationship."

The way he looks at me, I can almost believe that myself. I give a tiny lift of my shoulder as though completely unaffected. As though the way his mouth moves when he speaks doesn't do things to me. "You are quite something."

"You don't know the half of it, darlin'," he says, laying on his accent thick.

Why the heck didn't I think to make my imaginary boyfriend Irish? The two seem to go together like figs and honey. I roll my lips to wet them a little, and Matt's gaze drops there. His throat moves with a swallow, and I realize how close we suddenly are, both of us straining close like flowers seeking the sun.

"Can I get you anything?" A server appears to the side. Thank God. *Because I think I was about to climb into his lap.* "To drink?" White shirt, an apron, and a long blond ponytail that she swishes over her shoulder, none of which Matt seems to see as he barely glances her way, politely reciting his drink order.

"Whiskey. Please. A single malt if you have it." His eyes on me feel bold and kind of possessive.

"Champagne?" My request sounds like a question, my mind buzzing with the things I want but can't have.

"Absolutely." She makes a note on a little pad and moves to the other side of the table to gather some of the abandoned glassware.

"Should I be glad not knowing the half of it?" I ask, unable to keep myself from going there. Returning to the conversation from the careful distance of my chair.

"Worried you might miss out?"

"Well, I'm not gonna scribble your name in a bathroom stall or anything."

"'For a good-time call'?" His mouth curls in a reluctant-looking grin.

I bet a good time would be had by all.

"Forget I asked." Because this is dangerous territory. It feels entirely too flirty.

"If you don't want to find out, what should we do instead?" So much suggestion in that.

"Whatever that is on your face," I retort, "let's *not* do that."

"Spoilsport. All right." He leans in suddenly. "Tell me something."

"Like what?"

"Anything. Tell me anything."

My eyes slide over his shoulder to Josh, one of the back-office people, leaving the dance floor and walking our way. "Rumor has it that one of the techs is on OnlyFans."

Matt gives a chuckle.

"But that's not the juicy part. He has a wife and three kids, but his followers are predominantly male, if you know what I mean."

"Tell me something else. Something about you."

"Matt, we don't need to—this is just a one-night thing."

A very shapely eyebrow (for a man) lifts like a taunt.

"That's *not* what I meant."

That's what they all say, his dark laughter seems to suggest.

"Can you, like, not behave?" I demand a little too delightedly.

"See . . ." He slips his hand between his legs to pull his chair closer, as though he has a secret to share. "I can behave," he says, his eyes devouring me. "But Nate from Nine Inch Males? Sadly, he doesn't know how to behave in public."

"Nine Inch—" is as far as I get before I laugh. Part chortle, part snort. I do a bad job of smothering the heinous sound with my hand. "Nine Inch what?" I manage eventually.

"Males." I swear his taunting tone reverberates right through to my bones. "It's what I'd call my escort agency. If I *had* an escort agency."

"Oh, my God, please don't say that in here. Even if in some weird, alternate universe it might help put those knuckleheads in their place." *Or one of them, at least.*

"Help how?"

"Doesn't matter." I glance over his shoulder at the dance floor again. Granted, I can't see the idiots I work with, but they're probably propping up the bar. *Maybe doing lines in the bathroom,* I think uncharitably. Vices that almost come with the job.

"Doesn't matter?" he repeats, then begins to make chicken noises.

"Stop that," I say. I chuckle.

"Baaawk, bawk, bawk." Matt begins to move his arms like wings.

"Okay!" I splutter, still laughing at his impression. "I just meant that a man who's paid to . . . you know. He'd likely be packing." Obviously, I can't look at him as I say this.

"Sounds like you're asking a question."

"What?" I glance his way and blink. *I mean, if you're offering.* "No. Not at all. I was generalizing." Shit. *Shit!* What possessed me to say that? "Look, before I hired Cuddle Carl, I'd found myself on a couple of escort sites. And it just made me think. Premium rates must mean a premium service."

"So do you think escorts are paid by the inch?"

"No!" I splutter. Laugh. Then coax my eyebrows from my hairline. "You said nine-inch—can we just change the tone of conversation, please?"

"By the inch," he repeats, meditatively. "That is a question I've never thought to think, let alone seek the answer to."

"Maybe Nate from Nine Inch Males ought to know. For market research."

He taps a finger to his lips as though in thought. "Getting back to your idea," he says, smacking his arm down like an elephant's trunk. "I'm not at all sure slapping my massive man meat on the tabletop, at a wedding, is the way to go."

"Massive?" *Help!*

Almost ponderingly, he adds. "Maybe that's why I get paid the big bucks."

"Well, I'm happy for you," I say, struggling to keep it together while ignoring all the things. *All the things running through my head as well as flickering in my panties.* "And while you might be right, I'd still love to see their faces. It would seriously mess with their heads." Both of their heads, I think with a snicker. Along with the pressures of the job, the liquor drunk, and the coke vacuumed, I wouldn't be surprised to find one or two already have issues getting it up.

Ask me how I know, because I'm not talking hypotheticals here.

Despite that, half the girls in New York seem to be looking for a man who works in finance. I find the concept laughable and the species so overrated. At least, now I do.

"Maybe I could hire a stripper for the office," I say, propping my elbow on the table and cupping my cheek. Maybe I shouldn't have ordered that drink. Or inhaled the one on the way in.

"It might give you a laugh, but it's not adequate payback."

"Payback isn't what I have in mind." Playing them at their own game, however . . .

"Maybe *you* don't." He says this so airily, with so little consequence, my intuition is immediately tweaked.

"I didn't tell you how things are because I need someone to defend me."

"I'm aware. But also, I'm not someone you've hired."

"Meaning what?"

He sits back in his chair again, all lounging confidence. "I think you know exactly what I mean."

"No, or I wouldn't have said otherwise." I don't ever rely on others to fight my battles.

"Why do you think I'm here?"

"Because you're—" *Nice,* I almost say. "Because you felt bad for me."

He quirks his head slightly as though to say *Maybe,* or *That's not entirely it.* "Let me put it another way." Like a snake striking, he sits forward again and takes hold of my hand. "I'm not working tonight. I'm not taking orders."

I find myself blinking again, rapidly this time. And oh, the places my mind goes.

"But you don't need to worry. I won't fuck you over." Those eyes, they're beguiling. "As for fucking you . . ." There's something almost cautious in the way his gaze moves to the back of my hand. "That's lady's choice."

Chapter 6
RYAN

The server returns with our drinks as I try to talk myself out of what Matt just said—what I think he just said. Because I felt the truth of his words in the way his gaze gobbled me up. And I don't like that I love where this might be going.

It's not like I hired an escort . . . I just kind of got him on a free loan.

I mean, if I like. If I want to take him up on it.

Pretty sure that's what he meant.

But I couldn't. I know I threw out big words in that old bar, but I couldn't have sex with someone I'd normally have to pay. *Could I?* Only, I wouldn't be having sex with just someone. I'd be having sex with him. With Matt. If I want.

Check, please!

Only kidding. Kidding myself.

I bite the inside of my lip to stop myself from smiling because, hell, the way it felt to be in his arms makes me think I probably could. Except for one little problem. It's not a moral issue. Or even an ethical one. It's more that I get the feeling Matt might be the sexual version of a gateway drug.

I've been lonely since the split. Just because I haven't missed sex doesn't mean I haven't missed being touched, I now realize. Missed being desired. Held. But if I give in, do this once, who knows where it might lead. *Might as well transfer every quarterly bonus to him.*

"What?" My tone is almost accusing as I realize he's still watching me. Watching me digest his meaning.

"I didn't say anything." Amusement lingers in the delectable quirk of his lips.

"But you're staring."

"Am I? I think you'll find this is more a case of mooning."

"Mooning?" He does say the cutest things. It could be his accent, though.

"Not the one with the bare arse, obviously."

"Bare—yeah, don't do that." Cute *and* irreverent.

"Says the woman who was all about me slapping my cock to the table a few minutes ago."

"Let's try and elevate the conversation, shall we?" I reply, like I wasn't just imagining making it rain fifties à la Lil Wayne while demanding he peel off my panties. With his teeth. Sounds like the sort of thing you might pay an escort to do.

Lady's choice.

I wonder what a night with him would cost.

Stop thinking about it! His offer isn't something that requires examination. Or an answer, for that matter. I can just gloss over it. No need to dwell on the fact that he's into me. *Or why else offer? Unless I got it wrong, and* lady's choice *means I still have to cough up.*

Enough already! It's not as though I'm not gonna ask him for clarification!

"I'd just like to point out," he says, pulling me from my thoughts, "you're the one who dragged the conversation into the gutter in the first place. Not that there's anything wrong with the gutter from time to time."

I bet he doesn't do it in gutters. I bet his job is mostly hotel based. Thousand-count linens and fancy champagne cooling in a bucket by the bed. Caribbean islands. Yachts. Six-star hotels, sunscreen, and tiny shorts.

"Now you're doing it," he says.

"Do what now?"

"Mooning. You're pretty good at it."

"Ha." My retort comes out as just a breath. *I've gotta pull myself together.* "The time and place for a gutter isn't now. Or here." And I should know, given I've spent my adult life crawling out of that place. That girl from North Carolina is long dead. No more *y'all* or *yonder* or *fixin' to do* anything. I coached myself out of all that a long time ago.

"What should we do instead?" So much suggestion in that tone of his.

"For the purposes of this evening, what couples do, I guess."

"This couple." He motions a finger between us. "I sense they would canoodle."

"Sounds like something senior citizens might do."

"Second base. Sometimes third?" He pulls back as though something has just occurred to him. "Are you trying to entice me into the gutter again?"

"Maybe our relationship is more a meeting of minds. Maybe we're a couple that talks about art and philosophy."

"Do you know much about art? Because I don't."

"You're meant to. Well, Nate is. But no one here will ask you questions about art. Unless it's art as a means of tax avoidance. In that case—"

"I should rely on interpretive dance to confuse them?"

"Maybe feign laryngitis." My smile dissipates as my gaze drifts across the table, to where the glasses have been mostly cleared.

"You're worried about them, aren't you?" he says, following my gaze.

How weird. For a little while, I forgot the reason I'm here. "I just want to get it over with."

"Do they intimidate you?"

"I can handle them just fine." Mostly handle them. Or handle most of them. *Most of them but one.* "I just don't want to get caught out in a stupid lie. Though most lies are stupid, by my reckoning."

"That's some very black-and-white thinking. Some lies are told for valid reasons."

"Well, I have valid reasons for doing this—for going to these lengths. As the only woman on the trading floor, I have to be okay with the frat-house office mentality. I can take the daily shit throwing, but that's where the line ends." I learned the hard way that trying to laugh off or ignore inappropriate behavior only comes back to bite you in the ass. Some men seem to think *no* is open to interpretation. They can't help but test those waters, and if you're soft . . . God help you.

So I take no shit. And while the guys wear chinos or business slacks and Patagonia vests, I adhere to the dictums of Coco Chanel and dress like I'm about to meet my worst enemy every day. In other words, my office persona is Miranda Priestly. On crack.

My makeup is on point, my hair is pulled back, and I wear my glasses, not my contact lenses. It's my armor, and it very clearly states: *You'd better be talking to my face.* And it's always worked—the ballbuster version of me has always made them toe the line.

Until it didn't anymore. Which is why I've had to recruit some help tonight. Someone big and strong and male to help me get my point across. Which is kind of galling in itself.

I inhale deeply, not quite sure how much I'm ready to tell Matt. But I need to tell him something before they get back.

"Once upon a time, everything in the office was fine. I had a boyfriend, and my colleagues mostly treated me as though I was one of the guys. Not ideal, but I could deal with their lame jokes and zone out during their embellished tales of who they banged the night before. Fast-forward a little, and now I no longer have a boyfriend but an office nemesis, though Pete pretends that only one of us is affected by our split." *Bull. Shit.*

"And since the split, the office banter, if you like, has taken a turn. The kind of turn that some people would describe as sexist." *It's me. I'm some people.* I rub my lips together, not wanting to sound like that girl—the one who needs a man to fix things for her. "They're mostly harmless—"

"Even with the bet they've got going?" he demands.

"It sounds worse than it is. The issue isn't so much them as a collective as it is one of them."

"What's his name?"

"Brandon." My lips curl. "For reasons clear only to himself, he's under the impression it's his turn now."

"His turn?" Matt demands, his gaze flinty.

"Now that Pete's done with me, I guess."

"Fuck." Matt swipes his hand across his mouth as though tasting something offensive.

"He asked me out, and I turned him down," I rush on, wanting to be done with this. "And it's like that's made me some kind of challenge." It's gone from crude comments when he thinks no one else is paying attention to straight-up abuse.

"That's fucked up."

"It is, but it's a reality for more than just me. I was being harassed long before I could spell the word. I learned early on that I needed to harden the hell up and get used to being called a bitch—and worse—in the workplace. You get hit on, you turn them down, you get labeled a bitch, fine. But if you call them out, suddenly you're difficult.

"And before you say I should make an official complaint, it would be no use. He's too popular with the C-suite. His numbers are good," I add with a weak shrug. "But the fact that I faked a boyfriend in the first place is down to him."

"That's not surprising."

"It was to me," I say with an unhappy huff of a laugh. "At least, in the moment."

"What happened?"

"We were having drinks after work to christen the new guy's first week at work." I swallow and slide my hair behind my ears. "He'd survived that baptism of fire, and you've got to be a team player, right?"

Matt smiles, and I hate that I see pity there.

"An hour in, and I was getting ready to leave. I visited the restroom only to find Brandon lounging in the dim hallway on my way out."

Matt's smile falls, his expression a mixture of concern and trepidation.

"*Come on*," Brandon had said, all hands and beer breath. *"The more you fight it, the more I want it. It's gonna happen between us."*

Shock had washed through me like a tsunami. Fear, if I'm being honest. He wore such a feral look in his eyes.

"Nothing bad happened," I say. "I just pushed him out of the way as I uttered that lame phrase every girl whips out when she's not interested. 'I have a boyfriend.'"

"Hanging around dark hallways. *Making* you push him. Fucking hell, Ryan. That's the behavior of a predator."

I wave his words away. "I decided I might as well run with that story. Embellish it, even. So I began weaving my tale. I'd met a guy on vacation. An artist from Madrid." With my hand, I indicate him. "Interesting, glamorous, and not on the same continent. A perfect creation, really."

"Long distance?" I hear Brandon scoff. *"Never gonna last."*

"Fun while it does, though" was my retort.

He didn't like the idea of that.

"So that was my story, and I've stuck to it." Especially when his efforts intensified. Hair touching, fingers tracing the base of my spine or briefly touched to my hip, his opportunities chosen when he knew I wouldn't make a scene. An elevator dick brush that I tried to tell myself was an accident.

"We will fuck, Killer." This he said as late as last week, his assertion like a lover's whisper as he hung over my shoulder as though helping me with something. *"It's only a matter of time before it's my cock you're riding."*

"Pretty sure anyone willing to fuck you is just too damned lazy to jerk off."

"That mouth," he said, all growling and entertained. *"One of these days I'm gonna use it as a—"*

"What part of 'I have a boyfriend' don't you understand?" I demanded, rolling my chair back over his foot.

"The part where I've never seen him." His retort, always with an air of having the upper hand.

I give an uncomfortable shrug. "That's why I was so desperate earlier."

"Why the hell are you still working there?" he asks with a serious frown.

"I have plans," I say, not willing to give them away. To jinx them. "I know I'm not perfect, and in some ways, I've brought this on myself."

"Fuck that," he says immediately. Passionately.

"I just mean my smart mouth seems to encourage him. But you know that old saying, if you run into an asshole in the morning, you run into an asshole, but if you run into assholes all day, you're the asshole?"

"And that's not you."

"That's not me. I know I'm kind of prickly, but I'm more than aware of my own flaws." But even if Brandon's interest was genuine and he gave me flowers in place of intimidation, I still wouldn't date him. I won't ever get involved with another man in finance. Too much drama. Too much trauma.

"I just wanna get tonight over with." My words feel brittle. "We only need to stay long enough to make a point." And not long enough for anyone to realize Matt isn't a Spanish artist called Nate.

"And the point is that you're taken? Or that they should pull their heads out of their arses and join the new century?"

"Both works for me."

"Then I think we should dance. So you can show me off to the whole office, the big strappin' lad that I am."

I tsk. "Such a peacock."

"Are you gonna want to congratulate the happy couple?"

I glance down and smooth my hand over the tablecloth. "*Want* might be putting it a little strongly." Fun times to be had by all, right?

"What's he gonna think about me?"

"I don't give a flying fuck."

"But you know he's not gonna like it. He's still part of the reason I'm here."

I guess that's true—no point in arguing. "Pete traded up."

"Fucked up, more like. But getting back to me, the peacock."

I give a tiny laugh. "Oh, so you admit it?"

He almost rolls his eyes. "Do you want to know the reason I'm here? And I don't mean them." He glances across the table to the chairs yet to be filled. "The reason I came with you? It's because you intrigue the hell out of me."

Intriguing. That's more than I expected. Better than *pretty* or *hot* or any of that mundane stuff. And boy, do I soak up his regard like a sponge, no words between us, just a thousand crazy ideas. Then I remember what he does for a living—again—and the pleasure swelling in my chest pops like a painful blister.

"You're good at this," I say like I know what I'm talking about.

Something clouds his expression before he gives a nod, his fingers rubbing across a suddenly taut jaw. "The thing is, I mean it."

"Small talk," I almost shout. "We should . . . talk."

"I did suggest that earlier."

"Did you? I don't recall."

"Tell me something," he purrs, and I remember. "Tell me something about Ryan."

"Now, there's a can of worms you really don't want to open."

"Fuck that. Tell me all the things."

"You asked for it," I say. Though it sounds more like *Your funeral*. "I'm an only child. Adult orphan." I pull a stupidly sad face and make a crying gesture with my index finger before realizing I have no idea why I told him. "Favorite food?" I hedge, and he nods. "Carnitas, specifically from a Mexican place in FiDi. Oh, and zeppole. Can't forget zeppole."

"Specifically from?"

"Someplace midtown." Zeppole. My having-a-good-day treat, probably because the taste reminds me of times past. Of elephant ears, of podunk towns and country fairs. "Pastimes?" I rush on, conscious of revealing too much.

"Anything. Everything."

"I love my job—I think I already said that. If I'm not working, I'm thinking about working. It's the best thing ever when my instincts are on point."

"They must love you." That doesn't sound like a compliment.

"Yeah, especially as they got me cheap."

"The fuck?" he mutters. "You're really not selling this outfit."

But I know I was lucky to get a job here. I likely only got an interview because of my name. *Like they confused me for a guy.* I don't have an MBA from Harvard, and I didn't go to business school. I started at an investment bank with a degree from a mediocre college I worked my ass off to put myself through. The bank job was a back-end role, and I just got lucky. Asked a lot of questions. Learned about the business. And once I had my butt in the interview seat, my ego did the rest. But yeah, they got me cheap.

"I'm not complaining. The industry is notorious for underpaying women, but my bonus kind of makes up for things. What else?" I ponder, refusing to return to our stare fest. "I'm not big on friends. Or people generally. I'm impulsive, quick to judge, opinionated . . . and I can't cook."

At this, he laughs. And I love that I made him do that.

"Couples kiss, Ryan. They touch."

Yes, please. Sign me up for some of that lady's choice, whatever that meant.

"Your turn." My mind is a spaghetti mess of thoughts, and the second the words are out of my mouth, I remember he doesn't share. *On dates.*

"Let me see," he says, his mouth curling in one corner. *Like the cat anticipating a juicy treat.* "I have more siblings than is seemly."

My expression must reflect my surprise.

"I blame the poor choice of TV shows in Ireland during the '80s and '90s."

"Wow. Good for your parents!" Maybe he's not telling the truth—why would he tell the truth?

"What a deviant you are, talking about my parents' sex life."

"I am not! It was you who—"

"You know, when we first met, I wouldn't have believed you were the kind of girl who blushes at the drop of a hat."

"I am not blushing! And if I am, it's because you're shameless."

"Do you think my parents might be responsible for the field I've ended up in?" This he says with an air of *I dare you to ask*. "Not that I'm complaining about my chosen career."

In my head, it's my turn to make chicken noises. "I guess enjoying your job makes life easier," I answer uncertainly.

I've never had an opinion of sex work. Or even sex workers. I mean, I guess it's one of the oldest professions in the world, but if you'd asked me this morning if I'd pay for sex, the answer would've been heck no. Why pay when dick is only ever a swipe away? Not that I'm into that kind of dating life. But also, I guess not all dick is created equal. And not all dick owners are interested in anything more than getting their own rocks off.

I can see that making the choice—the choice to go pro—might be empowering. Like he said before, there could be an element of security in the decision. And with a man like Matt, there would be fun. Laughter. A genuineness of connection. And the kind of mind-blowing sex a girl would max out her credit card for.

Not that I'm considering . . .

No, I am not.

"Makes for happier individuals," Matt replies enigmatically.

I have no issue believing he leaves a *lot* of women very happy. "What else?"

"I tolerate my friends. Mostly," he adds with a humorous lilt. "I like to climb. Rocks, mostly. Food? I like food. All food. And I can cook, which is just as well, as I have a voracious appetite. In fact, right now, I'd eat you if you stood still long enough."

My laughter is loud and genuine.

"Though I reckon I wouldn't have to be hungry to nibble on you."

I feel what he's saying, even if I don't fully understand it—feel it physically.

"As for the rest, I like beer and Irish whiskey, and I dress on the right."

"Such quiet confidence." I roll my eyes for effect and try very hard not to let my eyes fall there. *I bet he's abundantly blessed.* "Anything else?"

"According to my ex, I'm rubbish at commitment."

A slip from the vault? So much for keeping his private life just that, though I kind of see her point. I would have issues sharing him. "But just look at how you committed to this!" I sort of explode because the images that flash through my head are more than a little disconcerting.

"Or maybe I should just *be* committed."

"You are not crazy for helping me out." I'm the crazy one for thinking the things I've been thinking. "You're nice."

He pulls that unimpressed face again.

"You—you're a gentleman!" A gentleman on the streets and a freak between the sheets. We'll call that an educated guess. "Give me your phone," I demand, holding out my hand. I need a distraction before I overheat. "I'll call your ex and set her straight."

His mouth curves as he takes my hand in his instead. "Thanks, but I'm sure that would go down like a one-legged man in an arse-kicking contest."

"And that would be a problem?" I feel a little pang in my chest. "Because you want to get back with her?"

"It is her wedding day."

"Oh, right. Sorry."

"It's okay." He puts our joined hands on his knee. "It's just been a weird day."

"Maybe a little weird," I concede, forcing my gaze upward. A thin scar bisects his left brow, and I find myself wondering about the cause. "But you've rolled with the punches admirably, and for that I'm truly—"

"Grateful," he finishes for me. Ungraciously. *What is it with him and compliments?*

"I am!" I insist.

"No need." His words gruff, he rubs his hand over the darkening stubble on his jaw.

Why does the motion only serve to accentuate his lips? And how come I didn't notice before how well shaped they are? Full and kissable, maybe even a little pouty right now.

"Matt, listen, I—" But whatever I was about to say is cut off as the clowns return to the big top.

"Killaaa!"

"Killer Queen!"

Lord, do I hate that moniker.

Brandon's over-the-top greeting is echoed by his sycophants, including the nerdy but sweet quant that recently joined Dreyland Cap from MIT. The kid must feel like he's crossed over to the dark side, all the liquor and party favors available to him.

"Knock that off," I complain, glaring at the ringleader clown. Meanwhile, Jared breaks into his off-key rendition of the Queen song "Killer Queen" as I stare at him icily.

"Come on, Kil—I mean, Ryan. It's totally a compliment!"

"So says you," I mutter. Someone must've told him his dimpled smile was cute. Probably when he was three or something. Someone ought to tell him that is no longer the case.

"Killer Queen" is a song about a high-class call girl, but that's not where the association originates. It's the dynamite and laser beams—the kick-ass themes. Their own twisted take, at least.

And though I'm no one's pussycat, and rarely playful at work, the song does speak to me in other ways. I like to a girl pretending to be someone she's not. *I might not speak like a baroness, but I don't speak like a girl from my hood either.*

"Who's this?" Brandon gives a jerk of his chin.

"My Nathaniel." My tone says: *Who d'you think?* "Like I said, I won't be hanging with you guys today." Cupping Matt's cheek, I press my thumb lightly against the corner of his mouth. "I have my favorite plus-one with me today."

"Didn't see you at the service," he grates out.

"Didn't you?" *Screw you.*

"Aww, shit!" Jared exclaims. "This is the guy—the one you met on vacation!"

"This is *the* guy," I agree.

"Fuck!" Kyle drops into a seat. "Someone took my drink. I was coming back to it." He looks my way as though I'm interested in his drunk-ass complaint. "Vodka, Red Bull, Fireball, and—"

"So go order another," Brandon doesn't so much suggest as order. "Aren't you gonna introduce us?" This he fires my way, his tone sorely lacking suggestion.

I've opened my mouth to tell him exactly what I think of his demand and where he can shove it when I find Matt's—I mean, Nate's—fingers lightly squeezing my shoulder. I must've been too focused on these idiots to realize he's moved closer and that his arm is now resting across the back of my chair.

"What's up?" Jared says, dropping into the seat on Matt's right.

"Nate doesn't speak—"

"*Buenas noches*," my imaginary boyfriend says in an accent that sounds convincingly Spanish. *And convincing is better than comical.*

"*¿Cómo estás?*" Jared returns, sounding like a bad actor in a telenovela. "*Mi nombre es Jared.*" Or maybe that should be a kindergartener in a Spanish class.

I almost give a whoop of joy at Jared's butchering of the language. *Even I recognize that much.* Before the wedding, I asked everyone in the office if they spoke another language, in a roundabout way, as damage control after I'd uttered my stupid lie.

Being hotheaded is such a curse sometimes.

"*Bien, gracias*," Matt—Nate—returns pleasantly. And without an ounce of concern.

Meanwhile, I've still broken out in a cold sweat. I send a silent prayer heavenward. *Please let him know a few more words, Lord.*

"You speak Spanish?" Jamie, another of the guys, directs Jared's way.

"Nah," he admits. "I just learned enough in high school to impress this Mexican chick I wanted to get with." He turns to Matt again. "*¿Hablar inglése?*" Jared says next.

"*Un poco*," Matt returns with a small gesture of his hand.

He sounds so convincing, especially compared to Jared. I find myself thinking about what he said—why I hadn't chosen an Italian pretend boyfriend, given I'd spent three miserable weeks in Italy.

Italy wasn't miserable, but I was. I'd sold myself the vacation as a summer to get over my broken heart. I had very firm plans of finding an Italian stallion to screw some sense back into me. Sadly, the only D I got while there was depression.

"You really don't speak the same language?" Jared looks as confused as a cricket in a hubcap.

"We converse freely in the only language we need." For show, and because I suddenly want to, I press my hand to Matt's left cheek and my lips to his right. He makes a low, purring sound of surprise, then murmurs a string of seductive-sounding words. Words I can't make sense of, though their effect feels like hot syrup sinking into me.

"Man, I love love." Jamie sighs sweetly.

In the periphery of my vision, I note how Brandon sends him a death glare. "What did he say?" he demands.

Beats me, I almost answer as my brain plays catch-up. My blood seems to have drained from my brain to my lap. Oh. My. Lord. His mouth—the shapes it makes. That melodic rise and fall of his words. The man speaks Spanish, hallelujah!

But why the hell didn't he mention that?

"I only know basic greetings and *es calinete!*" Jared says. "You're hot."

"*No, no, eso no está bien,*" Matt—Nate!—says with a laugh. "Not correct. *Él está caliente.* He is hot," he repeats before turning my way. "*Ella está caliente.* She is hot." This he kind of purrs as he strokes his hand down my face. "Ryan." *Holy rolling r's.* "Is beautiful."

"Whoa," someone murmurs. I can't be sure who, and I'm not looking because I'm too busy staring into my pseudo boyfriend's eyes. Eyes that seem to shine with a dark possessiveness. *Man, he's good.* He's obviously had a lot of practice, but good Lord, the man could melt the panties off a girl's behind with just one look—no accent required!

My hottie inclines his head as he murmurs more of that sensual-sounding language, pulling me closer to whisper those sweet sexy somethings in my ear. It takes me a moment to catch on to his meaning, but somewhere in the shiver-inducing cadence, the husky rise and fall, I hear the word *canoodle*.

We're a couple that canoodles. Fine by me, provided we don't come anywhere close to second base in public.

"What'd he say?" Brandon demands once again, like a school bully who doesn't get the joke. Maybe because he is the joke. And he is definitely the bully.

I flick Brandon a look that says: *Like I'd tell you.*

"So guys, this is my Nathaniel," I begin, pawing his chest for good measure. *It's a hard job, but someone's got to do it.* "Nate, baby, these are my colleagues"—also known as the clowns I work with—"Tyler, Jared, Jamie, Kyle, and Dipesh. Why is Dipesh asleep?" I ask, watching his nodding head, his chin bouncing against his chest.

"Can't hold his liquor," Kyle supplies.

"You forgot to introduce me," Brandon puts in.

"No, I didn't forget."

Five of the six offer varying degrees of lukewarm hellos, while Brandon just grunts.

"You just spoke to him in English."

"Your point?" I slice Brandon with a look.

"And he spoke to you in Spanish."

"Ten out of ten for observation."

"Well?"

"We're teaching each other. What the hell do you think we do all those hours on the phone?"

"I know what I'd be doing if I had a hot Spanish girlfriend," Jared puts in lasciviously.

"There's only so much phone sex one couple can have." *Or not, as the case may be,* I think as I stroke my hand down Matt's shirt. He feels like Michelangelo's *David* under there.

"*Sufriría una lesión una y otra vez por ti cualquier día,*" Matt murmurs as he takes my hand in his and presses it to his cheek.

"*Sí, baby. Sí,*" I say. Damn it. I should've googled some Spanish phrases.

"Killer, you're killing me!" one of the clowns moans.

"It wasn't an invitation to watch," I retort through gritted teeth.

"Then stop feeling him up," Brandon mutters.

I spear the shithead with a look. "Really? The number of times I've had to listen to your tales of *this* hot girl from a bar and *that* hot girl from Instagram."

Thanks to social media influencers, finance bros have become a hot commodity. The irony is these men are often the smartest in the room, but they're also idiots because they've bought into the finance bro hype. They see themselves as irresistible, like our job is all yachts and partying. In reality, it's long hours in the office, with even longer hours glued to our phones at home staring at market alerts, reading emails and texts, and dealing with phone calls from other time zones.

"Can't be much of a relationship if you can barely communicate." Brandon lounges back in his chair as he sends a glower Matt's way.

"We say all we need to in other ways."

"I didn't think you meant it," he mutters sourly. "That you were bringing someone."

"And I'm supposed to care what you think?"

He glares at me as the others make a kind of whistling sound, like fifth graders in the schoolyard.

"What'd I miss?" Dipesh says loudly, coming to like a lip-smacking jack-in-the-box.

"Killer Queen brought a boyfriend."

"The Spanish guy?" Dipesh asks, all wide-eyed drunkenness as he glances around the table as though trying to make out who is who.

"Yup."

"How tall are you?" Dipesh squints across the table at Matt.

I wouldn't be surprised if he's seeing multiple Matts. *Lucky for him.*

"Is he taller than five feet six?" he persists.

"Don't be a dick." I glance around the table with a look of disgust. *You assholes.*

"He's tall," Jared eventually offers up. "Six two would be my guess."

"And handsome," Jamie says.

"And more to the point, he's really Spanish," Kyle adds.

Dipesh nods as though taking this all in. Then he jumps to his feet. "Yeah!" He begins to hammer his fists to his chest like a puny Tarzan. "I win, motherfuckers! Pay up!"

Matt catches my eye, his expression seeming to say, *You have got to be kidding me.*

Chapter 7
MATT

Sufriría una lesión una y otra vez por ti cualquier día.

It's not every woman I'd offer to suffer a repetitive strain injury for.

By way of long-distance telephone sex.

Good thing no one at that table spoke Spanish, you eejit.

"He seemed kind of territorial." Aiming for casual, I turn us in a circle on the dance floor. Lucky for me, the band has turned to Billie Holiday for inspiration. And maybe I shouldn't be enjoying having my hands on Ryan this much, but fuck it. I should get some of the benefits. *Might as well be hanged for a sheep as for a lamb,* as the saying goes. "Bryce, was it?" I add, poking when she doesn't answer.

"Brandon," she says flatly. "The bane of my office existence."

"And the bet was his doing."

Her shoulder flicks. "He does seem to have it in for me."

He'd like to have it in you, a little voice in my head whispers. And I'd like to break it off. At the root. Preferably without touching it.

What the fuck is with that? I mean, I like to think I'm a decent kind of fella. I do what's right and stand up for those who can't stand up for themselves. But this feels different—the way I wanted to launch myself across the table and punch him in the face felt so real. And that was just for his stroppy fucking attitude. For the way he was looking at Ryan, I wanted to twist off his tiny balls.

So much for entertainment. And so much for lady's choice. I only realized what that sounded like once the words were in the air. Because it sounded like I might be touting for business instead of being genuinely interested in her.

I stifle a sigh. No point in backtracking. It's not as though she seemed interested in the proposition. Either of them.

"I thought that skinny fella was gonna break a rib when he started hammering at his chest."

"Hush." Her eyes dart left as an older couple smile, waltzing by us. "My boss is over there," she says, nodding toward someone I can't see behind me. "And you're supposed to be Spanish."

"I thoughta thata skinny fella—ow!"

"Knock it off, Spanish Mario." She lifts her foot from mine. "Why didn't you tell me you speak Spanish?"

"You didn't ask."

She narrows her eyes, a smile tugging at her mouth. "So are you Irish or Spanish or . . ."

"Soy lo que la señorita ordene." I'm whatever the lady ordered.

"That's *not* an answer."

"Sure it is. Just because you don't understand it . . ." *Go on, ask me what I said.*

"Show-off."

I stifle a disappointed sigh. "I'm half and half," I say. Half Irish, half Spanish, and all kinds of into her, despite the obstacles I've put in my own way.

"Oh. Cool."

"Do you want to know what I just said?" *Go on, say yes.* If for no other reason than it can be annoying when people say shit you don't understand. Like *You're not the kind of man women want to marry.* Or *You're a good-time boyfriend, not a longtime one.* Fuck.

"I'm almost afraid to know."

I make a chicken noise again. Ryan gazes, playfully unimpressed.

"You really want me to keep my mouth shut now that you've discovered my Spanish tongue?" *Go on, ask me what my Spanish tongue would do to you.*

"Such compliments," she deadpans.

"There are all kinds of ways to compliment," I say, devoid of suggestion. From my tone, at least. *"Porque con esta lengua rendiría homenaje a tu belleza."* Because with this tongue I would pay homage to your beauty. "Wanna know what I said that time?"

"Probably not."

"Come on, be adventurous." She can deny with her words, but those eyes . . .

"I'm kind of risk averse."

I give a soft chuckle. "You can't convince me you're frightened of anything."

Her gaze slides over my shoulder. And hardens. "How about murder on the dance floor."

"Something tells me you're not referring to Sophie Ellis-Bextor."

"Who?"

I open my mouth, about to ask how old she is, to complain that "Murder on the Dancefloor" is a classic. What comes out instead is "Your ex is behind me, isn't he?"

Her expression gives an almost imperceptible flicker, her gaze drifting over my shoulder again. So I press two fingers to her cheek, gently moving her gaze back.

"Eyes on me, darlin'. That fucker doesn't deserve an ounce of your attention."

"I'm just imagining his face as Bolognese again."

I give a soft chuckle and lift her hand to the back of my neck. "Let's give the bastard a show." Without giving her time to protest, I close the small space between us, pressing my lips tenderly to her hairline. Her head sits under my chin, and the heat of her body, its softness, just . . . *fuck*.

"Really, really messy Bolognese." There's a wobble in her delivery that makes me tighten my grip. "I don't know why I feel like this. It's not like I don't see him most days."

"Fuck him. He's not worth the salt of your tears."

"Oh, I'm done crying," she says with a heartening vehemence. "It's just . . . all this." It's not hard to guess what she's referring to. The hotel. The day. The felicitations. "He gets all this after the way he treated me. There's no justice, you know?"

But as I twirl us around, he doesn't look joyous. Not that I say so. "How about we send him a tiny *fuck you*?"

"What do you have in mind?" So much suggestion in her tone. So much interest in the brightness of her eyes. She gives a little gasp as my arm brushes her waist, but it's nothing compared to her expression as I pull her body tight, pressing my fingers to her peach of an arse.

"Try not to look too shocked," I murmur. "You're supposed to be used to my hands."

"It's not your hands that are shocking." Her lips clamp together, but the words are already out there. "Please ignore that I said that," she quickly adds.

I give a soft laugh as pleasure ripples through me. "I don't think I can. You called me a peacock, and now I feel like one."

"Is that what you have stuffed down your pants? Oh my good Lord," she adds in a hushed yet mortified tone. "I should *not* have chugged both glasses of champagne. It must've gone to my head."

Just like she's gone to mine.

"A peacock," I murmur ponderingly. "Well, it's not fully . . . cocked. Just a little interest, let's say."

"This is so inappropriate." But she's smiling, even if she's trying not to.

"You started it. But I can finish it," I offer, deftly twirling us again. "Finish you."

She blinks as she tries to discern my meaning.

"I have no words," she says, her lashes still fluttering. "But at least the view is better this way."

Now that I'm blocking her line of sight, she means. I have that pleasure, and he's not at all what I expected. Which was a finance nerd, the kind that gets off on spreadsheets and wears an overpriced fleece vest to hide his pigeon chest. He doesn't fit that stereotype at all. Six feet, at a guess, blond, and my money is on blue eyed, though it's hard to tell, considering the feckers are narrowed like slits currently.

That's it, arsewipe. Take a good look at who's manhandling her now.

"Your man is watching us awful closely for someone who's just gotten married."

"He's not my man. I also don't care."

"But he does," I say, dipping her for good measure, my eyes meeting his as I do. *Yeah, fucker, take a good look.*

"What are you doing?" Her tone is slightly panicked, though her leg slides against my thigh, her body fully on board.

"What Latin lovers do." Hand splayed against her sternum, my fingertips feather the smooth wings of her collarbones. I give a satisfied purr before I pull her up again. "Dancing is a vertical expression of—"

"A horizontal desire?"

"Old-school missionary, I was gonna say." I don't know whether it's the role I'm playing that makes me say these things or whether it's desire or jealousy. I just know I want more than this moment.

The beat changes, and it's like someone up there is looking out for me. I slide an arm around her waist and my thigh between her legs.

"What the heck—"

"Just go with it. He's still watching." Not that I'd know, because I'm no longer looking at him.

Dancing with Ryan is the next best thing to having her in my bed. The proximity. The touching, bodies moving with synchronicity. I lead, she submits. I give and she . . .

Fuck. I clasp my arms tighter, one hand on her backside and the fingers of my other curled around her ribs. And my God, can she move. Sultry, sinuous, all undulating provocativeness as I press my lips to the curve of her neck. She smells of exotic blooms and secrets and tastes like she might—

"Ryan." A man's voice, deep and assured.

Under my lips and my hands, she freezes. I straighten, pulling her in front of me as I slide possessive arms around her waist. Our bodies still flush, my front pressed to her back, I'm a bear hug of possessiveness. *And it feels so right.*

"Pete." Check out the pronunciation of that *t*. "And Annabelle." I almost hear her forced smile. "You look stunning."

"Thank you," the bride murmurs.

"Congratulations. To both of you."

"It's so good of you to come," the bride adds when the groom does not.

"Oh, I wouldn't have missed this for the world!" Such forced pluck barely drowning out those piss and vinegar undertones. "This is Nathaniel—Nate. My boyfriend."

All of a sudden, Pete looks like he's sucking lemons.

How about balls, Pete. Suck on these *balls.*

"*¡Enhorabuena!*" I begin, my congratulations all magnanimous obliviousness as I nuzzle my stunning girlfriend, besotted. "I wish you much 'appiness." A little bit of Mario isn't gonna kill anyone. Except my foot as Ryan presses the point of her heel to my toes.

"Thank you," the bride replies softly. Meanwhile, the groom can't take his eyes off my hands. On Ryan, obviously.

You snooze, you lose, pal.

I tighten my arms around her and whisper something suggestive sounding in her ear. *Suggestive sounding* my ass—there's nothing ambiguous about *I'm going to make you come so hard you'll forget what his face looks like.*

Good that no one around here speaks Spanish.

"I bought you chef knives," Ryan suddenly bursts out. "From the wedding registry. I figured you might want to use them. Someday."

"That's . . . so nice of you." The bride looks up, bewildered. "Isn't that nice, Peter?"

"Yes. Nice. Thanks, Ryan."

I can't see Ryan's expression, but I see his. Fucking entertaining, I'll say.

"Well, we'd better . . ." Ryan's words trail off.

"Things to see and people to do," I put in with a heavy accent as I turn.

"Things to *do*," the wanker corrects.

"No," I say, twirling Ryan around, then back into the cradle of my arms. I shoot him a wink over my shoulder. "I got it right the first time."

I'm thankful my parents made us learn how to dance in our early years. Irish, flamenco, ballroom. The future benefits might not have interested me back then, when all I wanted to do was be outside with a ball. I reaped the benefits once I reached puberty, though. And I'm reaping them again as I sense his eyes following us.

"You okay?"

"Yeah, I'm okay," she murmurs.

"He's not at all like I imagined. He's so aggressively . . . average," I say. *Okay, lie.*

"I feel kind of bad. For her, I mean."

"She's not your responsibility."

"Did you see that diamond?" she blusters. "Of course you did. Pretty sure they can see it from the moon."

"You did your good turn when you provided her with a murder weapon."

"I sounded weird, didn't I?"

"You sounded like a badass. I wish I'd taken a picture of his face. Almost better than Bolognese."

She laughs, and the sound gets me right in the feels. She should laugh always. Not like a crazy person, but she should be happy, content and loved, a woman like her.

"Thank you," she says quietly.

"For the appearance of Spanish Super Mario?"

"Even for him."

"Anytime, darlin'. And anytime you want to ride the mustache . . ."

"Oh, my God," she splutters, putting her hand to my chest. "You don't even have a mustache."

"For you, I'd grow one." I cover her hand with mine. "Because you deserve someone who treats you right."

And there, in the middle of the dance floor, Ryan stills. "I don't care what you say," she whispers, resting her hand on my chest. "I think you're one of the nicest men I've ever met."

"Ah, darlin', you're confusing nice with good mannered." As though to prove a point, I take her face in my hands. Fuck it all to hell. I don't care about consequences, the person she thinks I am, or the things I said were no good for me. Because right now, all I want to do is kiss her. Kiss her until she sighs. Kiss her until her body melts into mine.

Her eyes darken with anticipation as I move closer and slant my mouth over hers. And as our lips meet, I feel that spark of recognition again. Like we've done this before, maybe in some other time or some other universe. Is the familiarity in the flutter of her lashes or her tiny inhale? Or maybe the way she folds her fingers around my lapel? Because I sense it all. Feel it all. Like this is what I've been missing all along.

Fuck. Pleasure coils inside as the tip of her tongue glides against mine.

"You play dirty," I whisper, pressing my lips to the corner of hers.

"I prefer the term *creative competitor.*"

"Creative." So much suggestion in the word as I pinch her bottom lip between my teeth. Suck on her delicate gasp. "I do like the sound of that."

I'm too old for making out on dance floors. Too old for public displays of affection, of passion, yet here I stand, giving not one fuck for any of that. Another press of my lips, and her mouth yields once more, the dance floor dropping away, the people around us fading into the ether at the vibration of her tiny moan. I want her. I shouldn't, but I'm too far gone. Every press of her lips, every tentative brush of her tongue is nothing short of intoxicating.

"Oh, God," she whispers as I slow the kiss, pull back a little, and stare into her soulful eyes. Her tongue makes a deft flick to the bow of her top lip as though tasting our kiss.

Like I wasn't hard enough already.

"A friend said something to me earlier tonight," I whisper, stroking her cheeks with my thumbs. "He told me there's beauty in the spontaneous. Even magic sometimes."

"Tonight was certainly spontaneous."

I stare down at all that beauty. A hundred things I want to say, and not one of them makes any sense. "And magical, don't you think?"

"Yeah," she agrees softly.

"Good. Because that's why I think you should come back with me tonight."

Chapter 8
MATT

Outside, the air has cooled, but I don't think that's the reason for Ryan's shiver. If her blood is simmering half as much as mine, then it's anticipation.

"Are we walking?" she asks.

"Cab, I think." But there's something holding me back. Something I need to do first. *Need viscerally.* It's part of the reason I followed Ryan here in the first place, I realize. "I've gotta go back inside," I say, not letting go of her hand. I tip my head in the direction of the doors, the doorman vacillating, his hand still on the door. "I've forgotten something." Not a lie. Not exactly a lie. "I won't be a minute."

Her expression flickers uncertainly, so I make it right as I pull her into my arms and whisper something in her ear.

"Really?" Her incredulity hits the cool air in a chuckle. But with a dubious look, she allows me to pull her inside.

"Wait here, yeah?" I back her up against the arm of a couch only to find her fingers at the back of my neck.

"I can't believe you don't have condoms," she whispers with a giggle that tickles my ear.

"I feel judged," I say, pulling away with a grin.

"Well, I guess this is kind of a busman's holiday."

That again. My body kind of hedges as my brain weighs up the prospect of spilling my guts. *Now or later? In public or when we're alone?* I know I'll have to come clean—put her right. Admit I'm not someone who fucks women for a living. Not that I actually *said* I was an escort, but I've hardly disabused her of the notion either.

Because I'm an idiot, obviously.

"Hold that thought," I say, holding up my index finger. There's no easy way to pull myself out of the shit, but the best thing I can do is not tell her here.

"I'll be waiting." There is so much suggestion in her tone. Weird how it feels like there's a lead weight in my stomach suddenly.

Three steps away and three back before I'm pulling her against me again. Kissing her. Whispering, "I can't wait." Fuck, I want her so badly, but I have to do this first. Even if what follows isn't a night of unadulterated passion but a punch in the gob. "Don't go anywhere. I'll be right back."

"You'd better be."

My gaze falls over her one more time. She's all sass, her eyes lit from within.

Please, God. Don't let me have fucked this up.

Through the hotel foyer, my rapid steps echo as I weave through residents and guests, taut jawed as I ignore the men's room on this floor. I take the stairs—take them two at a time. Blood and adrenaline pumping hard through my veins, my desire for Ryan simmering just under the surface.

Out on the second floor, through the marbled entranceway. I pause as I reach the imposing ballroom doors. Straighten my jacket, then my cuffs, and slow my pace to sedate as I make my way inside and spot him almost immediately: One of the two men who deserve a little trouble.

I approach the table, keeping from his view, slowing my pace again as I draw nearer.

"I'm telling you, that bitch has some kind of pussy voodoo."

I halt at the fucker's words.

"You haven't gotta chance with her," one of the other men retorts. Jake, I think, his words slurred, thanks to the drinks. "She can't stand the sight of you."

"She'll come around."

"Bullshit."

"She'd better," he growls. "I want my turn."

A fucking turn?

"Voodoo, I'm tellin' you. She has all the best plays—I mean, where the fuck does she get her stuff from?"

"Instinct," Dipesh says. "She pays attention to the little things."

"And Brandon's gotta little thing for her," someone else quips.

"Fuck you," Brandon retorts. "You don't understand. Pete wouldn't be where he is without her."

"Pete got promoted because he's marrying in. He fucked Ryan over!"

"Yeah, but she made it so he got noticed. Pussy voodoo, I'm telling you."

I've heard enough.

I pass an empty table and swipe up a half-filled glass, then theatrically trip over an invisible chair leg. *Oops.*

"What the fuck!" Brandon jumps up, wearing his last drink of the evening.

"¡Disculpe!" I announce, throwing up my hands, my language a full-body experience now. "So sorry." I point a finger. "Bryce, no?"

He glowers and mutters, "It's Brandon," as he presses a stray napkin to his soiled pants.

A *tsk* of teeth and tongue. "You look like you 'ave pissed yourself." I give a chuckle, then move on.

I hit the jacks, the bathroom, as intended. Thankfully, there isn't an attendant on duty. There is a condom machine, and while I really don't have condoms on me, I do have them back at my hotel.

As I begin to rinse the spilled cola from my hands, the door swings open.

"This is a fucking Brioni fucking suit," Brandon begins, giving it the big man, throwing shapes—his chest puffed out and his arms positioned like he's holding a rolled carpet under each. *Fucking eejit.*

Water drips from my fingertips as I turn from the sink.

"Listen man, you're gonna—"

I flick the droplets in his face.

"What the fuck?" Stunned, he reaches up to wipe his face, and before he can utter another word, it's on. Two steps, and I grab him by the balls. A little unorthodox, I'll grant you, a little familiar, but there's method in this madness as I manhandle him until his back hits the wall. "What the fuck," he repeats . . . not in the same tone, obviously. A few octaves higher.

"I thought this is the way you like it," I mutter, keeping up the accent as I basically crush his bollocks between my fingers until he squeals. "Is this not the way you like it?" Without giving him time to answer, I knock the wind out of him some more with a right to his guts. Then I thrust my forearm across his neck for good measure. "It's not such a good feeling when it is happening to you, no?"

Men like him are the lowest. Men who claim space that doesn't belong to them are fucking abusers and violators, every one. They're nothing but scum.

"Hey, man," he stutters, tears clouding his eyes. "Stay cool."

"I am ice cool," I snarl, straining to keep my accent from straying Irish. "But I want to know what it is about my woman. Why you have such a fascination."

"I don't know what you're talking about," he bleats, his breath liquor-foul as I plant my fist in his kidney.

"Tell me!"

"She just . . . she just . . . knows, man. Everything she touches turns to gold."

"And you think she might rub your pathetic little lamp?" I long to smash my forehead into his nose . . . but I'm not about to leave evidence of this little chat. "She is mine. *¡Hijo de puta! ¡Malnacido!*" A jab to the guts. *"¡Cabronazo!"* Then another. Motherfucker. Son of a bitch. Bastard. Take your pick. "There is no place and no time on this planet when you will be anything to her, do you hear?"

When he doesn't answer, I jam my arm against his windpipe.

"Yeah, yes." A pained swallow. Tears and snot.

Fair fucks to him—no one without balls would understand how much this hurts. I could almost feel for him. *Almost*. "What was that?"

"I hear you—I fucking hear you!"

"You will treat her with nothing but respect. To you, she will be like a far and distant land—like ancient Egypt. Interesting but unreachable. Something you cannot touch. Unless you want to lose these for good." I make to grab him again, and he flinches. Like I want to touch his sweaty ball sack! It's a necessary evil, that's all. Something to get my point across. "In fact, I don't think you should even say her name."

"Okay. Okay!"

"Pussy voodoo," I spit, releasing him to collapse into a heap.

I wash my hands, muttering in Spanish and ignoring the sound of him retching and the sight of him on all fours. I'd call him a pig, but that would be insulting poor swine.

Bullies. Man, how I fucking hate them.

Chapter 9
RYAN

My heart is aflutter as I watch Matt cross the vast foyer, his gait all loose-limbed confidence and ease. Yet the look in his eyes speaks of intensity.

"I thought you'd forgotten me."

"As if that were even possible." He draws me to him as though this is an exchange we've had a hundred times. *A hundred hellos and a hundred goodbyes.* "They were out," he whispers in my ear.

"Out?" I pull back a little. A bathroom out of condoms?

"I had to try a couple of floors before I found a machine not empty."

"Really?" Pretty sure my eyes bug.

"Weddings." He shrugs, staring down at me half amused, half in lust. "They give everyone the horn."

"The what?" I ask with a chuckle.

"Everyone's up for it. Weddings are notorious places for people hooking up. Stands to reason, I suppose. People dressed to impress, free-flowing alcohol, and pheromones in the air. And that is a very lovely dress," he says as his eyes slide over me, all but taking it off.

"I like nice clothes." My words come out shaky as anticipation tumbles hotly through me.

I treat myself to quality in all forms. It's one of the perks of no longer being poor.

"Oh, it shows." He pulls me close again, and my eyes flutter shut at the caress of his breath against my neck. "I've been thinking about peeling you out of this dress, while trying to talk myself out of it," he adds with a dark chuckle, "since the minute you took my hand and demanded I come with you."

A thrill zips down my spine. "I'm not sure that's exactly how things went."

"Liar." He presses a heavenly kiss to my neck, his tongue a deft flick over my thudding pulse.

"Sounds like you're accusing me of being bossy," I say as he pulls back again.

"I'm saying I'm pretty sure you can do anything you put your mind to."

You. I want to do you.

"Also, I have an idea." There's that spark in his gaze again, a little bit of wrong wrapped up in all that nice. *The fun kind of wrong.* So this time, it doesn't catch me by surprise as he takes my hand. He takes two backward steps, and I see the flash of a grin as he turns. He strides in the direction of the check-in desk, pulling me along for the ride.

"I'd like to book a room."

"I'm so sorry, sir, we're fully booked," answers the first available desk clerk.

"A hotel this size?"

"We have several functions this evening," she offers apologetically.

This is New York in October. The hotel is likely overbooked rather than just booked. But then I notice the way her gaze flicks over him.

"However, we do have several suites available."

Obviously, I wasn't as astute in my observations as she was. Though it's not like the expensive cut of his tux would've marked him out as an escort. *My God, an escort.* A thrill courses through me with the thought. Maybe I'll get a taste for it. And maybe one day I'll be wealthy enough to be a sugar mama in my own right.

"That's fine."

Shit! I yank my head out of the clouds. A suite in the Pierre? That's gotta be like a down payment on an apartment.

"No, honey. There's no need," I put in, using the smile I perfected early in my adult life. The one that accompanies the lie *This refusal comes as a choice, not a lack of one* as I tug on Matt's hand. "We just need a room. We can—"

"A suite is fine," he says, half amused, half bemused, and already reaching for his wallet. "A bed's a bed. Darlin'," he adds, with a little bit of the devil again.

"Don't be ridiculous," I whisper hotly.

But then he puts down a credit card, and I do a double take. It's dark, sleek, and exclusive looking.

"Matt," I whisper harshly, tugging on his hand.

"Excuse us for a moment." He glances the desk clerk's way before allowing me to move us away.

"Are you crazy? A suite is way too expensive," I say before he can speak. *What kind of an escort has a black Amex anyway? One on a retainer? One with an expense account?*

I feel like I'm missing something, and I don't like it. Should I really want a part in this?

I want part of him, I think. Which is a lie, because I want every part of him. Every part of him over every part of me.

"Would it help if I said it's tax deductible?" His lips twitch with amusement.

You pay tax on horizontal earnings? In case that falls out, I bite my bottom lip. Until I find his thumb pressed there. My breath gives a tiny catch.

"How is it possible to be jealous of your teeth," he whispers, gently prying my lip loose.

How is it possible I'm about to swoon?

"I think there's a kind of symmetry in this. You. Me. This wedding. This hotel."

I feel my expression flicker. "I don't . . ."

"That might've been you." He tips his head, though barely. "The girl in the white dress, the one that should be pitied for tying herself to a fucknut like him."

White dress makes me sad, while *fucknut* gives me pause.

"You had a lucky escape, while he's already regretting his choices."

"You don't know that." *You don't know him like I do.*

"I saw it on his face. Saw it in the way he watched the places I touched you. Like he thought I overstepped. So here's what I propose. Suggest," he amends, his mouth curling at that irony. "You let me book the room—"

I open my mouth to protest again. To no avail.

"Then you let me take you upstairs and do what I've been dreaming of all evening." The intensity of his words and the look on his face—it's like my dress has already disintegrated. "Let's make the walls of this old hotel shake with your pleasure. I promise I'll fuck you so well the whole place will hear my name. But we don't need the whole hotel to know, do we?" His touch is a fleeting brush to my chin. "Just one man. One man who deserves to know for good what he's lost."

"I don't . . ."

"It's a poetic kind of justice, don't you think? Sung from the top of your lungs."

"Maybe you should've been a lawyer, because that's quite an argument you make."

"Oration isn't really my thing. Oral, however . . ." And there is that wickedness again.

Nerves and anticipation occupy my thoughts as he slides his arm around me, and we move back to the desk.

The key slides over the counter. "Can I get you some help with your bags?"

I don't think she's being facetious, but I almost die on the spot anyway. Nothing says *one-night stand* like a couple without bags.

"That won't be necessary." Matt is much cooler in his response—all suave insouciance. In other words, he has zero fucks to give.

I expect he's had more practice at this than me.

We make our way to the elevator, and moments later, the doors glide closed.

I'm doing this. Really doing this!

I'm going to spend the night with a modern-day courtesan, a man who pleasures women for money. I bite the inside of my lip, giddy suddenly with the notion, because there's no way Matt is a hired suit, a date to accompany you to a wedding or a business dinner. He's too accomplished, too sensual, too plain hot for that. He's definitely a full-service kind of escort, because what woman could keep her hands to herself?

I tense a little when his arm slides behind me, his hand cupping my hip. "You okay?"

I nod, not trusting myself to speak.

"See that handrail?" he whispers, pressing his mouth to my ear. "It's just the right height, don't you think?"

"Hush," I hiss, even as my attention slides to the brass rail running around the elevator car, when what I want to ask is *The right height for what?* A barre class? Something to hold on to while the man rocks my world?

I don't, obviously. We're not alone in this tiny space, thanks to a uniformed attendant just a step or two away. The hotel is old-world fancy, and fancy people must not know how to use their fingers. Something tells me Matt knows how to use his fingers as they tighten on my hip with a squeeze. Then slide around to cup the round of my ass cheek.

"To alleviate the height difference, darlin'," he adds, all feigned innocence and familiarity, as though we're an old married couple instead of a pair that just checked in without luggage. "Kissing you is always a delight, teacup. Sitting you on the rail would just give the old neck muscles a rest."

The elevator attendant, a lady of a certain age, glances briefly our way before smothering a soft, endeared smile. Of course, she's completely unaware of Matt inching the fabric of my dress higher from behind.

Teacup? I mouth, unimpressed. "Because I'm small and dainty?" I say, leaving off *fragile*.

"Of course." He leans closer, his next words a lower, hotter whisper. "And something I want to put my lips to."

I swallow a gasp as his fingers slide between my legs.

"Right. Here." His words are all hot breath against my neck as he curls his fingers in a torturous tease.

I close my eyes against the onslaught of images. His hands on my thighs, pushing them wide, the brush of his stubble, his tongue and his lips teasing, working me until I can barely breathe.

A *ding* sounds, and the attendant announces the floor number. "Have a good evening," she says as we step out.

"Thanks. Me too," I reply, turning beet red immediately. "You too, I mean," I add, ignoring Matt's chuckle.

"I thought you said you had nice manners." I point an accusing finger at him as the doors glide closed again.

"I thought you said I was nice." He wraps his hand around mine, my index finger still pointing. Everything south of my waist tightens as he closes his teeth over the knuckle. "I'm really not."

"It's all an act, huh?" My question sounds husky as his lips fold over my finger, and he gives a rumbling noise of assent. He watches me, his eyes playful, but there's an intensity there too. The kind that makes my heart thump and my body tingle. I feel like I'm burning, but for the cool, damp tip of one finger as he pulls back.

"I'm not nice at all," he murmurs.

"Are you trying to disappoint me?"

Matt suddenly pulls my body flush with his. My hand falls to his chest, the muscle and sinew underneath reacting deliciously to my touch.

"I wouldn't dream of it."

"Good. Don't wanna make things *too* easy for you," I whisper, tracing my thumb over a button on his shirt.

"You prefer to make it hard?"

A heady anticipation floods my veins as he gently tilts my head.

"Innuendo much?" I find myself whispering.

"You started it."

"I—"

He swallows the rest of my response as our lips meet in a kiss that's light and teasing. Notes of whiskey and champagne, lips lingering before those kisses deepen, until they're filled with aching and promise. His thigh suddenly comes tight between my legs, tenderness traded for hot breath and a desperate sort of gracelessness. He feels so hard and so real as my fingers run over him, when he grips my butt and my back hits the wall.

No, not a wall. A door.

We should stop. But the words are only in my head, our mouths fused and my knee sliding up his thigh. My hands twist his shirt and slide through his hair, greedy and grasping.

Then, from somewhere, comes the sound of a lock turning over. I'm too far gone to care where or why when Matt pulls his mouth from mine and slides me unceremoniously to one side. My mouth falls open in silent protest as I watch him step back from the door—the opening door—his expression turning from dark-eyed want to one of bewilderment.

"So terribly sorry." His accent is suddenly very posh and very British. "I don't know what happened there. One minute I'm walking along the hallway, and the next, I'm almost on my arse. I must've tripped over the bloody carpet!"

I press my hand to my mouth to stop myself from giggling. Or asking if he's into amateur dramatics. *Because that was surely dramatic.*

"Okay, sure," a masculine voice offers hesitantly. "Well, you take it easy."

"Thank you. And you." Matt kind of salutes and spins on his heel.

I begin a slow round of applause as the door clicks closed. Matt grins and gives a theatrical bow.

"You were convincing," I say, pushing from the wall. Hips swaying obviously as I saunter closer and reach up to tidy his hair. "*Almost* convincing." I allow my gaze to dip to below his belt. "I'm not so certain there's any disguising that."

"Sure there is," he replies, all silky toned. "Come with me, and I'll let you watch it disappear."

A swipe of the key, the click of the lock, and my stomach turns weightless in anticipation.

"Ladies first," he says, pushing the door wide.

"It's a nice philosophy." I deliver my taunting response over my shoulder.

His low chuckle. "One I live by."

"I guess I'm a lucky girl."

The suite's decor is tasteful but traditional, with a little French thrown in. A pair of pale Louis-style chairs and a coffee table flanked by low ottomans, the open door to my right leading to the bedroom. Because that would be too obvious, I cross the room to stand by the darkened window, wondering if I should flirt some more, pour us a drink, close the curtains—any or all of the above.

The door closes. Matt's jacket comes off and is abandoned to the back of the couch. One hand slung low in his pocket, he crosses the room while watching me with such intensity that I shiver.

"I have something I need to say. Something to tell . . ." His feet come to a stop at the same time as his words, maybe something to do with the way I've loosened my dress at the waist.

I make a small sound when the silk slides over my breasts, tantalizing my already-aching nipples through my bra.

"You were saying?" I'm not normally this brazen. At least, not in the bedroom. But then, I've never slept with an expert before. *I've never wanted someone as much as I want him.*

"Yes." He gives his head a shake, like a horse shaking off flies. "Yeah," he adds, his throat working with a deep swallow. I want to press my lips there. Press my teeth over the cording of muscles and bite. "Ryan, there's—"

A roll of my shoulders, and my dress flutters to the floor.

"Fuck me."

My core twists with need at the way he drinks me in, his gaze roaming hungrily over my La Perla lingerie. Green, to match my dress, the set was a treat to myself to cheer me up. It didn't work, or so I thought. It's sure making me happy now.

"You were saying?" I positively strut across the floor.

"Yeah . . ." His eyes. My breasts. It's a beautiful thing. "I was saying . . ."

"Are you married?" Coming to a stop in front of him, I tip onto my toes and slide my arms around the back of his neck. If he says yes, I'll adjust. *And choke him.*

"No, I'm not." His big hands cup my hips. Slide down to my ass.

"Are you committed in some other way?" I'm thinking specifically of a black Amex and sugar mamas and handsome, younger sugar babes. Though he seems a little on the mature side, a little too sophisticated for that title. Sugar zaddy? The tux, his air. But all those thoughts dissolve as he pulls my body tight against his.

"I wouldn't be here if I was."

The solid press of him does wild things to my pulse, my blood. Not that he realizes as I press my finger to his lips and coolly whisper, "Then it can wait."

"I don't think—"

I give a teasing sway of my hips, and the brush of my soft to his hard elicits *the* sexiest sound from him. "Less thinking."

His reply is a ragged-sounding curse as his grip tightens on my ass.

"Your eyes kinda match my underwear."

"You like green." His fingers slip under the elastic of my panties, caressing the place where my thigh and butt meet.

I like his green eyes. I like the way he's looking down at me. "What are the chances your underwear is green too?"

"Want to find out?"

"Well, one of us is wearing far too many clothes," I whisper, drawing my index finger down his torso, bumping over the line of tiny hindrances on his shirt. As I reach his belt, I tuck the tip into his waistband and take a step back. My eyes gravitate to what I felt pressed against me. *Oh my. The size of that thing.*

"I like the way you look at me." Honest words and his hot look.

Man, he's so good with his mouth. I bite back a smile at where my mind goes with that.

"There's kind of a lot to take in." I flatten my palm over the front of his pants, spreading my fingers wide over his *very* obvious interest. Just the thought of it inside me makes my stomach swoop like a fairground ride.

"I'd love to know what you're thinking right now."

"Just that . . ." I lift my gaze but not my head, watching his reaction as I touch him. As I curl my fingers around his solid girth. "This is gonna take some magic to make disappear."

The corner of his mouth lifts as though hooked. *God, I know I am right now.* "I might have one or two tricks up my sleeve."

"I sure hope you can deliver on those words."

"Oh, I'll deliver, Ryan. I'll even let you tell me where."

A giggle bursts free. So, *so* smutty. So, *so* delicious. "I thought you weren't taking orders tonight."

"We both know that's not true." His answer bears a lazy kind of mocking, his eyes burning with such heat and promise.

"I like the sound of that," I whisper. Pressing my hand to his chest, I push him backward. One step, two, until the backs of his legs hit the seat of a chair.

"I know. Because you're a bossy little thing."

"I prefer *assertive*," I purr, not sure where the words are sprouting from. But if there was ever a time to fulfill all a girl's fantasies, that time would be now. "Sit your ass down."

My heart pumps wildly as I follow, climbing onto his lap. The Louis-style chair is wide and easily accommodates my knees on either side of his thick thighs. I wonder if he can see that my heart is beating out of my chest or if he notices the tremble of my fingers as I tug on his bow tie. Like the ribbon on a gift, it loosens effortlessly, the soft whisper as I pull it free from his collar doing strange and wonderful things to my insides.

I trace the top button on his shirt, then flick it open as Matt tilts his head back in invitation. His throat is warm as I press my lips to the triangle of exposed skin, and he swallows as I kiss my way up his neck, groaning softly as I graze his jaw with my teeth.

I did that to him. I made him moan. I turned his eyes lust glazed and green gold. I made his breath short and his cock hard.

I rest my hands on his shoulders, pressing onto my knees, feeling every inch a goddess.

"Good fucking God, you make my mouth water." The hungry longing in his gaze answers a deep pulse inside me. His attention dips, transfixed now between my legs.

I crook his chin with my finger. *I can commiserate, my hot friend.* "You look like you want a taste," I whisper. *The tiny white scar on his brow. Where did he get that from?*

"Ah, darlin'. I want my mouth on you more than I want my next breath."

His words, how they affect me.

His dark lashes flutter like my insides as I draw closer and press my mouth to his. He gives a tortured-sounding groan as I take his soft bottom lip between my teeth, his fingers tightening on my butt.

"Ah, ah." Our breaths still mingling, I lift his hands away, placing them back on the chair arms. "No touching."

"You can't mean to be so cruel." His mouth tips upward, but he keeps his hands still, into this in more ways than just the iron rod in his pants.

"I think you like that I am." *I know I'm getting off just looking at you.*

Ignoring the tremble in my fingers, I unbutton the rest of his shirt, eyes avid as I push the sides wide. As I circle his flat, tan nipple, an unexpected tremor runs through him, his sharp intake of breath almost too loud for the room.

"I like that," I whisper. The sound he made for me.

"I like you."

I slide my fingers down his abs, his six-, no, eight-pack. *Gotta love an overachiever,* I think as I watch the muscles flex and contract. "You are so *nice.*"

A growl.

"You are, aren't you?" I whisper in his ear, the tips of my breasts barely brushing his chest.

"Come and sit on my face, and I'll show you exactly how nice I am."

A low chuckle stutters out of me. But I think he means it. Now, wouldn't that be something . . .

I push up and put my hands to the back of the chair, my arms setting the girls to their best advantage. A sight he can't fail to miss.

"Maybe you're not so nice." One hand in his hair now, I fist it, making him hiss. "Maybe you do deserve cruel," I rasp as I drop into his lap and rock over him.

"Fuck." His eyes slam closed as his body shudders.

Sensation heats and blooms, my skin hot and my pussy aching to be filled as I work over him again, loving how his attention turns inward, almost as though he's concentrating.

"Wait." Another swallow. "I think my brain just exploded."

"Just your brain?"

His expression turns a touch sardonic. "Darlin', you're good. But you've no worries on that score."

"Promise?"

His chuckle is so, *so* smutty that it makes my cheeks burn. I'm almost naked and dry humping him, but bashful at the thought of him coming in his pants? *Ridiculous,* I think as I put my lips to his neck again, swallowing the low rumble he makes as I press my teeth there.

"I don't need your brains," I whisper, working myself over him, loving how he throws back his head, eyes closing under the weight of this pleasure. "What I need from you is *here*." The feel of him. I have never been so turned on and can hardly believe the things I'm saying.

"Darlin', you want the whole package, believe me."

"All of you?" I taunt. I bite my tongue to keep from asking, *To get my money's worth?* It's just a fantasy, I tell myself, ignoring the pang in my chest. But it doesn't stop me from wondering how many times he's heard that. How many times has he been belittled or made to feel cheap?

We have that in common, he and I. Different careers, same judgment.

"You want my mouth, my fingers, my tongue, and my cock." His voice has a desperate, sandpapery quality to it. "Let me give them to you."

How his words ache. How his body strains. How my core clenches as those images splash over the walls of my brain. *His mouth on my breast. Midnight hair and his tongue buried between my legs.* From the tips of my toes to the roots of my hair, I'm so ready for this.

"Let me taste you, Ryan. Let me give you a night you deserve."

"You feel so good," I whisper, not giving a damn for my breathy, porn-worthy words as I drop myself over him. *Over his cock.* "I'm so wet for this. So wet for you."

"Show me." This sounds less like a demand and more like a plea for clemency.

I fall forward, my nipples peaked and brushing his chest through my bra's gauzy fabric. "How bad do you want that taste?" I whisper in his ear, closing my teeth over the fleshy lobe.

He hisses a curse, hips bucking, the heat of my pussy just out of reach. "So fucking much. Look at me—I'm desperate for you."

And he is as I push up onto my knees, arching my back with intent, cupping my hand between my legs. Those lust-glazed eyes light up my pleasure center like the Fourth of July.

"Ryan, show me more." His words sound despairing, like those of a man with an endless thirst. "Touch yourself, darlin'. Please."

My insides pulse with longing as I slip my hand under the waistband of my panties, making a slow slide down. I make a soft noise as the pad of my finger reaches the wet ribbon of my flesh.

"Fuck, yeah. Yes." His tongue swipes his lips, rendering them unbearably tempting. "Slip your fingers inside, beautiful."

I close my eyes to his expression and the temptation of his voice.

"No, darlin'. Open your eyes. Watch me want you."

And so I do. Our eyes connected, I touch myself, swirl and play, until I can't stand it anymore. I fall forward, our kiss instantly hot and messy and frantic.

"Let me." His fingers loop my wrist, his eyes bright as he brings them to his mouth, licking them clean, the sensations and the scene making my body buck. "Take off your bra," he demands as he works those digits like his favorite sucker.

"Who's in charge?" I whisper, dragging my finger down the ridges of his abs. "Who's on top?"

"No doubt about it, darlin'. But I thought the aim was to torture me?"

So much temptation in his expression. If he was a work of art, and he kind of is, I'd name the piece *Distracted Desire*. Maybe because it seems like he doesn't know where he wants to look the most. I'm not sure I help his conundrum as I slip one hand behind my back and flick open the catch, then slide the straps down my arms.

"Jesus." He blinks before his head drops back, and he stares at the ceiling for a beat. "I fucking knew it. Teardrop tits."

"I beg your pardon?" I almost reach up to cover them. But I guess he'd like that too.

"You have teardrop tits. The shape so perfect, they make a man want to weep."

"No need to cry," I croon as I lean closer teasingly. I don't even complain when he fills his hands with them, putting his thumbs to good use.

Complain, no. But moan . . .

He puts his clever fingers to work, learning me. A soft swipe of his thumb, a delicate roll. A tight pinch that rides the delicate line between pleasure and pain. I slide my hands into his hair, offering myself up when he takes my wrists, pulling them to the small of my back. The position changes the dynamic immediately as I go from torturer to captive. But I don't care, and the only protest I make is when he licks his thumb to paint the moisture over my nipple.

"Oh, God."

"You're so sensitive."

I shiver, the result of his soft-blown breath. But he's not unaffected, as I note the pulse jumping in his neck. Anticipation shoots like stars through my veins as he lowers his head, and I whimper, though not from an expectation realized, as Matt presses his teeth to the curve of my breast.

"Make that noise again." His eyes shine with a dark possessiveness.

"What noise?" So much for sass as I whimper again, thanks to the long stroke of pleasure he applies with the flat of his tongue. I arch my back, my nipples aching for more, and when he finally pulls the tight bud into his mouth, I cry out.

"So perfect." His eyes are like coal as he engulfs the other tip. I feel it everywhere and sense how it might be when he's finally pressed between my legs. Which I suppose is the idea, as he subtly sets me back. "Let me see." Puzzlement must reflect in my expression, as he adds, "Show me again how you like to be touched."

I don't need the invitation but take it anyway as I slip my hand inside my fancy panties. "Oh, God." I flex into my palm with a hum, my hips bucking needily, my body so very primed.

"Tell me, darlin'. Tell me how it feels."

"Wet," I whisper, sliding a finger where I'm slick, not quite able to believe I'm doing this. That I'm touching myself so blatantly, desperate to drive a man wild. And he does look wild, his eyes more golden than green. *More dark angel than man.*

"What else?"

"Hot." The *t* as sticky as molasses.

"So fucking hot."

"And empty." Playing my part, I give a little pout.

He gives a stuttering laugh that doesn't speak of amusement. "You're fuckin' killing me."

"I like that for me."

His hum seems to agree. "Deeper. Push them in deeper. Take away the ache."

His counsel so tempting, his words as hot as a fever dream, I can do nothing else but follow it. Because I want to. I want us both to get off on this.

"That's it, teacup. Right up to the knuckle."

My insides spasm, despite the misnomer. "I'm not a teacup," I pant, undulating into my palm. "Fragile and breakable." Fuck that.

"You're my teacup," he repeats. "Dainty yet practical. Delicate and curved." His hands cup my hips and slide up to my breasts. "And like a teacup, you sit so well in my hands." I don't have the wherewithal to complain as his thumbs slide across the pebbles of my nipples. "And my God, I can't wait to drink you up."

"Oh," I rasp, sliding a little wetness across my clit. *"Yes."*

"But you'd better be ready, because I'm a bit of a brute. A greedy drinker," he says, his words rougher, his touch too. "Too hard for a little teacup, maybe."

"No." Faster I swirl.

"Because I'll slurp and suck and gulp until you're so wet you'll drip all over my face."

"Yes!" I pant, my hand jerking in my panties, those nerve endings having multiplied somehow.

He pulls my mouth to his, the air between us all breath and want and heat as he kisses the fuck out of me. "Let me," he rasps. "Let me taste, Ryan. I'll make it so good for you."

I barely nod when he stands, his strong arms trapping me against his body as he carries me across the room. I jerk a little as something distinctly hard and cool touches my butt before we reach the bedroom. *Is that . . . the dining table?*

"What—" I get as far as lifting my finger, intending to point out the perfectly usable bed in the other room.

"I told you I was starvin'," he says, his accent so rough. He tears off his cuff links, his movements swift. "And surely it would be uncivilized of me to feast anywhere else."

I push up onto my palm, dazed. Pulsing. Turned on more than I ever have been.

"And I do intend to feast." His eyes burn as he strips off his shirt. "I'm gonna make such a meal of you."

Chapter 10
MATT

Her lovely face. Eyes dark, her pink lips parted like an invitation. *An invitation to plunder.*

As I circle her dainty ankle with my fingers, her body stretches languidly, and she seems to bite back a moan.

"Your ankles are one of the first things I paid attention to." My tone is conversational, as though there isn't an almost-naked woman spread out on the table in front of me. A woman who thinks I do this kind of thing for a living. *I should be so lucky,* I think. *If my only client was Ryan, at least.*

"My ankles?" Her lashes flutter as though her mind is playing catch-up.

"After your attitude, maybe. And these." I lift her leg and place the point of her heel between my shoulder and chest, leaning into it a little, relishing the pointed bite. "Dainty ankles, spiked heels. I had some quite graphic thoughts about both."

"Yet you still took some persuading."

If you'd flashed me those perfect tits, I would've shut my trap a lot sooner.

"But look at us now." Just look at *her*. When she slid her dress from her shoulders, it took everything inside me not to rush at her. I fucking love fancy lingerie—love the look of it, the gossamer stretch of fabric holding in all those lovely womanly bits. Lingerie is like an invitation, in the right context, and Ryan's dress fluttering to the floor was exactly that. But I still had to slow myself down because this night is all about her.

I will tell her the truth. After. And maybe it'll bite me in the arse. *It definitely will, and it'll be doubly my fault at that point.* I'm sure she won't understand why I didn't insist on telling her earlier. Or believe that, when she loosened her dress, I temporarily lost the power of words. How can I explain that when she strutted across the floor like a pint-size Victoria's Secret model, I just couldn't do it. I couldn't spoil the fantasy, her fantasy, not then. And not when she climbed into my lap, owning her daring and loving her choices.

How could I after all that she's been through?

What Would Fin Do . . . That fucker's voice echoes in my head again. *What he wouldn't do is to be so stupid as to sell this to himself as altruism.*

"Matt?"

Her heel is pressing hard enough to make a mark, and my hard-on is still raging. Yet here I stand, fucking . . . woolgathering? Cupping her heel, I lift her leg to suck on the tender flesh of her inner ankle.

"Oh, God. Why does that feel so good?"

Then I bite it a little. "Maybe I'm just *that* good." I press my smile into the taut muscle of her calf, loving the way she trembles. Another nibble. A lick behind her knee. All those erogenous zones, and I'm gonna taste every one.

"Please hurry."

"You got somewhere you need to be?" My tone is mild as I pull out a chair, hooking it behind me with my foot.

"No, I just need—"

"I know what you need, darlin'. But the more you try to rush me, the slower I get. When you have the right man for the job, he wants to do it well," I say, playing into my role, into her fantasy.

"You're gonna do me well?"

I lick a long stripe up her inner thigh, and the noise she makes ought to be bottled and sold as an aphrodisiac.

"What do you think?" I give a sucking pull that I hope will bruise. Then a scrape of my teeth as I work my way to her apex. She sighs as I press my mouth over her pussy, and squirms as I give a groan, all hot and fucking needy. "Ryan, you smell *amazing*."

"Oh, God. That's . . . *oh!*"

I nuzzle my tongue over the damp patch, pushing it inside her. "I'm gonna devour every ounce of you," I murmur, dragging my thumbs along her folds. "Then I'm gonna fuck you just like I promised. Do you remember that? What I said?"

"The whole hotel's gonna know your name."

"That's right, teacup. I'm going to fuck you so well that, when you think back on tonight, you'll wonder if you imagined it. If you embellished it in your mind."

"Like a tall tale," she whispers.

"Or a long one," I rasp, hooking my fingers into the elastic of her panties. I begin to slowly slide them down her legs.

"It was how big?" she says with a sigh, her body bowing as she takes her breast in her hand. *Pink nipples, red nails, and such dark eyes.*

"Big enough. Ah, darlin', just look at you. You're so fucking pretty." My voice is all groan as I use my thumbs to peel her open to my view. "Pink and wet and so lip-smackingly gorgeous."

She pushes up onto her forearms, staring down as I slide her thighs wider to study that piece of heaven. Diligent student that she is, she watches my appreciation and my fleeting touches.

"Listen."

Our eyes meet as I push a finger inside. We both hear the evidence of how much she wants this—how ready she is—even without her sweet little moan. And we both see it as I rub her pleasure between my thumb and fingertip. Her eyes darken as I bring them to my mouth, lips closing over the freshwater taste of her.

"Why is that so hot?" she whispers, a tremor running through the sentiment.

"Because you are." I push inside her again. Her head drops back, body melting against the table like ice cream on a hot pavement. My cock aches as I work that digit in, then out, loving her soft sighs and the way she feels like velvet. One finger, then two, and her moans deepen. Another finger and a twist of my wrist, and she cries out, undulating against the invasion.

"Oh, God. Don't stop." With languid, midnight eyes, she reaches between us to grab my wrist. As though there's any chance I would. As though I don't want to see this.

"You're so beautiful, every inch of you." Her body begins to tighten, and her thighs to shake. "Yeah, just like that," I croon. "I can't wait to be inside you, feeling you pulling me deeper and deeper."

Still holding my wrist, she begins to writhe. "Please, more. I need you."

"Not yet," I whisper. "Not until I kiss you here." Her back arches from the table as I lick my thumb to slide it over the bud of her clit. "Would you like me to do that?"

"*Yes.* God, yes." Her desperation a thing of beauty.

"You want me to put my mouth on you?"

"Yes!"

"Feather kisses over your pretty little clit?"

"Yes, please."

"You want me to kiss your pussy? To make out with it?"

"Yes, Matt. Please! I want to have sex with your face!"

"Now, there's an invitation . . ." I slide my hands under her arse and pull her down to engulf that swollen little bud. Her body spasms with relief as I suck it. Lick her. As I press my face to her pussy like I'm trying to make a mold.

"Oh, God, yes! Yes!"

"You're a thing to be devoured, teacup. I want to sup and suck," I rasp. "Drown myself in you."

She crests—peaks. Pulls on my hair so hard, I think she might leave me with a bald patch. *Worth it, though.* And she's fucking vocal, which is the icing on this cake. A cake I want to gorge myself on as her cries ring through the room.

"Oh, my God." Panting. Happy. Smiling. She's maybe even a little shocked. "That was so, so good."

"So fucking good," I growl, not yet done.

"Matt . . ." She squirms. Pushes on my head. "Please."

"Stop tryin' to wriggle away. I'm not done here."

"I am!" she exclaims, part exasperation and part giggle.

"You just think you are."

"Matt." She pulls on my hair, and our eyes meet. "I can't."

"Yeah, you can. And I want it, Ryan." My dare, then her grip slackening.

"You're trying to kill me," she groans.

"But what a way to go." Lowering my head, I suck her clit into my mouth.

She says my name again, softer now. And her moan? Hands down the sexiest sound in the world.

"I'm greedy, darlin'. So greedy." A swirl of my tongue. A delicate graze of my teeth.

"Yes . . ." Her body working with me, growing wetter. Hotter.

"I won't be satisfied until I taste you again. Until you come all over my tongue."

"Oh!"

My fingers still inside her, I feel the strings of her orgasm, tied so closely to the previous. She arches against my mouth, unable to resist the tide of her body. Fingers, tongue, stubble—I put the unholy trio to work until her thighs begin to tremble and her whole body flushes pink, demanding more. Insisting that I get her there.

And I do. Fuck, yes, I do, until she's boneless and blinking at the ceiling. All that gorgeousness stretched across the wood, sweat soaked, pink and shiny.

"Wow. Just wow. I have never . . ." She lifts her head as I stand, watching as I run the back of my hand across my wet mouth.

"Never what?" My mouth quirks. So much amusement in those tiny words.

"I've never done that before."

"I've never heard that before."

"Heard—"

"Never has anyone demanded that my face have sex with them."

"Urgh. Stop!" She throws her arms across her eyes.

Are women who hire gigolos meant to be this fucking cute? "I liked it," I kind of growl. "I liked it a whole fuckin' lot."

Her arm doesn't move, but she holds up two fingers. *Not an insult.* "I've never come twice in such quick succession."

"No?"

"I'm pretty sure I saw stars being born."

I bite in a smile, not wanting to be accused of being a peacock. *Ah, fuck it.* "Ever seen a supernova?" I pull a condom from my pocket, from a packet I picked up in the second jacks—bathroom—I visited. *So not a complete lie.* Placing it on the edge of the table, I unbuckle my belt and begin to strip.

"You are so cocky." No prizes for guessing where her eyes fall. "I guess you have the goods to support the hypothesis?"

"So *this* is where you expect me to slap a massive schlong on the tabletop," I say, hearkening back to an earlier moment. A previous conversation.

"A girl can hope."

Hope we're paid by the inch? I push the thought away. Inchwise, I'm doing just fine. It's my dodging of the truth that ought to bother me. And maybe it will. *When the blood has returned to my brain.*

Belt buckle loose, my pants drop to the floor, and I kick them away. With a deep exhale, I run my hand down my chest and the ridges of my stomach, playing my part. Only, this doesn't feel like pretend or just getting my rocks off. It feels . . . like everything that can be right between two bodies. Between two souls.

"You're all about the tease, aren't you?" Despite her bold words, her voice wavers. Maybe because I've stuck my hand into my boxers to give my poor, neglected cock an experimental tug.

I give a low groan as my head rolls back. "Takes a tease to know a tease." My answer is low and rumbling as I slide my other hand under the waistband.

"Two hands?" she asks, before her teeth dig into her lip.

"I thought two hands were supposed to be better than one."

"I guess we'll see," she whispers, and with that, she brings one heel to the table. She lets her knee fall, exposing the center of her femininity.

"Teacup," I say on a groan, "you don't play fair."

"Never have, never intend to." She swipes a slow finger through her wetness. Fuck me, she is amazing. "Oh!" she adds as I whip off my pants.

I flip the condom up and tear the corner with my teeth before unceremoniously sheathing my straining cock. Like I've done hundreds of times. But never like this. Never with a tremor in my hand and a desperation clawing at my guts with a need to plunge. To pillage.

I grab her hips and slide her to the edge of the table. My hands look huge against her, my skin dark where she's pale. I grit my teeth as I line myself up, white-hot need pulsing through me.

"Matt?"

I glance up. "You really are a good man."

I don't answer—can't for the sudden lump in my throat. Guilt, I think. Contempt for myself, maybe. But desire wins out. *Isn't it always the trump card?* Especially as her hips tilt to meet mine, her fingers reaching out to curl around my shoulders.

"You're worth a hundred of them," I whisper. *A hundred of me,* I think as my mouth catches hers. Breath frozen half in and half out—both of us. I drive my way inside, swallowing the sound she makes.

This. The sentiment beats in my chest as I hold her there, pulsing around me. Me in her. Her in me, somehow.

As I retreat, her back arches with a silent plea.

"Please, I—"

I grant her appeal, dropping my head to her shoulder with a curse as I watch the wet, ruddy slide of my cock. *"Fuck."* My whole body quivers as she draws the inside of her foot along my thigh. I kiss her, wetly and messily, and the noises we make are multilayered. Feminine moans and rough grunts, sharp gasps and ragged breaths. *"Me encanta el sabor de tu coño."* I love the taste of your pussy. Fuck, yes, I do.

"That sounds so hot." A gasp. "Spanish."

"You're hot," I say, surprised I slid into the language. "And you feel so fucking good."

"Not . . . not . . . that I don't like the way you usually speak. I should've made my boyfriend Irish." Her words almost run together.

"You like a bit of the Irish," I assert, laying my accent on thick.

"I like it from you." Her eyes are dark and glossy as I slide my hands under her backside, her body an elegant arch. I bring her closer. Closer to me. To the edge of the table. To ecstasy.

"Ryan," I whisper, rolling the *R*, using my raciest of intonations. "You've an arse like an onion." I tighten my grip on said excellent arse.

"What?" Her mouth curls, but with a snap of my hips, she cries out.

"It makes me want to cry, because it's so fucking lovely."

"That is . . ." Amusing, judging by her expression.

"C'mere till I get ahold of ya," I say, wrapping my arms around her, pulling her body with mine as I fall back onto the dining chair. "Let me wear the face off ya."

She's all smiles as she leans back a little. "Gonna need a translation."

I grip her thigh, and fuck me, the sight of her. All pink and wet, stretched around me. I can barely stand it.

"It means I want to kiss you." My hand almost covers the entire back of her head as I bring her mouth to mine and do just that.

"Wow." Her mouth falls open in a soft O as I thrust and simultaneously pull her down against me. And again. *"Yes!"* On the tips of her toes now, riding me. "God, you feel so big."

"Just the right fit." Her velvet walls pulse around me, stealing my wits. But I'd seriously become an idiot for this. "Give me your mouth," I demand, dragging her lips to mine again. *I can't get enough.*

Joined in two places, we're all swallowed moans and lewd sounds as our bodies meet. With each flex of her hips, I drive myself deep. No teasing, no games. This is primal. Primitive. From the way her nails pierce my shoulders to the overwhelming war rising through me.

This, my pulse pounds. *Mine.* I want to own her. Make her bend. Fill her. Fuck her until she submits.

"Yes!" As though hearing my thoughts, she cries out, her pussy grasping me like a fist.

"That's it, darlin'," I rasp. "That's it."

Her back bows, her pussy throbs, and I swear by all that is holy, her eyes roll back in her head. But I've no time to dwell, to enjoy the signs of her pleasure—of a job well done—as demand rushes through me. My pleasure swells, heat and sensation spreading through me as my body is pulled under by the rhythm of hers.

Chapter 11
MATT

I wake to rain lashing against the windowpane. And the other side of the bed cold.

As I stretch out, enjoying the ache in my abs, my ears strain to hear sounds other than the miserable weather. Ryan might be making coffee or taking a shower. Checking her phone while curled on the couch?

But these are all wishful, optimistic thoughts. Thoughts contradicted by the gnawing ache in my chest. She's long gone, and I have no one to blame but myself.

"Fuck," I mutter, dragging myself upright and raking my hand through my hair. I feel kind of robbed. If I'd considered for one minute that she might . . .

Feck it. No use crying over spilled . . . champagne. And strawberries, I think as I pull on the linens half hanging off the bed and stained with both. A bit of chocolate too.

I ordered room service during a break in the fun, so hungry that my stomach had started eating itself. I also ordered a bottle of champagne, given that's what Ryan had been drinking, and I felt like celebrating. We both laughed when it arrived accompanied by a bowl of chocolate-dipped strawberries.

My mouth lifts on one side, as though hooked, as I remember how she took the piss—busted my balls over this.

"Oh, honey, how sweet. You ordered the Valentine's package?" Her expression—so much for never wanting to be held for an hour. Or fucked for an hour.

I paused in the action of shoveling one in my gob—I would've eaten a photo of the Last Supper if that was all that had been delivered—and decided strawberries, a steak sandwich, and frites could wait. Because someone needed that gloating look kissed off her face.

My smile falters as the memory fades, and with a sigh, I drag my sad and sorry arse out of bed.

There isn't one sign of her here, in the suite. No stray earring. No scribbled note with her phone number. Just the lingering scent of her perfume and the aftermath of our marathon fuck fest. Stained sheets, half hanging off the bed. *A bed well used and linens she rolled herself in, like a burrito, as she slept.* Plates of half-eaten food and an empty bottle of champagne. Throw cushions and towels strewn around the place. We fucked in the shower, then out of the shower, thanks to the temptation of slipping towels.

There's a handprint on the still-gray window and a heart-shaped arse print on a wall mirror, which also reveals the hickey on my neck, my fucked-up hair, and a bite mark on the inside of my bicep as I reach up to straighten it.

What my reflection doesn't show is my aching abs. And a heart full of regret. Not that last night happened but that she's not here.

The perfect ending to a one-night stand, some would say, naming no names. *Fin and Oliver.* So why do I feel so hollow?

I didn't get to tell her the truth. *Silver lining or a fuckup?*

The latter, I think, because that also means I didn't get the chance to explain the rest. The rightness of being in her company. The connection I felt.

Did she feel it too?

I guess not, or else I wouldn't be standing naked and alone, staring out through the rain.

Chapter 12
MATT

"Uncle Matty, you don't got the right color hair for Prince Charmin."

"*Charming*, Clodagh," Leticia, my sister, corrects as she straightens her daughter's sparkly crown.

"The other stuff is toilet paper," I say, plucking at a cheap gold-colored button on my chest. "Which I suppose is apt, considering I feel like something you wipe your arse on. I mean, what are these meant to be?" I demand, now flicking the gold fringing dangling from my shoulder.

"Epaulets, you heathen." My sister gives a pitying shake of her head. "Prince Charming is obviously some sort . . . of military man."

I look down at the pale-blue velvet frock coat, complete with gold braiding, belt, and satin sash. It's an outfit Sebastien, our younger brother, promised he'd wear when he took Clodagh to the theater before gallivanting off to Spain last minute. The tickets were supposed to be my contribution to the outing! I didn't think for one minute I'd end up dressing like a pantomime prince and taking her there myself. I must be soft in the head.

"Some sort of feckin' tool," I mutter as I eye the matching white gloves distastefully. "Ow! What was that for?" I clutch my bicep after Letty catches me a good one with her pincerlike fingers.

"For behaving like a tool."

"Did you see that, Clo? One of the ugly sisters just walloped Prince Charmin. What do you reckon—off with her head?"

"Mommy's head isn't ugly."

"Isn't it?"

"No! Not Aunt Lo's and not Aunt Lou-Lou's, neither!" she says, using her nicknames for my younger twin sisters, Lola and Lucía. "And you gotta potty mouth, Uncle Matty." Clo's brows pull down.

"For saying *feck*? *Feck* isn't swearing. Prince Charmin wouldn't swear."

Clo gives me a doubtful stare.

"It's *Charming*." Letty's hiss is delivered through gritted teeth. "Which is something you know nothing about. Honestly, Matt, do you think I don't have enough problems without having to police your language where there are impressionable ears?"

I glance down at a confused Clodagh as she gingerly touches her tiny shell-like ears. "Our own father cursed like a sailor—in two languages—and we turned out all right."

"Debatable." Letty's gaze slices my way, looking me pointedly up, then down.

"Come on, sis," I cajole. "'Tis a long way from smashed avocado on toast we were raised."

"True," she reluctantly agrees. "Gentle parenting back then meant being threatened with a slipper rather than a shoe."

"Verás como saque la zapatilla!" I say, impersonating our father as I slap my hand with an invisible slipper. Letty laughs.

"Who are you pretending to be?" Clo asks, her cute little face perplexed.

"Your grandpa."

"My lelo wouldn't hit anyone with a thlipper!"

"A slipper?"

Letty elbows me in the ribs.

"The sins of the parent are not visited upon their grandchildren, obviously." I send Letty a speaking look.

"Lelo did smack Uncle Matty with a slipper when he was a kid because he was a terrible tearaway."

"I think you must be confusing me with Hugo."

That puta, she replies silently, smiling as she mouths the insult.

I slap the gloves down on the console table. "Did you just call the apple of our mother's eye a very bad name?" To be fair, Letty has a point. At the ripe old age of thirty-two, Hugo is yet to grow out of his whoring phase.

My heart gives a sudden duplicitous pang. What I wouldn't give to be in that position again. Whore. Pretend or not. For one woman only. One woman I'll likely never see again.

It's been ten weeks nearly to the day since I woke in that suite at the Pierre alone. Sixty-nine days since the best sex of my life. One thousand six hundred sixty-four hours (give or take) since I last held Ryan in my arms, sated and glad, as we'd finally fallen into bed.

We screwed on almost every conceivable surface, from the table to the bed, the bed to the shower, and the shower to the sofa. And against the window overlooking a purple-skied predawn Central Park. I played the role until my abs hurt, but it didn't feel like pretend.

The morning after, it was like her absence had left me hollow, and somehow, I'm still feeling that loss weeks later.

I give myself a mental slap. Fucking woolgathering again. What-ifs and maybes don't make a bit of difference to my current reality. My current predicament. My current state of dress. You can hit the big time. Be touted as one of the top forty under forty. Be a mover and a shaker, see your own face staring at you from the front of *Forbes*. But none of that will get you out of a stupid feckin' frock coat when it comes to family.

Good thing Clodagh is cute.

"He's only the favorite 'cause he's not here," Letty says.

"Fair fucks," I agree.

Seb is visiting Hugo, who plays midfield for Real Madrid, which is probably part of the reason he hasn't settled down. Hugh is a footballing god over there—everywhere he goes, he's trailed by wannabe WAGs. Ironic, given he wants neither wife nor regular girlfriend. Ironic and unfair. *He doesn't want a girlfriend, and I can't keep one.*

"As in, not here teaching my child unsavory words." Letty pinches me again.

"Shit—I mean, ow! What in the name of arse was that for?"

"Guess," Letty demands as she draws the sides of her cardigan closer, suddenly the very image of our mother. Not that I'd say so because I prefer not to wear my testicles as earrings. This divorce is really doing a number on her. It seems to have sucked all the fun out of her.

And my guess? I glance down at Clo. "Sorry," I offer.

"That's three more times, Uncle Matty." Clo holds up three stubby fingers.

"Ah, come on," I cajole. "That last one didn't count. *Arse* isn't really a bad word. No worse than *ass*, at least—which they say a lot where you've been living."

"They don't say *ath* a whole lot in kindergarten." Clodagh gives a twist of the lips that's far too sardonic for someone who's yet to reach the age of six. "Uncle Matty? Why does Uncle Seb say you get more ath than a toilet theat?"

"Oh, for feck's sake," Letty mutters, rolling her eyes.

"What does that mean?" Clo persists.

"It means you shouldn't listen to your uncle." I sweep her up into my arms, which is no easy task, thanks to the hoops of her sunshine-yellow princess dress. "Haven't I told you all boys are idiots? Especially Uncle Seb."

"You got that right," Letty murmurs.

Clo begins to giggle as I swing her around, almost knocking an original George Condo off the wall. But the sound is enough to lighten anyone's heart.

"Put her down." Though the words are delivered like a complaint, my sister's expression is merry as she sweeps up Clo's coat. "Let's get you into this."

"That's a bit small for me. Oh, well." I stick out my hand as though I'm about to put it on.

"Uncle Matty, that's not your coat!"

"Isn't it?"

"You're too big!" Clo answers through a delightful-sounding giggle. "Anyway, printheth don't wear no coat."

"Prin . . . princesses don't wear coats?"

This kid needs a speech therapist. Maybe I should've paid for sessions instead of theater tickets for Chrithmath. I mean, Christmas. "That's because princesses don't live in London in January," I say, taking the woolen duffle coat from Letty and shaking it out. "In you get."

"Thucks," she complains, shoving her fist into the armhole.

"Clodagh!" her mother chastises.

"Well, it does. You gonna wear a coat, Uncle Matty?"

"I most certainly am." To hide this ridiculous getup, if nothing else. I pull my phone from my pocket as it buzzes with a text. "Car's here."

"You sure you don't wanna wear the matching pants?" Letty taunts as I slide my phone back. "Personally, I think the golden edging was very fetching."

I send her a less-than-friendly look as Clodagh begins to bounce on the spot.

"And the boots! Please, please! We'll look like we're going to the ball!"

"They don't fit, remember? My feet are bigger than Uncle Seb's?"

"You mean your ath," my sister adds with a snicker.

"Jealousy is very unbecoming, pancake pants," I reply, patting my sister on the head.

"But you gotta give me the wothe," Clo says, cutting off her mother's—judging by her expression—unpleasant response.

"The what?"

"The wothe," Clo repeats, her hip jutted and her palm facing the ceiling. She eyes me like she thinks I'm an idiot. My vacant expression probably confirms her suspicions.

"Belle needs a *wothe*, Uncle Matty."

"Uncle Matty doesn't have a rose for you, baby. He's never seen the movie," Letty says softly, "so he didn't know to bring one."

I feel like I've been punched in the guts watching Clodagh's little face fall. She's already been let down twice today by the men in her life. Once when her father forgot to call, and the other when fuckin' Seb conveniently forgot their plans. *Ah, fuck it.*

"Not a problem," I say, scooping her up again. "We'll stop at a flower shop on the way."

◆ ◆ ◆

After we've secured a red rose, Dave, the driver, drops us as near as permitted to the theater. As he pulls away from the curb and the stupid satin sash whips me in the face, I realize I've left my coat on the seat.

Fucking thing, I think as I tuck the shiny piece of shit one-handed into the belt. At least it isn't raining, or snowing, I decide as I take Clodagh's hand. *I'm not sure I would've gotten my coat on anyway, not with the size of these feckin' shoulder pads and epaulets.*

The Palladium is in the West End, the London theater district, and is currently buzzing with theatergoers. But as far as I can see, we're the only ones dressed for the occasion. And drawing a few funny looks. Some indulgent ones, mostly from the female population. The blokes, however, seem to silently agree *Rather him than me*.

"Come on, slowpoke," I say, tugging on her little hand. Apart from feeling a bit of a tit, I'm feckin' freezing! "Pirate code says stragglers will be left behind."

"We aren't pirates!" she answers with a giggle.

"Course we are. Captain Prince Charming and First Mate Belle."

Clodagh's expression turns immediately pensive.

"You okay?" I ask, slowing my pace.

"Just thinking."

"Anything I can help you with?" I know Letty's doing tough with the divorce, but with Clodagh, it's harder to tell how she's feeling. She seems to have adapted well to her new school and country, but she barely mentions her dad. Not that he'd be winning any prizes in the father stakes.

"I'm just thinking maybe next time you can be Gaston."

"Gaston?" I say instead of *Next time?* They've been staying with me up until recently, but this is the first outing alone for me and Clo. Frankly, the responsibility is terrifying.

"You look like Gaston," she says, nodding her little blond head. "Not handsomest prince."

"Oh, really?" *Cheeky little shite.*

"But you got the same color hair as Gaston. And a butt chin like him."

I give a hearty chuckle. "So what I'm hearing is this Gaston fella is good looking." *Out of the mouths of babes.*

"And he's good at spitting. Plus, he's hairy, same as you."

"He sounds . . . grand." We reach the line of theatergoers queuing for general admission. If I thought I'd be here, I might've made some other arrangements. *A box or something*, I think, eyeing the group of kids a little way in front of us. I don't know kids. I also don't want to know kids. Or sit in among them.

"He isn't grand, Uncle Matty. He's a handsome, empty-headed jerk. He doesn't love Belle. He just thinks she's the prettiest girl in town, and because he has a very high 'pinion of himself, he thinks she should be married to him. He just wants to own her. That's what Mommy says. But Beast, he has a good heart."

There is so much to digest in her little speech.

"Well, that's what you want, isn't it? Someone with a good heart." Though I think it might be a bit early to be talking about men and love. Clodagh is still only five years old.

"You're not like Gaston, Uncle Matty. You say things that make Mommy laugh when Daddy says things that make her cry."

"Mommy cries?" I thought she was done with all that.

"Only when she thinks I can't hear her."

My heart gives a little twist. I'd finish that shitebag off, physically and financially, if I didn't think that would give him something else to bleat about. Some other thing to blame her for. *Waste of fucking oxygen that he is.*

"You have a heart like the Beast."

"Well, that's . . ." Enough to bring a lump to my throat. "Very lovely to hear. But, you know, Clo, when you get to be a big girl, and you date?"

"I gotta be at least thirty-five before I do that. Mommy says so."

"Good. I like that plan."

"Aunt Lola says Mommy should've taken her own advice."

"Yeah, maybe." Feckin' Lola. "Anyway, what I was trying to say is that it's not up to you to find the prince within the beast."

"What do you mean? Inside like he ate him?" She looks horrified.

"No, nothing like that." *Jesus.* How to put this? "Well, the Beast, on the outside, is all rough and tough and growly."

"But he has a good heart."

"Yeah, I know. But you shouldn't have to dig for it. He should be able to show you it, shouldn't he?"

"Like, under his fur?"

"No, not quite like that—"

"Hey, Matt!"

I glance up to find Mila standing in the line ahead of us. *The Lord works in mysterious ways, his miracles to feckin' perform!* Why the hell did I think it was a good idea to give dating advice to a five-year-old, again?

"Excuse me," Mila murmurs, smiling in apology as she makes her way back along the line toward us.

"Hi!" I think I might be smiling too much or too weirdly, judging by Mila's expression as I press a kiss to her cheek. I'd be happy to see her any time, but I'm feckin' ecstatic not to have to dig myself out of that. "How are you?" *And bless you for saving this poor, wretched fool.* I'm hardly fit to give dating advice.

"I'm good, and kind of surprised to see you here. Aren't you supposed to be with Fin and Oliver?"

"I'm meeting them later." So I'm a soft touch because, yes, I had plans of my own, but after Seb's selfishness, what could I do but step in? Letty has had so little time to herself since she came back. I mean, I offered to get her help—a nanny or an au pair—but she says it's too much. It's like she thinks she can negate her ex's lack of parenting by overcaring or something.

"And who have we here?" Mila asks, hunkering down in front of my niece.

"This is Clodagh, my niece. Clo, this is Mila, my friend." She's also Fin's wife. She might even be the making of him.

"Hi," Clo answers shyly, holding her rose to her chin.

"Hello, Clodagh. I love your dress."

"I'm Belle, and Uncle Matty is Prince Charmin," she says, glancing up at me.

"That's me. Prince of the toilet paper. Are you here to see *Beauty and the Beast*?" Stupid question. Or maybe not, as her expression flickers.

"You mean *Aladdin*?"

"I thought we were here to see *Beauty and the*—" I halt and glance at the Perspex-covered ad poster on the theater wall. "*Aladdin*. Right." I glance down to my *date*. "You think your mother might've mentioned it."

"But you got the tickets," Clodagh says, tapping me with the rose.

Aubrey, my personal assistant, did. But there's no need to let her take the praise. The line begins to move up ahead, so we do too. "So *Aladdin*," I say, sending Mila an apologetic look.

"Yep, *Aladdin*. I'm here with a youth group."

Although still very busy with her wedding-planning business, Mila does a lot for charity, particularly with underprivileged kids. By extension, Maven Inc. does a lot for charity too. It's fair to say that since the pair announced their surprise marriage, Fin thinks a lot less about himself. These days, he's often to be found squeezing money out of friends and clients in the name of his wife's causes.

"I suppose I should be grateful I'm not wearing harem pants, a vest, and a fez." I'm pretty sure my nipples would snap off in this weather.

"I was just about to mention how fetching you look."

"Thanks." I narrow my eyes playfully. "No need to mention it. Like, ever."

"No need to mention it . . . to anyone in particular?"

"I see you're picking up what I'm putting down. Don't tell your bollix of a husband, and you and me will be grand."

"I'm sorry, Matt. Fin and me, we don't keep secrets," she says with a grin.

I harrumph. Like a grumpy old bastard. "What's it gonna cost?"

"I have no idea what you mean," she says, trying not to let her grin get any wider. But I know her game.

"I'll give you fifty grand," I mutter, gesturing ahead to her youth group. One of them waves, and I realize it's Ronny, Mila's assistant. "Hey, Ron," I call out. "Got any secrets about your boss you'd like to trade?"

"Nah, fam!" she calls back with a stuttering laugh. "Me and Meels are tight. We go way back."

"Miss Mila." Clodagh tugs on Mila's hand. "Is that lady your family?" I guess it's Ronny's vernacular that prompts Clo's question.

"It's just Mila, love," she says, dropping down to my niece's level again. "Ronny *is* my family. Some family you're born to. Others you choose."

"So you chose her?"

"I did."

"Because she's 'portant to you?"

"Exactly."

Clodagh's head tilts my way. "Can you unchoose family, Uncle Matty?"

"You're stuck with me."

"I was just asking," she mutters.

"Back to my outfit," I say. "That and the price of your silence."

"It's really that important to you?"

I love how Mila doesn't bat an eyelash at both the bribe and the amount. I suppose it means she no longer feels out of place or uncomfortable. I mean, I get it. I wasn't born with a silver spoon in my mouth either. Not like the other Maven two.

"You know if either of those eejits gets wind of this," I say, tugging on my sash, "I'll have to leave the country."

"I think it's adorable what you're doing." She gives a sassy one-shouldered shrug. "How you look."

"That's because you're not a piss-taking arsehole." My eyes fall closed. *Fuck,* I silently intone. I glance down and, with a sigh, say, "Sorry, Clo."

"Uncle Matty," she says, her own sigh filled with disappointment. "You're not 'posed to curse where my ears are, remember?"

"Maybe I should just take your ears off." As I reach for those tiny things, she gives a delighted squeal, slapping her hands over them.

"Not my ears!"

"I'll get them later. It'll be easier with scissors."

The poor kid a few places ahead in the line glances back. Horrified, he huddles closer to his designated adult.

We eventually reach the front of the line and have our own tickets checked, and then we're in. It turns out we're all seated together—no doubt Aubrey booked Mila's tickets too. But by tacit agreement, we head to one of the bars first. A plan the kids agree on when I offer to buy them all ice cream.

"Chocolate for you, Clo?"

My niece nods with relish.

"Can I get you and Ronny a glass of wine or champagne? And the kids? How many of them are there?"

"Sixteen. And while I'd say more than a couple of those kids would be thrilled at the offer, let's not get you arrested today. Besides, I think they're more the cider-in-the-park furtive kinds of drinkers."

"Got it." I shoot her a quick salute. "Wine only for those of age. Ice cream and sodas for everyone else."

"Thanks, but I'm good. Ronny will probably have a Coke. She's on duty right now."

"Makes sense." You can drink around your own kids, but you probably shouldn't be throwing them back when you're in charge of someone else's.

"Can I have a thoda, Uncle Matty?"

"A . . ." Soda! "Sure?" I glance Mila's way. "Five-year-olds are okay with fizzy stuff, right?"

Mila holds up a hand. "I'm unqualified to offer advice."

"Ah, shit, I'm sure it'll be fine." Fuck. Again! I glance down at Clo, who sends me a long-suffering look.

"Don't worry. I won't tell Mommy. *This time.*"

I suck at this whole kid thing.

"Maybe you should get Uncle Matty a swear jar," Mila suggests.

"For him to whisper the bad words into?" Her tone sounds full of doubt.

"It's more about teaching Uncle Matty not to swear, because with a swear jar, every time he says a naughty word, he has to put money into it."

"Who gets to keep the money?" Clo asks suspiciously.

"If it's your swear jar, you do."

"I need a jar!" the kid says, pivoting to face me, and I'm sure I see dollar signs light up in her eyes. "And then you can say all the bad words you need."

"I'll end up broke," I protest with a chuckle.

"That is a distinct possibility." Mila has been to enough dinners to know this to be true.

"Jar later. Let's hit the bar for now. While I can still afford to."

"I wanna stay with Mila. I need to hear more about the jar."

"We can do that," she says, taking Clo's hand.

"Fine, but no scheming," I say, waggling a finger between the two.

At the bar, I ask a bewildered server if soda is illegal for five-year-olds. Apparently, it's not, though a nearby group of mothering types eyes me with such distaste, I almost ask the server to stick a vodka in it for the five-year-old.

Anyway, I order enough soda and snacks to fuel an army. I also get a few cans of alcohol-free mojitos for Mila and her companions, plus a beer for myself. As I turn from the counter, arms full of contraband, I wonder if Letty might have reservations about me taking Clodagh out again. That is, if I take her home buzzed to fuck on sugar.

Hmm. Come to think of it, I'll be the one dealing with her for the next couple of hours. *Maybe I should've gotten her water,* I think as I belatedly come to realize my footsteps are slowing. It's not because I'm reluctant to return to Clodagh with all this junk, but more like my brain is trying to make sense of something. Of what I'm seeing as, through the crowds, I spot my niece talking to a woman. Short and slight in stature, especially hunkered low in front of Clodagh, she seems familiar somehow. Maybe it's the coat she's wearing. *Emerald green.* Or maybe it's the way she flicks her dark hair over her shoulder.

Mila still has hold of Clo's hand, seemingly part of the conversation. But it's the woman who has my attention, everything around me seeming to shift into slow motion. Objects and people around me blur, my vision tunneled and focused. Though I see *her* as clear as day, and my anticipation dials high as I wait for her to turn.

"Watch it, mister!"

I come back to my surroundings as a group of kids is herded across my path. I momentarily lose sight of Clo and . . . I pick up the pace.

"Maltesers!" Clodagh reaches for the packet balanced in the crook of my arm.

"Who was that?" I ask as my gaze sweeps the space for her. "The woman you were just talking to?"

"The one in the green coat?" Mila asks. "No idea. She stopped to talk to Clodagh when she heard her accent."

"She picked up my wothe when I dropped it." Clodagh pulls a bottle of Sprite from my hand. "She's 'merican too."

"Did she say where she was from?"

Clo shakes her head. Then shakes the bottle.

"She was perfectly nice," Mila puts in. "And I didn't take my eyes off—"

"Course you didn't." I don't mean to be curt, but I can't throw off this prickling sensation. It's like fire ants are crawling all over me, like if I don't find the answer, they'll start to bite. "I just thought I recognized her." Or I hoped. "It's fine," I add, plastering a smile across my face.

"The lady was buying tickets to another show," Clo says, passing her soda back, impatient for it to be opened.

"Was she?" I loop my fingers around the top.

Clodagh nods. "She just moved to London and said hearing me talk reminded her of 'merica."

"That's nice, darlin'." I begin to twist the bottle top, though the violent-sounding hiss makes me tighten it again.

"I told her we were going to see *Aladdin* and that you had gone to buy me a thoda."

"That I had?" I ask quickly.

"Her uncle," Mila answers, looking at me strangely. Can't say I blame her.

"Are you gonna open that?" Clo taps the bottom of the plastic bottle.

"This?" I hold it up as though I'm not even sure what it is, and Clo nods. "Not just yet." I make to slot it into my pocket before realizing this stupid frock coat doesn't have any pockets. "Maybe when we get to our seats. Speaking of"—I glance Mila's way—"they're going to deliver the rest to us in there."

"Thank you, Matt. That's so kind of you."

"I told the lady they don't have a popcorn machine here."

"Popcorn?"

"Yes." Clodagh frowns. "Are you not listening to me?"

"Of course I am. You said they don't have popcorn here."

"Yeah. I told her I love popcorn, but the lady's favorite thnack is thomething else they don't got here."

"Too bad," I answer, careful not to repeat my mistake.

"She likes zeppole, and I said I like it too. That my daddy sometimes buys me it from a truck when we visit him at work. That's a good memory I have," Clodagh says a little sadly. "She said she likes it because of good memories too. Zeppole reminds her of country fairs, that's what the lady said. She has a boy's name. But she was a lady, not a man."

"What kind of boy's name, Clo?"

"Same as a kid in my class. I don't like him. He picks his nose."

"Ah, that's rotten. But what was the lady's name, again?"

"Ryan. Her name is Ryan."

"Ryan?" My heart lifts a good couple of inches.

"Uncle Matty, you keep saying the same things as me!"

"I know, pet. And I'm sorry." The apology shoots from my mouth as my heart begins to beat frantically. "But you're sure the woman in the green coat was called Ryan?"

"That's what I said, didn't I?"

"You did," I say, glancing around distractedly. *It can't be her. Can it?* "Did she say where she was going? Next, I mean?"

"To catch her tube, whatever that means."

The Tube—the nearest station is just minutes away! My heart pounds against my chest as though it will break through my ribs. "Mila." My head jerks her way. "Could you keep an eye on Clo for a bit?" Without waiting for an answer, I thrust the concession stand treats into her arms.

"Yeah, but—" A bag of crisps falls. I swipe it up.

"You help Mila, Clo?" The little girl nods. "You'll be okay for a few minutes, right? That's a good girl," I say as she nods. "I promise I won't be long."

Clo says something in response, but I'm already turning away.

A fool's errand. The words whisper in my head as, outside, frigid air hits me in the face.

"The Tube," I mutter to myself as I dodge a family crowding the steps, then take the remaining three in a long-legged leap. *Oxford Circus is the nearest station.*

I turn right out of the theater into the pedestrian thoroughfare full of shoppers, theatergoers, tourists, and teenagers deciding between burgers and noodles.

Hope is a thing with wings, so they say, and it's hope that carries me to the end of the street like a man fucking possessed. I don't feel bad about leaving Clodagh with Mila, though I'm sure it'll come. And I'll probably cop it from Letty thanks to her current hypervigilant parenting. But I don't have the headspace for any of that right now.

"Scuse me! Sorry!" Turning shoulder first, I squeeze through a large group of dawdling tourists, almost slipping on the damp pavers as I swing a right at the end of Argyll Street. I leave them gesticulating and yelling in something that might be Mandarin.

"Oi! Do you need glasses, mate?" Not so difficult to understand is the cabby after I dodge into the road, narrowly missing his black cab. *Or maybe it misses me.*

I hold up my hand in apology. No time to stop.

I know it's her. It's got to be, I think as I pelt to the other side. Then, impersonating an Olympian, I sprint away, all powering legs and robot hands.

Ryan, wait for me. I'm coming for you. Because how many women called Ryan in the world can there be—women who like green and eat zeppole? The thought that she might be here, in the same city—well, the feeling is indescribable. The wings of hope themselves.

Oxford Street, and the circular red-white-and-blue signage is my bull's-eye. The sight calls for a spurt as my lungs work like bellows and my legs like pistons.

"Excuse me—excuse me!" I shout, descending into the station. Taking the steps three at a time, I dodge between commuters, the correct side of the stairwell be damned.

In the bowels of the station, my breathing echoes in my ears as I turn one-eighty, scanning the barriers and the escalators beyond, hoping to see a hint of green coat or dark hair.

"Fuck," I mutter, turning back, ignoring the way the tails of my velvet frock coat flap like dodo wings.

"Cool coat, bro."

"Lost your horse and cart?"

"Fucking carriage," I say, mostly ignoring the hoodie-wearing brigade in favor of stalking over to a London transport worker.

"Have you—" Heavy breathing. I need to get back to the gym. "Have you seen a woman in a green coat? Dark hair." I ruffle my hand through my own hair as though the fella needs a hint.

The man straightens and leans his elbow on the top of his sweeping brush. "Green coat," he ponders. "Green coat . . . I think I see one *fine* lady taking the escalator southbound," he says with a vague sort of wave.

"Great. Thanks." I swing away.

"Wait!"

I swing back again.

"It was northbound, I think. Maybe the Central Line."

"Thanks. Again." I make for the ticket barrier as I reach for my wallet. "Fuck. Shit!" I pat my chest and my back pockets, my skin turning clammy in that instant. It was in my hand when I shoved the snacks into Mila's arms. I must've left it with her.

I become aware of a terse *tsk*. A sigh. Then a huff. I'm holding up a line of commuters. I know it's no good appealing to them. London commuters are intolerant at the best of times.

"There are other barriers," I mutter, moving to the side. I consider hopping over the thing once this lot is through, but then I remember the videos of a man with his nut sack caught in the barrier after trying to jump it not so long ago. "Fuck it." I slip in behind a bloke tapping his card, hustling him through the barrier faster than he'd planned on.

He huffs, all aggravated bluster.

"It's for a good cause," I call over my shoulder as I dodge past, heading for the northbound escalator.

"What a fuckin' liberty," the man shouts. "That's theft, that is!"

"From Transport for London, not you," I mutter, taking the escalator two steps at a time.

A fool's errand.

This time, the words take up more space in my head as I remember how this place resembles a rabbit warren. She could be anywhere.

Off the escalator, I turn right onto the first platform. *Empty.* Which means the train just left. *Fuck!* Undeterred—because what choice do I have? I know she's here somewhere. She has to be—I race along the platform. Back out again into the tiled warren of corridors, the stupid satin sash flapping in my face. Another escalator, the treads two at a time again. I dodge left, then right, sweeping the corridors to check the platforms as I pass them.

"Watch it, numpty!"

I murmur an apology, my thoughts on the southbound platforms next. Up the stairs, my thighs screaming now. Along the corridor and down again.

"What's your hurry?" someone shouts.

"I'm looking for a woman in green," I call back.

"Aren't we all!"

A laugh. One I don't stop for.

"Green coat? I saw someone."

I stop and pivot on the sole of my shoe to find a pair of girls a little way in front of me. They're probably in their early twenties. Puffer jackets and Ugg boots, hairstyles from the 1970s—the flipped-bangs one that seems all the rage now. "You saw . . . what?" Who.

"Lo." One girl clutches the other one's arm. "He might be a stalker," she whispers.

"I wouldn't be much of a stalker dressed like this," I say, plucking at the lapels of this stupid jacket. Sliding my hands through my sweaty hair.

"Not much of a Prince Charming either," she says with a disdainful look.

"Farther along. Heading for platform 3," the other girl says.

And I'm off again, another burst of energy, another burst of *scuse me*s and *sorry*s. Left onto the platform, one that's pretty packed.

. . . the train approaching is . . .

I slow my pace at the announcement, working myself amid the mass of commuters, peering over their heads. Would I even see her here, that little teacup, among all these people?

. . . please stand back from the platform edge.

The train pulls in with a cacophony of squealing brakes as the warm updraft moves my coattails.

. . . Oxford Circus. Change here for . . .

People pile off as people pile on, the crowd beginning to thin. My heart beginning to sink.

Until someone moves left, and I spy the back of a green coat!

"Ryan!" I bellow, my feet propelling me forward again. "Ryan!" Louder this time.

She disappears onto the train.

The alarm sounds.

The doors begin to close. I pivot left, making for the nearest. She's so close—she's fucking here! So close until . . .

The doors meet before I can reach them.

"Ryan!" I bang on the thing with my fists, drawing lots of looks, but no recognition. She's in a different carriage.

My heart drops to my boots as the train begins to move, then disappears from my view. Despondent, I collapse to a nearby bench, panting and out of breath. I press my elbows to my spread knees, all kinds of curses and mutterings flowing through my head. Until something kindles in my chest. A realization.

She's here. In London. *Somewhere.*

It's just a question of finding her.

Hope is a fire that burns bright.

"Excuse me, sir."

I tilt my head to find one of London's finest—the transport police version—towering over me. "Do you realize fare evasion is a criminal offense?"

I break into a smile. "Fucking worth it, though."

Chapter 13
MATT

"Here he is—Prince Charming!" Wearing a grin of shit-eating proportions, Fin raises his glass in toast as I cross the floor of Oliver's almost-empty club.

Oliver's club isn't a nightclub or a sports club. It's the kind of place I never thought I'd see the inside of. Heavy furniture and leather chairs built to last but not necessarily for comfort. Poor lighting and antique paneled walls, the timber dappled with sword marks. *Allegedly.* And my least favorite aspect, ugly portraits of long-dead white men staring disapprovingly down.

Ah, they'd be turning in their graves to know they let Irishmen—and women—in these days.

The club is a private members' establishment, formerly known as a gentleman's club, renamed so as not to be confused with the kind of place with poles, stages, and scantily clad women.

"I think you've got that the wrong way around." Reaching my so-called friends, I pull out one of the ugly leather chairs around a small table. "You're the one with the hair *and* the charm, pretty boy." I give my head a theatrical shake, a bit like a Thoroughbred Iberian. Or a social media influencer in front of a camera.

"But you're the one with the silky sash and shiny buttons." Fin makes feckin' spirit fingers over his chest, vicious delight in those sparkling blue eyes of his. "Or so I've heard. Wear it for me sometime, baby?"

I make a noise of disgust as I wonder what else he's heard, the least of which would be that I dumped his wife with a kid she barely knows. Thankfully, the pair of them seemed to be getting along like a house on fire when I got back to the theater just before curtain-up. I had hung back before taking my seat, waiting for the lights to dim to hide the fact that I was mildly disheveled, sweaty haired, and red in the face. Mila would've probably assumed I'd been up to no good. Worse, she might've insisted on answers.

As it was, I spent the first half of the show with my brain reeling between plans to find Ryan and excuses to provide Mila with because telling Fin and, to a lesser extent, Oliver seemed like a fate worse than death. But Mila was far too polite to ask and, during the intermission, merely murmured a quiet "I hope you caught up with your friend." She didn't wait for an answer, turning to speak with one of the kids from her youth group instead. *She's one of the good ones, Mila.*

Good that Evie wasn't there, is all I can say. She's also a good woman, but it definitely wouldn't have gone the same way.

As for Clodagh, she's yet to mention my excursion to her mother, mainly because she was so enamored with the show, and yapped about it all the way home. The only other thing we talked about was getting her a cookie jar. Apparently, a jam jar won't be big enough to store all my sweary transgressions.

"I knew about the romance novels," Fin taunts. "But I didn't know you were into fairy tales."

Jaysus, you make one reference to *Bridgerton*, and you're forever labeled. So I cracked the spines on one or two of Letty's novels. So what? I know I'm not the only one.

"I hear romance books are more your line," I retort with a careless gesture.

"I already have an abundance of romance in my life."

I scoff, mildly pissed off. "It's like you don't even remember you snagged Mila by accident. Personally, I'm still not convinced she isn't suffering from Stockholm syndrome, given the beginning of your relationship. An isolated island, no one to turn to but you. Sounds more like the beginnings of a true crime podcast than a romance."

"What wrongs have I committed to deserve spending my Saturday evening with you two?" Oliver's tone is withering as he reaches for his wineglass.

My attention pivots. "How long have you got?"

"The time it would take to list them would turn your wine to vinegar," Fin adds.

"My conscience is as clear as the driven snow." Oliver gives a haughty sniff.

"I wasn't aware you had a conscience," I say.

"Sure he has. It's a recent addition to the stiff-upper-lipped, stick-up-the-ass Brit model. A conscience called Evie." Fin's attention glides my way again. "But back to you. What's this I hear about you haring around London after a woman?"

"I don't know. What is it you hear?"

"Enough to pique my interest." He glances down, lowering his lashes like a coy debutante.

"That might work on Mila, but it's not working on me."

"Come on, give it up. Who is she?"

"Why, Fin. You're practically frothing at the mouth."

"Yeah, yeah. Creamin' in my panties too."

My answer is to borrow Oliver's glower.

Fin continues to poke. "Am I not allowed to be happy for my friend getting back on the proverbial horse, *Mr. I'm-not-interested-in-women*?"

"When did I ever say that?"

"When you were in New York in October, and things haven't changed since. Frankly, I've been worried you might be considering the church."

"Be fair, Phineas," Oliver says with a wave of his glass. "After a day spent in the company of ex-girlfriends, we might all consider becoming men of the cloth."

I frown again, Oliver's way this time. It's very fucking clear these two have been talking about me.

"So imagine my surprise at what my darling wife had to tell me after the theater this afternoon."

"I said I wasn't interested in casual sex," I retort, pointing a finger Fin's way.

"Please let's get this over with," Oliver adds almost wearily. "I would like to eat dinner sometime this evening."

"Are we eating here?" is Fin's only (complaining) response. To be fair, the food here is atrocious—like something served out of history. I'm convinced they're still using Mrs. Beeton's cookery book. *Tough beef and soggy veg, but at least the whiskey is good.*

"I wouldn't," another voice puts in. "It's duck à l'orange. Or the Dover sole. Again."

Oliver gives a pained expression. "Thank you, George, but we aren't dining in this evening."

"Thank God," Fin mutters.

"You are, however, just in time to furnish Matías here with a drink."

"Right you are, sir," the waiter replies happily.

"Howya, Cyril," I greet him, ignoring the dictums of this arcane establishment, whereby all members of staff are referred to by the name of George. *Every one of them. So yeah, fuck that.*

"Hello, sir. I haven't seen you in a while."

"Busy times." I've been avoiding these evenings, mainly because Mila and Evie often meet us for dinner. Though my friends' wives are great, I can't help feeling like a spare prick at a wedding when sitting with the four of them.

"What can I get you?" Hands behind his back, Cyril leans onto his toes and back again, like an old-fashioned policeman.

"I'll have a pint of the black stuff and a whiskey chaser, thanks."

"The Bushmills 21, sir?"

"That'd be grand."

Cyril retreats, and I find myself shifting uncomfortably in my seat. There are only so many excuses a man can make to avoid hanging out with his friends and their wives, but right now, I need to be here. I need their help in finding Ryan. "Right, so," I begin. "Not that it's got anything to do with you, but I haven't gone off women."

"Oh, we know," Fin says with relish as he leans back in his chair. "Tell Daddy Fin all about it."

"I think I've just been sick in my mouth."

"Oh, for God's sake." Oliver crosses one leg over the other like a declaration.

"There was a woman. *Is* a woman."

Fin's brows rise high on his forehead as though to say, *No shit, Sherlock*. And though neither man says anything, they exchange a look.

"What the fuck is going on between you two?"

With a pained sigh, Oliver reaches into his inside jacket pocket and pulls out his wallet. He places two fifties onto the table before pushing them Fin's way.

"Nice doing business with you," Fin says, holding one of the notes to the light. It's an act of showmanship rather than checking for counterfeits. "Ryan, wasn't it?"

I make a noise, part dismissal, part *get fucked*.

Fin positively beams. "So tell us all your news," he says like some teen drama queen as he slides the money into his top pocket.

I hold up a forestalling finger as Cyril returns with my pint of Guinness and single malt.

"Who won?" the waiter asks, setting them down.

"Not you as well," I complain.

Cyril gives an apologetic half shrug.

"I did," Fin replies.

"I'm glad to hear it." Cyril turns Oliver's way. "No offense, Mr. Deubel."

"None taken," he returns with equanimity.

"Well, I'm very glad to hear the news," Cyril adds. "And I hope to serve the lucky lady a drink or two very soon."

"We'll see," I mutter, lifting my pint. Cyril retreats almost soundlessly. God knows what Ryan would think of the place, but I'm getting ahead of myself. "So." I put my pint down, turn it thirty degrees or so to the right. "I met her in New York," I say, studying the condensation on the glass. "The night of the wedding."

"Perhaps you ought to give me my money back," Oliver murmurs. "Sounds like I was right."

"He hasn't finished yet," Fin says with a dismissive flick of his hand. "Go on."

"After the wedding, and after I hung up on you, I more or less bumped into her." Which is better than the truth: that she accosted me.

"That's what's called a meet-cute," Fin says for Oliver's benefit. "No need to kidnap a woman from her own wedding."

"Hilarious," Oliver drawls, unimpressed.

"So you bumped into her," Fin says, turning my way. "And . . . then you lost touch? Until you saw her again today."

"Which is just another way of saying it was a one-night stand," Oliver says without judgment. He makes a gesture with his hand: palm facing the ceiling, finger curling in and back. Sort of *give me my money back*.

"Since when have you two become gossiping auld women? Ah, that's right," I mutter, folding my arms across my chest. "Since the pair of you got married. Slippers and pipe by the fire and stickin' your noses in other people's lives."

"Oooh!" Fin intones. "Someone's got his panties in a wad. Green panties, to boot."

I can't help but smile. He means *jealous*, but I'm thinking of green gossamer lace and the treasures beneath. *All that loveliness.* "Look, we spent the night together, and she left while I was sleeping."

"A perfect ending." A pause. "What?" Oliver glances between us. "At least in my experience. My *previous* experience."

Fin looks momentarily confused. "Do you not know how to use that thing?"

"Eh?" But I follow his drift as his eyes drop to the table. I make a noise of disgust.

"Being hung doesn't mean you don't have to put in the work."

"*Jaysus*," I mutter. "It was nothing like that."

"If she didn't stick around, then maybe she thought it wasn't worth repeating."

"He might have a point," Oliver puts in. "Back in my single days, I was usually the first to leave. After morning sex. It was quite convenient living in a hotel."

"Would the pair of youse just shut the hell up for a second?" I demand, slipping into the vernacular. "She didn't leave because she didn't enjoy herself. She left because she thought I was a fucking escort!"

Again, the pair says nothing, maybe because my retort seems to echo rudely in the room. Oliver gives a sudden nod, one that's preceded by an indignant huff and the violent shuffle of a newspaper from a nearby table.

"Good evening, Viscount Radler," Oliver offers, biting back a grin. "You'll have me blackballed," he murmurs, turning my way.

"He'd be doing you a favor," mutters Fin.

"Thrown out of my own club for entertaining undesirable sorts?"

"I thought he was asleep," Fin says.

"I thought he was dead." The two of them glance sharply my way. "What? He's got feckin' muttonchops—men haven't worn muttonchops for more than a hundred years." And he's always there in the same position, hiding behind a copy of *The Times*. "I thought maybe he'd been stuffed or something."

"Unlike your girl," Fin retorts as quick as a flash.

I slide him a look that very eloquently says, *Get. Fucked.*

"What do you mean she thought you were an escort?" Oliver leans in, all discreet drawl and disdain. He slides his fingers over the base of a glass of wine, which is probably something unpronounceable and ridiculously expensive. To be fair, my taste in whiskey runs the same way.

"Just what I said." I adjust the cuffs of my shirt under my jacket, the thing suddenly no longer fitting right. "She even left me an envelope stuffed with cash. My fee or my tip or—"

"Whoa, whoa, whoa." Fin holds up a hand. "You *charged* her?"

"Fuck, no!" I retort. At checkout, my heart leapt when the receptionist mentioned there was a message for me. Maybe she'd left me her number after all? *No such fucking luck.* Though there were looks. Weird ones as I opened the envelope and a good chunk of cash almost spilled from it.

"That's not what it sounds like." Oliver remains impassive; meanwhile, glee dawns slowly on Fin's face.

"You American gigolo, you." The bastard enunciates each word slowly, delightedly.

"Isn't that an old movie?" Oliver looks mildly confused.

"Yeah, with Richard Gere. Though he's more like Richard's *gear*," Fin adds, pretending to grab his junk under the table.

"I don't understand why you'd do such a thing."

"It's not like I set out to," I complain.

"The road to hell is paved with good intentions," Fin says, reaching for his glass. "Not usually envelopes stuffed with cash. Seems I've been missing a trick."

"Literally," Oliver adds dryly.

"Hilarious. Fuckin' comedians." I fold my arms across my chest. "Go on—don't let me stop you. Yuck it the fuck up." This is why I didn't want to tell them. It's not like either of them is a paragon of virtue, but I'm not in the mood to waste my breath.

"Sorry," Fin offers. "It's quite a tale. Kind of hard to resist."

"I honestly thought I was doing the right thing. At least initially. I didn't want to encourage her—pretty and pretty crazy can go hand in hand. And she had this wild story from the minute we met. I wasn't sure she was serious. Or right in the head."

"The crazy ones do have their attractions." Fin nods sagely. He would know.

I glance between the two of them and their frowns, and as succinctly as possible, I tell them what went down. I touch on how we met, my sympathy for Ryan's plight, and my reluctance to go to another wedding. I explain how she misunderstood me, and how I just played along with her assumption—I was so feckin' sure I wouldn't be going to another wedding. I tell them about her ex and the sickening company culture she worked in. Describe her fucknut colleagues and how their misogynistic bullshit culminated in that despicable bet. And I tell them how all this swayed me. How I played the part of a doting boyfriend and how, as that boyfriend, I dealt with the ringleader. Then I admit our mutual attraction carried us to a hotel suite.

From there, the tale is a closed door.

"Sunk cost fallacy," Oliver says out of nowhere.

"What about it?" Fin asks.

"Matt's lie. I can see he was trying to protect himself, but his mistake was investing so heavily in that lie that he couldn't give it up. Even when it became apparent that the truth would've been the more favorable strategy."

"Not true," Fin interjects. "The truth would've meant the evening ending with nothing but angry words. Not amazing sex." He glances my way. "Or the potential for more."

"But he'd have a clear conscience."

"My conscience is just fine," I snap. "And I am actually sitting here, so stop fucking talking about me as though I'm not."

"His conscience is just fine too," Fin says, glancing at his watch. "I expect she's a couple of cocktails deep with my wife." *His conscience named Evie.*

"Sex wasn't the reason I didn't tell her." But I silently admit it was less about her in that moment than I told myself.

"Sex was definitely part of the reason." There's no bite or teasing to Fin's response. "I think it's more the case that you've been hoisted by your own petard. If you'd admitted the truth, you wouldn't have gotten to spend the night with Ryan. And you wouldn't be filled with what-ifs right now."

"Dreyland Capital," Oliver puts in, cutting off my retort.

"Yeah. You know the outfit?"

"I know the company. Heard of them, at least."

"Good or bad news?" Fin glances Oliver's way.

"There have been some . . . less than complimentary reports, as I recall. Not that I'd hold that against them."

"Yeah, well, I hold it against their fuckin' throats."

"I'm not defending them. I'm merely pointing out that we, the three of us, can be as ruthless as the next cutthroat in business."

"But you'd no more sexually harass a woman than you would your wife's fluffy dog."

"Fluffy demon dog," Oliver corrects, brushing his hand over his thigh as though it's covered in dog hair. It's not.

"Bo is more likely to sexually harass Oliver," Fin adds merrily. "In fact, he has."

"Don't remind me." Oliver's tone turns icy.

"I know the industry is . . . old school," Fin continues, "but it's hard to believe there's still shit going on like that. At least you knew where to find her, right?"

I rub my jaw. "She doesn't work there anymore." A fact that is obviously good for her but was pretty shit for me when I went looking. "I haven't been able to track her down."

A look passes between the two.

"I'm sorry, I don't understand," Oliver says. "You tried to track her down because you wanted to . . . offer her a job or return her envelope of money?"

"Because I want to see her again." Desperately. "To tell her the truth. To explain that . . ." I just can't stop thinking about her. "Look, that night was the weirdest night of my life. But it was also the best. I couldn't bring myself to walk away from her. I had to help. And I just thought the safest bet was to play up to her assumption."

Fin reaches for his glass. "I'm kind of curious how she reached that assumption."

"It doesn't matter," I say. "I thought I was making myself unobtainable. Undesirable, or something. And after the afternoon I'd had, there was no way I was interested in a casual fuck."

"Said no single man ever." Fin slices me a look I choose to ignore.

"But there was nothing casual about that night, and things just haven't felt right since."

"Is that why you stepped in for me?" Fin sits forward, steepling his fingers over the tabletop. "To keep yourself busy?" He glances Oliver's way. "I'm pretty much obsolete as far as client relations go."

"Hardly," I answer uncomfortably. "It was just a few dinners here and there."

I stepped in ostensibly to allow Fin more time with his new wife. So much of his job is spent entertaining and schmoozing our wealthy business partners that it takes up a lot of his personal time, which wasn't an issue before Mila. But the man is newly wed and in love. So I said I'd help him out.

But I had an ulterior motive. While I introduced Chinese moneymen to the best Irish whiskey in London and arranged a private couture show in Milan for a bunch of Qatari investors' wives, I was also networking. These past months I've spent time and effort building relationships, when before I was only interested in building sites and building wealth. And now I'm on first-name terms with the kinds of financial big hitters that have fingers in lots of international pies. *Including the States.* These rich feckers love me—they love my common touch and my earthy (or sweary) *craic*—so, of course, should I decide to drop a few hints their way about mismanagement of a certain hedge fund, I'm sure they'd be all ears.

As the saying goes, revenge is a dish best served cold. That's not to say there isn't something satisfying in making a man see the error of his ways with a more . . . primitive response.

"Well, you took to the role like a duck to water," Fin says, studying me.

"You're not the only one who can be sociable."

"But that's not what it was about." He sounds impressed, not that I'll admit his suspicions. "You're one motherfucker."

"You've gotta take opportunities as they're presented," I answer, sticking with my poker face.

"So your plan is to what? Fuck Dreyland Capital for messing with your girl?"

"She's not my girl." At least, she isn't yet. *And she won't ever be if I can't find her.*

"You want to punish them?" Oliver asks, perplexed. "For what? They're just one of a hundred companies that operate in the same way."

"You mean chauvinistically? Archaically? Fuck that. They should be put out of their misery."

"Along with a good portion of the finance world?" Oliver asks.

I lift my ankle to my knee and straighten the pleat in my pants. "I didn't say it made sense. I'm not sure I understand it myself. But it was almost as though she expected that kind of treatment. Not in a way that made her seem downtrodden, because that's not her. She's all kind of kick arse. Resilient. As hard as nails. On the outside, at least." I look up to find my friends examining me. "It was like her self-sufficiency had been long ingrained."

"In this industry I can believe it," Fin murmurs.

"It was more than that. Worse than that. So yeah, like any man with feelings, I want to help her."

"Help?" Fin repeats.

"Fucking . . . protect her. Do better. Punish her ex for making her suffer, for ignoring what was happening in that toxic space. I mean, it's less viscerally exciting than smashing my fist into his face, but he married into the family business. What better way to make him pay than by causing that business trouble? Maybe even failure. I'd make it his fault."

"Sounds like you've given this a lot of thought," Oliver says.

"Maybe more to the point, it sounds like a *you* thing, not a her thing," Fin adds.

Oliver turns to face Fin. "But faint heart never won fair lady."

"Whatever the fuck that means," I mutter.

"It means we both get it," Fin replies. "Look, you're a good man. Principled and fair, but have you considered how Ryan will feel about it? She might not appreciate your interference. She might see your actions as undermining hers, taking away her individual power. Especially the way you describe her."

"She's not here, though, is she?" I say, toying with my whiskey glass.

"All the more reason—"

"I want to fucking crush them," I growl, my grip tightening on the glass.

The table falls into silence. Until Fin breaks it.

"Because you love her."

My head jerks immediately up. "Cop onto yourself," I scoff, lifting my drink and ignoring the twinge in my chest. "You can't love someone you've spent less than twelve hours with." I throw the whiskey back.

"Yeah, you can." Fin's tone and his smile feel like compassion. "Ask me how I know. Ask him."

But I don't.

"You didn't tell us what happened when you caught up with her today," Oliver says. "I take it you didn't mention your plans."

"That's just it. I didn't catch her. I followed her into Oxford Circus Station, where she got on the 1:54. Victoria Line." I press my palm to my jaw and flex; everything inside me so fucking tense. "I was so close, yet . . ." I blow out a breath. "Where she is now is anyone's guess."

"And you're sure it was her?" Oliver asks, reaching for his phone.

"Positive." I know what I heard, and I know what I saw. "I just don't know where to go from here."

"Transport police." Oliver's tone is matter of fact. "CCTV footage."

"Yeah," I scoff. "It's not like they'll just hand it over." It wouldn't be my first rodeo with them, not after today.

"No, but you will be able to view it. Tomorrow," he adds, setting down his phone. "Expect a call. Personally, I've never had an issue bending the rules or playing dirty."

"And this is news how?" Fin deadpans.

"It's not news, per se. It's strategy." Oliver glances my way as though formulating what he wants to say. "Aside from finding her, what exactly do you want from Ryan?"

"A chance. A chance is all I can ask for."

"Then how about we investigate the possibility," Oliver suggests.

"The possibility of what?" Fin's head pivots so fast.

"Of devastating Dreyland Capital. Destroying them not for the sake of it, but because harm has to be answered."

"I don't know," Fin says doubtfully.

"Just an investigation, Phineas. A look at how we lock down their deal flow, should Matt decide that's what he'd like to do."

"Steer away their investors?" Fin frowns.

"What's the use of having market influence if you don't use it to get what you want?"

"I just don't get how this will benefit *her*?" Fin says, looking my way.

I shrug, unsure. The only truth I have seems to lurk in a very primitive center of my brain: for better or worse, I want to protect her.

Chapter 14
RYAN

"Who are you all tarted up for?" Martine asks as she passes by, all slinky hips and sass.

"Girl, not who; what," I answer, my attention remaining on the empty meeting room. The office is pretty empty too. Just me and Martine so far, everyone else still suffering from post-Christmas blues, it would seem.

I like to get into the office early, as a rule. I usually check the foreign markets while drinking my first coffee of the day. Maybe get a start on any paperwork before the office fills and the day is inevitably eaten up communally.

"Why do you suppose companies insist on meeting rooms like this?" Arms folded, I nod toward the glass box with its catwalk of a table and the dozen or so ecru Eames chairs. "There's nothing about the room that would set people at ease or even encourage a flow of openness and trust."

Martine laughs. "Openness and trust—are you sure you've done this job before?"

My smile reflects in the glass.

"It's all for show, the whole space-age interior thing," she says with a dismissive wave. "Because the walls of glass are so they can keep an eye on us. Fapping on company time is not allowed."

I cough out a laugh as I glance over my shoulder at her. "I think it's probably more a productivity thing than a fapping thing."

"You have your theories, and I have mine," she retorts, all playful pique. "And I've been here longer than you."

"Well, that's true," I agree, turning to face her fully.

"Wow, check you out, Miss Thing." She snaps her fingers as her gaze falls over my outfit. "Very stylish, the assassin-favored high-ponytail-and-oversized-blazer look. Also, very Y2K. Of course, I remember it the first time around."

"When you were twelve?"

"Why, thank you, dollface." Batting her lashes, she presses the backs of her fingers under her chin. "It's all thanks to the tweakments." She blows me a kiss as she takes a couple of steps backward. Then she turns and sashays her tight ass away.

"Is that dress Dries Van Noten?" I call after her, coveting her style, from the leopard-print kitten heels that I'm sure are YSL to the fine-knit claret-colored wool hugging her figure.

"A Mango knockoff," she replies without turning.

But I don't believe her as I pull at the front of my shirt. *Underdressed? Too young? Too of the hour?* Second-guessing my Veronica Beard pantsuit, I slide off the oversize blazer and cross the office to hang it in the coat closet. Or cloakroom, as they call it here, which is just another piece of English whimsy that appeals to me.

My heels echo against the floor as I make my way back. A slow smile spreads across my face for no other reason than the sight of dust motes dancing merrily in a shaft of weak wintery sunshine. It feels like a good omen, the sun shining today. Maybe because

London has been nothing but gray since I arrived. Not that I'm complaining. I'm stoked to be here, whatever the weather.

When I applied for the job at DLC Capital Management in the fall, I didn't think for one minute I'd wind up working for one of their subsidiaries in London. Freakin' London! In my secret reveries, I'd long imagined myself living here, sipping cocktails in fashionable clubs and beer in old pubs with roaring log fires. In Knightsbridge and Mayfair, shopping till I dropped. Brunch at Soho House and discovering retro treasures at Camden Market. Winter walks through Hyde Park with a coffee in my hand. Being here is like a dream come true.

The city is iconic and cooler than cool, from the chimes of Big Ben to the trundle of black cabs and red double-decker buses. It's the quaint street names and cobblestone lanes, history and culture, ancient buildings, museums, and galleries. It's the Square Mile of towering glass but also the pristine parks and tranquil woods. It's the world-class restaurants and hotels but also ye olde pubs. It's the home of philosophers and explorers, artists and poets, and yes, grouchy commuters on the Tube ignoring crazy drunk people singing show tunes. And as of last month, it's also home to me.

I'd probably put up with ten Brandons and their bullshit to live here, but the icing on the cake is I don't have to. Theta is a hedge fund, still largely male dominated, but (so far) without the level of noxiousness of Dreyland Capital.

"Any idea what today's meeting is about?" Martine asks, reappearing next to me.

"You're a lifesaver," I say as she passes me a coffee. I inhale the fragrant steam. There's just something special about the first coffee of the day. Though I'll admit coffee in London hasn't been *quite* as enjoyable. *Maybe it's the water over here.* "No idea. I was just invited to sit in." My new job is a promotion. I'm a PM—a portfolio manager, though I'm still getting to grips with how things are done within the organization.

"I wonder if all three of them will turn up together?" Martine slips a hunk of her expensive, colored honey-blond hair behind her ear.

"All three of who?" Bringing the coffee cup to my lips, I blow gently on the scalding dark liquid. Before I realize what I'm doing. *Low-class Ryan escapes again.*

"Maven Inc. It's who the meeting is with this morning, or so I've heard on the old grapevine."

"Should I have heard of them?"

"Only if you're interested in the most prestigious PE firm in the city. Or their hot-as-fuck principals."

I make a face. Private equity? Not my specialty. PE are longtime investment specialists, whereas hedge funds are all about making those quick bucks. Also, men? Not necessary, because I'm still living on the fantasies of October's Mr. Killer Jawline. Mr. Talented Tongue. Mr. Cost-me-two-grand-for-the-night. *He was worth every penny.*

"You okay?"

"Hmm?" I realize I've zoned out, daydreaming about my audacity and his great big—

"Maven has three primary partners. Each one of them is as rich as Croesus and as *hot as fuck*," she says, enunciating the latter heavily.

"Thanks for the heads-up." Martine is a little older, twice divorced, and her cynicism matches my own. Also, we seem to have scarily similar taste in men, at least, according to our occasional lunch dates. She likes them younger, and I do not. Which is where we meet in the middle. Though it's an academic kind of appreciation, as neither of us has time in our lives for men. And I have no interest, especially after . . .

"Tell me something."

I stifle a sigh at the echo of his voice in my ear. It's not that my libido is still on the fritz, because Matt certainly reignited *that* flame. But I have a sneaking suspicion that he might've ruined me for other men. *It's such a cliché, but clichés are a thing for a reason.*

I take a sip of my coffee and try not to grimace as I burn my tongue. One way to make sure I don't recoil at the taste is to burn off my taste buds, I guess.

"Of course they're all married." Martine glances my way. "The good ones always are."

"Or payable by the hour."

"What?" The word bounds from her mouth, full of mirth.

"It's just a thing," I say evasively, hopefully, as I set my cup on the sill. Maybe I'll water the ficus with it when it's cool.

"A good thing, I hope. Though it would have to be a *really* good thing to pay for it."

"I've never . . ." Only, that's not strictly true. Not after that one time when I forced myself to visit the two ATMs nearest to a certain Manhattan hotel, the morning after what I have come to remember as the Night of My Life. *Capitalization required.*

As I stuffed what I was able to withdraw from my account into a mooched hotel-branded envelope, I told myself it didn't matter what the desk clerk thought. It needed to be this way. No matter how special my night with Matt had been, I had to draw a line under it. And I told myself that it was just a momentary madness that'd made me consider checking his wallet while he slept to see if he carried a business card.

Nate from Nine Inch Males. I stifle a soft sigh at the memory.

I briefly considered including a note, but what would I have said?

Thanks for the night of my life.
Kudos, sir. You railed me good.

You should be paid by the inch and the minute.

Or maybe it should've just said . . . thank you. Just . . . thank you.

I still don't have the words to adequately express what that night was, what it meant to me. So instead, I scrawled his name on the envelope, then handed it over to the desk clerk before I could change my mind. *And deliver it myself.*

The money made me just another satisfied client and not someone who'd pine or lust after him. But the night, the experience, was truly something special. Revisiting it could only end in obsession. And eventual bankruptcy.

"I don't judge," Martine says loftily. "I mean, I'll listen. If there's a tale to tell. But no judgment here, my friend."

"There's no tale," I insist.

"Pity. I don't know why we women don't avail ourselves of the services of a professional more often. I mean, I hire a personal trainer to keep my ass in trim, and a dermatologist for my face. Why not a specialist for my vagina?"

"I think that would be a gynecologist."

"I've got one of those too. But there's more than one way it should be taken care of, right?"

I chuckle.

"Makes me think, though," she says, turning to the window and the gray-blue view over the city. *Winter daylight hours are short.* "Another couple of years in this place, and I'll be able to get me one of those on retainer."

"One of what?" My question stutters out in another chuckle.

"A professional." She gives a wiggle of her brows. *Her aesthetician must be great.* "Sounds pretty perfect to me. None of the complications and all of the orgasms."

Until you can't stop thinking about him. Which leaves you with more complications. But also, more orgasms. Self-administered.

Time to move the conversation on.

"Do you think the men who build these glass-and-metal towers realize they all look like penises?"

"Ryan, men are almost always thinking about their dicks without even realizing it."

"So that's a yes?"

"They have two heads, but they can only use one at a time. I think it must be like being tied to the village idiot sometimes."

"It would answer a lot of questions, I guess."

"Everywhere you look in London, from Nelson's Column to the Shard, there are dicks as far as the eye can see."

"The Shard would be a very unfortunate penis," I say. "Kind of stabby, all that unbalanced girth and pointy end."

"We need more female architect leads, because it's only going to get worse. I mean"—she moves closer as though ready to divulge a secret—"there's a building currently going through planning called Undershaft. *Undershaft.* Can you believe that? Wasn't there a consultation over the name?"

"That's kind of . . . special."

"If there was a consultation, you can bet your sweet arse it didn't include women. Or not enough of them. Of course, you know what's under the shaft, don't you? Balls," she adds with a decisive nod.

"Oh, my Lord." This is a conversation and a half!

"And you didn't hear it from me, but Maven Inc. has its sticky fingers in another project I heard they've internally christened the Dildo."

"Internally? *Really,* Martine?"

"Would I lie to you?"

"You've got to be making that up."

"Sadly, I'm not that creative. Or else I wouldn't be working in finance." A pause. "Did you get up to anything interesting on the weekend?"

"Yeah, I forgot to tell you. I signed the lease on my new apartment—no more serviced accommodation for me!" It's been a bonus, but there's nothing quite like having your own space.

"Well, that's wonderful!"

"I get the keys this week."

"Congratulations. Sounds like you're about to become a real Londoner."

"High praise," I say with a laugh, lifting my coffee to my lips again.

"Praise is my love language." She gently jostles my shoulder with hers. "Well, that and blow jobs."

"What the hell!" I splutter, spraying coffee all over the window.

◆ ◆ ◆

Nine a.m., and the office has come to life, though the vibe is a little different from usual, the buzz increased. The floor of a hedge fund isn't ordinarily a quiet place to work. There are quiet spots, but mostly the offices are full of go-getters and proactive folk. As hard work is usually only acknowledged at bonus time, and by money and rarely by praise, people tend to be loud about their achievements in their day-to-day business. But they're not bigging themselves up this morning. Strangely, the buzz seems a little hushed. Awed, maybe?

This is interesting to me, but not as interesting as the smorgasbord of breakfast foods a catering company has laid out.

"What have you got there?" Arthur, one of the junior traders, asks, hovering by my shoulder.

"This? A Portuguese tart, I think."

"Sounds like my last girlfriend."

"What would she call you, I wonder?" I don't quite manage to keep the bite from my tone.

Arthur pauses as though giving my question some thought. "Probably 'that workaholic wanker,'" he answers candidly, then reaches for a Danish pastry. "Gor, dees are goog."

"I'm not sure they're a one-mouthful kind of pastry," I say with a chuckle as I add a little fruit to my plate. Melon, papaya, and pineapple. I avoid the grapes because you know they're just gonna roll right off my plate. "Why are we the only ones eating?"

"Post-Christmas diet blitz and New Year's resolutions to maintain for, oh, at least ten days."

"You're funny."

"Funny enough for you to buy me dinner?"

I think the local vernacular would refer to Arthur as a chancer.

I slant him a look as I pop a small slice of pineapple into my mouth, mainly to stop myself from responding *Umm . . . how about ah-hell no*. "Ew." Suddenly, my mouth turns down, filled with sourness.

"The prospect's not that unappealing, is it?" Amusement twinkles in his not-wholly-unattractive blue eyes. *Pity green is more my thing these days.*

"It's this pineapple. It's really sour," I say around the half-masticated mush. While I consider spitting it into my napkin—because I'm classy like that—I swallow it down instead. *Urgh.* I give in to a shiver because that was really unpleasant.

"Dinner?" he prompts, his blue eyes still twinkling.

"On me?" I respond eventually.

"If you insist."

"No!" I say. *Or laugh.* "What I meant is, do you really think that's a winner, asking me to buy *you* dinner?"

"Equal opportunities and all that. Plus, you've gotta earn more than I do."

Can't say that makes me feel bad, even if Arthur is a chancer. And kind of cute with it. Not that it means anything.

"Well." I pause, searching for a kinder word than *no*, when, through the glass, I notice the arrival of the senior execs in the outer office. *Or as they call them here, the big nobs.* "Earnings aside," I say as the lift dings. "I don't . . ." My words trail off as I track Nigel, the CFO, ushering a group through the office.

"Earnings aside?"

"Hm?" But my attention is elsewhere, Martine's words echoing in my head. *"Rich as Croesus and as hot as fuck."* Boy, she wasn't kidding.

Rich men seem to have an aura, a presence. It's more than just the cut of their suits or the $500 weekly hair trims. It's something as intangible as air but just as real, and I sense it in the room the moment they step over the glass-walled threshold.

Hottie number one is tall, dark, handsome, and kind of imperious looking.

Hottie number two is tall, fair, and handsome, with an air of Californian perfection.

Hottie number three, with his head bent over his phone, is tall, dark, and—

Fuck. My stomach plummets, and it has nothing to do with the rancid fruit as I roll my lips together, like the start of his name. *Matt.* I'm thankful when no sound comes out.

I can't make sense of this, whatever this is. Why would he be here? In London—in this office? Short of this man being Matt's doppelgänger.

"Ladies and gents, if I could have your attention."

As Nigel speaks, Arthur touches my elbow as though to say we should take our seats. But my mouth isn't the only thing that isn't working, my feet having somehow turned to Jell-O.

Matt isn't in finance. He doesn't work for a private equity company in the heart of London, because that would mean—

"While I'm sure there's no need for an introduction . . ." Nigel's mouth continues to work as he casts his gaze over the room, a pinch in his brow evident as it bumps over me. ". . . Oliver Deubel, Fin DeWitt, and Matías Romero . . ."

There. Matías. Not the same name. Except . . . *Half Spanish, half Irish.*

From the other side of the room, the man's eyes lift from his phone as, like a counterweight, his hand lowers. Seconds and milliseconds seem to slow as he blinks, his lashes long and thick. Then the inevitable. Our eyes meet, his widening with disbelief. Lips lifting with warmth and recognition.

Meanwhile, I feel like I've been plunged into an icy-cold pool. I press my hand to my mouth as the power of speech and motion comes back to me in a rush. Which is just as well, as my stomach revolts and I become aware that I'm almost certainly about to vomit.

Chapter 15
RYAN

It's not a ploy, cunning or otherwise, to avoid a scene, as the soles of my shoes feel suddenly slick against the industrial carpeting. Palm pressed to my mouth, I move toward the door while my brain belatedly lodges the minutiae of Matt's reaction.

Confusion. Doubt. The jolt of his body like he'd stuck a fork in a toaster. Doubt. Then maybe delight?

At the door, I yank on the chrome handle that's almost as tall as me, the stupidly heavy glass door too slow to open for my liking. I sprint from the meeting room, knowing I'm going to be so pissed. I'll have an awful lot of words to say, and some of them very unpleasant, but right now, I have more pressing matters to deal with.

"Ryan?"

I register Martine's frown, but don't stop. I will not demean myself—I will *not* barf in an office made of glass.

I make it to the bathroom not a moment too soon and seem to be in the stall for the longest time, given the meager contents of my stomach.

"You okay in here?"

The door tentatively opens, Martine appearing around the edge of it.

"All over but the dry heaving." I swipe toilet paper from the dispenser and pat my sweaty head, feeling all kinds of sorry for myself. "That was . . ." *It couldn't have been him. No way.* Vomiting *and* hallucinating. What vile ailment are those symptoms of?

"Food poisoning?" Martine offers. "Maybe a bug?"

I press my lips together because I just don't know.

"Try not to die, anyway." She opens the door wider.

"Can I choose to?" I lean back against the sleek stall wall.

"I can think of better places to haunt."

I try to smile, at least until she reaches for my wrist.

"Come on, out you get," she says as though talking to a little kid.

"I don't want to," I answer, sounding like one.

"No need to be embarrassed. Unless your reluctance is something to do with a certain dark-haired stud."

Deny, deny, deny.

"He shot out of the meeting room hot on your heels, sweets."

I huff out an unhappy-sounding laugh as I pull my wrist from hers. *Stud*, she called him. She doesn't know how close she is to the truth. To my truth. To his lie?

Motherfucker. I tip back my head and stare at the marbled ceiling as my anger flares. Anger I can deal with. Anger is better than shock. Better than feeling sorry for myself.

"Did you say he had a wife?" I demand, my gaze slicing her way.

"No wife."

My stomach swoops at the sound of Matt's voice. That melodic accent. He comes to a stop behind Martine, his smile tentative and sort of beautiful. But they say even the devil was an angel once. Not that he's the devil. He's just another man. Another man who's no good.

"Though you did meet my niece on Saturday."

"What?" My frown is reflected back at me in the mirror above the washbasins.

"Blond hair. Yellow dress. We were at the Palladium? Never mind." His shoulders move with a deep inhale.

"I'll just . . ." Martine begins to move toward the door.

"Don't," I say quickly. She stills, and gives a quick nod that feels like relief. "I can't do this," I say, still looking at her. I can't look at him. I can't be here. I can barely think. Martine nods and turns her body sideways as though to shield me from Matt. Head down, I move toward the door.

"Ryan." My name seems to bleed with regrets as his fingers settle around my upper arm.

I glance pointedly down at the same knotted cuff links peeking out from under his jacket sleeve. "Let go." If my voice sounds calm, it's because I'm now icy cold inside. He lied to me—about everything. He isn't who he said he was, *what* he said he was.

Oh, my God. My entire skin suddenly prickles as I realize exactly what—exactly who he is. He's fucking Midas! There was no sugar mama paying for the suite in the Pier because he's absolutely loaded. *How mortifying.* The things I said, talking up my job, my personal wealth, when my salary, my net worth, is probably his spare change.

"Were you laughing at me the whole time?"

"What?" His brow furrows like he can't make sense of what I'm saying. "No. Ryan. I never . . . I'm sorry. I'm so sorry. For everything. But most of all, I'm sorry you weren't there in the morning."

"You think that would've made things okay?" I demand, incredulous.

"I was gonna tell you."

"Nice. Tell me after the fact but before now, right?" My voice increases in volume with each word spoken. At least, until I come back to my senses. "Let go of me."

"You told me you didn't want to know." But at least his fingers loosen.

And there's that unhappy laugh bubbling up inside me again. "I can't do this," I mutter, breaking for the door. I didn't want to know this—any of this.

Like a good soldier, Martine falls in behind me. She murmurs that I should leave, that she'll tell management I'm ill. I turn right out of the bathroom, so grateful for her help when she even shoves my purse at me, pulled from under my desk as we pass.

"Ryan, please," Matt calls.

"Not now," I hear Martine say, her voice calm.

"But I need to speak to her."

"She doesn't want to speak to you." There's no malice in her reply, only an evenness.

"You don't understand," he retorts stridently.

I pull on the stairwell door.

"If you make a scene, she'll never forgive . . ."

I don't hear the rest as the door creaks closed behind me.

But she's right, I won't forgive him. *Ever.*

◆ ◆ ◆

"Starbucks is all that's wrong in the world."

Why would he think that? Because it's readily available? Made for the masses?

Asshole, I think as I stir my second coffee of the day, this one in the 'Bucks in the Westfield shopping mall. A coffee I can't seem to stomach.

Maybe Starbucks is beneath him. Maybe a wealthy man like him refuses to drink out of anything but a gold-plated Hermès espresso cup. Maybe there's nothing but Black Ivory beans in his office—the stuff that's fermented in an elephant's stomach before it's shit out at a thousand dollars a pound. *Or something like that.* It strikes me that it's a pretty apt analogy for how I feel right now. Shit out, though without the gold dust price tag.

I hope I never set eyes on him again. I don't need to hear his bullshit excuses. It's wildly apparent why he didn't tell me the truth. Because he never thought he'd see me again.

He was probably laughing at me the whole time.

He's no better than the rest of them—no better than Brandon. *Than Pete.* Well, fuck him. Once you've broken my trust, that's it.

I pull the sides of my jacket closer, my shoulders rolling agitatedly. It's not that the jacket is ill fitting. More that my skin feels too tight right now. I've had enough therapy to know why. The past. *Isn't it always?* A childhood like mine doesn't come without scars. And right now, I feel like my skin is transparent, like my whole sordid history is on show.

And boy, does that make me feel inadequate.

Poverty and neglect can do that to a soul. Poor little white trash girl.

The jacket I'm wearing is new. I just picked it up from a store called Whistles, thanks to mine still being in the office and the weather being god awful. *The office. Shit.* I hope they bought Martine's excuses. Her earlier text said that the meeting looked to carry on without me. And, apparently, without Matt. Not that I asked. Not that I care.

I've also emailed HR, apologized, and said that I'm sick.

It's not a lie. I'm sick of being lied to. Sick of feeling like I'm not enough. It's the reason I ended up at Whistles. Then the next clothes shop . . . and the next. I glance at the multiple bags at my feet. *It's just a temporary tumble into old habits,* I tell myself. It's what I have done, since I could afford to, to make myself feel better. Can't say it's cheered me up any today.

Fuck it. The chair legs protest as I stand abruptly, the squeak drawing attention in the busy coffee shop. Whatever. I'm not going to sit here marinating in self-pity a moment longer. Liar or not, it was only one night. It's not about to change the course of my life.

I am young, free, single, solvent, and successful, I remind myself as I loop the numerous bags over my wrists and fingers. I don't need a man to fix me or make me feel good. I pay my own bills, and I take care of myself. Me. Nobody else. And I am not going to sit here and wallow one moment longer.

Straightening, I throw back my hair and pick up my cup and take it to the counter, because I'm not a sociopath.

I'm going home. To the serviced apartment, at least. Tomorrow, I'll go back to work, force everything to return to normal, and by the end of the week, I'll move into my own place. London is big enough for us both. He's bound to want to continue the conversation. I expect he wants to deliver his apology to ease his conscience and make himself feel better. I also expect I'll hear him out, for no other reason than to make my own feelings clear.

Then I'll never need to set eyes on him ever again.

I take an Uber home and, at the last minute, call into the nearby Little Waitrose, which is like a bodega and Trader Joe's had a cute store baby together. I mindlessly grab something for dinner, along with a bottle of organic sauvignon blanc, which I almost put immediately back. But the bags hanging from my wrists remind me my vice is my own, and not my mother's.

"Looks like a good night," the cashier says as I heft the wire basket to the checkout counter.

"Er, yeah. I guess," I agree as he begins to pull out the items to scan.

It seems dinner consists of a sharing-sized bag of tortilla chips, a small tub of *labneh*, and another of spicy *muhammara*. Plus a jar of dill pickles, a packet of HARIBO Tangfastics, and a pint of vanilla Häagen-Dazs, the latter three of which I seem to have planned on eating together.

That's as weird as hell.

I guess tonight's food choices are thanks to whatever made me ill earlier. Or maybe my body is just craving the familiar, thanks to food in London not tasting quite right to my foreign taste buds. *I'm sure it'll just take time.*

The cashier scans the final item—the wine. "You know what they say. A little of what you fancy does you good."

"Turn that frown upside down before people begin to think you don't fancy me."

I find myself grabbing the countertop at the phantom of Matt's voice. The things he said that night in October and the way he looked at me.

Immediately, my mind begins to whir, snapshots of my day flittering through my brain. My bad-tasting coffee. The awful fruit. Vomiting. The bra that I thought must've shrunk in the dryer. There was the bar of chocolate I couldn't eat last night and the weird metallic taste I've had in my mouth for days.

When was the last time I had my . . .

But I've been busy. Stressed! Moving to the other side of the planet can do that to a girl. My argument is silent, my denials adamant. But it's all there, even if my brain is trying to convince me otherwise.

No, that can't be right, because then it would mean—

"You okay?" Concern etches itself in the cashier's face.

I realize I'm clutching the counter and breathing heavily. "Am I . . ." I give myself an internal shake to scatter those frightening thoughts. "Let me get back to you on that," I say, my words sounding so very far away as I lift my hand and point to the shelves of medication behind him. "Could I get one of those too?"

I swallow and tell myself it's just a precaution. There's no way I can be . . .

"A pregnancy test? No worries. So do you want the generic or the branded?"

Chapter 16
MATT

I'm outside the building when she arrives the next morning. I recognize her gait before she's close enough for me to see her face, her hips swaying as they do in my dreams. Despite the distinct lack of light at 7:30 in the morning, I see she's wearing dark glasses.

Did it upset her that much to see me yesterday? I hoped she was ill when she ran for the bathroom, rather than the sight of me making her sick.

According to Fin . . .

Well, what does he know.

But there's no escaping she was shocked to the core, and I hate that things unfolded as they did. I know she will, too, because her professional life, her success, is something very important to her. That's why I'm here so early this morning.

That, and her colleague suggested it might be a better time.

My stomach cramps as she draws nearer. Trepidation. Anticipation. The desire to sweep her up in my arms and just fucking . . . kiss her. I huff out a chuckle. *There's an invitation to a swift kick in the balls if I ever heard one.*

Ryan passes by without a second glance, and she doesn't turn back at the click of the car door as I climb from the Audi with a frown. For a woman who used to live in New York, she seems sorely lacking security smarts. *A lone car, a virtually deserted street, her vision obscured by dark glasses.*

Before I know I'm doing it, I call out her name.

She halts. Turns. Gives a faint but humorless smile. Her outfit is all business, her heels killer. And though her hair is slicked back from her face and secured in a ballerina bun at the nape, it's not the hairstyle that makes her expression seem pinched.

"The early bird," she says, like she was expecting to see me all along.

"More like the worm. At least, in your friend's estimation."

"Martine?"

She seems to like that, not that the admission wins me any brownie points as her expression hardens. I want to ask why the glasses, but maybe I'm afraid to know.

"I'm sorry if I startled you. Same goes for yesterday."

"Yesterday was . . . I couldn't . . ." She exhales a frustrated breath.

I nod like I understand, words and excuses and reasons all straining at my tongue. "It was a shock," I eventually manage. "I get it. It was a lot to take in, but I'd really—I'd really like to talk to you." My words sound rushed, strangled, and uncomfortable all at once.

"Would you?" *Get fucked:* That's the tune of her answer. The underlying score.

"Yeah, I would. And maybe you think I don't deserve it, but I'll be turning up day after day until you hear me out."

"At my place of work?" she says, unimpressed. "That sounded like a threat."

"I'm not in the building," I say. "I won't cause you any trouble there. But I am a persistent fucker, and you deserve—"

"You must have a lot of time on your hands."

"I'll make time," I say without bite.

"So just a lot of parking tickets for you in the meantime." Her eyes flick to the yellow markings in the road. "But I hear you can afford it." Which is the point she was trying to make anyway as her gaze moves to the car. Low slung and sporty—I suppose it did set me back nearly two hundred grand.

"You're right," I eventually say, shoving my hands into the pockets of my dark jeans because all I want to do is step closer and hug her, even if she is all high heels and *fuck off* attitude. But it's just a veneer. *I think.* But those dark glasses. What the hell is going on under there? "There are other things I want to say. Things I need to explain."

The soles of her shoes scuff against the pavement, and I worry she's about to turn away.

"Do you wanna . . ." I gesture at the car at the same time as she says:

"Fine. But not now."

It's weird how little relief I feel. *Tell me something.* Tell me why my hands itch to touch you. Why my insides vibrate with need. Why I'm worried you might get on a plane and I'll never see you again.

"Later. After work. I'll meet you there." She nods, indicating a wine bar on the other side of the street.

"Okay." I nod a little too eagerly. "What time?"

"When I'm done."

"Right." I almost laugh. But I get it. This is on her terms. *Again.* But that's fine.

She turns away, ending our conversation. I open the car door and slide in, feeling . . . less than elated. But why?

Nothing else for it. The engine rumbles to life. I suppose I better head to the office to fill in the time between now and whenever "later" is.

◆ ◆ ◆

"How'd it go?"

"Creeping feckin' Jesus!" I exclaim as I open my office door to find Fin looming on the other side. "Is there something wrong with your office?" I demand, glancing at the espresso cup balanced in his palm.

"Yeah. It's being redecorated," he says, stepping out of the way.

"But we went through that not too long ago." And a pain in the arse it was.

"I said *my* office, not *the* offices." He throws this over his shoulder as he makes his way to my desk.

"Mila?"

"She's taken a budding interior designer under her wing . . ." His words trail off, his shrug kind of *you know how it is*. He sets the tiny cup and saucer on my desk, then leans back against it.

"Right." It'll no doubt be some talented individual from a disadvantaged background. Adding the offices (or office) of Maven Inc. to their portfolio will be a grand start to a career, I imagine. She's a good person, Mila.

"I offered up my office, as it'll be less disruptive than having the bedroom ripped apart," he admits.

"Those were your choices?" It's hard to keep amusement from my tone.

"Pretty much," he answers happily. "I didn't stand a chance."

"Ah, you love it," I scoff.

"Married life is a blast. And speaking of love . . ." This time when his words trail off, he gives a comic wiggle of his brows.

"I'm meeting Ryan later," I say, slipping off my jacket.

"That's something, I guess." His eyes dip as he crosses one ankle over the other.

"I think so." Something fucking terrifying.

"Especially after yesterday."

"No more jokes, Fin."

"I wasn't gonna! I wouldn't dream of saying something like . . . the sight of you made her ill."

"Grand. Thanks for not mentioning it." I cross the office, and at the alcove at the side of the Adam fireplace, I open the concealed fridge and pull out a bottle of water.

"Any idea what you'll say?"

"I'll just play it by ear," I say, cracking the seal on the lid. "Want one?"

He holds up his hand: *No thanks*. "You think that's the best move?"

"Well," I say, the bottle hovering at my lips. "I could prepare a PowerPoint."

"Not a bad idea," he says with a chuckle. "You could include hearts and flowers."

"Piss off."

"Pissing off," he says, straightening. "Oh, we had the transport police yesterday."

I frown. "Was it about the CCTV footage?" That I no longer require.

"No. They wanted money. Jesus, Matt. Is that what it costs for jumping the ticket barrier these days?"

"Nah, that was an on-the-spot fine of fifty quid. The rest is a donation to their charitable fund because I was . . . just because." Just because I'd seen her again. Just because there was a chance I might get to put this right. High on exhilaration and excitement, I'd decided I might just be lucky enough to have her in my life.

And now . . .

Now lucky is the least of what I feel.

Chapter 17
RYAN

I see him before he sees me. I watch him from the back of the bougie wine bar as he steps in from the rain, slicking his hand through his wet hair.

When I'm done. I give a little huff. My reality is so different since I said that this morning, all *fuck off and die* vibes. I wasn't ready to speak to him then, and I'm even less ready now. But there are things in life you have no control over, no matter how hard you try.

Point number one: my news. The potential to rock both of our worlds.

Point number two: me camped out in this wine bar since midmorning, after giving Matt the impression he'd be waiting on me way after office hours.

To be fair, that was the plan. Hell hath no fury like a woman, if not scorned, then made to feel less than. *On several fronts,* I think as my throat moves with a deep swallow.

As far as new starts and new years go, this one sucks.

Matt's expression changes with the tilt of his lips, and he lifts his hand in a tentative wave. *Like I wasn't a colossal bitch to him this morning.* Not that he didn't deserve it. And I deserve an explanation. *The explanation I told myself I didn't need.* But that was before. And now I'm living a whole new reality. Even if what happened in October has suddenly shuffled lower on my shit list.

He makes his way toward me, unwinding a blue woolen scarf from his neck.

"Hey," he says, reaching the edge of the booth of amber velvet. It's *U* shaped and deep, and I've chosen to sit here for privacy. I also planned to arrive early to gain the high ground. I just hadn't planned to be here most of the day.

I'm sitting in the deepest part of the booth. The power spot, I guess. I decided it wouldn't do to sit opposite him. *Getting lost in those eyes. Being tempted by the tiniest quirk of his smile.* But mostly, I'm not sure I want to see what's on his face as I break the news.

But I couldn't keep it to myself. He has the right to know, though I tried to persuade myself otherwise.

"Hi." I resist the urge to stick my finger into my hair to loosen this bun. My head is thundering, the thing having pulled tighter and tighter as the day passed. But at least I'm no longer wearing dark glasses like a desperate-to-be-seen C-list celebrity. Someone ought to make a concealer for swollen, cried-out eyes. They could patent it and make a fortune.

"Can I get you another drink?" he asks with fake cheer.

I give a short shake of my head. *Ow.* "You go on ahead, though." I tighten my hand around my cup of tea, my other gripping my coat under the table as though I'm ready to bolt at a moment's notice.

"Right. I will." He strips off his dark woolen coat and drops it to one end of the booth, the smell of rain and wool and cologne assaulting my nose. *I didn't even know rain had a smell.* "Back in a bit."

"Better make it a double," I mutter once he's out of earshot. "Lord knows one of us should be drinking." A pain shoots up my left wrist, and I realize my fist is clenched. It's a physical manifestation of stress that hearkens back to my childhood. What might be a natural reflex to a developing nervous system gave me carpal tunnel more than once. The fact that I'm feeling like this now—again—makes my eyeballs prickle.

No, and hell no. I'm not going there again.

I cried myself dry a long time ago.

I'm usually much better at keeping my emotions at arm's length. I am not enjoying my visit to the past, and these reactions feel alien after all this time. Overwhelm is nobody's friend.

"Name five things you can see."

An old therapist's advice comes floating back to me. I've had my fair share of therapy on my way to becoming the person I am today. It helped me rationalize my mother's shortcomings.

Not so much my own, though.

I push the insidious thought aside in favor of finding my five things. The rain on the windowpane, sparkling like diamonds. My shaking hands, the earthenware cup they're wrapped around. My coat by my leg and that ass and those dark jeans.

A laugh bubbles up inside me. Oh, the irony of a lingering attraction. I force myself to move on.

"Four things you can hear." Music. The ambient kind that gives off good drinking vibes. The chink of glasses, the buzz of my phone with an incoming message I don't want to read. Matt's chuckle as the bartender flirts with him.

Touch. Three more things. My cooling cup, my forehead slightly damp to the touch. The smooth wooden tabletop.

Deep breath.

Smell. Two things. My herby tea and the hint of liquor long ingrained into the walls.

Taste. One more thing to concentrate on. I lift my cup and grimace at the tepid liquid.

He turns, his expression open. Why not guarded?

My leg begins to bounce, but I force it not to, jamming my hand under it as he pulls out his wallet. *Good Lord, that is an ass made for jeans.* I wonder if he has a personal shopper. Whether in a tux, a suit, or jeans and a fine-knit sweater—and I'm digging those rugged worker's boots—he probably always looks like he's just stepped from the pages of a magazine.

As he taps his card to pay for his drink, I snatch up my phone and pretend to be engrossed in it, rotating my aching wrist out of sight. But there's nothing I need to see on my screen—the earlier text was just junk. I have no markets to watch, no reports to read, no calls to return. *What the heck will I do with myself?*

Matt gives a polite cough as he reaches the booth, and I look up.

"This is a nice place."

"Yeah, it is." A pause. "I was surprised how big it is inside." Small talk, urgh. I'm not sure it makes it better or worse that we've seen each other's genitals. Seen, touched. *And the rest.*

"Like a TARDIS," he adds. The reference goes over my head, but I don't ask him to explain. We're not friends. "Do you mind if I . . ." He gestures to the booth.

I give a careless flick of my wrist: *Have at it.*

"Have you been here before?" Putting his glass on the tabletop, he slots himself in at the end of the booth.

"Once. After work." Last week with Martine, toasting the new year and our future success.

Here's to being ambitchious! To being a better bitch.

Where did that Ryan go?

"Thanks for meeting me," he says carefully before he brings his glass to his mouth. That lush, talented mouth.

"Thanks for being flexible." So very flexible, as I recall. *Urgh. Stupid brain, knock that off.* "With your time," I add coolly, glad he can't read my thoughts. "I get that you're busy." *Just not busy getting busy,* my mind supplies, in all its inappropriateness.

"I'm sure we both are." His fingers flex around his glass. "So, yesterday." The words are expelled with a deep exhale, signaling a change of conversational gear. "I genuinely didn't know you'd be there. That you work for Theta."

"I get that." At least, my brain registered his surprise, then laser engraved it inside my head. "What were you doing there, incidentally?" *And as an aside, did you have anything to do with my humiliation today?*

"We're looking for a collaboration on an acquisition. I don't know how that went," he says, raking his hand through his hair. "I didn't . . . Too much on my mind, I guess."

For the first time I notice the dark circles under his eyes. The pinch between his brows.

You think you have a lot on your mind now? Well, I'm about to blow it.

"Look, Ryan, let me just say that I'm so sorry for not telling you the truth in October. And for yesterday. I'm gutted that seeing me knocked you sideways."

"It did, as you say, knock me sideways." I glance down at my manicure, the pale tips against the dark wooden table. I'm not sure it was purely shock that took me to the bathroom.

"But here's the thing. Cards on the table, and peelin' back my skin. If I could go back and do it all again, I'm not at all sure I'd change a thing."

My bun hits the back of the booth. *What now?*

"I don't think I could risk the experience, because God knows I have thought of little else since."

My stomach does a traitorous little flip, shock replaced by pleasure, those recollections fluttering to life inside me.

"Are you okay?" he asks tentatively when I don't offer anything. "Feeling better, I mean?"

This isn't a throwaway line but a genuine question. A real concern as he studies my face. But my impassivity is first class. A mask I have worn for years. Even if my internal world feels like it's crumbling.

"Seeing you yesterday . . . I can only imagine how you must've felt."

Goddammit! I screw my eyes tight as they begin to prickle. I will *not* cry.

"Ah, darlin'." His hand moves to cover mine, but I snatch it away, using it to lift my cooling tea to my mouth. *When in Rome, right? I'd rather be drinking wine.* An inappropriate laugh bubbles inside me. *Not for the next few months.*

"I'm fine," I say, mastering both my tears and my ridiculousness as I set the cup down again. "It's just been a weird twenty-four hours." Understatement of the century.

"Yeah," he agrees in a low rumble. "It must've been an absolute head fuck, and then being ill, on top of everything."

Sick, not ill. Like the two are unconnected. "It wasn't the sight of you or anything." My tone makes a mockery of my words. I don't expect him to bite, but I also don't expect the tiny hint of his smile.

"Like I say, I can only imagine, because it felt like my own heart was in my mouth when I saw you there. And I had the advantage. I already knew you were in London."

"How?" I feel myself frown. That sounds stalkerish, right? "How could . . ."

"I saw you on Saturday. At the Palladium."

"Oh, right." In the office bathrooms he said as much, I guess. I just wasn't taking anything in or even thinking straight.

"You had a conversation with my niece. She's a dotey little thing," he adds, holding out his hand in a height approximation that spells out *little*. "Yellow dress, red rose, duffle coat? Dressed as a princess?"

"Belle, I remember." I smile despite the situation. *My situation.* "She'd dropped her rose."

"Yeah, Clodagh said. That's her name."

"Yeah, she told me." I told her she had a pretty name, and she asked me why I had a boy's name. I'd gone to the box office to book a show as part of the full London experience. A London experience that's turning out to be shorter than the one I envisaged, for sure.

"At first, I thought it must've been wishful thinking."

"Wishful?" The word is a hopeful little sound floating in the air between us.

"That I'd imagined you there. Mistaken you for someone else. Someone else with dark hair and a green coat." Another small smile, like he's remembering my dress, not my underwear, as I ignore that hopeful flutter. "But then Clo told me about the zeppole fan club you both belong to, so . . . I ran after you."

"You ran?" There goes that flutter again. "Ran where?"

"Clo said you had a Tube to catch, so I legged it to the Oxford Street station."

I put my elbow to the table and my palm to my face. "But that place is like a maze." As someone who's lived in New York, I have found the London Underground network more than a little overwhelming. Add in the DLR, the Lizzie Line, and the sheer size of Transport for London's network, and, well, I've gotten lost more than a couple of times. And don't get me started on the misleading station names: East India. Barking. Pudding Mill Lane. Swiss Cottage. Elephant & Castle, where there is neither elephant nor castle. And what's with Cockfosters?

"Yeah, it is a bit," Matt agrees.

"There are so many corridors and escalators and platforms," I add in a murmur as a curiously warm sensation spreads through my chest. *He was looking for me.* "But you couldn't possibly have—"

"Found you?" His green eyes are all pleased and sparkling. "But I did. I was knackered, sweaty and breathless, and my thighs were burning like mad. Then I saw you. I called your name, but you didn't hear."

"I didn't know," I say softly, wondering how that meeting might've changed some things. *Not all things,* I think, my brow flickering with consternation.

Don't get sucked in. Everything is about to change anyway.

"In hindsight, it's just as well you didn't see me," he adds. "Not given the state I was in. I wasn't exactly looking my best."

My eyes flit over him, and I hope he can't see my doubt. He'd make a sack look appealing.

"I'm not sure a satin sash and tasseled epaulets are really my thing."

"Tasseled what now?" My response is part chuckle, part huff. For the world, I can't see him dressed like that in my head.

"I was the prince to Clodagh's princess. I had on this sky blue frock coat and white feckin' gloves. I looked like a complete eejit!"

I laugh despite myself. I'd forgotten how easily he made me do that. Right or wrong, I feel the tension inside me melting as I process the fact that not only is Matt an uncle, but he's also the kind of uncle who'll play dress-up for his niece. The kind who spends time with her and takes her to fun places, who'll make himself look silly for a little girl's whims. Maybe just to see her smile. And that fills me with gladness. It makes me feel happy. *And a little sad at the same time.*

"That sounds like something I'd pay good money to see."

Matt coughs into his fist, and my cheeks instantly turn radioactive as I realize what I've just said. *I'd pay him. Again?* Man, this blushing thing. I don't know where it's come from or why it started.

"I just meant—"

"Apparently, next time I've got to be Gaston."

I let out a breath, grateful we're not lingering on my embarrassment. "Because of your chin," I rush on, nodding a little manically.

"Is it really that bad?" With an amused expression, he brings his fingers and thumb to it.

"No, that's not what I meant!" *What the hell is going on with me?* "You just have a superhero chin." *That's not any better, stupid brain!*

"Apparently, Gaston is a bit of a shit."

Again, I'm thankful we're not dwelling. "I guess that's the thing about a pretty face. We sometimes get blinded by it."

His happy expression falls. "I didn't set out to hurt you."

"Don't have to mean it for it to hurt," I murmur.

"You're right," he replies solemnly. "I'm sorry that I didn't tell you. I should've insisted."

A memory instantly flickers to life. *"Are you married?"* I'd asked, standing in front of him.

"I wouldn't be here if I was." His eyes looked so green, so lust glazed, and my own desire reflected back at me. *"I don't think—"*

"Less thinking," I'd whispered. God, how I'd rubbed myself against him like a cat. He didn't really stand a chance.

"I shouldn't have let myself get carried away."

Matt's voice yanks me back to the moment, my perspective altered somewhat. I've been blaming him since yesterday. Blaming him for his choices and ignoring my own part in that first heated moment.

"I fancied you pretty much from the moment I set eyes on you in that grotty pub. From the second your palm landed on my chest. It sounds pathetic, I know, but I just said something stupid, and you misunderstood. Instead of putting you right, I just rolled with it like a complete eejit."

"But why? Why did you do that?" Because it makes no sense. Matt is as hot as any man I have ever met. I know it wasn't to impress me.

"It was a precaution," he says, visibly uncomfortable. "I didn't want to end up spending the night with you."

I say nothing. And he says nothing, like there's nothing more to be said.

"Wow," I manage eventually. "I hope that sounded better in your head."

"What? No, that's not what—"

"Maybe you should've practiced first. Said it to a mirror a few times."

"Fuck it," he says, slumping back and kind of throwing up his hands. "Well, here's something else you won't believe. I don't do one-night stands."

"Like you're not an escort?" I retort, my words ugly.

"I'd make a really shit escort."

Au contraire, my brain offers. *You hit all the high spots.*

"I want an emotional connection as much as the physical. I want to be in your head, and want you to be in mine, as much as I want to be inside you."

Something in his tone, his sincerity, allows my mind to slip back in time again. In his lap, skin to skin, nothing between us but the look on his face and the way he said my name. He was inside me, and I him. And suddenly, I believe him.

"Remember, I'd also spent the afternoon at an ex's wedding. I had some idea of what you had to look forward to. Or not. And I tried to talk you out of it."

"Fine, but what happened still happened, whether you meant it to or not. And you still lied to me," I retort, hanging on to that line of blamelessness despite my slippery grip on it. "Do you have any idea how I felt yesterday? What I'd thought back on as a perfect night suddenly turning so sordid."

"Sordid," he repeats with a curt nod. "Kind of like how you left me an envelope stuffed full of cash."

"Which I feel *so* great about now," I mutter as something painful blooms inside, like a poke to an old bruise. Embarrassment makes me defensive and mean. Those old familiar hurts make me want to crawl out of my own skin. "Feel free to return it." I fold my arms across my chest. "You with all your success—I'm sure you don't need it."

"I get why you did," he says, without bite now. "But we both know that the money, the lies, none of it detracts from the night we had. I know I should've said before we got to the suite, but I wanted to tell you in private, not where those arseholes might be hanging about. I was so into you, and you were amazing." Words begin to spill from him. "So beautiful and brave, and I wanted you more than I've wanted anything. I told myself it would be worse to tell you once your dress was on the floor—you were already half naked, and I'd already half lost my mind. But that's not to say it was altruism. I just wanted you so much."

Grief and hope bubble up inside me, the sensations taking me by surprise so badly that I give a sharp sob. Because no matter how sincere he sounds, no matter how heartfelt his words, I'm about to tell him something that's about to change both our worlds.

And maybe his mind.

"Hey, now," he says, moving closer.

I press my palm to my mouth, vehemently shaking my head. *Don't touch me. Don't come near. Just . . . too late.*

"Sweetheart," he croons, rubbing his big palm in circles across my back, the fingers of his other hand folding over mine. "I didn't mean to make you sad."

"You—didn't—make—me—cry," I gulp out between sobs, my chest and shoulders jerking with each word.

"But I have. I'd punch myself in the face if I thought it'd do any good."

"You—didn't—make—me—sad." I suck in air like a woman who's preparing to be drowned by a wave. "You—made—me—pregnant."

Chapter 18
MATT

Tell me something. But maybe not that.

I slump back in my seat, my hands falling away. Then rubbing at my chin. Pressed across my mouth. I glance away, down the length of the room to the windows, and watch as the lights turn clinging raindrops the colors of Smarties. A couple seated there plays footsie as the bartender pulls a pint. The door opens, and someone leaves. Someone else walks in. Ordinary actions, ordinary lives that are unchanged by the moment before. Meanwhile, as my world is . . .

Holy fuck!

Exploding? Imploding?

"I'm sorry," I say, turning back to Ryan's lovely face. "But can you say that again?"

"Sure, it's not like it'll undo anything." She sniffs, her words watery and jerking. "Matt, I'm pregnant." She sniffs again and, after reaching for her purse, begins to rifle through it. "Where is a stupid Kleenex when you need one."

I reach for the cocktail napkin that came with my drink. "Here."

"Thanks," she murmurs without lifting her eyes. She dabs at them, then her nose, which seems to have turned red. Under other circumstances, I'm pretty sure I'd be in bits about this—about her tears, I mean. But right now, I can't seem to feel anything.

"We used condoms."

"I'm aware." Her sharp glance seems almost weaponized. "I was there too."

"Sorry. Stupid thing to say." I frown, but before I know it, my mouth is off again. "That night, when you slipped off your dress, I could literally feel the IQ points falling off me. Fuck," I mutter. "I know this isn't the same, but I think I might be just as dumb for a while."

"Okay." She twists the napkin between her fingers.

"Pregnant," I say as though trying the word out. "Fuck me. When did you . . ."

"I took a test yesterday afternoon. After I left. After I was ill. It was mostly to rule out the distant possibility," she adds with a really unhappy laugh. "I've been feeling a little off. Mostly, things I like haven't tasted right. My sense of smell has been . . . well, elevated, I guess. I just thought London smelled weird. Bad enough to gag a maggot sometimes." She gives in to a harsh shiver.

Gag a maggot? Given the circumstances, I temper my smile.

"I didn't think for one minute the test would be positive."

"I'm kind of glad it wasn't the sight of me that made you sick." Despite the tangle of my thoughts, my lips tug upward.

"That was shock. Maybe."

"Are you okay? I mean, isn't yesterday a bit late to find out?" I'm thinking specifically of Letty's pregnancy. A couple of my cousins' too.

"I'm sorry my reproductive system hasn't adhered to best practices," she retorts, that tentative ease between us popping like a pin in a balloon. "But I have just moved across the Atlantic. I've been a bit occupied." She presses the tissue to her nose again. "My schedule has been pretty hectic. Life has been new and exciting but stressful."

"Right, yeah. Sorry."

"Stop saying that."

"What?"

"That you're sorry. Even if you are."

"Okay, right."

"Now I've told you," she says, turning her attention to her purse. "And now I'm going to leave."

"What? Wait—what do you mean you're gonna leave? You can't just . . . leave!"

"I'm not asking you for anything," she mutters, beginning to shuffle her bum across the seat.

"Please stay." I reach out, laying my hand on her arm.

She halts. Turns, blinking rapidly as though digesting my words.

"I'm sorry that I don't know what to say."

"Welcome to the club." She glances away. But at least she's not trying to *get* away as she relaxes her grip on her purse.

"How many weeks along . . ."

"Maybe ten." She pauses, her eyes not moving from my face. "You know there's no way I'd be telling you this if there was a chance some other man was responsible, right?" Her delivery is, well, challenging.

"Understood."

"But I guess you've only got my word for it right now."

"Your word is enough, Ryan."

She gives a breath that seems to lower her shoulders. "I guess I'll need to see a doctor to be sure of the exact timeline," she says, softer now. "I don't know much about pregnancy."

"Me either." I find myself wondering exactly how effective home pregnancy tests are as I swallow over the large ball of words lodged in my throat. How the fuck? What the fuck? When the . . .

well, maybe not when. "Does that mean you're . . ." I rub a finger along my nose as my gaze inadvertently dips to her flat stomach. "That you want to keep it?"

"Yeah." She gives a firm nod. "Yeah, I do."

That feels . . . not wrong. I mean, it's terrifying, but also—

I snap back to the moment when I realize Ryan is still speaking.

". . . it's kind of crazy, and all kinds of frightening, but I'll cash in some of my investments when I get back to the States. Get a house or an apartment, depending on where I decide to set up home. We'll be okay."

"Wait." I hold up my hand. "Rewind a bit? Say that again . . . would you?"

"When I get back to the States?"

"Yes. Yeah. You're going back?" Ice drops into my chest, cooling a tentative warmth. *Huh.* "But why?"

"Rewind further?" Her brow quirks. "I got let go this morning. Fired, to be more precise."

"Shit." But she can't go back—not when I've just found her.

She clears her throat a little. "That about covers it."

"What for? I mean, what reason did they give?"

"Performance issues, which is bullshit. I hadn't been there long enough to make a difference either way."

My heart sinks. Could I be responsible for this after yesterday? The meeting was something I actioned, and Fin said the whole thing went pretty much tits up after . . . *yeah, that.* After we left.

"But the market is kinda volatile at the moment," Ryan carries on, unaware of my disquiet. "I'm sure I don't have to tell you the market dictates everything in this business. But I don't know," she adds, her tone weary. "Maybe I didn't make a difference fast enough. Maybe my face didn't fit. Maybe they decided someone's nephew could do the job."

"Yeah, that happens."

"All this to say I really don't know. Not that it matters. I was within my probation period, so it is what it is."

"You're taking this very calmly."

"I know." Her mouth tips humorously. "My life is about to implode—might as well push the nuclear button."

"Is that why—" I halt, not sure I want the answer. Not sure I have a right to the question either.

"Why I'm going ahead with things?"

Things. Pregnancy. Parenthood. Life-altering decisions.

"I'm not judging," I add quickly. "I just remember your career means a lot to you."

She pauses before answering. And when she does, it's without an ounce of hostility. "The short answer is no." Another pause as I watch thoughts flicker to life on her face before fading away. "I guess I just knew. The minute shock wore off, at least. Maybe it's my age." She gives a quick smile, and I bite my tongue to keep from asking. "I'm thirty-five," she says anyway.

"I didn't ask."

"Maybe not verbally. You?" She allows her gaze to flit over me. I like how it feels.

"I'm thirty-eight."

Her brows lift.

"Good genes," I say with a grin.

"Do you really come from a big family?" Her question is tentative, like she doesn't want to give too much away. *She remembers what I said.*

"Yeah, I do." My reply is kind of expansive as I lean back against the booth. "I didn't tell you lies that night. Well, with the exception of . . ."

"What you do for a living," she whispers.

"My family is huge," I put in quickly. God knows how this news will go down with them. It'll give them something to yak about, for sure. Something to worry about. Something to bend my ear over. "I have three sisters and two brothers. All younger than me."

"That must be nice," she answers quietly. Softly.

"It's grand. Sometimes. And other times, not so much."

"I don't. Have a family, that is." Her gaze falls to her cup, and she looks about to pick it up before changing her mind. She pushes it away.

"Should I get you a refill?"

She refuses with a shake of her head. "But thanks."

"No family at all?" I begin again.

Another headshake.

"There's just you?"

"Just me left. But there was only ever me and my mom growing up."

"I can't imagine that."

"I wouldn't bother." Her chin lifts. In defiance? "It wasn't the easiest of childhoods, which I know now wasn't my fault."

Knows *now*? Something from the depths of my own upbringing flares to life in my head. *Children of God are without blemish.* My parents were very unimpressed when, aged eight, I'd plucked this Sunday school learning out of my brain. They also weren't convinced it was adequate reason for the hole in their new TV. It's been upcast plenty in family lore, but I didn't spend my childhood suffering for it.

I don't know what to say, except to point out the obvious—that I'm sorry, that it's shit. But she's rebuffed me already. So I reach out and put my hand over hers.

"I never knew my dad." Her smile says *Fuck your pity*. But Jesus—I think I get it. She was leaving because that's what she knows. And she was leaving first because that's what she assumed I would do. *Like history repeating itself.* "I always thought I'd have a family. Before, you know." Her eyes dart away. She means with him, the bastard who dumped her and turned her life upside down. "And while this feels crazy, it also feels right. It's not like this"—her words trail off as her hand drops to her stomach—"has willed itself into existence."

"No, I get that."

"But you don't have to worry," she says, looking up at me. "I take full responsibility. I don't need you to step up."

"Fuck that." My hand tightens on hers, my voice low and vehement. These are my feelings, and they have nothing to do with her childhood, her past. "I want to be part of this. Don't shut me out."

"I didn't—" She swallows thickly. Sets her shoulders. Composes herself. "I just meant I'm not out to trap you. That I get this is my decision."

"I want to be part of this."

"But I'm going back to the States. Monday."

Something like panic bolts through me.

"Though I get the impression Theta would've preferred to get me on a flight before then."

"Can they do that?"

"I agreed to it. Signed the paperwork and everything. I guess I wasn't processing information too well. Maybe because I spent more time than I care to remember curled over a toilet bowl this morning. Then I was called into the office and blindsided. But I don't really have any choice. My visa is dependent on my employment, and I'm living in accommodations on the company dime. I'd just signed a lease on a new apartment, and they said they'd cover any penalties."

"I should fucking think so."

"They're also paying me to the end of my probation period. It seemed like there was little point fighting it."

"It sounds to me like they're trying to get rid of you with undue haste."

"It doesn't matter, not in the bigger picture. Women who have babies, kids, they don't thrive on the trading floor. Each requires too much commitment. Can't be in two places at once."

"But it should be your choice, not theirs. This is wrong, Ryan. Don't stand for it." Because I fucking well won't.

She drops her head quite suddenly, beginning to gulp in air.

"Ah, darlin'." She doesn't flinch when I put my hand to her back.

"This is all so, so fucked up." She begins to cry, quiet hiccuping sobs, and my heart twists as I pull her in to my chest. "I'm sorry for the waterworks," she says, her words all snuffling and wet. "I'm usually more . . ."

I crook her chin and dip my own, bringing my gaze level with hers. "Aloof?"

"Stoic."

"Tears are just a valve, you know." I use my thumb to swipe one from her cheek, amazed when she lets me. "They aren't a weakness. Everyone needs to let off steam sometime."

"I've gotta be all out of steam by now. This morning, after you left, I was so upset. I didn't know if I should tell you or not. Would you blame me? Think I was after money?"

"There now," I croon as her words echo in my chest. "It's gonna be okay."

"I didn't know what to think, what you'd think. I couldn't use the elevator in the state I was in, so I took the steps and, halfway up, dropped to one like I was winded."

Something squeezes my heart. To think that under that cool exterior was all this worry and pain.

"I pressed my head between my knees," she says, lifting her watery eyes to mine, "and sobbed and sobbed as the cold from the concrete penetrated my pants, freezing my ass."

"That's how you get piles."

"What?"

That ache turns to a pinch as Ryan pulls away, all red nosed and flushed. I just want to pull her back. Keep her there. "It's what my granny used to say if she'd catch us sitting on cold pavement or a wall. 'You'll get piles!'" What the fuck am I saying? I guess it's better than *I know something else that'd like to penetrate your ass.*

"I'll . . . bear that in mind," she says, her words creeping higher in pitch.

"Although you might get them now anyway." *Ah, Jaysus. Move over, Casanova.*

"What the hell, Matt!" This comes out in a shocked but watery laugh.

"I know. What the fuck."

"More like, How would you know?"

"Because sadly, my family doesn't believe in boundaries." My expression twists. "You can blame my sister, Leticia, for oversharing. That's Clodagh's mother."

"Well, it's something to look forward to, I guess." Her brows pinch with consternation.

"I reckon Letty is a bigger pain in the arse than hemorrhoids," I mutter.

"What will they think about this?" Her eyes flick warily my way. "About you becoming a dad."

There's something about that word that tugs at a place deep inside me. "A dad. I'm about to become a dad." I slide my hand through my hair. "How fucking amazing is that?"

"I guess it won't matter what they think," she says softly as she presses her hand to my chest. *Over my heart.* "We're really doing this?"

"Yeah," I say, covering her hand with mine. "We really are."

Chapter 19
RYAN

I can't believe I'm doing this—that we're doing this.

That he wants to be part of this.

"Ryan Hoffman?" The doctor looks up from an iPad, and holy hell! I am shook—the doctor is such a hottie! His white shirt strains against broad shoulders, his face the kind of handsomeness that's rugged and a touch lived in, while his dark hair has a little salt and pepper around the temples. He quirks a brow, and I begin to wonder if I have crumbs on my face. I just ate crackers. With jam. The sweet-salty combination was just . . .

I realize I'm just standing here. Like a dummy.

"Yes. Yep, that's me. And this is Matt, my . . ." I half turn toward him at the same moment I run out of words. My pretend escort turned real mogul turned ultimate surprise? My one-night stand baby daddy?

"The father," Matt says, linking his fingers between mine. He gives them a reassuring (or forgiving) squeeze. And if the doctor is handsome, then I don't rightly know what Matt is. Handsome plus?

"Pleasure to meet you both," the doctor says, his tone matter of fact. "Take a seat." He casually indicates a pair of leather chairs on the other side of his huge desk.

The room's proportions are oversize, the accents understated Georgian splendor. An original marble fireplace, crown moldings, and window shutters, contrasted by the high-end spa feel. We're at some fancy-assed obstetrics clinic on Harley Street, the place in London world renowned for medical excellence.

Matt suggested he arrange the appointment, but I argued there was no point, given that I wouldn't have a visa or medical insurance for many more days. The reality was more that I refused to give Theta the satisfaction of seeing charges for prenatal *anything*. No need for them to congratulate themselves more on their decision. But Matt was adamant we should be reassured that all is as it should be. I assumed it was more that he needed to be sure I was telling the truth. At least until he said something that blew those thoughts right out of my head.

"You're carrying our child." He reached for my hand, taking it between his own. "I can't help you do that physically, but I would be honored if you could try to let me shoulder some of the responsibility in the ways I can."

I couldn't argue, thanks to the emotional lump that filled my throat. My God, tears are bad enough, but I detest feeling like a vessel of seething emotions. I can only hope this is a short-lived symptom of this pregnancy. A temporary madness that won't last the full nine months.

Of course, the practical side of me wonders exactly what kind of help Matt will be to me when I'm back in the States. *What kind of father, even.* But I owe him this much. So two days later, here we are.

We take our seats as Dr. Hottie—I mean, Dr. Travers—leans back in his chair.

"Thanks for fitting us in," Matt begins, all business himself. "We appreciate it."

"Yes, so much," I agree, shooting the hot doc a bright smile. We're in this together, Matt and I. Parents-to-be, not together, but civil all the same.

In the daily course of my job, my former job, I made decisions involving huge chunks of wealth, and I have a pretty great track record. Some might attribute my success to historical data or trends, some to the availability of highly technical mathematical modeling. Others might say it's a learned knowledge. Or nothing but luck—the way the wind blows, how far Mercury is in retrograde, or how many roosters I sacrificed on my altar that morning.

Seriously, I was asked that on the trading floor once.

But the truth is, much of my success is down to an innate gut judgment system. I know intrinsically when and how to trade. Where and with whom. And when to hedge. It's probably a kind of sixth sense developed during my childhood. Knowing when to be present and when to be invisible saved me a lot of stress and whuppings.

It maybe even saved my life once or twice.

So when I stared at the pee stick test three days ago and read the little proclamation of "PREGNANT," despite the shock, deep down, I knew I'd be going through with this. It wasn't a decision exactly, because there was little rational thought involved. It was just something I recognized deep inside. The right path, I guess. My life was altering, my body was preparing to become a mother, and that was that.

What I didn't factor into this new future was Matt's involvement. I didn't give him much of a thought. And when I did spare him a little brain space, I just assumed I wouldn't be able to get out of the country fast enough for him. In other words, his reaction has been unexpected. To say the least.

"It's my pleasure." Hot Doc Travers smiles widely as I play back my words, wondering if I've spilled all that, rather than keeping it all at a cerebral level. "Really," he adds. "An extra hour in the office means I miss my youngest's piano lesson."

A relieved chuckle bursts out of me, though I turn it into a cough delivered to my fist.

"It's bad enough listening to him plink-plonking on the thing," he says, his fingers drumming the air above his desk, "but the bloody dog has to join in, howling along. The place is like a madhouse," he says with the slightest hint of a Scots accent. "Aye, well. Parenthood is the best kind of madness. Something you'll learn for yourselves in due course. Let's get down to business, shall we?" He picks up a pair of dark-framed glasses and, slipping them on, adds two more attractive points to his tally. "So. Ryan, how are you feeling?" he asks, reaching for the iPad again.

"I'm pretty sure I feel pregnant. And according to the home test I did a couple of days ago, I am."

"Then pregnant you are."

"For sure? Don't I need a blood test or something to confirm it?" I could've been making it all up. Should I have brought the pee stick?

"Well, there's a chance that you might feel like a bit of a pincushion by the time we're through. But no, home tests are very accurate these days. You're in the right place."

"Oh, right. Well, I guess I'm pregnant," I say, glancing Matt's way, who slides me the kind of look that makes my heart go pitter-pat.

"So you're thirty-five years and one month?" The doc glances at the tablet again.

"Yep. Yes, the nineteenth."

"It was your birthday last month?" Matt glances my way again. "Sorry I missed it," he adds quietly.

"You weren't to know." Oh, my Lord. This is grade A awkward, especially as I glance back to the doctor to find him looking at us over the rim of his glasses. Thankfully, he's too professional to comment. "And that makes me a geriatric mom-to-be."

Next to me, Matt scoffs.

"That's a thing," I say, my eyes sliding his way. "Google it if you don't believe me."

"It's nothing we'll worry about just now," puts in the doc. "Looking ahead, I typically work out of Chelsea and Westminster Hospital. I assume you were told that at the time of booking?"

"Yes, the receptionist did mention it," Matt answers.

"But this is just kind of a preliminary . . . appointment," I put in, landing on the right word. "I'm going back to the US soon." Very soon. Monday, in fact.

"Right," Dr. Hottie says, sliding Matt a look that appears more than a little judgy.

"We haven't sorted out the finer details," I add, coming to his defense. "This is all very new. We're still trying to get our heads around how everything will . . ." My words trail off as I flounder, not able to adequately express my thoughts. My expectations. My hopes.

"We'll make it work," Matt intones, reaching over to touch my knee. The spot still feels warm as he lifts his hand away.

"Symptoms?" the doc asks next. I appreciate that his manner is very matter of fact.

"I feel as sick as a dog. Nothing has tasted right since I got here, and now I think I know why. And I've been sort of tired, but I put that down to work."

"You're a hedge fund trader." His attention flicks to the tablet again.

"Yes." I filled out the form almost by rote. What I do for a living is part of who I am, even if I'm not doing it right now.

"I imagine that's quite a stressful career."

"It can be." I glance down at my hands in my lap. *You're about to be a mom, no longer a mover or a shaker.* I push the tiny fear aside. "Maybe not as stressful as delivering babies."

"I have the best job in the world," he says with a genuine-sounding pleasure. "But your symptoms all sound very normal."

"I've been . . . emotional too."

"Also very normal," he says, beginning to rifle through his desk drawer, pulling out something that looks like it might be used in a middle school math class to measure angles. "You haven't included the date of your last period."

"I don't know," I admit. "My cycle is kind of erratic." I feel my brow crease. "I guess I had some spotting a few weeks back that I thought was my period."

"Right."

"I mean, I have been under more stress recently."

The doctor's gaze slides Matt's way again.

"Work-related stress," I qualify.

He drops the angle-calculator thing to the desktop. "Not to worry, we can use the—"

"Would the date of conception help?" Matt offers up suddenly.

"I'm sorry," I offer the doc before shooting Matt a glare. "That was a little—"

"Inappropriate?" Matt's tone is unrepentant as he adjusts one of the pleats in his pants. "I'm sure the doctor knows how babies are made."

"Aye." Dr. Hottie's gaze bounces between us, filled with humor. "That I do. Theoretically and practically," he adds under his breath as he scribbles something down on a pad. Honestly? It looks like a delaying tactic as he composes himself, as he tries not to give in to the urge to laugh. "So the date?" he manages eventually. Without looking up.

"The twenty-fifth of October. Or the twenty-sixth," Matt adds as his gaze captures mine.

I look away as my cheeks turn nuclear.

"So you're looking at the eighteenth of July as your due date. We'll check that out with a scan in a bit."

"A scan?"

"Aye. If you'd pop into the next room, Jenny will weigh you, take your blood pressure, do your bloods, and so on."

As though summoned by his words, a nurse, Jenny, I presume, materializes in the room. "This way, my lovely," she singsongs.

I spring from the chair and make it as far as the door before I realize Matt isn't behind me. I turn. "Do you want to . . ."

He's on his feet before I can blink.

After having my height measured (no change) and my weight checked (very minimal change), I hop up onto a white padded bed, as instructed, to have my blood pressure taken and a little blood drawn.

"If you could lie down now," Jenny instructs. "Then lift your top and wiggle your bottom down a bit, my love."

I came prepared for being poked and prodded, if not scanned, maybe made to wear a paper gown? So I'm dressed in my easy-access pants, which I wriggle over my hips before lifting my shirt, all while pretending Matt isn't in the room.

"Would you like me to wait outside?" he asks as the pale roll of tissue under my back rustles louder than thunder with each of my unintentional squirms.

"No, don't be silly." *I'd never win an Oscar,* I think as my eyes follow Jenny, who dips out of the room. "This shouldn't feel so awkward," I mutter. "What's a little skin when we've literally had our mouths on each other's genitals."

"Ready?"

"Shit!" I jump as the doctor enters the room. Matt begins to cough like a man who's swallowed his own tongue. "Sorry, I mean yes." *Did he hear me say that? If he did, I'll just die right now. Get it over with.* "All ready!"

"Need some water?" He slides the question Matt's way.

"No." Composing himself, he thumps his chest with the side of his fist. "But thank you."

"Pull your shirt up a wee bit more. Perfect." Dr. Travers tucks more of the tissue into the lowered waistband of my pants, the motion perfunctory and long practiced. "Cold squirt," he instructs, squeezing cold lube over my stomach.

My eyes meet Matt's again as the doc lifts a wand that's a lot like my old Hitachi, er, massager. *Yeah, let's go with that.* From the bottom of the bed, Matt's brow quirks questioningly. Teasingly. I bite back a snicker.

The lights dip, and the wand is applied in a less fun way than my Hitachi, thank the Lord. There's something soothing about the dimly lit room, until—

"Oh!"

"There we go," the doctor murmurs.

An ache instantly creeps up the back of my throat, my whole being focused on the *whoosh-whoosh-whooshing* and the almost ethereal image on the screen. "Oh." I suddenly find my hand in Matt's and look up to find him staring down at me.

"Nice and strong," Dr. Travers murmurs from somewhere outside our bubble. Me looking at Matt, Matt looking at me, our baby's heartbeat filling the space between us.

"Tell me something," I find myself whispering.

Matt smiles, his eyes turning glossy. "This is so fucking amazing."

Chapter 20
RYAN

La-di-fuckin'-da. Just look at you now. You're no better than me.
No better than I said you'd be.

I jolt upright, dragged from my sleep like a person pulled from the deep as I press my hand to my chest and gulp mouthful after mouthful of air. It's still dark outside as I reach for my phone and realize it's past seven already. *A lie-in,* I think, like my heart isn't still thundering as I use the back of my hand to brush the hair from my face.

As my panic begins to recede, I throw back the covers and swing my legs out of the bed. I thought I'd forgotten what my mother's voice sounded like. That her accusations were no longer my problem.

Better than her. Lord, I'd like to think I've made better choices, but whether that makes me a better person or just more obstinate is anyone's guess. I knew from a young age I wouldn't be following in her footsteps. Not as long as I had breath in my body.

I'll never be dependent on my looks or a man. I'll never get myself so twisted up that I forget my responsibilities.

How can you forget about a child? My feet softly pad across the carpet as I head for the bathroom. How do you forget to pick her up from school? Or forget she needs to get there in the first place. How could you put your need for liquor above her tiny stomach?

I won't ever be her, I think as I pass my suitcase on the luggage rack, both items that signify my temporary state in this place. The arms of my pink sweater hang from the case. What story do they tell? The need for a hug? A bolt for escape?

It's too early to start analyzing myself this morning.

The sweater is a manifestation of my manic attempt at packing last night after Matt brought me home. *My temporary home.* The phase that lasted less than twenty minutes and seemed to achieve nothing but piles of clothes dotted on every surface, and a few dumped to the belly of my $2,000 RIMOWA suitcase.

What to take, what to leave, and how the heck did I end up owning all this stuff anyway? I've only been here a matter of months. But the January sales were just too tempting. It seemed almost rude not to treat myself to a new wardrobe to match my new life. *Nothing to do with filling the empty space in my life with shopping, right?* And not that my new clothes will do me any good in the coming months.

After, though. I become aware of a flutter of anxiety in my chest. I will return to work after this, though what I'll be doing is anyone's guess at this point. Babies and trading aren't exactly a marriage made in heaven. I have only known women in more-senior positions who've made it work, but at what cost? You take a few months out of the game, and your clients are handed off to others, which is bad for income. For networking. For morale, and the Lord only knows what else.

It'll be fine, I reassure myself. *Something will turn up—there isn't anything in this world I can't do.* Including raising a child by myself, if it should come to that.

I pee, brush my teeth, shower, and all that stuff, while my brain revolves around a never-ending list of unknowns I'll be facing in the coming months. There's the literature the doctor handed me last night—the dos and don'ts, the what-to-expects, including a bunch of stuff I hadn't even thought of.

And then there are the practicalities of my return to New York next week. From getting a new phone number to finding somewhere to stay, beginning with an Airbnb. And, of course, discovering how Matt will fit into all this. Also, if how he's feeling right now will last. The safest thing is not to buy 100 percent into his involvement. It wouldn't be the first time I have been stung by a man.

Pretty sure the pattern began while I was in utero.

Out of the shower, I examine my body in the mirror. It looks exactly the same as it did yesterday. Except my boobs *are* a little bigger, so maybe my favorite bra didn't shrink in the dryer.

Maybe I'll be one of those moms-to-be with a cute bump, I consider, both hands splayed there. All round and petite like I swallowed a soccer ball. Considering the size disparity between me and my baby daddy, maybe I won't. So maybe I'll elect for a C-section to save my poor hoo-ha.

Something else to consider.

Or not.

It's weird to think I've been undergoing changes for weeks without even realizing. It's also good to know that the food and water here don't really taste weird. It's just that my taste buds are a little . . . hormonal. Slipping into my fluffy white robe (another recent purchase), I consider how externally, things are pretty much the same, while internally, my world has shifted.

I make my way to the kitchen, with a detour to the bedroom to grab my phone. I find a text from Martine asking how I'm bearing up, not that she knows anything but that I no longer work for Theta. I'm beginning to text out a reply when my phone vibrates with an incoming text from Matt.

MATT: Fancy some breakfast?

ME: A girl has to eat.

I feel way too fluttery for my reply. *It's not a date,* I remind myself. It's just breakfast. With your baby daddy. The one you'll be leaving in a few days.

ME: Don't you ever work?

Last night, Matt was insistent on taking me home after our appointment, despite my reassurance that I'd be fine in a cab. The standoff over, I sat in his passenger seat, holding the ultrasound image of our little bean as the radio played low in the background. It's the strangest feeling in the world to know I'm currently cooking a small human. *Such a lot to get my mind around.* I guess he must've sensed that as he pulled up outside the building.

"Whatever else," he'd said, taking my hands. "I promise you're not alone in this."

Which is a whole something else to get my mind around. I have a bazillion questions about how this will work—the logistics, for one. And his family—will he tell them? Will our little bean have involved aunts, cousins, maybe uncles? Grandparents, even, who'll live so far away? Will he visit? Will he want to bring the bean back for the holidays? Will he be there for the birth? And how long can I expect before our little bean gets a stepmom? *How is it I'm already jealous of her?*

My phone dings again.

MATT: I'm not saying I'm lazy, but if there was work on a bed, I'd sleep on the floor.

And then a second follows.

MATT: Now imagine that in my dulcet *Oirish* tones.

And then a third text.

MATT: In other words, there has to be some perks of being the boss, right?

I want to smile, but I won't. The man is entirely too cute for his own good. Even when he's being incomprehensible. Which might be another problem, if I let it go that way.

See you at 10? comes his next, and final, text.

Should I draw the line at being picked up? I'm not his girlfriend—he shouldn't be running around London after me. The traffic is enough to make you want to tear out your hair from the roots. On the other hand, I don't think I could stomach the hot-metal-and-grease smell of the Underground this morning.

I give in to a whole-body shiver at the thought of all that stale air and the carriage rocking.

Maybe I'll draw that line another day.

Chapter 21
MATT

"You look nice."

"Thanks." She twists, reaching for the seat belt, though I still note the tiny pinch in her brow as she simultaneously reaches for the door handle.

"I've got it," I say, making as though to close it. "That's okay, isn't it? Paying you a compliment. Telling you you look nice." Because she does. Whether it's the clothes she's wearing, the muted tones, the fabrics that seem soft and inviting right down to her woolen bobble hat, or the fact that she seems to be glowing, I don't know.

Or maybe it's more because I've been thinking about her for weeks. Fantasizing. Wondering what if. Anyway, who knows why I feel the way that I do. Mother Nature and the mysteries of the world. What I do know is Ryan was the last person I thought about before I dropped off to sleep. And that she was on my mind the instant I peeled my eyes open.

"Yeah. I guess." Her answer is nothing if not hesitant. "You look nice too."

"Thanks." I grin and close the door with a solid *thunk* before I say or do anything stupid. Like *High five! I put a baby inside you.*

What the fuck is with that? Why does that make me want to preen? As if bombarding her with texts this morning wasn't enough idiocy for one day.

"Where are we going?" she asks as I climb in and start the engine.

"For breakfast, if you can face it. You're not sick or anything, are you?" *Fucking calm down!*

"I'm kind of starving and jonesing for a coffee. Decaf from here on out, I guess."

"I know just the place."

After a period longer than I bargained, thanks to the traffic, I pull to a stop just off Kensington High Street.

"It says 'restricted parking.'" Ryan points to the signage. "There on a pole."

"So it does," I say, muting the engine anyway.

Audi before, Range Rover today. I'm not a petrolhead. A car is to get you from A to B, as far as I'm concerned, though I do own a few of them. One of the perks of being worth a penny or two is the ability to buy a new motor without the inconvenience or necessity of having to sell the previous one. Anyway, I left the Audi at home in favor of something more solid, my responsibilities this morning already feeling quite profound.

I loosen my belt, and Ryan is out of the car before I can get there to help.

"I was joking about the parking tickets before," she says, straightening her oatmeal-colored coat. "But maybe you weren't."

I find myself staring at her. At least it's not raining today, because her coat doesn't even have buttons. She is as cute as a button, though. All that dark hair flowing from under her adorable bobble hat, coat almost trailing her ankles.

"Matt?"

"Huh? What?"

"Don't tell me." She's all taunt and mischievous grin as she tightens the belt on her coat. "You're frowning because you wanted to open the car door for me."

"Well, yeah." *But not as much as I wanted to stick my hand up your sweater to see if you have an undershirt on. For starters, at least.* What the fuck is wrong with me this morning? "There's nothing wrong with a bit of chivalry, is there?"

"What do you suppose God gave me these for?" she retorts, making jazz hands.

"Maybe for this," I say, taking one of them and linking my fingers between hers. We set off along the road.

"So we're holding hands now?" she says, slanting her gaze my way. And by that, I mean upward. Her boots aren't heeled, which really emphasizes the height difference between us.

"Looks that way." *Sure, she's only two hands higher than a duck,* I hear my mother say. I can't wait for that lot to meet her. I've just got one or two things to take care of first. Like getting her to stay. "And you look to be enjoyin' it, what with your cheeks so pink."

"Dream on," she retorts as she tries to pull her hand from mine. *Not a chance, darlin'.* "It's just cold." She uses her free hand to adjust her hat as though to prove her point. "What? It is!"

"Give it up," I say, flicking its baby blue pom-pom. "It's positively balmy out." The sun is shining, at least.

"And that's why my breath is half ice particles?" To prove a point, she purses her lips, blowing a breath of air like a kiss.

Lucky air.

"Wait till February," I retort. "Then you'll know what cold really is." The second the words are out of my mouth, I'm cursing them. Beside me, Ryan falls quiet and stares at her feet.

"It's a nice neighborhood, isn't it?" I try again after a minute or two.

"Let's see if you're still saying that when we get back and you've been towed."

"Nah, not today. I'm feeling lucky."

She glances around at the houses, a mix of redbrick and white stucco, which I've always thought look like old-fashioned Christmas cakes.

"Looks like a pretty pricey neighborhood," she says, glancing at a street sign. "The Royal Borough of Kensington and Chelsea," she says, eyebrows raised and a touch of hoity-toity in her voice.

"I know. Can you believe they let the likes of me walk the streets?"

"You think they don't like nice guys around here, huh?"

"*Well mannered*, not *nice*."

This time, she refuses to look my way.

A few minutes later we walk under the green-and-gold canopy of a tiny hole-in-the-wall Italian bakery.

"Pastries for breakfast?" Ryan says. "Do you have a secret sweet tooth?"

"They do great coffee here," I say in lieu of telling her the truth. That I have a hankering for the sweet saltiness of a girl called Ryan. They also have something I hope she'll like. Something that Clodagh might like too. *Maybe I'll get her takeout and drop it off for her after school.*

The bell above the door chimes as I push it open. It's not a café, just a bakery. No tables and chairs. Not that it matters, as we have another destination.

We join the short line, Ryan like the proverbial kid in a candy store, her fingers pressed against the glass pastry case.

"What do you want?" I murmur, bending so my head is almost at her shoulder.

"A girl. I'm thinking it has to be a girl."

I give a delighted little laugh, caught off guard by her candor. By the moment and where her thoughts are right now.

"But that's not what you meant." She turns her head and gives a playful roll of her eyes.

"No, but that's a bit more important than your breakfast order. Why a girl?"

"I don't know how boys work," she says, turning back to the glass.

"I seem to remember differently," I say, pressing my hand to her hip. It's a brief touch, and she doesn't move away from it, but maybe she doesn't notice because of her coat.

"What can I get you?"

I glance up at the twentysomething fella in a green apron. "A *cortado*, please, mate. And . . ."

"A cappuccino. Decaf?"

"Make them both decaf," I say.

"Matt, you don't have to—"

"We're in this together."

"You gonna give up whiskey too?"

My expression twists, conflicted.

"You don't have to do that either," she says, amused.

"Anything else?" the bakery bloke puts in, his tone bored.

"May I please have one of these buns filled with cream?" Ryan presses her finger to the glass.

"*Maritozzi*," he says, more North London than Italiano.

"That's what you're having?" I feel my brow furrow.

"Yeah." She glances my way questioningly.

"That's what you want?" The words escape without thought. And Ryan's expression? It's not much impressed.

"You brought me to a bakery for breakfast, so don't think you can give me a hard time for my food choices."

"What?"

"You don't have to tell me about the risks associated with gestational diabetes."

"No!" I say, backpedaling quickly. "I just thought you might've wanted zeppole."

"They have zeppole?" Her eyes widen, then dart to the baker. Sales assistant. Whatever.

He nods and moves down the counter, tongs hanging over a row of pretty pasties swirled with cream.

"That's zeppole?" Her tone is doubtful.

"Yeah." The bloke frowns and snaps his tongs: *Yes or no?*

"With raspberries *and* custard?"

"Yeah." He still sounds bored.

"Wow, y'all's zeppole is way fancier than the ones I've had before."

"We'll take a zeppole," I interject with a chuckle. *Y'all's?* Ryan's not from the South. Is she?

"*Zeppola*," he corrects, monotone. "That's one. *Zeppole* is multiple."

"Yeah, all right. Thanks for the Italian lesson." Fuck's sake. You try to do something cute, and this is what you get for your troubles. "I tell you what. Give me a half-dozen box and a couple of the pistachio pastries." *What a miserable fecker.* Me, not him. It's not like I was expecting cartwheels, but I wanted this to go better than it has. *I'm a fucking try-hard.*

We move down the counter to pay and wait for our coffees. I glance down at a tug on my sleeve.

"Thank you."

My heart lifts a good inch from its cavity. "It's just breakfast," I murmur, all pleased anyway.

"Not for breakfast. Thanks for remembering."

"I don't know if anyone has ever told you," I say, pressing my thumb to her chin. "You're kind of hard to forget."

Chapter 22
MATT

"Look at that," I say as we get back to the car. "Not a parking ticket in sight."

"Okay, smart-ass." She pulls an unimpressed face. "So you got lucky."

"I told you I was feeling lucky. In fact, I'm always lucky."

Call me a romantic, but her hand moves very slightly, almost as though she's about to touch her stomach. She doesn't follow through, because that would be too revealing. Instead, she sends me a look: *You're crazy.*

Maybe I'm crazy about you. "I wonder if . . ."

"Where are you going?" Her face is an absolute picture as I begin to wander up the driveway of the house I've parked in front of. Large, detached, with a Regency-period facade. Picture-box perfect, really.

"I'm just gonna have a look."

"You can't—that's trespassing. It's someone's property! Matt, seriously," she hisses as I saunter away. "Come back!"

"In a minute."

"If you don't come back here, I swear I'll . . ."

I halt in my steps, feeling a slow smile spreading across my face. "Make it worth my while?"

"Urgh!" She crosses her arms. "I won't call emergency services when you get bitten by a big-ass guard dog."

"To be fair, it does look like the kind of place that should have security." I glance up at the camera in the roofline. Then give it a wave. "Oh, look—it has."

"Matt!" she kind of growls this time. Like an annoyed Chihuahua.

Because I don't want to stress her out too much, I pull a key fob out of my pocket. "Who knew you were such a little Goody Two-shoes?"

"There's nothing wrong with following rules," she retorts pertly. "Rules are created for reasons. Mostly for reasons like you." But then her mouth clamps shut as the security gate begins to close between us. Then open again almost immediately. "You live here?" she accuses.

"Yeah, I do." I make my way back down the driveway and go to take her hand.

"Asshole," she says, snatching it away. But she's smiling. Reluctant and unimpressed (or pretending) but smiling anyway. And that makes me strangely happy.

"Would you like to . . ."

"It's a little too late to ask me if I'd like to come back for coffee." This she says with a cocked hip and a pat to her stomach.

The sight . . . that attitude. The suggestion in her words? It feels like a shot of stardust blown by an angel through my veins. "At least you know I can't get you pregnant." Too soon?

"At least, not again," she concedes evenly.

At least not for a while, I think as she follows me up the driveway, and I bite my tongue to keep from saying, *We'll have such fun trying.*

"I bet you're one of those guys who loves his toys," she says, spotting the Vanquish.

"Weird," I murmur, studying it. I thought it was parked in the garage.

"It is a little weird. Unless you're Batman."

"You're funny." I input the security code at the front door. The locks disengage, and it clicks open.

"I see you got Batman's front door too," Ryan says as I press it wider and usher her inside. "Oh, my." She turns a slow circle in the entrance hall, her soft-soled boots almost silent on the black-and-white tiled floor. She takes in the sweeping staircase, the antique table in the center of the hall with a silver urn that's supposed to hold flowers, and the massive chandelier above it. "This is like something from *Bridgerton*." Her voice sounds awe filled.

"Without the flowers," I say. Ryan jerks around and stares at me as though I've grown another head. "I haven't seen the show," I add quickly. "Just the trailer and the advertising shit plastered all over the buses."

"Which still leaves me kind of curious if you've read the books."

I keep my expression bland to her questioning one. "Have you read them?"

"I'm impressed you even know what I'm talking about."

"Behold." I hold out my arms, the paper bakery bag dangling from my left wrist. "A modern man." I give a theatrical bow. "Also, one who has sisters," I say, straightening again. "There might be one or two of their romance books lying about," I add knowing full well there are. Because Letty left them. Like unsubtle hints.

"That sounds like a line," she says with a crook of her head. "A cover-up. Are you a closet romance fan, Matt?"

"Not closeted at all. Who doesn't love love, Ryan?" I don't wait for her to answer as I put down the pastries and help her from her coat. And she lets me. I chuck it over the newel post, and she pops her bobble hat on top before fluffing her hair.

"What?" she asks, catching me watching her.

I'm pretty sure the appropriate response is not *I want to gobble you up*.

"Nothing." I shove my hands into the pockets of my dark jeans, shoulders up around my ears. "Kitchen?" No grand tour. We should probably avoid rooms with soft surfaces—beds and stuff.

"Sure." She nods, and I swipe up the bakery stuff. "Did you grow up in a house like this?" she asks as we make our way downstairs to the garden level, where the kitchen is. That's the family kitchen, not the outdoor kitchen. Or the catering one. Or the kitchen in the empty housekeeper's apartment.

"Nah. Growing up, home was a redbrick semi on the outskirts of Dublin. My dad sold insurance, and my ma worked in the office of the local school. What about you?"

"I didn't grow up in a house like this." So bland a delivery tells its own story as we enter the kitchen. A story that seems to have nothing to do with bricks and mortar. "My mom had . . . issues. Alcohol and anger mainly," she says, hopping up on a tall stool. "Like a good Beaujolais and hunk of Brie, they went real well together. She also had a lot of boyfriends," she says, looking anywhere but at me. "I couldn't wait to get out of the place."

"I'm sorry," I murmur as I set the bakery bag on the counter and pull out the box.

"Not your fault."

I can still be sorry, whether she wants me to be or not. "Where'd you grow up?"

"In a pissant town in Bumfuck, North Carolina."

I cant my head like an inquisitive terrier. "I did wonder about that hint in your accent."

"I do not have an accent. Bar the obvious one," she adds with a flick of her hand. "I worked very hard to get rid of it. *Y'all.*"

I smile, mainly because there's nothing I can add. Nothing she wants to hear, at least.

"Can I get you a drink?" I make my way to the other side of the kitchen. "Juice? Tea? Water? Another decaf?"

"Water. Sparkling, if you have it."

"Got it." I turn to the concealed fridge, the size of a catering one.

"You have a beautiful home," she says, taking in the dark cabinetry and fancy marble countertops. "Really, just gorgeous."

"Thanks." The Sanpellegrino bottles *clink* as I pull one from the shelf. I crack the cap. "The place had been split into flats when I bought it," I say, pouring the effervescent liquid into a glass. "It's been a labor of love."

"You didn't . . ." She circles her finger in the air. "Your labor?"

"Well, I didn't put in an underground basement, gym, and swimming pool, but everything I could do, I did. I designed the kitchen," I add as I put the glass and bottle down in front of her. "Helped fit it. Repaired the Georgian moldings, stripped a hundred years of paint from the staircase."

"You're pretty good with your hands. I mean—"

"Glad to see you don't have a bad memory." Pleasure pulses through me as her gaze dips behind the curtain of her hair.

"It wasn't your hands that got us into this predicament," she murmurs, maybe not for my ears. I laugh anyway as I pull out a couple of side plates.

"Some might say *predicament.* Others might say *blessing.*"

"I like that."

I pause and consider how I must've acted in the wine bar. I hope I've made my feelings clearer since then. "Yeah, I do too." I pull open a drawer and lift out a couple of linen napkins. *Now, wouldn't that impress my mother.* "I know there's still lots to think about, logistics and such, but yeah, I'm excited."

"Good." She nods a few times, maybe in surprise. Or relief as she blows out a slow breath. "That's good to hear."

"I'm glad," I say as I untie the string on the pastry box before spinning it around and setting it between us. "There's a reason I brought you here today, rather than out somewhere for brunch."

"As long as it doesn't include a basement and handcuffs."

I tsk again. "There you go spoiling my surprises." I reach into the box, pull out a random pastry, and drop it to my plate.

"You're a trip," she says, following my direction with a slow, exaggerated shake of her head. I get a little kick of pleasure when she opts for the zeppole. A zeppola? I can't feckin' remember!

"That's part of what I wanted to talk to you about. Trips," I repeat. "Specifically, about you leaving."

She keeps her eyes on her pastry for a beat. "It's not going to be easy. But like I said, this is on me."

"No, this is not a *you* thing, Ryan. Not anymore."

"I appreciate you saying that, but you don't need to feel as though you have to make things right." Her attention drops again as she turns her little zeppola between her thumb and forefinger. "We had one night together, and it was amazing. Just what I needed, as it turned out." Her eyes meet mine again. "And an amazing but unexpected thing will come out of that night, and it's great that you want to be part of it all, but that doesn't mean anything more than that."

That told me, didn't it?
Well, fuck that.

"Anything more than becoming a father," I retort. "And wanting to be involved in a child's life? *Our* child's life." That's my pivot, of course. I'm not giving up.

The thought of Ryan walking away . . . it's unthinkable. Because as much as I want to be in this child's life, I want her too. It's early days, and I get that these are big words and promises, life-changing sentiments. But I want her in my bed. In my arms. In my life. I want this to work.

I want that chance, at least. And I can't have it while she's living somewhere else.

"Turn off your skeptic's radar for just a minute and listen to what I have to say. Please."

She gives a lift of her shoulder. A tiny *if I must*. But I sense her discomfort. Feel her stubbornness creeping in.

"We didn't plan this. I know the timing is rough. I mean, Monday? But you didn't come all this way to just end up going back, did you?"

"I don't have much of a choice," she murmurs, gathering her hair to pull it over her shoulder.

"But you like it here? In London, I mean."

"Yeah. I was just beginning to find my feet."

"So stay. Stay for you."

"Matt . . ."

"Okay, stay for me. Stay and let me be part of this experience. I don't want to miss out, Ryan."

"You really mean that?"

"This is how much I mean it. Move in with me."

"What? No!" She almost recoils, but for the back of the stool. "We barely know each other."

"Isn't that a reason you should, then? We're gonna be parents, and we barely know a thing about each other. How can we raise a child on that basis?"

"I just . . ." She looks so small right now. I mean, she is small, but her presence, her fucking aura, should be as apparent as the

Burj Al Arab. But I suppose she's had a rough few days. The stuff she's gone through must've felt like a colossal head fuck.

But still . . . back to me and my role in this.

"I want to be part of this kid's life."

"I hear you."

"I just don't think it's right for him to come into the world and learn his parents didn't really know each other."

"I don't want that. I don't want her to think she's a mistake." Her eyes are so solemn, her next words so quiet, I'm sure they aren't meant for my ears. "Or the regret of her mother's life."

My heart instantly aches for her. "Hey." I touch her shoulder, like we're mates.

"How to Mess Up Your Kid's World 101, right?" She shoots me a sad smile as she reaches for her glass. That way she doesn't have to be responsible for moving my hand.

"No child deserves that." *And she didn't deserve you.* "And our child isn't a mistake."

"No, I don't think so either."

"A blessing."

"Right," she whispers.

A blessing in disguise. I clear my throat, but it's not so easy to clear the emotion. "We need to know about each other—to learn about each other—so when birthdays roll around and he asks us what kinds of things the other likes, we can tell him what his mother's favorite investment strategy is and name the name of his father's favorite rugby team."

"Okay," she says, a little bemused.

"That way we get a decent birthday present and not any old shit."

A laugh jumps out of her before she presses her hand to her cheek. "This is madness, though. Isn't it?"

"It's just building a foundation, a solid one. With stories and experiences to reflect upon. It's not like we'll be on top of each other." *At least, not immediately.* "I haven't shown you round the place yet, but you can see the house is huge."

"Matt, come on. Be reasonable. You can't expect me to do this."

"Yeah, I can. It's not like I'm asking for a huge commitment or anything." *Again, not immediately.* "I just want to be part of this—and I want to be with you through this. Shoulder the responsibility in all the ways that I can."

With a sigh, she slides her gaze to the gray, cold garden. So I pull out my trump card.

"The house has a self-contained apartment. You could stay there." *Though I'd rather you stay in my bed.* "You could work. Or not. And we could hang out, get to know each other. After all, we've a lifetime to be together."

"A lifetime?" Her gaze slides back slowly, her expression unreadable.

"Our child's life," I answer quickly.

Fatherhood. It's something I always assumed I'd get to experience, though the details were hazy beyond that fact. I suppose even after Ryan told me, I don't think I took it all in. It didn't truly become real until I heard our child's heartbeat. Everything changed then because there was power in that sound, something ancient and inevitable pulling at me. Probably the weight of responsibility, but the sense of it felt—feels—so right.

"Last night, I spent a long time staring at that grainy image." The ultrasound. "I had a glass of whiskey in one hand and all this . . . feeling inside me."

"It's a lot, I know."

"I wasn't overwhelmed, unless there's such a thing as a surfeit of happiness. I was feckin' swimming in the stuff." I give my head a tiny shake at the admission. "But then I thought about you not being here. Me not being with you. With both of you. I came to a decision. And that's if you can't be here, then I'll need to be there." And I mean that. I don't know how it'll work, except that it'll be a lot of fucking work. A lot of travel—a home in one country and a business in another—but I'll do it if I have to because I want this.

"There? You mean in New York?"

"I know we're not together, but I'll do what it takes to be part of this. I'll need a while to sort everything out, but if you're leaving Monday, then expect me to follow."

Unless Fin and Oliver kill me first.

"I won't be able to offer you anywhere to stay," she says with a watery laugh. "I haven't even found a place for myself yet."

"Do you want to go back?"

Her pause. That's my answer.

"So stay. With me. Until . . ." Something in her expression says I've gone as far as I can with that. "Until whatever. Just give me this time. We can sort the logistics of later out . . . later."

"I can't believe you would do that."

"I'll do what it takes. But also, for what it's worth, I know a good employment lawyer. There might be something you could do with Theta, and it would be easier if you were here for that." I haven't even finished speaking before she begins shaking her head.

"I don't want to be anyplace where they don't want me. Where they don't appreciate me."

Good for her. "But there might still be something in it for you. An unfair-dismissal claim might mean money. A payout."

"Screw them. I want nothing from Theta. I don't even want to see their name on my résumé."

"Fair enough." I lift my pastry and take a bite. I'm sure in other circumstances it would taste amazing. But right now, I might as well be chewing sawdust, because all I want to do is experience the softness of her fluffy sweater. Maybe rub my face across it. *Before*

I take it off. Run my fingers through her silky hair. *Before I wrap it around my fist.*

I've heard of pregnancy hormones increasing a woman's sex drive but not that they're meant to make the dad a horny fucker. I doubt pregnancy porn qualifies as anecdotal evidence, not that I've partaken. Not that it stops my thoughts from turning dirtily in on themselves.

Hey, darlin'. How would you feel about watching some dirty movies on my flat-screen mirror this evening?

Fuck, I'm definitely losing my marbles.

"I'll pay you rent."

My head snaps up at the sound of her voice, her words bypassing my brain and affecting my body immediately. Happy confetti bursting in my chest! I just about restrain myself from offering her a fist bump.

"Rent," she repeats, her expression firm. "Which makes me your *tenant.*"

"You can pay me if you want. I'll put that money aside for Matt Junior." Next thing, I'm picking a raspberry out of my hair. "Or Matilda," I say, putting it in my mouth. "I'm open to either. Unless you prefer Pierre."

She gives a soft, husky laugh as, this time, the raspberry hits my forehead.

"I'd say you're open to disappointment," she says, licking the custard from her thumb. "On both counts." Her eyes catch mine, and a jolt shoots through me—through us both. We're on the same page and thinking the same thing. The hotel. The chair, her body inches from mine. I caught her wrist as she pulled her hand from her panties. *Like a good girl, following my instruction.* Her fingers in my mouth, that first taste like a drug. I licked and sucked as she watched.

We gravitate closer as I realize, as if for the first time, the effort it's taken not to touch her. When all I want to do is haul her closer and suck the goodness right out of her.

"I must have some rights," I murmur, my heart pumping and my cock beginning to throb.

"You think?" She's all cleavage and sparkling provocation as the tip of her tongue swipes at the corner of her mouth.

"Well," I begin, capturing a silky lock of her hair. "I did put a baby inside you."

Her eyes glitter like blue flames, her plump lips pursing as she begins to respond. But that's as far as she gets—her attention jerking upward. From the floor above, the front door slams loudly shut.

My apology is a quiet groan as I hear my sister's muffled complaint. *Jaysus, Letty. You pick your fuckin' moments,* I think to myself. I begin to pull away, halting when, from the stairwell, a little voice makes itself heard:

"Uncle Matty, how did you put a baby inside the lady?"

Chapter 23
RYAN

This is awkward. On top of awkward. With a side of awkward.

"So what is it you do, Ryan?" Leticia—or Letty, as Matt calls her—has an accent that bears more than a transatlantic hint. Clodagh, meanwhile, sounds as though she's from the States.

"I'm a trader at a hedge fund."

"Wow. Interesting." Her gaze slides Matt's way. I'm guessing she's thinking my job makes me perfect for him, like we're peas in a pod. Or maybe she's thinking the opposite, like he needs a stay-at-home wife. Or maybe I should just stop overthinking every goddamn thing, because it's none of my business. "In London or . . ."

"Oh. New York, though I was offered a position here a month or so ago. It's just a pity it didn't work out." *A pity* is one way of putting it. And the other is a plain euphemism. I swear I wouldn't ordinarily be so laid back about this, but for my life being a kind of take-a-ticket shit show currently.

Do I want to stay? Matt asked. I was so excited to be here. The achievement felt immense. *Do I want to go back to New York?* Not really. It's not my home. But then, nowhere is.

"Really?" I'm not sure if that's pity or consternation pinched between her brows. "I'm sorry to hear that."

Maybe she knows what it feels like.

"Thanks," I murmur, actively keeping my eyes from Matt. My skin still feels shivery when I look at him after our little interaction. *"I must have some rights,"* he said. And then that line that made me feel like I was about to burst from pleasure. *"I did put a baby inside you."*

Lord, the husky timbre of his voice and the suggestion in his delivery. Was I imagining things? It felt like we were about to kiss. And that's a whole can of dangerous worms. It simply can't happen, not if I want to stay. And I do want to stay, I realize. I think it would be a good thing.

Modern families come in all guises, and I want my little bean to have more people in her life than just me. *People who love her.* I could do it on my own, for sure. I've done everything else in my life solo. But that doesn't mean it's the best way. So I'll stay here for now. And if things work out, maybe I'll give birth here.

"How do you two know each other?" Letty asks as the old-fashioned kettle whistles and Matt moves it from his fancy-looking range.

"We met in Manhattan last year." *Just a few months ago, for one glorious night.* "At a wedding."

Her eyebrows lift as she stares at her brother's back. "You keep your cards close to your chest."

"What?" he replies, playing ignorant. This probably feels so weird for him too.

"New York," she says again. Muses, maybe.

As Matt turns, a whole but silent conversation seems to pass between the two. Like I said, awkward, topped with awkward, with a side of awkward.

What am I supposed to do in this situation? Or even say?

If I'd known his family was coming, I might not have agreed to move in with him right at that moment. If for no other reason than to save us this . . . situation. There's the kid. Clodagh. And her little wiggling ears. Though that feels like a bullet dodged right now as she watches TV. Cartoons seem like a pretty good distraction for a five-year-old. But I feel like an interloper right now. Though Leticia seems nice enough, her reception seemed tinged with a light frost. Or maybe I'm imagining things.

I wonder what she'll think when she finds out about our little bean. Or the fact that I'm moving in. *She'll probably think I'm a freeloader out to trap her wealthy brother.*

Maybe I should insist on a tenancy agreement and have some paperwork drawn up. Something to reassure them both. All?

I usually make a point of not giving a flying fuck for the opinions of others, but this baby will be part of their family. I want them to not hate me, at the very least.

I hope they're a nice family. They sure raised a good man.

"I didn't realize I had to keep you informed of my movements." Matt pours hot water into a floral china cup the size of a soup mug. He glances my way and winks and—dammit—my boobs begin to tingle.

I fold my arms immediately. My nipples are probably blinking like disco balls—and that is not my fault given he's the guy that turned my sexual faucet back on after it had happily been on the fritz. I guess hormones could be to blame, which would still make it his fault by my reckoning. I haven't once suffered a pregnancy scare in my life, so I'm blaming our current reality on Matt's super jizz.

"So . . . you guys are dating?"

"No," I say at the same time as Matt retorts:

"Nosy much?"

"Don't be giving out to me," she says with a laugh.

"My family," he begins with a pained glance my way. "Sadly, they're as mad as a bag of spiders."

"And he's the king of them," she says, leaning in. "You should see how smart he looks in his frock coat with the fancy golden epaulets."

"Sounds like something I ought to see," I say, like this is the first time I'm hearing this.

The pair begins to bicker in a way that makes me both happy and sad. They say you're not supposed to miss what you haven't had, but I'm not sure that's true. There are plenty of times I've yearned for a connection. For family. And just as many times I have thanked Providence there wasn't an *us* to suffer.

"Uncle Matty, may I pleath have a hot chocolate?" Clodagh asks from the huge sectional on the other side of the room. Which is pretty much where Matt led her the minute she appeared at the bottom of the stairs. So much for cartoons being a perfect distraction as she kneels on the cushions to wave at me. I wave back and hope she's not in the mood for asking more awkward questions. Because kids aren't dumb. They're perceptive.

"Why not," Matt says. "But we're out of marshmallows."

"This house is bullthip!" Clodagh playfully thumps the back of the sectional.

"Excuse me?" her mother demands. "What did you just say, young lady?"

"This house is bullthip," she replies happily.

"Where on earth did you learn that?"

"Uncle Seb. When he was back from university."

"Your brother is at university?"

"He's the baby of the family," Letty replies.

"A happy surprise," Matt murmurs. "Or so the story goes."

That look. I bite my lip to stop myself from smiling back at him.

"At least he's no longer a teenager," Letty says, oblivious to the look that passes between us. "They're God's cruelest gift to parents, I'm sure."

"He was a pain in the arse for us all," Matt interjects. "You're not gonna be a rotten teenager, are you, Clo?"

"No, I'm gonna be a printheth!"

"Good girl."

"God, I hope so," Letty mutters. "Because it seems unusually unfair to spend the first twelve or thirteen years learning on the job. You don't drop them on their head, they learn to speak, to say nice things, and become tiny, funny humans." She glances her daughter's way, her eyes soft. "You think you've got the job cracked—you're nearly there. Then puberty hits. And you realize you're rubbish after all. Because they tell you so. Often."

"Wow, that sounds rough."

"It is. I've watched friends deal with theirs. Teenagers," she adds with a sigh. "You can understand why some animals eat their young."

"I couldn't eat Seb. He stinks," Matt says, as he sets a fancy cup and saucer in front of Letty.

"Not anymore. Not now that he's into girls. Thirteen-year-old boys think a bar of soap is for hiding their pocket money under," Letty says, turning my way as though the information might be useful. *Good thing we're having a little girl.* "Then at sixteen, they seem to remember what sopa is actually for."

"Not me. I didn't stink," Matt insists.

"You're the eldest, so who would tell?"

"Have a pastry," he says, sliding the box her way. In other words, shut up about smelly boys.

She gives a slight lift of her hand. "Thanks, but no."

"Clo can have one, though?" He glances his niece's way.

"Sure." Her mother shrugs. "Why not."

235

"Yum!" the little girl hollers as she clambers over the back of the sofa.

"Clodagh," her mother scolds. "You know better than that."

"Ah, leave her. It's only furniture. Ryan?" Matt kind of pivots on his heels to face me. "Would you get me the hot chocolate out of the pantry, please?"

"The pantry?" The pantry in a house I have never been in before now. But I guess I now know why there aren't appliances (or pretty much anything) cluttering the countertops.

"Yeah." He jerks his head left like he's trying to send me a signal. "I think I left it next to the mixer."

"Cool beans." Is something I've never ever said in my life as I slide from the stool. But he obviously wants me out of the way. As I cross behind Leticia, I point to the only solid door I can see, the other one glass and clearly leading to a fancy-schmancy wine cellar, one that seems to contain a decent amount of whiskey too. Anyway, Matt nods, so into the pantry I go.

It turns out not to be anything as simple as a pantry but a whole other room—a whole other kitchen, almost. Maybe Matt preps meals in here. He did say he could cook, as I recall. Or maybe he has a fancy chef and this is his domain. I can't decide if the setup is excessive or a really good idea as I make my way to the shelf at the end, where the fancy-looking mixer seems to be stored.

"Got it?" Matt calls out.

"It isn't next to the mixer," I shout back. A few seconds later, the door opens. "What am I doing in here?" I whisper as Matt steps inside.

"This." In front of me now, he rests his hand on my shoulder and leans in, bringing with him the warmth of his body and the scent of soap and cologne. Everything south of my waist pulls tight at a sudden and very visceral memory. The moment is over in a blink as he pulls back, gently shaking a jar of hot chocolate mix. *Harrods, of course.*

"If you knew where it was—" I give a little squeak as he ducks quickly and presses his mouth to mine. Just a peck, nothing sexual, but a sneak attack. And he looks all kinds of pleased with himself. *I'd better not be having a boy,* I think, staring at him. He's too much.

"I wanted to get you alone. Not like that," he adds as I open my mouth to protest. His hand hovers over my waist for a moment, ultimately dropping to his side. "Should we tell her?"

"About the baby? Shouldn't we wait?" A chicken begins to cluck in my head. "I know twelve weeks is what they say." The rest of my sentence echoes in my head. *But I'm not ready.*

"What they say? Say about what?"

"Twelve weeks seems to be a convention. People wait until then in case . . ."

His hand finds mine. "Don't think like that. Not at twelve weeks, fourteen, or forty."

"We'll tell her before forty weeks," I say, trying to joke while feeling anything but funny.

"We don't have to say anything to her. Not yet."

"But do you think Clodagh might blab?"

He gives his head a quick shake. "I don't think she knew what we were talking about."

I pull a face, unconvinced.

"She probably just repeated what she heard."

"I don't know." But the way he's looking at me is distracting. It makes me feel all kinds of unnecessary things.

"Besides, that's what cartoons, pastries, and hot chocolate are for."

"Distractions. Good thinking."

His reply is a quick, reassuring squeeze to my fingers before he turns. I follow, of course. Because that ass. I mean—

"It was on a high shelf," he announces as he exits the pantry.

"Short joke. Great!" I retort as though this is our regular shtick. Rather than taking my seat again and enduring another undignified hop and heave, I lean against the end of the island and watch Clodagh do it instead. But first, she takes a quick detour into the kitchen.

"I didn't say anything," Matt says, holding up both hands.

"But you used the cup," she says, producing a glass cookie jar full of money from a low cabinet. *The kind of money that folds.*

"You can't even read!" Matt scoffs.

"Can too," she retorts, all short-person adorableness as she clambers back into her seat.

"What does it say, then?"

"I'm f—" Clodagh stops as she finds her mother's hand over her mouth. "You tried to trick me!" she complains as it drops. "That's not very nice, Uncle Matty!"

"Neither is the cup," her mother murmurs, tapping the rim of the saucer.

I glance down and realize there are words printed among the flowers, twining like vines. *I'm fucking radiant,* the twining script reads.

"He has a few of these," Letty offers. "One of them looks perfectly ordinary, until you've finished your tea and look down and read *You've been poisoned.*"

"Matt!" His name comes out in a gurgling chuckle.

"Do you have brothers?" Letty asks.

My gaze dips, but only briefly. "I'm an only child."

"Lucky you," she adds, but I can tell she's only kidding.

"Ahem!" Clodagh shakes her cookie jar again.

"No way," Matt complains as he pulls milk from the fancy fridge, then fires up an equally fancy coffee machine. "The deal is you only get money when the words come out of *my* mouth."

"I have words." The little girl frowns at her uncle's back.

"They'd better not be rude ones," Letty censures.

"Mommy." Clodagh turns in her seat to face her mom. "Where do babies come from?"

My heart literally plummets, and Matt's arm pauses midair as he reaches for a cup.

I know the answer to this one, the answer in our case, at least. *Alcohol, reduced inhibitions, super sperm, and defective prophylactics.*

"Well, honey, that's not really a conversation for right now." Her mother brushes Clodagh's hair from her face, the gesture quite tender.

"Yeah, but where do they come from?"

"Amazon," Matt says, now pouring milk into a little pink cup. "They have everything."

"No, Uncle Matty," the little girl says with a laugh. Is it me, or did that have a tiny edge of gleeful malice to it?

"Then maybe the machine at the arcade." He makes a snapping motion with his hand without turning around. "The one with the claw."

"Please, Mommy. I want to know!"

"You know where they come from." Her mom's tone turns firm.

"Yeah, but how do they get in your tummy?" she demands, pressing her hands to her torso.

"Why have you got such a bee in your bonnet about this right now?"

"Clo," Matt interjects, "come and press the button on the coffee machine. It'll make your hot chocolate extra frothy."

But Clodagh knows her uncle's game as she looks her mom dead in the eye and says, "Because I want to know how Uncle Matty put a baby in Ryan."

Chapter 24
MATT

"Oh, look, the part-timer is back," Fin taunts as I enter the meeting room the following Monday morning. Oliver glances up from the printouts in his hand, acknowledging me with a nod.

I took a few days' personal leave—not that I feel I *have* to report in, but I haven't seen the pair since the day after the meeting at Theta went tits up last week. It's been a while since I've taken time off, and I'm slightly surprised this pair didn't send out a search party. I'm glad that they didn't, as they would've only intruded on my Ryan time.

I'm pleased to report she's moved in. Well, into the basement apartment, which was originally intended as staff accommodation. It's nice enough, but I'm working on getting her upstairs. *Into my bed. Into my life. The whole shebang.* Which is not quite how I framed it to Letty yesterday.

After Clodagh's perfectly timed question—well, I thought it was kinda hilarious; there are no flies on that kid—I drew a look of gratitude, maybe even admiration, from Ryan as I explained the situation to my sister.

"We're having a baby," I announced. "And though me and Ryan are in this together, we're not together."

Ryan's shoulders sagged with relief. Letty, meanwhile, slid me a squint-eyed look. None too attractive.

"And while you're here, I might as well tell you that Ryan has agreed to move in with me so I can be part of the whole experience."

Letty's next look was incredulous—she looked at me as though I'd grown another head.

Clodagh's input was kinder. "You'll like it here, Ryan. Uncle Matty gives the best kind of hugs."

And I like to think that I do.

I called my sister later and listened to her rant her concerns. When she was done, I reminded her that I'm thirty-eight, that I've amassed a wealth that most people couldn't spend in a lifetime. And that achieving those two things didn't happen by accident.

In other words, mama didn't raise no fool. I know what I'm doing.

Now there's just these shitehawks to deal with. And the rest of the family to tell, though there's no great hurry as far as they're concerned.

"Aw, babe," I say in response to Fin's flapping gums. "You missed me?" I pull out a chair at the head of the table and drop into it, then stretch out my legs. "Howya, Andrew." I send Oliver's assistant a short wave before he slips out the door and closes it behind him.

"*¿Qué es la craic?*" Fin asks in a mixture of Spanish and Irish slang.

"The craic is grand," I answer agreeably.

"*Muy bien.*"

"Well, I think it's pretty good."

The craic. Such an Irish concept. You can have good craic, and bad. Savage craic, which is also good, or *the craic might be ninety*, which is the pinnacle of a good time spent. *What's the craic* is "How are you?" or "What's going on?" And if you're described as great craic, that means you're fun to be around. If you want to go deeper, craic is prana and it's chi. The life force that governs us, that flows through us, that simply is.

Fuck, that got a bit deep.

"Well?"

I shrug: *Dunno what you're talking about.* "Did I miss something?"

"You don't answer your phone . . . you don't call." Leaning back in his chair, Fin gives a careless flick of his wrist. "I was beginning to think you didn't love us anymore."

"Babe, you know I'll always have time for you in my life."

Fin flips me the finger, and Oliver gives a pained sigh.

Sitting up, I reach for the bottle of water we each have set in front of us, along with a portfolio including the meeting's agenda. Oliver is a stickler for protocol. Ignoring the accompanying glass, I crack the lid and gulp it down.

It's all good—this is typical Fin and me. I'm prepared to catch some shit for dropping off the face of the planet for a few days. Some things are just more important than making money.

"What is this I'm seeing?" From his seat at the middle of the table, Fin waggles his finger as though to indicate my face. "This is something new."

"What?"

Fin sits straight and gives a gasp, like Oliver's maiden aunt. Not that he has a maiden aunt, but if he did, she'd sound like that. "You've won her over, haven't you?" Fin's demand is narrow eyed.

"Well . . ." I bite back a burgeoning grin. If only he knew.

"So that's where you've been? You hydrate, my friend," he says, tipping his own water bottle on its side before rolling it down the long art nouveau–era meeting table.

Oliver gives a pained wince at the sound.

"We'll get you some electrolytes," Fin adds as the bottle rolls off the edge and into my hands. "Call Andrew back," he says, glancing Oliver's way. "Let's get this man a protein bar, stat."

"Thanks for your concern," I drawl with good humor. "But I'm all good."

"Yeah, I can see that. You're smiling like a lunatic."

"That's because I have news."

"News other than you've won her over?" From the far end of the table, Oliver examines me over the rims of the dark glasses he doesn't like to admit he needs.

"That the sight of you no longer makes her sick?" Fin puts in.

"Har-dee-fuckin'-har."

"So when do we get to meet the unlucky lady?" Fin waggles his brows ridiculously.

"Soon, I reckon."

The idea of waiting twelve weeks before announcing the pregnancy went out the window with my sister's visit. *Thanks, Clo.* Letty's reaction was better than I'd expected, to be honest. She seemed pleased. Or maybe *pleased* isn't the right word. *Vindicated?* Looking forward to me joining the parenting club? I'm not sure. Though I am certain she has thoughts and opinions, she was kind enough to keep them to herself. For now.

"We should have dinner," Fin continues. "I mean, as long as that sickness isn't contagious."

"Definitely not contagious." I brush a finger against the bridge of my nose, my words seeming to end in a curl. "She was, ah, sick for another reason."

"I imagine it was shock." Oliver's gaze returns to the papers in his hand.

"A bit of that. A bit of something else."

"What something else?" Fin pulls a face—a suspicious twist to his expression. Then, "No. No fucking way!"

"I'm gonna be a dad."

Oliver lowers his papers slowly this time. Fin, meanwhile, looks like his jaw just unlocked at the hinges.

"She's pregnant?" Oliver calmly lays the documents on the table.

"Yeah."

"Congratulations."

"Thanks." I turn Fin's way. "You can shut your mouth now."

"I am *shook*."

"You've been hanging around with Ronny too much. But also, I know how that feels," I add, rubbing my finger at the edge of my smile to temper it.

"But you're okay about it. I mean, you look fucking happy."

"Yeah, I am okay. And slightly terrified, naturally." The terror comes from the shedload of pregnancy books I ordered, which has left me wondering if too much information is a thing. Reading some chapters makes me feel all sorts of warm and fuzzy and smile like an eejit. Other bits—and here comes the terror—leave me wondering if the human race would still be a thing if blokes were responsible for birthing babies. *Or maybe it would just end if it was left to me.*

Women. The fairer sex, for sure. The stronger sex, no doubt. And I don't care what anyone says, the recent uptick of dipshit social media "We're pregnant!" announcements makes not one bit of sense. Women bear the burden—generally speaking, and not to diminish anyone's gender identity—they experience the pregnancy. Growing a whole new-arsed human is a 100 percent solo activity. Their partners might be lucky enough to be involved in the fun start, but to my mind, we're entitled to zero of the kudos.

I'm all for sharing and mutual responsibilities. I'm committed to equal parenting, and of course I'll support Ryan wherever and however I can. *Where she'll let me.* But I'll be sure to let her know that she deserves my endless gratitude for taking this one for the team.

"How far along?" Fin's voice brings me out of my thoughts.

"Fourteen weeks."

"A Manhattan October baby."

I slice him a look. "That's fucking weird."

"That I know the last time you had sex? Agreed."

"Whatever blows your hair back."

Fin snorts. "If my internal joy was waiting on you getting your rocks off, I'd be miserable most of the time."

I just haven't been interested in anyone else thanks to this massive Ryan hangover I've been suffering. *But it's over now.*

"And things are all right?" Oliver's inquiry turns the conversation sensible. Thank the feckin' Lord.

"Yeah, she's okay? Happy, healthy, and shit?" Fin puts in.

My smile falls a touch. "She's happy," I answer tentatively. "But we're not together."

Oliver says nothing.

Fin says, "Oh, shit."

"The official line is we're in this together but we're not together. Until I can change that."

"Right." Only Oliver speaks this time.

"It's sudden, but things will improve." I'm more than willing to do the work. To make her feel safe enough to let down those walls. Let her see in her own time how good this could be for us. *For the three of us.*

"So . . . what are you gonna do?" Fin asks.

"Be there for her. Literally. She's agreed to stay with me."

"She's moving in?" Fin asks with wide-eyed astonishment.

"Well, yeah. The timing isn't great." My hands open in a gesture of *what the fuck*. "Theta fired her. It kind of caught her off guard."

"What the fuck? Because she blew chunks on their carpet?"

"On what grounds?" Oliver translates for him.

"Performance issues, though she disputes that strongly. But she also says there's nothing to be done about it, thanks to her probation period."

"That does muddy the waters," Oliver says. "Unfair, but perfectly legal."

"Legal maybe, but also fucking immoral." Fin might be a dick sometimes, but he's a good friend.

"The law is the law," Oliver says. "And business is just that."

"Which is kind of how Ryan feels about it," I admit. "She's been pretty stoic about the whole thing. Me, not so much. Especially as they'd booked her on a flight back to JFK today."

"Fuck," Fin mutters. "So that's why . . ."

"She's staying with me? Part of the reason. She's gonna pay me rent," I say with a dark chuckle.

"Ah." Fin gives a sly yet understanding grin. "It's like that, is it?"

"Well, I don't have a private island." I give a shrug, and Fin's grin widens. The tale of his and Mila's marriage had its own obstacles. "I just need time and a little space to win her over."

"From gigolo to baby daddy." Fin sounds fucking tickled.

"From one-night stand to forever." Because that's what I'm aiming for.

◆ ◆ ◆

Following our monthly meeting, I call in at one of our projects in East London, where I've agreed to meet the head quantity surveyor. I could ask her to meet me at our offices, or even her office in Canary Wharf, but I like to see how things are progressing with my own eyes.

The project, an urban regeneration, will include a shopping mall, businesses, and youth centers. It'll be a huge bonus to the area, and I'm happy to see the foundations have been constructed. I know Mila will be too, given this is her old stomping ground.

After the East End, I make my way back across the city, mentally planning an impromptu visit to Theta Investments sometime in the not-too-distant future. My plan is to ambush one of the big nobs and discover the real reason for canning Ryan. Even if she's telling herself she's not interested in the reason she was fired, I'm sure she will be at some point.

And I'm more than a bit curious myself. As well as suspicious, because when I think back to those turds in tuxedos at the Pierre, and replay the things their ringleader, the head ball bag, bleated in the jacks, it's hard to believe she was fired for anything performance related.

Those bollixes seemed almost deferential around her. It was a weird kind of respect. With the exception of the ball bag, of course. He was just jealous. And deluded. Which I put down to brain shrinkage from all the happy dust he probably shoved up his nose. Who the fuck thinks having sex with a successful woman will make *you* successful?

Stuck in traffic now, I roll my shoulders and rotate my neck. Just thinking about those bastards makes me want to book a flight to New York to break a few noses.

As for Ryan, trading is a precarious business at the best of times. No less so as part of a hedge fund. It's a common phenomenon that when the P&L edges toward the red, heads begin to roll. But I can't see that being the case here, not after they went to the expense of recruiting and relocating her.

So yeah, I'm curious. She will be too. She's just got a lot on her plate right now.

"Dial Ma," I announce on a whim, and the car's Bluetooth does just that.

I suppose I better get it over with. Tick another one off my list.

I wonder who Ryan has on her list. She must have people, right? How strange must it feel, being alone in the world. Well, she isn't now.

As usual, Ma doesn't pick up. She's a bit of a gadabout, is old Catherine. Sixty-seven years and the doyenne of the Irish Countrywomen's Association's local guild. If there's money to be raised, she's doing it. Shit to be learned, she's adding it to her skill set.

She takes on the arrangements for the Christmas party at the old folks' home, the Easter parade and egg hunt for the local kids. She bakes lemon cakes made with olive oil for fundraisers and knits tiny cardigans for the premature babes in the neonatal unit.

Tuesday is for bridge, Wednesday is her knitting circle, and if you call into her home on Saturday afternoon, expect to be served *aperitivo* no matter who you are. Marinated olives, *jamón ibérico*, and Manchego cheese. Maybe *patatas bravas*, and a glass of dry cava or a bitter-tasting afternoon cocktail.

She lives a full life, and that's without the fair chunk of time her and the old fella spend in Spain, where my ninety-six-year-old *abuelo* is still kicking about.

"Ma, it's me," I begin as the phone connects with her message bank. "Just checking in. I also wanted to ask what your plans were for July. Specifically around the eighteenth. D'you fancy coming over to London for a few days? I need someone to watch the cat while I'm in hospital watching your new grandbaby be born. Anyway, let me know if you're free. And no, I haven't gotten a cat. But I have just gotten someone pregnant. Ciao!"

I chuckle to myself as I end the call. She's rubbish at checking her messages, so feck knows when she'll hear it. But I'll know the minute she does.

"Call *mi mujer*," I say next. My woman. She just doesn't know it yet.

"Hey." Ryan answers on the third ring.

"Hey yourself." I can't help the smile that seeps through my words. "How's it going?"

"The unpacking? Pretty much all done."

"Well, don't overdo it."

"It's just some clothes," she says with a soft laugh.

"Some?" For someone who's only been here a matter of weeks, she has enough clothes to open her own shop.

"Yeah, okay. Lots. But what was I gonna do? The postholiday sales were too much to resist!"

"Hey, it's your life. I'm just enjoying being in it."

"Speaking of being in my life, I still need your bank details."

A threat? "I'll get them to you eventually. When I've got a minute," I add, so as not to sound too flippant.

"Matt." She gives my name a warning tone.

"There's no great hurry."

"Maybe not for you. I like to pay my way."

"And you will," I say insincerely. "Or you could just keep it—cut out the middleman. I'm only gonna put it into an account for the baby."

"And that's *your* choice. But I will be paying you rent." By her tone I can tell she's trying not to get annoyed. "And while we're on the topic, I think you should have some paperwork drawn up by your lawyer. I want to reassure you and your family that I'm not out to steal your money."

"My family would be over the moon if they thought you were. They're always telling me I have too much of the stuff."

"Matt," she growls.

In my mind's eye, I see her hands balled into fists. My angry little Chihuahua, not that I'd ever say so. I like my balls where they are, thank you very much.

"If you don't get the details to me soon, it means I'll have to visit the bank and withdraw cash. And that would be a pain in the ass. You really don't want to put me through that inconvenience, do you? Braving the Tube and the cold weather, and not to mention the dangers of carrying cash through the city."

"Feck's sake," I mutter. "I'm still trying to recover from the last envelope of cash you left for me." A light chuckle sounds down the line. She knows she's got me. "You love to play dirty," I mutter, my mind instantly bending to the first time I accused her of that. Kissing on the dance floor. Lips soft and eyes full of promise.

Dirty to follow later.

"And like I said before, I prefer the term *creative competitor*."

Her answer is all business and zero teasing. My disappointment feels distinct.

"It would be easier to write you a check, but the bank didn't give me a checkbook when I registered my account."

"Checking accounts are pretty old school."

"Pretty convenient if you ask me. Look, just send me the details, or I might just end up buying more clothes."

"You might need to yet. Muumuus, I reckon."

"This baby better not be a giant, or I will never forgive you."

"What? It's not my fault I come from good country stock!"

"I swear, if I need a vagina reconstruction after this, you're paying for it."

"Okay."

"What?" The word bounds from her mouth.

"If that's what you want, but I think it's only fair I should keep an eye on your vagina as part of the proceedings. What's with the gasp? You said *vagina* first."

"It's not your use of the word!"

"It can't be my perfectly respectable offer."

"You think?" Hearing her laugh is such good medicine.

"I'd just check in. Periodically. Or maybe a daily debriefing might be better. You know, seeing as you're concerned about it."

"I didn't say I was concerned, but I might be now."

"I think it's good idea, keepin' an eye on your undercarriage." *Ah, fuck.* I almost slap myself. Talk about unsexy.

"I'm not a car! Also, I don't remember reading any of those suggestions in the literature from the clinic. Surely the doctor would've mentioned something like that, don't you think?"

"I'm not sold on that doctor," I say. Grumble. *Bitch?*

"I thought you said he was the most sought-after obstetrician in Europe—that he delivers all the royal babies."

"So I was told." He does come highly recommended. "There was something not quite right about him. Something off."

"If by *off* you mean *gorgeous*, then yeah. Agreed."

"You noticed that."

"Hard not to. But I would never date a doctor. The God complex does nothing for me."

"Right. Well . . ." This is fun. *Not.* She's treating me more like a fucking girlfriend.

"Was there anything else?"

"Yeah, I called to say I'll be home about seven. I thought I could bring us some dinner. Anything you fancy? Thai? Mexican? Ethiopian?"

"I'm good, thanks. I'm kind of beat. I'm gonna take a shower and turn in early. See you tomorrow maybe?"

"Sure." My spirits immediately sink.

"And don't forget to send me your bank deets, okay?"

"*Yeah, all right*," I say in a tone I've heard my father use when worn down by my mother. "Wait—don't hang up."

"What?"

"Steak or sushi?"

"I just said I—besides, I can't eat sushi." Her excuses fall quickly, her tone slightly panicked. And I don't think I'm imagining it.

"On July nineteenth, which would you pick?"

"Why?"

"Play along," I say. Cajole. "Gotta make the most of my opportunities in getting to know you." *I'm a patient man, Ryan. But feck knows you're taking every opportunity to hold me at arm's length.*

"I somehow don't think little bean is going to take me for steak or sushi on my birthday," she says, hearkening back to our earlier conversation. But I hear the relief in her tone.

"Of course he will. Matt Junior is a gentleman."

"Sushi," she answers.

"Good to know. Now I'll have an answer to his question, when he inevitably asks."

"What about you?"

"Steak or sushi?"

"Yeah."

"The caveman in me says steak all the way. Sushi is all well and good, but I'm a growing lad." *Growing dafter,* my mother would probably say if she could hear me. "Sushi feels more like a snack."

"A snack?" The upward inflection to her voice is curious. "I bet you're looking like a snack right now."

"I'm not always hungry," I retort a touch defensively.

She's laughing as she hangs up, which makes me wonder what I've missed.

Chapter 25
RYAN

Fifteen weeks, and well into the second trimester, where I've resolved to spend less time with Matt. So much for the pregnancy honeymoon period, though I was pretty lucky with my symptoms for the first trimester. Which were mostly defective taste buds and emotional instability. Though I guess the second is still hanging around a little.

Since I moved in, Matt and I have eaten dinner together most nights, and that new normal is starting to feel way too comfortable. So for the past two days, I've gone cold turkey. Which means we're conversing mostly by text. *Cold turkey for real, because there's a definite risk of becoming too dependent on him.*

And then there was the dream I woke from two mornings ago, flushed and sweaty, my insides pulsing emptily. As I lay in the murky gloom of the early morning, listening to the rapid beat of my heart, I allowed my mind to drift. Something I hadn't done since I'd moved in, which is probably why my somnolent brain took me on a trip down (smutty) memory lane.

Since I'd crept out of the hotel back in October, I'd been using the memory of Matt and our night together to get myself off. But that was before. Before I knew the real him. Before I moved in with him, when I told myself it had to stop—that it was wrong. Not to mention dangerous. But that morning, it was my unconscious mind that conjured him. I wasn't to blame. He was already in my head, and I was already wet and tingling.

What was the harm in one more tiny indulgence?

So I closed my eyes and dipped back into my memories. We were lying in that huge bed. My body was mostly covered in a fluffy hotel robe, wet from the shower, my face bare of makeup. Yet he stared down at me as though I was a rare treasure, sifting his fingers through the strands of my hair. His touch felt so good, and I curled into him like a cat.

Between us, there had been passion and craving and moments of connection that felt almost transcendental. Moments where, if not for the weight of his body, I might have floated away. But that particular moment, lying there with my head on his chest, was one of pure comfort. Something I hadn't known I'd needed.

This is connection, I thought as my hand wandered aimlessly over the dips and valleys of him, like a cartographer exploring a new and wonderous world. My fingertips inadvertently brushing his thick cock.

"Come up here." His words were raspy, as though his voice had been long unused.

"Not yet," I whispered, cupping the heavy weight between his legs. Delighting in the growl of his next breath. "Can I . . . can I do this?"

He laughed. "You're asking? You never have to ask."

"It's polite," I almost simpered. "So can I?"

He threw his arm across his eyes. "You're gonna torture me, I can tell."

And oh, I wanted to.

He submitted to my touch, my exploration, and that felt sexy as hell. I brushed the silken head, the satin steel of him against my palm. I climbed to straddle his legs, and he groaned my name, the muscle of his thigh contracting as I pressed my hand there.

His eyes turned to coal as I wrapped my fingers around his shaft and bent to swipe my tongue there. "Yeah." The word was just a breath, and next, a low growl. "Lick it, darlin'. Make it nice and wet."

Oh, the effect his words had on me.

"Like this?" I whispered, dragging my tongue along his length. From base to tip and back again. Swirling the tip.

"That's good. *So good.*" He swept my hair from my face—a tender gesture—but I knew it was so he could watch as he said, "Put it in your mouth."

"You should do audio porn," I whispered, glancing up the length of his body. A body that shook with laughter. And when he stopped, he moved his hand to my head, pressing it down.

That one tiny act of dominance, and I was done.

With my mouth stretched around him, he watched me work. And the noise he made as I took him deep could've blown a house down.

"You're so good," he rasped. He gave a thirsty swallow, his head tilted back, exposing the strong line of his throat. *The tremor in his Adam's apple.*

I felt like a goddess. His taut breaths and his stuttered praise were my creation. Mine alone. I made his body shudder and his eyes turn molten.

"Yeah, like that. Just like that, darlin'." Desperate then, his jaw taut and his words running together. "Don't you make me come, Ryan. Don't you dare make me come."

It felt like a challenge. A gauntlet thrown. I was going to give my white knight the ride of his life. Drive him to the edge of his sanity, to the point he was unable to do anything but . . .

Let go.

Give in.

Give it to me.

And those memories are why I'm hiding out in my rooms like a troll under a bridge.

Because I'm not my mother. I can resist a man.

Because I will never be her, and I'll always put my child's needs first.

I'm just down here, cooling things. *My blood mostly.* Lines will not blur. Hearts will not get hurt.

I tell myself this is just a temporary state. Pregnancy hormones. And they are a blast.

As in, if I don't keep them in check, they're likely to blow up in my face.

◆ ◆ ◆

Sixteen weeks.

> MATT: Do you know Matt Junior is the size of a tomato this week?

I can't help but smile at Matt's first text of the day. It's hard to believe a man can be this sweet. *And hotter than the devil, when he invades my dreams.*

Yeah, that's still happening, though I'm not sure if it's truly hormones that make me feel this way or if it's just him. Dark haired and funny, caring and kind could be just my thing.

Not that it matters.

> ME: Beefsteak or plum tomato?

> MATT: A lemon-sized tomato.

> ME: What I'm hearing is baby Ryan is the size of a lemon. Good to know!

MATT: It's a bit vague, don't you think?

ME: What is?

MATT: Is he the size of a lemon from Valencia or one we get at the greengrocer? There's quite a variance, size-wise.

ME: . . .

MATT: Calm yourself. I know you live for my scintillating conversation.

More than he knows.

MATT: Anyway, all that to lead up to the fact that I know you already know how big he is because you keep unfolding the corner of the pages of my pregnancy bible.

The pregnancy bible is one of a number of parenting books that have appeared in the house over the past couple of weeks, but the pregnancy bible, as he calls it, is kept on his nightstand. It's super stalkery, I know, but I look at it every day after he's left for work. Though I'm careful to replace it each day exactly as I found it. *Or so I thought.*

I guess there's just something heartening in reading the pages Matt has read the night before. The facts he learned before dropping off to sleep, maybe to dream about them. The cute facts, not the horrifying ones. The stuff of dreams, not the stuff of nightmares.

Anyhoo, my stalking gig makes me feel connected to Matt in a way that negates my fear that he'll discover what that connection costs me.

ME: Not me.

MATT: So that wasn't one of your many many hair ties I found on my bed?

Damn. I roam around his big, beautiful house every day while he's out working, discovering little things about him without him knowing. I've learned he's a closet romantic (not such a stretch of the imagination) thanks to the romance titles I found slotted among the business, philosophy, and history books on his shelves. I don't believe for one minute they all belong to Letty.

While he once said he can cook—back in October, when I admitted I couldn't—I have yet to see evidence of this. Instead, he has a private chef called Mary. Mary is a grandma of three and an absolute darling. I know this because we've chatted as she's prepped dinner.

In fact, I love how chatty Mary is. Almost as much as I loved hearing how Matt pays her full time but tells her not to bother coming in every day, but just to keep him stocked up in meals instead. She also let me in on the secret that Matt has a bit of a sweet tooth, not that you'd know it from looking at that body of his. But she showed me where his stash of candy is. By the sheer amount, I can tell the man loves strawberry licorice. Think Twizzlers.

But his condom stash I found all on my own. *In his bathroom vanity. Left-hand top drawer. At the back.* I might've counted how many were in the box. I might also know that number hasn't altered since I moved in.

It seems Matt is also a bit of a slob, though I'm not sure I wouldn't be too if I just dropped stuff and a team of (paid) fairies relocated those items to their rightful spots. I guess that's why he's teased me about my own habits. He said it's like I think I'm being graded on my tidiness.

Old habits, I guess. Except for the hair ties he teases me endlessly about.

These and others are the little nuggets of Matt I stash away like a squirrel hoarding nuts. Facts, knowledge, thoughts, and feelings that I'll save for future reflection. Some day when it's too late to cave, because every day I'm fighting my growing feelings. It's hard not to be seduced by the idea of a man who'd give up his world to follow me. *Me and his baby.*

And that's what I tell myself is at the heart of our connection. That Matt is a good man, a decent man who's doing the best he can after finding himself in this situation. While I battle the idea of him and me, he's given in to the temptation of family. *No matter how less than ideal, less than pristine, our origin story is.*

Coming clean would be a disservice to him. Worse, maybe even a repeat of history. And I will do everything in my power to avoid passing on my own traumas to this innocent. Every time I rest my hands on my stomach, I swear to the life inside me I'll be the best mom I can.

Which includes my very careful response to his accusation.

ME: I really don't know what you're talking about.

MATT: Unfolding the pages that I've folded feels like a judgment...

ME: It is. Only heathens don't use a bookmark.

I thank the Lord and all the stars above that this is what he chooses to call me out on. Instead of the fact I've been lurking in his bedroom. *Lying on his bed.*

MATT: I'm pretty sure the definition of heathen is a person (or persons) who makes another lose their place in a book they're currently very avidly reading.

ME: Fine. I'll order my own copy.

MATT: Don't. I like that we're reading the same copy. I wouldn't even complain if you read it over my shoulder.

ME: Now *that* is the behavior of a heathen

How is it he seems to know when I need to smile? I ask myself as my phone vibrates almost immediately again. Sliding the message open, I pad across to the kitchen to fill my water glass. The apartment is modern, neat, if not a little institutionally sparse. Two bedrooms, one bathroom, and a through-lounge diner, plus a tiny galley kitchen, which I barely use. Because I can't cook. Currently. Maybe I should use my current free time to hone my culinary skills. Can't feed a toddler on takeout leftovers.

MATT: Harry Potter or Twilight?

He has his ways of learning about me. And I have mine. *Snooping and grilling Mary.*

ME: HP. Ravenclaw all the way!

MATT: I had you down as Gryffindor.

ME: What's wrong with RC, Hufflepuff boy?

MATT: I'm probably more Slytherin in a Hufflepuff cloak. And just so you know, my wand is at the ready ;)

The danger in that offer isn't getting pregnant twice.

Chapter 26
RYAN

Seventeen weeks, and my pants no longer fit.

Just last week—three days ago—they were fine. Then, bam! I seemed to wake up and find my external world matched my inner. Like, *Hello! Pregnant lady here!*

Thankfully, I can still get into a couple of pairs of my casual pants, mostly with the aid of a hair tie looped through the buttonhole, then twisted around the button. *Classy, right?* But I can forget wearing the black Reiss cigarette pants I bought in the January sales. And the wide-legged cream wool ones. For now.

Matt and I had dinner last night—one of our sanctioned conferences—so we won't be repeating the occasion tonight. Is treating myself meanly making me less keen? The jury is out on that one.

I'm still trying to balance things. To mitigate risks. I don't want to make it obvious that I'm avoiding him, so I'm trying to play things cool. I make a point of texting him most evenings to ask if he's home, even though my stomach flips like that of Pavlov's dog when I hear the rumble of whatever car he's driving that day pulling into the driveway.

I might text something like Hey, what's up? Kind of *frat boy seeks booty call.*

Ha! I wish. Wish it could happen without the tangle of feelings, maybe.

Those hormones, I tell ya . . .

I still allow myself dinner with him two or three times a week, courtesy of Mary's culinary skills. He'll ask me how I'm feeling, what I've been up to, and I try to make my answers sound interesting, because life is pretty dang boring at the minute.

Worse than boring is my rising anxiety. I've never been unemployed before, not once since I began working as a teenager. No matter what else has gone on in my life, work was once my one constant. Something to get lost in when life outside that bubble got tough. That I don't have that distraction right now is . . . hard.

I try not to worry—to keep my shit together. For the sake of the bean, if nothing else. What if she feels what I feel? I read that my stress might release cortisol, which, in turn, could affect her development.

Stop. I'm doing it again. Worrying about things I can't control.

I'm treading water, that's all. I'll return to the swim soon.

It's safe to say that it's better if we stick to the topic of Matt's job over dinner. I enjoy hearing about his work and his partners—I gobble that shit up. *Even if I'm still avoiding meeting them.* They sound like really good friends, as well as solid business partners. Frankly, I'm worried what they might say about me. *They probably think I'm trying to trap him.*

Fuck. I'm doing it again, allowing my mind to run wild. Since when have I begun to care about what people think again? I close my eyes and take a deep breath, slow and easy.

Fuck it, I silently intone. *It's not my business. It's not my problem, and I'm not gonna worry about it.* I allow my eyes to flutter open a moment later. It might be a poor mantra to some, but it's always worth reminding yourself that you can't control the actions of others.

Hell, sometimes I can't even manage my own thoughts.

Which is why some evenings when Matt gets home, I'll say I've already eaten. It's usually crackers and cheese for dinner then, or maybe something zapped in the microwave of my tiny galley kitchen, me eating it from the carton as I stand at the countertop. Life as usual.

I do enjoy our dinners together and find Matt really enjoyable company. He's smart and funny and irreverent, his edges a little rough. *Deliciously so.* Sometimes I'll catch myself watching him eat and wonder if I'm borderline developing a fetish.

The days we don't eat together, maybe I'll join him after dinner, or maybe I won't. But when I do, he'll drink a whiskey, and I'll pretend to enjoy a cup of tea. And I will absolutely not think about asking him for a taste of his tongue.

Ah, the memories.

Sometimes we'll eat ice cream at the kitchen island. A pint of Ben & Jerry's and a couple of spoons. Maybe the rugby (kind of like football without the right precautions) will play on the big screen at the other side of the room. Maybe music will play in the background instead, and after an hour or so, we'll say good night and go our separate ways.

He might go downstairs to work out or upstairs to shower. And I go back to my temporary home and try not to think of him doing either of those things. *Try and usually fail.* I'll imagine him, his body wet, his skin gleaming. Muscles straining, veins prominent, his cock standing proud in his hand . . .

Because those are the kind of exercises I imagine him undertaking.

But most days of the week I manage fine to keep the bulk of our contact text based, and when he asks if I'm coming up, I'll say I'm tired, that I'm turning in early. Or that I'm off to catch up with Martine from the office, though we've only done that once since my awkward parting with Theta. I feel a little like her dirty secret, but I'll persevere. Gotta cultivate those future work contacts somewhere.

Chapter 27
RYAN

"Hey, Martine. It's just me . . . again. I'm sure we'll catch up at some point! Or maybe not," I mutter as I hang up, trying not to feel despondent.

Twenty weeks, I think, catching a glance at myself in the darkening window. That's more than halfway. *I look like I'm majorly bloated.* The garden beyond is still barren and gray as I rub my hand over my little bump, kind of like when I have a stomachache. *But this is no fart,* I think to myself as I turn away from the window.

My professional life, however? That seems to be nothing but stale air. I can't even get Martine to return my calls, which might be less to do with work and more that, outside the office, we've found we have nothing in common.

I knew looking for a job while pregnant and here in the UK and on the wrong visa would be difficult, but I didn't think it would be impossible. I assumed I'd make it work, that I'd dabble in freelance. Maybe make some independent trades on behalf of some old clients I'd kept in contact with, those I'd made money for in the past. I'd built a pretty solid network in the States. *So why the hell can't I get anyone to take my calls?*

I heft myself onto a stool and scroll through my sad call log. Could Pete have had a hand in this? The asshole was pretty pissed when I handed in my resignation. I like to imagine he pisses green every time he thinks of me being in London. In hindsight, he did seem to think my success came at a cost to him. *Fucking men.*

"Sorry, bean." I press my hand over my stomach in apology. I know Matt and I both joke about the sex (of our child, not the sex that got us here), but I'm aware there might be a boy growing in here. It's a distant possibility, I feel. But it warrants consideration.

"I don't really care what you are, as long as you're healthy," I find myself saying. "And I'm doing my best to make it so, taking all the advice, vitamins, and shit. And when you get here, I'll do all I can to make you happy. And keep you safe." I feel a sense of ease and contentment as I run my hand over my bump. A kind of warmth that gladdens my heart.

And contentment is better than all that other stuff. The fear and the worry. The stress from thinking about what might happen if I can't get a job later, when the baby is here. When I overtax my brain imagining how things might be if I'm forced to go back to the States, knowing Matt won't ever be a real dad if I do. The weight of responsibility and pressure feels immense.

I mean, how would it even work if I went back?

I know I'd get something, even if my contacts aren't answering my calls right now. Put me in a room with one or two of them, face to face, and I'll work it out. Win them over. Make them remember. But what then? A nanny and a job that means I'm not there to feed her breakfast or tuck her into bed. A weekend mom, at best. Or maybe I'd have to fight to be in her life at all. Would Matt contest my leaving—take me to court to prevent that reality? And who would blame him for putting the needs of his child first? Not me, because he's a good man. One of the best I've ever known.

So much for doing my best—I realize my thoughts are a mess and I'm gripping my phone so hard that my wrist hurts. I set it down and press my fingers and palms to the cool marble to ground myself. I breathe in, expanding my lungs to capacity, before letting the air out slowly. "In . . . out . . . in . . . out."

"Name five things you can see."

I glance out at the garden. Gray skies and ripples in the surface of the pond. A crow sitting in an oak and a willow's branches sweeping the ground in a low lament. I look down at my feet. Can't see them, so that doesn't count. My bump. New life. I rest my hand there.

Four things I can hear. The low hum of the fridge and the pad of my feet across the kitchen. The sound of water hitting the sink as I turn on the faucet, and the distant rumble of pipes. The sweet symphony of a home.

Three things I can touch. The cool porcelain of the Belfast sink and the sensation of cold water running across my skin. The squish of a natural sponge.

Two things I can smell. I close my eyes and inhale. Coffee grounds and the lingering scent of toast. Matt's breakfast, I guess.

One thing I can taste. Both of those things in his kiss.

I wish.

I open my eyes, give a sigh, and redirect my thoughts once more. *Away from Matt this time.*

I have money and time. I'm comfortable and stable. What will happen will happen anyway, whether I stress about it or not. I just need to keep my head in the game. Be positive. Keep busy. Make sure my baby isn't swimming in cortisol.

So it looks like I'm about to book a cookery class.

◆ ◆ ◆

UNKNOWN NUMBER: Hi Ryan, this is Letty, Matt's sister. I hope it's okay that he gave me your number. I'm in the area and wondered if you were home.

Home. Yeah, I guess I am home. My temporary home. I hate the addendum, that intruding thought. But it is what it is. It is what it has to be right now.

ME: Hey Letty. It's good to hear from you. I am home, actually.

LETTY: Fancy some company? A party of two.

ME: Sure! I'd love that.

LETTY: Great! See you soon.

And she must have really been in the area, because five minutes later, the doorbell rings.

"Hey!" Letty gives a little wave from the doorstep, her arms laden with shopping bags.

"Mommy has a key," Clodagh says, appearing from behind her mother. She trots up the steps, and her head quirks as she stares up at me. "But she didn't want to use it."

"It didn't feel right," Letty says with a shrug as Clo skips into the hallway. "There's an intercom, you know? In case you get visitors you don't want to see."

"All visitors are welcome." I have nothing else going on. "Shoot," I say, stepping back from the door. "Where are my manners? Come on in." *Don't be weird, Ryan!*

"Thanks," she says with a grateful look.

I close the front door as Clodagh begins to skip around the antique hall table.

"We used to live here, you know," she says. "And Mommy used to buy flowers to put on the table."

"Ryan is too busy for that, honey."

As I tear my gaze from the silver urn, her mother shoots me an apologetic look.

"I guess I could buy flowers," I say. But I won't, because this isn't my home and I need to remember that.

"Just don't expect Matt to notice," Letty says. "I'm desperate for a cuppa. Shall we put the kettle on?"

"Yeah, sure."

Still holding her shopping, she bustles her way down to the kitchen area as Clodagh and I follow.

"You don't mind, do you?" She drops her bags to the counter, her glance pensive as Clodagh throws herself over the sectional, dragging her little backpack with her. She begins to unpack the contents.

"No." Mind what? The shopping? The tea? Her dropping in? I don't mind any of it. "I'm really happy to see you."

Letty looks relieved, her expression relaxing instantly. "It's just, I know you and Matt aren't together, but this is still your home, and I don't want to intrude."

I laugh a little at that. "This house is huge. An army could march through it, and I probably wouldn't notice it."

"Well, that's true." She moves toward the kettle before taking it to the sink. "The *huge* thing, at least."

A few minutes later, tea is made and we're sitting on the sectional.

"So," Letty begins. "How've you been?"

"I'm good. All good," I say, resisting the urge to touch my stomach. Lord, I'm turning into one of *those* women.

"And Matt? How are you two getting along?"

"Good. Really good." *All the* goods. God, I'm such a liar, because sometimes, I am so very far from good. But it's not as though I can just say: *I think your brother's great, but I'm scared of commitment. Scared of the future. But that doesn't stop me from wanting to have sex with his face.*

No, not saying any of that.

"Matt's a really decent guy. One of the best," she says. She lifts her tea and takes a sip. "I know he's my brother and I'm supposed to be in his corner, but if he was a shit bag, I really would tell you. Before you had the babe." Her eyes dip briefly to my stomach. "The way I look at it, some people don't deserve to be in their children's lives."

Her ex, I guess she means. Matt told me she's in the middle of a nasty divorce; that's why she and Clo were living with him until recently.

"Yeah, I get that," I say, pulling on a thread at the hem of my sweater. I know it, even.

"Do you have friends here? In London?" She tightens her grip on the teacup handle, and a little liquid sloshes over the rim. "Balls," she mutters, swiping the droplets from her pants. "You don't mind me being a nosy old baggage, do you?"

"No. And no, you're not." Old, at least. I give a little smile. "I guess I haven't been here long enough to make friends."

"I've made friends," Clo pipes up, looking up from her coloring book. "I have lots of friends at school."

"Aren't you a lucky girl." Gosh, she's as cute as a button.

"I'll be your friend, Ryan. We can be family and friends at the same time, can't we, Mommy?"

"Of course, honey."

Clodagh returns to her pencils, and we both watch her for a minute or two.

270

"It's tough when you move, I know." Consternation knits Letty's brows. "It can be hard to make friends and stuff. But once the baby comes, you'll have baby groups and other mommy things to keep you occupied."

"And work. I hope."

"Well, yeah. I mean, that's important too. A sense of self. Because it's easy to lose yourself in motherhood. Oh," she says, putting her huge teacup down. "I forgot. I brought you something. Just a little thing." She kind of pauses. "You're not superstitious, are you?"

"I'm way too practical."

"Just thought I'd check. Matt said you hadn't started to get things in for the baby yet." Her delivery is halting and awkward.

"Yea-aah." My answer is dragged over too many syllables. I've been avoiding all conversation of baby things. It all just seems so . . . "It's kind of overwhelming. I just don't know where to start. Do I need a crib or a cot, or are they the same things? Do I choose a stroller with a car seat—one of those three-in-one things? What kind of baby monitor do I choose, and do I really need a white noise machine? Also, what the hell is a butt spatula?"

"It's like a whole new world," she says with a laugh. "I'm no expert, but I could help you, if you like? We could go shopping, head into town. It might help you to get your mind around things even if you order what you want and need online later."

"Really?" I feel my shoulders stiffen, as though I'm asking her for a limb. "You wouldn't mind?"

"Who doesn't like to shop?"

"I do love a little retail therapy."

"We'll make a day of it. Have lunch," she says, rounding the couch as she heads for her shopping bags.

"That would be so good. I also think I might need new pants soon," I murmur, stroking my stomach now.

"Oh, you'll need a lot more than pants before you're through," she singsongs in a tone of one who knows all the secrets and isn't telling. That's fair, I guess. Can't scare people to death the first opportunity you get them alone.

"This is for you," she says, coming back and setting a buttermilk-colored box next to me. Tied in a white satin ribbon, the box is so pretty.

"That's so kind of you," I murmur, running my hand along the edge. I don't remember the last time someone bought me something. *Well, there was coffee and zeppole. And before that, a night in the Pierre. Room service and champagne.*

"Are you gonna open it?" Clo asks, looking across at me.

"Would you like to help?"

Her mother laughs. *Boy, would she ever.*

"Yes!" The little girl abandons her pencils and scrambles from the couch. "I'll pull the end of the ribbon." And she does.

My heart. Letty's gift is so, so thoughtful. A selection of upscale lotions and potions for expectant mothers, and a bunch of the tiniest socks rolled to look like pastel-colored rosebuds.

"This is for when the baby gets a little older," Clo says, handing me a fabric rattle. "It's soft, see? So it won't hurt its head," she adds, giving a short demonstration.

"It's so cute."

"I picked it. It's a zebra," she says. "Because babies like black and white."

"Do they?"

"The lady in the shop said."

"Well, thank you," I say, smoothing her blond hair from her cheek. "It's perfect, and I'm sure the baby will love it."

"And this one here is called boob tube." She hands me one of the fancy lotions. "It's for your boobies."

"Thanks?" I give a stuttering laugh.

"I can say that because it's not a bad word, right?" She glances her mother's way but doesn't really wait for confirmation. "*Bangers* isn't bad either."

"Clo!" Her mother laughs, exasperated.

"Or *ta-tas*, or even Brad Pitts. There's another name I heard Uncle Seb say, but I can't remember it."

"Thank God," Letty mutters.

"I think it was *thumb bags*, but that doesn't make any sense. Why would boobies look like a bag of thumbs?" Shrugging the thought off, Clodagh skips happily back to her pencils and book.

"I'm gonna have such a conversation with that man," Letty grumbles, kind of red cheeked.

Embarrassment, not anger, I think, as I pull the last item from the box. A beautiful hardback book, embossed in gold with the words "Baby's First Year."

"I hope you don't mind I got in first with that," she says softly.

"Oh, it's so pretty. The illustrations," I whisper, turning beautiful page after beautiful page, each with a space for a photo, a thought, or a memento.

"Ma will probably bring Matt's baby book when she comes to visit and bore you half to death with tales of himself and his grand escapades."

I look up. "You all have a book like this?"

She nods, her flash of surprise evident. "At least one each."

"That's so sweet," I say, looking down again, embarrassed by the slip.

"I'm gonna draw the baby a picture," Clo says, filling the awkward pause.

"That's a grand idea. Scuse me," Letty adds, pulling her phone from the back pocket of her jeans. "Ah, shit!"

"I better get my swear jar." Clo drops her pencil and clambers from the cushions.

"No time. We've got your parent-teacher conference in half an hour. It's a good thing one of the other moms thought to remind me." She shoots me an apologetic glance. "Honestly, baby brain lasts for years."

"I don't wanna go," Clodagh whines. "You said I could have a hot chocolate at Uncle Matty's."

"Maybe later. Come on, we don't want to be late."

"I know we don't want to be late, because I don't wanna go!"

"Why don't you leave Clodagh with me?" I suggest, surprised by the offer myself. But the little girl is really not keen, and her mom looks so frazzled. And I just put my foot in my mouth.

"You're sure?"

I nod. Because I can't really say, *Lol, jokes, no,* can I? But really, how hard can it be? Clodagh is five—practically self-sufficient! Or maybe that was just me.

"I'll be an hour. Ninety minutes tops," Letty says, grabbing her purse after shoving one arm into her jacket. "Her teacher is a bit of a gasbag. It's hard to get away sometimes."

"That's fine. I'll be here." As usual.

A quick kiss to her daughter's head, a grateful smile for me, and she's gone.

◆ ◆ ◆

Things start out well enough. We sit on the couch with Clodagh's coloring book.

"This is you," she says, pointing to a triangle with a pin head and stringy hair. "And this is Uncle Matty."

"I can tell." Because his triangle body is upside down, narrow at the bottom and wide at the shoulders. Story checks out, but for his pin head.

"And this is me next to you, and see, you're holding your baby."

"I do see. Is it a boy or a girl?"

"I think it might be a guinea pig."

"Cool. I've never had one of those."

"Ryan, if you weren't already family, I would choose for you to be."

"Oh, Clodagh. That's so nice of you to say." My heart does the Grinch thing. I'm not gonna correct her. This is her family and my babe's family too. But I'm not part of them. I don't belong here.

"I'm thirsty."

"Then let's get you a water."

Next, Clodagh is hot chocolate thirsty, so I make her one of those with cream and sprinkles and marshmallows, because apparently, she's allowed all that before dinner.

Then she's hungry for grilled cheese. Given that it's almost 4:30 in the afternoon, I don't see the issue and think I might even be doing her mom a favor. Until I consider allergies. Clodagh settles for a piece of fruit instead.

Then her legs begin to ache, and apparently, the antidote is a run around the garden. Because "growing legs need things to do." So a run around the garden she gets. Which then necessitates a change of clothes after she skids in the wet grass and mud.

"Don't worry," she says as I stare in horror at her once-pink leggings. "I have clothes upstairs in my old bedroom."

So that's where we go, and as she pulls on some clean leggings, I take my eyes off her for two seconds. And poof! She disappears. Gone. Like aliens beamed her up out of nowhere. As in, no sight or sound of her is available to me.

I look in the closet and under the bed, the same in the next room, and the next. And so it goes, my voice echoing from the walls as panic begins to spout and grow, twining around my ribs like ivy strangling a tree.

"Clodagh!" Each time I call her name, I sound more than a little desperate, even to my own ears. "Clodagh, sweets, where are you?"

The doors are all locked—where the hell could she have gone? Unless . . . she's tall enough to open them from the inside. And has gone looking for her mom.

She wouldn't, would she?

I thunder down the grand staircase and check the doors. The kitchen, the pantry, the garden, my rooms, as my heart continues to beat like runaway hooves.

At my wits' end, I grab my phone and decide there's nothing for it—I'll have to call her mom.

So hey, Letty. I don't quite know how to tell you, but the house ate your daughter. Yep, that's what I said. She's gone.

"What's up, buttercup?"

"Oh!" I turn and practically fall into Matt's arms. "Oh, thank God!"

"What is it?" he demands, his arms tightening around me.

"Letty left Clodagh with me while she went to her parent-teacher conference." The words fall so quick, I'm surprised he can follow. "And everything was fine until we went upstairs to get her changed out of her muddy leggings, and now she's gone!"

"What do you mean she's gone?"

"It's not funny, Matt!" I thump his chest with the side of my fist. Because the man is amused. Amused!

"She hasn't gone," he says, gathering me close. He folds me under his arm as he turns his attention to the staircase. "Oh, what a pity," he calls upward. Loudly and with a theatrical exaggeration. "How will I ever survive without my Clodagh!"

"You think she's hiding from me?" I almost whisper.

"She's five. And a little shite."

"But she's so sweet," I protest.

"They all are. Until they're not. You can't have lost her," he says, giving a reassuring squeeze. "She can't work the locks on the external doors. She'll just be winding you up."

"What about the swimming pool?" My stomach sinks.

"Also locked by a code. And she's been swimming like a fish since she was two. Come on, let's find the tiny terror. I bet she's run you ragged," he says, slanting me a look.

"No, she was . . . yeah, she really did." We set off up the stairs.

"That's kids for you."

I wouldn't know. I don't know how this works. *Parenthood. Kids. Any of it.*

"Raaah! I'm a monster!"

"Fuck me!" On the first floor landing, Matt's arms tighten around me as he moves me behind him, shielding me with his body. Instinct, I guess. Not that the threat is too terrifying.

"Uncle Matty, you said a bad word!" the little girl yells, her hands still held in the air like claws. Latex claws. Because hanging from each of her fingers is an extra-large condom.

Chapter 28
RYAN

I can't sleep.

It's not the pregnancy. Not the physicality of it, at least. But maybe the emotional realities. The fact that I barely coped looking after Clodagh for an hour. *Maybe I should take some parenting classes along with those cooking classes I have yet to book.*

Most of the stuff I've read seems to make it sound like motherhood is instinctual. I just hope that instinct will kick in, because I feel so out of my element right now. But maybe I should cut myself a little slack and remember this is, in fact, my first rodeo.

I didn't know my father, and my mother was a mess. My upbringing was chaotic. Toxic. I felt powerless, and I was often scared. But I knew the world had other plans for me. Be it God, or the universe, or some other deity, I had certainty. I just knew I wasn't going to perpetuate the cycle, that I was going somewhere. I'd grow up, get smart, make money, become happy. Be safe. And never look back again.

I did that—I did all that. I did the work, studied hard, and found my place in the world. But now I'm rudderless. Out of my depth. And if I let my mind dwell, it becomes a scary place. My job was such a big part of my life, and it feels a little like, well, maybe I don't know who I truly am without it.

Ryan the mom-to-be isn't Ryan the killer queen. As much as I hate the moniker because of how it speaks to the past—a past that no one but me knows about—I do wish I felt a little more like that girl. Kicking ass and taking names, not caring for anything but success.

Instead, as I stand in Matt's kitchen, the cabinet lights the only illumination in the room, I feel truly lost.

I'm in the big kitchen because I've run out of the tea I once pretended to like but now actually enjoy. There's something soothing about the preparation of tea, a kind of mindfulness in the boiling of water and the waiting for the tea leaves to steep. *Steep, not brew. I've already been schooled there.* And then there's the drink itself, which I find now to be like a warm cup of comfort.

As I wait for the leaves to infuse, I pull myself up onto a stool and open the stock-trading app I recently installed on my phone. Time to redirect my thoughts and channel a little positivity into this evening. *Hormones. It has to be.*

It's been years since I've dabbled in the market privately. Working for a hedge fund pretty much exempts you from doing so, and I was never interested in putting my job on the line. Instead, I invested in the employee fund, which, while lucrative, wasn't as much fun. Or as personal.

Hedge funds trade on loans and lines of credit. Meanwhile, I'm playing with my own savings. So I'm playing conservatively but using the same parameters as I watch the market for specific events, things that might influence the price of stocks or derivatives. *Affect the price either way.* Whatever your poison is, the name of the game is to get out at the optimal time. The optimal time for profit. And so far, I'm doing pretty well.

Haven't lost my touch, I'm thinking, allowing that small win to soak in, when an email notification flashes up on the screen. My stomach flips as I realize it's from a business contact back in New York.

Dear Miss Hoffman . . .

Weird, considering he and I have shared many a lunch together.

Thank you for your recent email . . . *blah, blah, blah* . . . currently aren't in need of advisory services in any capacity, nor will we be in the future.

What the hell? That's not what my email suggested. Hinted at, maybe. I basically just asked if he had time for a call. The asshole was willing to listen to my advice before! What's with the formal language and the curt brush-off?

Mother . . . *fucker.*

As I set down my phone, I find the sting is more than just in my cheeks. The rejection burns, maybe because it's from someone I thought was . . . not a friend, exactly. A friendly contact. But also because this isn't the only rejection I've had since I sent out a bunch of speculative emails, looking for work. True, most of those rejections have come in the form of silence. *Which I tried to sell myself as something other than outright rejection.*

What the hell is going on? Maybe news travels continents, and that's why I'm running into walls. Maybe they know I got fired. *Or that I'm pregnant.*

What is my life right now? I can't manage a five-year-old, and I can't get anyone to answer a call or reply to an email. It's like my identity is slipping from my grip.

Something catches the corner of my gaze. There, on the countertop, lies my gift from Letty. *Baby's First Year.*

I feel . . . in need of something—a distraction—as I draw the book closer and lift the cover. I turn the pages, losing myself in the cute illustrations, each page a place to record our child's milestones. Until I'm struck by the realization that no one recorded my history. The arrival of my first tooth. My first tentative steps. My first word. I hardly remember ever receiving a kind word, let alone having someone take a photograph. There were probably photographs, but I took nothing when I left home. I didn't want the reminder. Like she didn't want me.

"Think you're so goddamn clever."

"All you'll ever be is a hole for a man to fuck."

Those were her parting sentiments.

Projecting, Mama? Oh, how you loathed your little girl.

But this book. These people—Matt, Letty, Clo. There is so much love. My experience won't be hers, because this baby will be watched with awe. She'll be encouraged, cherished. *And oh, what a life she'll have,* I think, my heart aching with this gladness. And still a little sadness.

Matt spoke of foundations, and I'm beginning to see what he meant. *The heights she will reach standing on the shoulders of that man.*

My heart skips as I hear soft, padding footsteps and look over my shoulder to find Matt coming toward me, dressed for bed. A pair of checkered pajama pants barely hangs on to his hips, the fingers of his right hand curled around a book.

"Sorry, I didn't realize you were in here."

I make a careless gesture—he shouldn't apologize—as I turn back to the book, dropping the end of my braid as though it's burning. It's an old childhood habit, brushing my lips with the end. "It's your kitchen." *It's your world. I'm just living in it for a little while.* I flick my gaze back his way, unable to resist a second look.

His half-nakedness makes my blood feel part lava, part champagne because he's all hollows and dips in this low light.

"I was hungry," he says, answering a question unspoken.

"Aren't you always?"

"You know how it goes," he says. "Why are you sitting in the dark?"

"It's not dark. It's comforting."

"And why are we whispering?" His shadow falls over me as he places his book down. *The Expectant Dad's Handbook.* He said it was a gift from Fin.

"Because it's nighttime." And a good thing too, as my nipples draw tight under the cotton of my nightdress. I shouldn't be here. *We* shouldn't be here. Whispering and ready for bed in all kinds of ways.

Why does my breathing sound so loud?

"What are you looking at?" he asks, leaning over my shoulder.

"The gift Letty brought earlier. It was so kind of her."

"She owes you more than that after Clo—"

"She owes me nothing," I say as I angle my head his way. A mistake, as I watch him reach back to rub the nape of his neck. The flash of dark hair under his arm shouldn't twist my insides. The pop of his bicep, the muscle and sinew flexing in his chest, I'll forgive myself for, at least.

"What do you think our baby's first word will be?"

"I don't know," I say with a low chuckle. "But something tells me you're about to say *daddy.*"

"Daddy," he repeats. "Mind blowing, right?" When his gaze catches mine, his pleasure just shines.

"Yeah," I whisper. "And look at these." I reach for one of the tiny white cotton rosebuds from the box. "They're socks." I press my finger under one, unfurling the bud to reveal that truth. "Look how small they are," I say, my demand awe filled.

"And they'll probably be too big. Initially, at least."

"You think?" I watch his face, wondering if he's teasing me.

"When Clo was born, I could fit her whole body on my forearm." He moves to demonstrate, his hand cradling an invisible head. I have two very different thoughts, seeing that. One, it's good that one of us has held a baby before. Two, my God, I can't wait to see Matt bare chested and cradling our babe.

"Oh!" I make a wholly involuntary noise as I suffer a sudden twinge in my back and arch from the stool, trying to relieve the tension.

"Put your hands on the counter."

Feelings riot through me at the command, need crawling through my insides like kudzu. "It's just—"

"Your back is sore. Let me give it a bit of a rub."

"There's no need." I shake my head, even as every fiber of me yearns to do as he says. "It was just a little twinge."

"It might do some good. It helped Letty when she was carrying Clo."

When he puts it like that, it sounds so normal. So unsexual. So why are my nipples as hard as doorknobs?

"I promise, no funny business."

"That's not . . ." Come on, idiot. Matt is nothing if not a gentleman. *Except when he's not.* A time I remember fondly. And often. But this is a dangerous game I'm playing, my head and my libido at odds. Maybe this is what happens when you're touch starved. *And feeling a little bruised. A little vulnerable.*

"Ryan?"

"Okay." I give a vigorous nod to seal the unsexy deal. Because this means something different to him.

"Yeah?"

Can't blame him for his surprise. "Why not." I flip the book closed, ignoring the tremble in my hand as I slide it across the countertop. This is not a question of getting an itch scratched but—

"Good girl," he whispers, moving to stand behind me.

My hand stills on the book. Man, that tiny phrase feels like *life goals*. Even more so as Matt slides my braid over my shoulder, the edge curling like a question mark around my right nipple.

Lord, give me the strength to survive this.

"Deep breath," he murmurs, pressing his palms against the backs of my shoulders.

I inhale, exhale, and he does too, judging by the air that skims the nape of my neck. A moment later, he begins to work, to apply his magic really, his fingers and thumbs easily unknotting the tension in my too-tight shoulders.

It's nice. So nice. Being touched like this, almost held. Being cared for.

A long stroke from neck to tailbone makes me sigh.

"Good?"

I nod my head, and Matt repeats the motion again and again, like a cat kneading a blanket. Only a blanket doesn't bite its lip to keep from moaning or demanding more.

"How's the pressure?"

Building, I think. *Bursting like a dam if we're not careful.*

I nod, not trusting myself to answer as his low tone adds to the effect, stroking like a caress.

"Push back. Yeah, just like that."

Why does everything sound so sexual? Not that I fight it, and I do as he says when he presses his palm to my tailbone.

"Oh, God!" My word dam breaks on that, the exclamation like a long, pleasure-filled sigh.

"Good?"

"You don't know . . ." *what you're doing to me.*

"It would be better if you were lying down."

My stuttering laughter sounds almost like an agreement.

"No, really." Amusement lightens his answer, too, and all I can think is it's a good thing he can't see my face. "Let me..." He moves to the side, his arm coming around me. "Just for balance," he reassures me, his arm pressing just above my bump. "Jesus, that feels—"

"Don't stop," I whisper, capturing his arm with mine and holding him there.

The air around us stills, and I tighten my eyes like a toddler's version of *It wasn't me*.

No, no. I didn't ask you to hold me while you keep rubbing that spot, because for some dang reason, it's getting me off. How is that even possible? I just know that it is as my body begins to vibrate like a struck tuning fork.

Meanwhile, Matt says nothing. I can't even hear him breathe.

Meanwhile, my breath is definitely audible as I suck in a long breath.

"Like that?" he asks, his palm returning.

I nod as he presses tighter, then rotates. I bite back my direction of *Harder, more*, my fingers piercingly tight where I grip his forearm.

"I..." I can't make myself stop.

"It's just tension, Ryan."

"Hormones," I whisper. *Whore moans,* it sounds in my head. God, I want to make some. "I can't believe..."

"You've never been pregnant before."

"I've never felt like this. Never needed."

Another pause, those words sinking in.

"Then... let me."

The pleasure kudzu explodes, twining through me and pulling tight as thoughtless words spill from my mouth. "I sincerely hope this didn't happen to your sister."

He laughs, and I'm glad he does. Because that sounded so weird.

"Teacup, let me help relieve this pent-up pressure."

I drop my head with a sigh. *If he only knew how much pressure.* It's one thing for him to touch me in a nonsexual way but quite another to admit that my brain and body have twisted that touch into something else. Something that makes my insides pulse and ache as though I'm moments away from climax.

"Let me make you feel good." Such temptation in those quiet words. Understanding, even. "It's just a massage."

But we both know that it's not.

"And what happens tomorrow?" My whisper sounds almost panic filled.

"Nothing. Unless you want me to do it again."

"Be serious, Matt."

"Whatever you want," he says so softly. "We can talk it out. Or pretend it never happened. Lady's choice."

My insides, oh, how they pulse with remembrance. "It complicates things."

"It doesn't have to." His voice is smoky. Sexual. And his hand curls around my hip, but doesn't hold as it glides upward, his thumb like a tiny mallet dragged along the xylophone of my ribs.

I guess I must be musical too, as I give a little hum.

"Ryan." His hand makes a frame for my breast, cupping the weight of it. "You can tell me to stop. And I will."

I bite back a pleasured whimper as his thumb swipes over my hard nipple.

"Would it help if I said how much I've dreamed of this? How I've imagined touching you. Tasting you."

"Hush." Don't talk. *Don't make this too real.*

"Then be a good girl. And turn around."

"What?"

"Didn't I tell you I was hungry?"

I allow him to turn me, and like iron filings to a magnet, my fingers are drawn immediately to his chest. *So warm and solid to the touch.*

"You're beautiful." His eyes shine golden as he reaches for the end of my braid, bringing it to his mouth.

"You were watching." Pleasure threads through my accusation as he swipes it across his lips.

"Enviously."

I give a soft, flattered laugh.

"I'd like to kiss you." A beat passes, and when I don't object, the light turns his dark hair glossy as he dips his head. Lower than I imagined, because his mouth is hot and wet and magic as it closes over my nightshirt-covered nipple.

I moan. Oh, God, how I moan, the feeling immense as that sucking pull resonates deep between my legs.

"Can I?" His question is tentative as he tugs on the cotton of my nightshirt.

"I don't . . ." *know.* I feel so conflicted. I want this, but—

"Please." That word, the need in it, undoes me. I begin to gather my nightshirt myself, and we both work to pull it over my head.

Heavy lidded, his gaze drinks me in. My breasts, the hard pebbles of my nipples. My rounded stomach, my softer hips. My simple cotton panties.

"You're so beautiful, Ryan."

I give a tiny gasp as his hands cup my breasts, and his mouth returns, his tongue swirling across a stiff bud. My moan sounds ragged as he sucks it hotly into his mouth.

"You're so, *so* lovely. Strong. Yet delicate, my little teacup."

My body seems to understand before my brain does as he dips, his hands coming around me as he lifts me to the countertop.

And then it's all over but the crying out.

Chapter 29
MATT

Romero family group chat, without the *aul wans*. The old ones, also known as the parents.

ME: I have an announcement to make.

HUGO: Yr gay?

SEBASTIEN: But not the good kind.

LOLA: Yeah, not the actual gay kind of gay.

LUCÍA: He's not cool enough for that. Matt is the late noughties, crap kind of gay.

LETTY: When are you lot gonna grow up?

HUGO: When you lick the back of my ballbag.

LETTY: That's a charming thing to say to your sister.

HUGO: Sorry. I'm not well. I'm still in my bed.

LETTY: What's wrong?

HUGO: Whiskey mostly.

SEBASTIEN: And a run of shite games.

HUGO: Do you wanna go home in a box?

ME: Getting back to me ...

LOLA: There he goes, main charactering again.

LUCÍA: That's where Matt gets it from. The aul wans are all for main charactering.

LETTY: Are you two talking in tongues?

LUCÍA: Story checks out. The parentals think this thread is for arranging their birthday presents and stuff.

ME: Fuck's sake. Are you all done?

HUGO: Done in. Can we get this over so I can go back to bed?

SEBASTIEN: You're in bed right now. And not alone, dick fingers.

LOLA: Dick fingers? Actually, don't answer that.

SEBASTIEN: Because everything he touches, he fucks.

HUGO: You're just jealous because you didn't pull last night.

MATT: SHUT THE FECK UP, THE LOT OF YOUSE!

HUGO: But at least you get more action than Matt.

SEBASTIEN: Father O'Flannery gets more action than Matt.

LUCÍA: Matt, *youse* isn't a real word.

LOLA: No wonder he doesn't have a girlfriend.

ME: Hilarious. But you're all wrong because I'm about to become a father.

HUGO: You're such a gobshite.

LETTY: It's true.

LOLA: HE TOLD YOU FIRST?!?!

ME: Blame Clodagh and her flapping lugs.

SEBASTIEN: Clodagh knows you used a surrogate?

ME: Feck off.

LETTY: Her name is Ryan. She's very nice. And she's living at Matt's place. They're in this together but not to-GETH-er.

ME: Thanks for that, Letty. Next time I'll let you break the news.

SEBASTIEN: Matt . . . she already did.

ME: Ah, Letty. Fuck's sake.

LETTY: Sorry. I was too excited for you.

SEBASTIEN: Congrats, big bro.

LOLA: Yes, congratulations, Matty!

LUCÍA: Same.

HUGO: I'm pretty sure there are wiser beings out in the fields chewing grass than you.

ME: . . .

Well, that went about as well as I expected.

Chapter 30
RYAN

Twenty-five weeks, and my bump no longer looks like it might be the result of a big meal. Matt's baby bible informs us that the bean is a big as a cucumber now, but I'm thinking this bump looks more like half a pumpkin. And I cannot contemplate what half a pumpkin might do to my vagina, never mine a full-grown one.

I might never have sex again.

And speaking of, the day following my needy kitchen cave, I couldn't look him in the face. Meanwhile, true to his word, Matt carried on as though everything was normal. As though my hormones weren't responsible for turning his back massage X-rated.

In the cold light of day, alone and in my own bed, I googled my reactions, and it turns out I wasn't losing my mind. A person can actually orgasm from a massage of the sacral region. Of course, the orgasm that followed had nothing to do with a back massage.

But I'd felt so close to Matt, and his touch was . . . Well, I needed it. The connection and closeness. I needed his hot breath and whispered words. His fingers, his tongue. All that bliss.

The experience certainly hit the spot. *A couple of times.*

And because I'm not as good at pretending as Matt is, I brought it up. Spoke the words. Mainly to say it couldn't happen again. And he was so casual about it—"Yeah, okay."

His response should've helped, not stung, right? But ignorance is bliss, so they say.

Not that I could feign ignorance at my next clinic appointment. As I lay on the bed trying not to react to the weight of Matt's dark gaze on me. Or remember how his tongue felt inside me.

Hot Doc Travers, as I now refer to him—though not to his face, obviously—had suggested we might learn our baby's sex during the scheduled scan. We declined. Matt is a fan of surprises, so he says. Me, not so much. But discovering our baby's sex seems like a reality I'm not quite ready for. I'm not sure that even makes much sense.

MATT: What's on the menu tonight?

I give in to a tiny smile. Matt's afternoon text is right on schedule.

ME: You tell me. Mary is your chef.

MATT: Yeah, but you can probably smell it.

ME: How do you know I'm home?

MATT: Because I didn't see you last night.

ME: And that means . . .

MATT: That means, statistically speaking, I will tonight. Not that you're avoiding me. Or rationing our time together or anything, right?

I frown down at my phone and take the coward's way out.

ME: Statistically? Are you a secret quantitative data gatherer?

MATT: I've been called worse.

ME: Does that stuff get you hot?

Danger! Danger! I need to rewind time, because my fingers were too quick for my brain!

MATT: I think you know what gets me hot, Ryan.

ME: Yes, but we agreed not to speak about it.

MATT: And I know what gets you hot.

ME: Matt, we can't have this conversation.

Not when it already has me hot under the waistband. Not that I have a waist currently.

MATT: You started it.

ME: And you're riding too much into it.

ME: Reading—you're reading too much into the conversation, I mean.

Riding was something I dreamed of last night. And not a horse in sight. Matt is hung—
Stop.
I guess it's safe to say our little dalliance last month didn't really help my hormones any.

MATT: But am I? I don't really think so.

My heart gives a little pinch. I was hoping he didn't care either way.
No, that's not true. I was hoping he wouldn't notice.
Okay, so that's a lie too.
I know he's not dumb, but I was mostly hoping he wouldn't call me out. *Rationing our time together.* That's exactly what I've been doing.

MATT: By the way, my parents are coming to visit next month. I hope that's okay.

Is it strange that I love that Matt texts in whole words? I like a lot about him, and I know he likes me too. And the time we spend together is companionable. Mostly. Mostly if I ignore my back-massage hiccup.

I tell myself we're friends, that our chemistry is natural, given our brief but very real past. But that it's not something we needed to act on. *Again.* Except, sometimes I see the way he looks at me and I get butterflies deep down inside. But it's more than just a physical attraction, because the way I like him as a person, a human, a man, feels bone deep.

ME: It's your house.

MATT: And it's your home. Plus, they're not coming to visit me. Not really.

ME: They know our situation, right?

MATT: I told them. I'm not sure it makes much sense to them, but when they're here, it will.

I'm not sure it makes much sense to me sometimes. It makes brain-based sense, at least. The heart and the libido are other matters entirely.

MATT: I did wonder how long it would take the aul wan to check her message bank.

ME: The aul what?

MATT: Aul wan is how we refer to our mother in the Irish vernacular.

ME: Old one, I'm guessing?

MATT: You guessed right.

ME: I also guess you don't call your mother that to her face.

MATT: I would never say such a thing in her hearing. Not without expecting a slap around the ear.

ME: You're never too big for one of those.

MATT: Never too big and never too old, apparently. Also, I told my siblings about us.

Us. So many thoughts and feelings and meanings in that tiny word. So much confusion. Opportunity. *Temptation.*

ME: How did that go?

MATT: Fine. Nothing to report. I expect we won't see them until after the baby is born.

ME: Okay.

MATT: Seb has uni, supposedly. It's the middle of the football season for Hugo. And the twins, Lucía and Lola, are currently working their way around Australia.

ME: You didn't tell me they were twins. Wow, biological bullet dodged!

MATT: Our hypothetical twins would be nothing like those hellions. But the longer that lot stay away, the better. They're like a swarm of locusts. They fly in. Consume all the beer and food in the house, and piss off again before you know where you are.

ME: Your siblings or your mom and dad?

MATT: Ryan made a funny.

ME: Hey, so, what do you call your dad?

MATT: Antonio, when he's not listening. Otherwise, aul fella. The pair is also referred to as ma and da. And collectively as the aul wans.

ME: Just so you know, this child will not be referring to me as an aul wan or ma. Maaaaaaaa! Sounds like a sheep.

MATT: We'll be Mammy & Daddy? Or Mommy in your speak.

That sounds so weird. And also kind of nice.

MATT: Anyway, I've told Letty she can unmuzzle Clo now.

ME: I do hope you meant that metaphorically.

Two minutes later my phone buzzes again.

MATT: Cats or dogs?

ME: For dinner?

MATT: Ryan made another funnee.

ME: I'm here all week!

MATT: I was hoping to keep you much longer than that.

My heart gives a little pinch.

MATT: So which one?

ME: I've never owned a pet.

I should've just chosen one. There was no need to admit that.

MATT: Not even a goldfish?

ME: Oh, yeah. I had a fish once. I got him at a county fair when I was 12.

MATT: What was his name?

ME: David Swimmer.

MATT: Ah, a preteen FRIENDS fan.

ME: Reruns were always available.

MATT: So not a cat or dog person but a fishy friend.

ME: I can't really say. He only lived a handful of hours.

Hell, why is all this stuff coming up now?

MATT: Fairground fish aren't destined for longevity, sadly.

Not with the stepfather I had at the time. Stepfather of the month, probably, though it sometimes seemed as though they were only around a matter of days.

My mother bitched about a fish needing a fishbowl and where the hell was I gonna get one of those. I put him in a plastic dish and said I'd figure it out tomorrow. I'd probably go into town, to the dollar store. They'd have something there. Maybe I'd even wait until the afternoon, when she was sometimes in a better mood. Mornings were rough for her, coming down from last night's liquor and the fighting with the boyfriend du jour. By afternoon, she would be well on her way again, but there was often a short period between hungover and drunk where she was more amenable. Or less mean, at least.

Not that I got to test that theory after the asshole boyfriend sneaked into my room that night, claiming he just wanted to help. We were friends, weren't we? He said he'd give me some money to solve my little problem. *No doubt if I helped him with his.*

I told him to get out—that if he didn't leave *right now*, I'd scream so loud they'd hear me in the next county. I also told him I slept with a knife and that I wasn't afraid to use it. By that age, I was well versed in fighting talk.

His revenge was to make my goldfish disappear overnight and said if I told anyone about our "little conversation," I'd be the next one to vanish.

It's weird how sad I was about that damn fish for months.

Also weird is how I've never thought of that night in years. It's not really a story worth recounting. I haven't before. I'm not about to do so now as I send my last text of the exchange.

ME: It was nice while it lasted.

I wonder if Matt will say the same, looking back on this experience. I'd like to think he'll have fonder memories of me than I have of my fish.

Chapter 31
MATT

Fucking Theta.

I hate that my instincts were on point. That I was right about them and her prick of an ex.

I pull out my phone as I thunder along the street, my mood as black as the clouds overhead. I should've looked into this earlier, but I've been so caught up with work. *And with her.* Maybe I could've done something, mitigated the damage. Though would she have wanted to still work there? I know the answer to that would be *Fuck no*.

It's so fucking wrong. Gender bias. Pay imbalances. Glass ceilings. Harassment and discrimination. The finance world is like a boys' club, and the proof is in the conversation I just had with Theta's CFO.

According to him, it seems news of Ryan's transfer to London—and her effective promotion—reached the ears of her weasel of an ex. Because that fucker took time out of his day to have lunch with the fund manager of Theta's New York office, then pretty much destroyed her character over prime rib at the Grill. And bad news travels fast, whether it's true or not, because people just *love* to share the misfortunes of others.

Well, fuck them, which is pretty much how our conversation concluded.

And fuck you, Nigel. You've crossed the wrong man.

Not only have they lost a valuable asset, but they've also pissed off the man standing behind her.

I press a button, and the call connects.

"Matías." Oliver's cut-glass tone echoes down the line.

"You know how we're looking for collab partners for the North 1 project?" A mixed-use urban redevelopment in Manchester. We're diversifying our partners. Looking for new ones, basically.

"Yes." His one-word answer sounds pretty suspicious.

"Well, Theta isn't it."

"According to the feedback I received from Nigel, they're very interested."

"Is that Nigel, the CFO?"

"Yes, that's him."

"That'd be the fella I just told to stick his dick in his ear."

"Any particular reason?"

"I believe I implied—*no*. Actually, *implied* isn't a strong enough word. I *instructed* the spineless arsehole to stick his dick in his fucking lughole to see if he could shag some fucking sense into his own head!"

"And is there any reason you're yelling that at me?"

"Sorry, no. I'm just fucked off. Annoyed." I rake my hand through my hair when what I want to do is punch something. *Someone.* Preferably the man at the root of all this.

"Understood. Well, I suppose I'll inform Andrew to strike them from the list."

"Probably for the best."

"Are we removing them from one list and adding them to another?"

"What other list?"

"The 'hurt-my-woman-and-I'll-fuck-up-your-world list,' I suppose we can call it. Or perhaps the 'list of destruction'? Yes, I prefer that."

"Why, Oliver," I begin, my footsteps slowing and my lips tipping upward, equally as slowly. "You sentimental old . . ."

"Less of the *old*, thank you."

"Is this what the love of a good woman does to a man?" My smile, there's no reining it in now. "I thought it was supposed to make you soft."

"Soft with them, Matías. Ruthless with everyone else. And if anyone crosses them, hurts them. Well, then we rain down hell."

I don't answer. The man hit the nail on the head.

"And then, of course, there are the times we hurt them. Usually with our egos. Then we do what we can, what we must, to make it up to them. I don't suppose I have to tell you that."

I give a long sigh and catch sight of myself in a nearby window. I look like a mad fucker, my hair standing on end, like the kind of person you dread sitting next to you on the bus. Not that I've been on a bus in a while. And why do I look like a mad bus-riding vagrant? Because someone slighted Ryan and because I want to fucking crush them.

But that's about me, like Fin said. It's about my ego, not hers. And the thing I've been preparing for? The thing I said I wouldn't do without her say-so? I might've already changed my mind.

"I will say that I have a particularly tender spot for men who mistreat the women they once claimed to love," Oliver then says.

"You do, do you?"

"Yes. A particularly tender spot I like to hurt them."

"That sounds like dirty fighting."

"I meant their wallets, Matías."

"Of course you did. No common thuggery for you." *Leave that to me,* I think, pressing my phone between my ear and shoulder as

I crack my tense knuckles. I recall a beating I administered without her knowledge. *Or say-so.* "We can't have your ancestors turning in their graves, now can we?"

"Mausoleum."

"Of course." I roll my eyes and set off walking to the car again. "How silly of me to think they'd be put in common ground."

"I have things to do, Matías. Are we adding Theta to the list and waging war on hedge funds on two continents?"

"Not Theta," I say. I think Nigel might think twice now before believing industry gossip. My ego can calm the fuck down.

"Understood," he murmurs. "It's been a while since I ruined someone's livelihood."

"You sound like you're looking forward to it."

"This is not my play, Matías. But I wish you good fortune in your endeavors. Though I will say we are yet to meet the lady in question. The reason for all this."

"Yeah, I know. Soon," I add, almost crossing the fingers of my right hand.

"Not that I'd add undue pressure, but I might suggest you step up your security before Fin turns up on your doorstep."

I chuckle. The golden retriever of our pack. Well, he's not shagging my leg.

"It's just a question of time. Ryan's had a lot of adjustments to make."

Or am I just making excuses for her?

◆ ◆ ◆

"This wine is delicious." Ryan sets down her glass and leans back in her chair, arching the small of her back a touch.

"I ordered it from Oliver's wine merchant," I say, trying not to let my mind drift back a couple of weeks at the tiny reminder.

She looked so luscious draped across the counter, all dark eyed and replete.

I hope to God it isn't long before I can taste her again. To hold her in my arms as we look forward to our future together.

"The fella said you can get pretty decent nonalcoholic varieties of wine these days." Which is total shite, because the man wanked on and on about alcohol being needed to soften the tannins and smooth out acidity. He might also have bemoaned the "diabolical effect the process has on the mouthfeel." Christ, I wanted to feel his mouth with my fist by the time he shut up.

But I digress.

It's date night. At least, it is in my mind. Though the number per week is still mandated—*nay, controlled*—by my lovely companion, I look forward to these evenings over anything else.

A delicious meal, at home, of course, because anything outside these four walls might be misconstrued by the rest of the world. Little does she know we've been having romantic rendezvous at this table for months, and not just that time I pressed her to the countertop and ate her out.

God, I'm such a romantic.

But if we don't have romance, at least we have sex. Sort of. Or maybe that's just me, given I've taken to wanking myself half to death when she leaves to go back to her tiny apartment.

Tonight will be no different, I consider, as I allow my eyes to roam over her. She's so fucking beautiful. *Bountiful* is the word that springs to mind, not that I'd say it out loud because she'd probably misconstrue it as a variant of *large*. Even if her breasts are—no word of a lie—huge. Magnificent, even.

Her body is so much fuller this month. She's like a peach I want to sink my teeth into. In short, she makes my mouth water.

"How was your day?" *Dear,* I add mentally. *Mi mujer. Mi amor.*

"Fine." Her gaze slides to the table, where she moves her napkin an inch to the side. "I did a little research. Looking at a couple of new opportunities."

"Work or investments?"

At this, her gaze lifts. "Work is dead in the water."

"A temporary thing."

"Can't make connections in the UK. And I can't get my US connections to play ball."

"It'll all work out in the end."

"It better," she mutters.

"How's your portfolio going?"

"Looking for tips?" She gives a humorous twist to her lips.

"Always." *God, I love it when she wears her hair down,* I think with a happy sigh, watching how it curls softly around her shoulders. I also love finding her hair ties dotted around the house. It's like the Ryan version of a "Hansel and Gretel" breadcrumb trail.

"I'm up double figures."

"And that's why it'll work out," I say, pointing her way, my other fingers still wrapped around my glass.

"Thanks, Matt."

"What for? It's the truth. Who could resist those figures?"

Or that figure. Her outfit a soft gray woolen two-piece—ribbed for her comfort, not for my viewing pleasure, though I'm enjoying the vista just the same. Square necked and sleeveless, her dress clings to her body like a sheath, all the way to her ankles. Her arms and shoulders are covered by a matching and very cute little-old-lady-style cardigan. It looks kinda like an old-fashioned bed jacket, rounded at the edges and joined at the neck by a ribbon tied in a bow.

How the hell do I know what a bed jacket looks like? No idea. But I'd like to see it on my bedroom floor. And that ribbon . . . *Open me,* it seems to taunt. *Pull on my end!*

I wish Ryan would—

Fucking brain. I discreetly adjust myself under the table. I'm definitely losing my marbles. By the day, it seems.

Ryan reaches for her glass again, holds it up to the light, and says something. Something about the wine, probably. I don't know exactly what, my attention still pinned to that bow and all that lovely cleavage and the *now you see it, now you don't* effect.

Fuck, how I ache to get my hands on her.

"Are you done?"

That I hear, though it's more the tone that pulls me from my musing. Perving? Anyway, I lift my gaze to her very pointed one, but not without noting how glossy her lips look.

Did she just lick them?

"Done for now," I answer in an easy tone. I drop my napkin to the table and lean back in my chair.

"I wasn't talking about dinner."

"I know you weren't. But you can't blame a man for looking. Not when you're irresistible."

"I'm practically the size of a house," she scoffs.

"Must be a very compact house. A bijou abode."

Her mouth curls reluctantly, though she ducks her head to hide it.

"Actually, come to think of it, can I move in?"

"You." That's all she says. *You.* Though her cheeks turn a lovely pink hue. She also gives a long-suffering shake of her head.

"I'll take that as a no."

"As you can see," she says, putting her hands to her rounded stomach, "there's no room at the inn."

"Hmm. I do see. And you know what occurs to me?"

"I dread to think."

"While it was no immaculate conception, it was pretty fuckin' spectacular."

"What has gotten into you tonight?"

You, I want to repeat. *You've gotten into my head. And my heart.* But she's not ready to hear those admissions. Maybe it's just practice she needs.

More time on the countertop?

I get that she's alone in the world, that's she's had a shit upbringing, and there's probably more to it than a lack of pets and a bad mother. I wish she'd confide in me.

And at the same time, I know the reveal has to be on her terms.

I can't imagine being alone. I can't even imagine being an only child, though plenty of times I wished for it. Especially in a house with as many kids as my parents had, where the arses outnumbered the bathrooms. But adolescence aside, I'd hate to be without my siblings. My parents. My friends. How does she cope? Who does she turn to when she needs a pep talk or a kick up the arse? *Or a hedge fund ruining.*

No wonder being dumped by that prick did a number on her. And it did, because let's face it, no one goes to the lengths she did to be at his wedding. It wasn't just about the dicks she worked with. Or maybe I should say *about one of them*. It was about saving face.

It was about saying: *I'm here. I stand. You didn't beat me.*

How can anyone not admire her for that?

But I worry about it too. Her once-bitten-twice-shy attitude and her hyperindependence. Just the fact of these dinners, our time rationed, is absurd. Especially when I see how relaxed she becomes in my company. And how she looks at me when she thinks I'm not paying attention. I know I'd be good for her if she'd only let me try.

I've got time, I tell myself. There are more than ten weeks left of her pregnancy, for a start. Or maybe our time will come after the babe.

I just want that time now.

"So," she says, her tone and her discomfited wiggle signaling a change in the conversation. "What's new at the office?"

Work is such a big part of Ryan's life. Not being in the office must feel a bit like losing a limb. *Not for long, though.*

"You know how it is. Another day at the coalface, preserving the time value of money." The theory that a dollar today is worth more than a dollar next week due to its earning potential in the period between. In other words, investments. It's what Maven is known for. We invest in real estate mostly, and at the moment, we're big on urban redevelopment. This is partially down to Fin championing Mila's social causes. And that's fine for all concerned because we're still making a shit ton of money. Though Oliver maintains he's in debt up to his (still very wealthy) eyeballs, but that's down to his love for Evie. And how she persuaded him a stately home and safari park would make a good fixer-upper project.

Lions and tigers and labradoodles, oh, hell!

The things they've done for their wives. The ways they've changed and bended for love—I find that shit amazing.

"You make it sound like a calling," Ryan says, a light taunt to her tone. "Like you're doing it for the greater good."

"Well, the greater good counts."

"The greater good of your pockets."

I love it when she's in a feisty mood, when she's all hot and . . . clever. I love her hair down, her scattered hair ties, and when she has her glasses on . . . ah-mazing! She can be my demanding boss anytime.

"Are you saying you work in finance for the love of it, not for the money?" I parry.

"I don't know whether you've noticed, but I'm not working anywhere right now." She half stands and reaches across the small table toward my whiskey glass. "Can I just . . . sniff it?"

"Sure." I beat her to it, passing it over, relishing the brush of our fingertips like this is some Regency romance. *One that's not fade to black, please.* "Any particular reason?"

She gives a short inhale. "Maybe a weird craving."

"Did you have any of those? They happen earlier in the pregnancy, right?"

She nods. "Just for a few days. Pickles and ice cream. Together." With one last sniff, she passes my glass back, sliding it back across the table.

"What do you think?"

"Smells like malt and wood."

"Oak. From the barrels."

"And something sweet."

"But you don't like the taste?"

"Ask me again. After." Another tentative touch to her stomach as our gazes hold, and in the silence, I feel every beat of my heart. "So. Work." Her gaze darts away. "Let me live vicariously."

"Ah, you'll be back at it soon enough."

"I don't know. Do you know many mothers in hedge funds?"

I open my hands: *No idea.* My only interest is the mother-to-be sitting in front of me.

The one I'd like to eventually call my wife-to-be.

"I loved my job, and I was fucking good at it. What are you smiling about?"

I sit forward, putting my elbow to the table as I rub my hand across my jaw. "Do you know when you curse or say something . . . bad, for want of a better word, you put your hands to your stomach? Like you're covering Matt Junior's ears."

She frowns. "I don't—do I?"

"It's adorable."

"You think? Maybe you're just strange."

"The word you're looking for is *enchanted*."

"Enchanted," she repeats, sliding me a doubtful look.

"Like magic."

She lowers her eyes, her lashes veiling her thoughts. But I hope she's remembering a conversation about magic and spontaneity. And about disappearing body parts.

"You were saying?" I prompt. "About work?"

"Just that I'm looking forward to being a mother, but I just . . ." With a sigh, she lifts her shoulders and lets them fall. "I'm worried, I guess."

"I think that's entirely natural. I mean, I get moments of *My God, what happens if I drop him on his head*?"

"At least you've held a baby," she mutters.

"I have, sure. But this is different, Ryan. Like I've said before, we're in this together."

"I know you say that. I know you think you mean it, but I'm the one having this baby," she says, pressing her hands to her stomach again. "I'm the one whose body will bear the brunt. Whose brain will frazzle. Whose sleep and time will be taxed. I'll be the one responsible for the bulk of the caretaking. The one whose career will suffer."

Has suffered, I think with a frown.

"I can't help you carry this baby or deliver it, and honestly, thank Christ for that. If it was left up to men, the world would come to an end. But the rest is on me as much as it is you."

"The practicalities don't work that way. I'm gonna need to go back to work sometime, and—"

"I'll help."

"Help what?"

"With the baby. When he's here. And when you're ready to go back to work."

"Sure." She looks a little frustrated.

"You don't believe me?"

"I bet you usually work as many hours as I do. I know you're as passionate about your job as I am. Was. Unless your contribution is a nanny?"

"If that's what you want. I mean, yeah." I give a shrug. "It's not a bad idea as backup for when we're both up to our necks. But that's not what I'm talking about. I'm gonna be a hands-on dad, Ryan. That's the plan. I mean, realistically, neither of us knows what we're in for. But this is *our* baby, not just yours. Equal responsibilities. That's what I hope for."

"You'd really do that?"

Though I'm not sure she's convinced, her expression hard to decipher right now.

"Why wouldn't I? Especially when you'll be looking after my money."

"Your—what now?"

"I've decided to invest some money with you."

"But I'm not working." She shakes her head as though she can't have heard right.

"But you miss it, yeah?"

"Of course. It's all I've ever known."

Well, that's something. I have her intrigued. And that she hasn't shot me down is a good sign.

Chapter 32
RYAN

Equal responsibility. Can he really mean it?

"And I'm thinking the easiest way for you to help me, and for me to help you, is by proprietary investment."

"Um, what?" Weren't we just talking about babies, not business? *If he knew about the past, he wouldn't trust me with his money. He wouldn't trust me with his child.*

I push those thoughts away as he slants me a look that's pure indulgence.

"I know you don't need me to explain the term to you."

"I know what it is," I retort. "They're kind of the cowboys of the finance world."

"Some might say so. But I generally don't give a fuck for the opinions of others, especially where money is concerned. Besides, I won't have to worry about reputations with you at the helm."

"At the . . . I don't know what you're talking about." He seemed so sincere about parenting. And now this? It's not baby brain that's making it hard to keep up with him.

"I thought about setting up a hedge fund. But honestly, the regulations here in the UK are tough. The whole process would be a total ball ache. A lot of paperwork, and hoops to jump through.

Headaches and legalities. Plus, these things take forever to set up. And you're at a loose end now." He opens his hands. "This is the right way forward, I think."

"The right way forward is a prop fund? Right for who?"

"It's not perfect, but it'll work. For now. As for who, this will be a prop fund with me as your only investor."

"Matt, I can't take your money—you can't do this." He's already done way too much for me.

"Let me shoulder some of the responsibility in the ways I can."

Is that what this is? Or is it an act of charity?

"I think you'll find I can. I know I can. Have, in fact. I've been working on this for weeks."

"But why?" I press my hands to my cheeks as though their burning doesn't answer that question loudly enough.

"It's good for a portfolio to have diversity. You don't think I have all my money in Maven, do you?"

"I don't know." I heard Maven mostly deals in real estate. Big deals. Billion-dollar stakes. Stately homes, phallic towers, and vast urban developments. Not daily trading. That's small potatoes. *Isn't it?* "I don't know what you do with your money, but I do know you're no rube. You must already have reams of people investing on your behalf."

"Not in the field I want you to invest in. On my behalf."

"So get someone with a track record," I answer. "Don't do this for me."

"For you. For me." He pauses, his expression hardening. "Do you think I haven't checked you out? That I haven't done my due diligence? We're having a baby together, sure. But that's not why I'm investing. Shit, Ryan, you should be asking why *not* you."

"I don't need you to tell me I'm good—I *know* I'm good. Which is why it's been so hard to accept my situation. Why won't those fuckers return my calls?"

"Come on," he almost cajoles. "You know why."

"I don't. But I can surmise." And I have surmised. I just didn't want to acknowledge the truth. *Because it feels like one more thing out of my control.*

"Stinky Pete." Matt lifts his whiskey as though in a toast. But he's not toasting Pete, so what could he be . . . "Shall we fuck him up?"

"For revenge?" Something blooms instantly inside me. Is it excitement or alarm?

"We could do it just for shits and giggles. Or we could do it because he's a misogynistic twat who deserves what's coming to him."

"There's more than just him to consider." There's Annabelle. Why would I hurt her?

"And if we *really* want to do it well, we could get the SEC involved."

"Then you'd be ruining livelihoods." But he'd do that for me, make Annabelle lose her standing and her town house. But the people I worked with would also lose.

"Maybe, but not mine. And not yours," he says casually.

"This isn't you, Matt."

"Because I'm a nice guy?" His jaw tautens and his gaze turns flinty, but the change is fleeting, as his expression clears and he adds, "It's just food for thought. Of course, you might want to do it yourself someday."

"Do I strike you as the vengeful type?" I ask him quietly.

He gives a shrug, and ugliness bubbles up inside me. Because I have ugly. There's a side of me that no one sees. A part of me I keep on a very short leash. But the joys of retribution are short lived. Revenge might be sweet, but it weighs heavy on the soul, I know.

I have a choice—I always have a choice. And my choice is not to live that way.

Not ever again.

"I think he's probably done now, anyway," he adds. "You're out of his reach. His little range."

And under Matt's arm. At least, metaphorically.

"He's tried his best." Matt sighs. "And I'm sure his mother still loves his disappointing face."

"I hope Annabelle has an affair with her personal trainer," I say, swiping up my glass. So it seems I'm not *quite* done with ugliness, though I've tried to ignore the fact that he was at the bottom of my unanswered emails and calls that rang out. *Low-life bastard.*

"You can do better than that."

My head jerks up, as though Matt heard. "I am doing better than that," I retort. "Let him live in the past and plot revenge. I don't dwell, and I don't think of him."

"That's something I'd raise a toast to." He toys with his glass but doesn't lift it yet. "And the other . . . my proposition?"

I put down my wine and roll my lips together as I allow myself a moment to look long into his play. There are pitfalls, sure. Emotional ones. He's already offered me so much, but at what cost? To me? To him? On the financial side, the worst that could happen is I underperform—which I won't—and he takes his investment elsewhere. Which would leave me right where I started.

Across the table, he cants his head, his eyes so gold right now. He's like a cat watching a mouse tread carefully around a pretty cheese-laden trap.

"You invest for yourself. Why not for me?"

"It's not the same. I'm just doing it to make up for lost salary." And to keep myself sane.

"What are your numbers like? I heard you say *double figures*, but what's the exact number?"

"I'm up twenty-three percent since I started."

"Those are good numbers," he says, with an impressed tilt of his head.

"I know" comes my somewhat cocky answer. "But my track record isn't long. If you want to know how I did at Dreyland—"

"That I already know." He taps the side of his nose. "Due diligence."

If he knew the real me, knew what I've done in my life to be where I am, we wouldn't be having this conversation.

"Twenty-three percent," he repeats. "Reckon you can do that for me?"

"Matt, please." *Stop tempting me with your pretty words and your pretty mouth.*

"We'll start with an initial investment of two million."

"I haven't invested two mill of my own," I say quickly. Because I don't have that kind of money available. *Is that like pocket change to him?*

"But you've done it for clients."

"Clients of a hedge fund. That's a different game. A different kind of investing—rarely is it personal wealth."

"But if you had two million of your own to invest, would you let someone else run those plays?"

"No," I answer immediately as my palms begin to itch. God, I want this, the old Ryan pushing at me. The girl with an instinct for a good deal.

"That's because you know no one can do it like you."

"With the backup, the office systems, the quants and stuff. But this? It's a lot of money, a lot to gamble with, which is essentially what you're asking me to do."

"At a rate of twenty-three percent? I'll take that gamble. Let me invest two million with you."

Under the table I ball my hands into fists. I want to—it's so goddamn tempting. I love what I do, what I did, but this is essentially another favor he's doing me. One I can't hold at arm's length by paying him rent.

"If not you, I'll just take the money elsewhere."

"Not to a prop fund, you won't."

"Well, not your prop fund. Think about it, Ryan. It's not the mode that interests me. It's the returns."

"What would you expect from me?"

"Have I expected too much from you so far?"

I give a tiny shake of my head. He's demanded nothing but given so much. "It's not just the returns, though." *It's not the real reason we're having this discussion.*

"No strings, Ryan. I'm investing in you. I have faith in *you*."

Faith. It's such a small word with a huge meaning. *Fuck it.*

"What are the terms?" I demand, looking up. *Like a fish unable to resist a pretty lure.*

"Two million, no drawdowns. We cap the risk at two hundred grand. Lots capped at twenty." Which means I'm not getting the money in small, drawn-down amounts. I can hit the ground running. It also means an individual investment can't go above £200K, as a way of protecting his money. *Smart.* Plus, I can make a maximum of twenty investments at my discretion.

"The risk?" I demand next.

"I'll bear it."

"And the profit split?" My heart begins to beat. If he makes it ridiculously beneficial for me—or worse? *Then I'll tell him to shove it up his ass.*

"Sixty-forty." He makes a gesture with his hand. "To the trader, obviously."

My heart does a little two-step beat. That's not terrible.

"Seventy-thirty," I counter with an imperious lift of my chin.

He pretends to consider it for a moment, when I cut in.

"And I'll want to revisit that when I get you to twenty-three percent."

"You drive a hard bargain, teacup."

Is he impressed or amused as his mouth curls almost reluctantly? Whatever it is, the moniker falls directly into my lap, thrumming away down there. Sensations, so many of them. Thoughts and feelings and fears and gratitude, none of which I can afford to lift the lid on.

"Those are my terms." I'm so glad my answer doesn't betray my internal world. "Your money. No other clients. I work on behalf of you only."

Matt leans across the table, holding out his hand. "You've got yourself a deal."

"Good." My smaller hand meets his, excitement and pleasure flowing through my veins.

"Tell me something." He puts his hand over mine, effectively trapping me. "Tell me anything."

"We're still playing that game?"

Until I know all your secrets, his eyes seem to say.

Not in this lifetime.

"Oh!" I press my free hand to my stomach before my attention snaps up. "The baby just moved!"

"Really?" His eyes wide, he drops my hand and rounds the table so fast. "This the first time?" he demands, dropping to his knee, his words full of wonder.

"I . . . yeah. I've had these kind of tiny butterfly sensations, but nothing like this," I say, feeling a twinge that I haven't shared this with him. But our kitchen encounter . . .

"Can I—can I feel?"

His tone is so sweet. I nod and swallow as he allows me to take his hand and press it where I felt that flurry.

A beat passes. Two. Three.

"Nothing." He stares down at my stomach, his smile not quite holding.

"It'll happen again—more and more," I answer quickly, trying to reassure him.

"Course it will." His expression turns soft. Then bright as his head jerks up. "I felt that!"

"Me too. It feels like a goldfish bumping the side of a plastic bag."

"We're not calling him David Swimmer!" The words bound out of him delightedly. "How about Flipper," he says, staring down.

"It's gender neutral, I guess."

"Flipper, you and your gorgeous mommy just made my day."

Chapter 33
RYAN

Twenty-nine weeks, and I have two million pounds in an investment account. I also have an office—a home office on the same floor as Matt's—with a window overlooking the garden and a picture-perfect window seat.

The room wasn't an office the day little Flip did her thing—that's how we're referring to the baby now. From me, it's still "She's moving—Flip is kicking—come quickly and feel!" And from Matt: "So strong, Flipper, my maneen—my little man. We'll have you kicking conversions for Ireland in no time."

Another game we're still playing, but I digress.

The morning after Flip's first flip, my office was a bedroom. By the end of that day, it looked like something out of an interiors magazine. In fact, an interior designer turned up that morning unannounced, carrying a half dozen concept boards, mood boards, and Lord knows what else.

We chatted, I made my choices in a daze, and then by the time Matt got home that evening, the contractors were already finished. My complaints fell on deaf ears, but my thanks were well received when I threw myself against him in a hug.

And he hugged me back, and his hug was solid. Fortifying. Like a power pack, recharging my world.

Working from home—though not *my* home—is pretty great. It's warm and it's comforting, and I can pop down and chat with Mary when she's here. I have everything I need—software, hardware, a desk the size of a runway, and an office chair that looks like it belongs in a spaceship.

Got to take care of those back muscles. And I don't mean by spontaneous orgasms.

The work isn't taxing. It's fun and exhilarating—like playing the slots. Sometimes frustrating, but that's okay because I love it. And it means I have something else to concentrate on and something else to talk about when Matt is home.

"They always leave. Did I not teach you anything, girl?"

I press my hand to my stomach as though to protect my baby. Protect her from who, though? My mother is dead.

Who's gonna protect her from you?

My heart begins to pound, and I practically stumble like a drunk to the pretty window seat. This is not happening now, I recite silently as I drop to the cushions. I made my peace with my past, with my decisions. I stepped away from all that rage, all that hate . . .

I put aside my yearning and my mother want. I made peace with the reality she couldn't be that for me.

Merciless. The word echoes in my head.

How could she expect mercy when she had so little for me?

I glance out the window, the aged glass distorting the view of the garden ever so slightly. Spring sunshine spills over a lawn recovering from a cold winter. Birds hop around a pond; a willow's branches seem to offer a hug to the ground. Inside the room, I wish there was someone to hug me.

All I wanted was to be loved. To be shown a little kindness.

In the place of that embrace, I wrap my hands around my stomach.

Matt would hug me, given the chance. Because he's decent and kind and generous and good, and maybe that's what happens when you grow up in a regular family. You learn to be loved. And how to show love.

He loves our baby. He'd love me too, if I'd let him.

But I won't let him, because if he knew the truth, it would ruin everything.

He deserves someone better than me. Someone better than a killer queen.

Chapter 34
RYAN

Thirty-four weeks, I think, glancing down at my bump. Baby Flip is the size of a cantaloupe, according to the baby book. And according to Hot Dr. T., she's ahead of the curve and probably not far off the size of a small watermelon.

Because her daddy is country strong.

As the sentiment echoes in my head, my mouth curls before I let rip a giggle because there's no one around for me to have to explain to. It's one of the things I remember thinking about Matt the night we met. Despite the tux and his polished appearance, the man looked country strong.

And it seems his offspring is following in his footsteps. I'm gonna have a daughter who'll play basketball. She'll be eight years old, and I'll be holding her hand while looking up, not down, at her. But that's okay because I'll love her so much. As will everyone else.

Little Flip is ahead of the curve in another way too. Her head is already engaged. And though that sounds terrifying, Dr. T. assures me it's perfectly normal.

I'm having a baby. Real soon!

Last night, Matt had arranged a group call with his family, so I got to meet them virtually. His parents hadn't visited as they had planned. They were needed in Spain after Matt's grandfather took a nasty tumble. He broke a hip, but he's had surgery and is on the mend.

Meanwhile, Matt thought chatting with me might be a good distraction for them, something to lift their spirits. Can't say I have ever been referred to as uplifting, but I understood his sentiments. That's not to say I wasn't looking forward to the call like I would a pelvic exam.

Anyhoo, next thing, the call became a whole thing—a group call with the Romero tribe. Letty and Clo from their home in North London; Sebastien and Hugo, his brothers in Spain; the supposed hellion twins, Lola and Lucía—who seemed very lovely—from their apartment in Sydney; Catherine and Antonio, Matt's parents; and even his cute *abuelo* from his hospital bed in Cádiz.

My baby has a grandmother, a grandfather, and a great-grandfather who all can't wait to meet her. And uncles and aunts who laughingly said they were good for gifts but not to put them down for babysitting duties. Except for Letty, that is. Matt replied that was fine—that he wouldn't trust them with a guinea pig. Which then prompted Clo to ask where her Uncle Matty got a guinea pig and say how unfair it was that she wasn't allowed one. The call was a blast! Raucous and loud, people talking over each other, arguing and laughing and calling each other names while Antonio, Matt's dad, played the straight man.

This family. They just vibe. I'm so happy little Flip will get to be one of them. So happy she'll be loved by them.

◆ ◆ ◆

Thirty-four and a half weeks, and I am huge. Just enormous! My stomach has grown so much, I feel like it's changed my center of gravity. But my skin is fantastic—I'm frickin' glowing—and I have the hair of a supermodel, all swishy and glossy.

On the not-so-good side, I'm as horny as all get-out.

My poor wand will be worn out by the time this baby arrives.

I caved and bought a new one after Matt and I . . . yeah, that.

I didn't bring my favored model from the US—I dumped it before I left. There were the voltage issues to consider, but more than that, no way was I going to be stopped coming through customs with that thing.

Anything to declare?

One overworked sex toy and a crush on an Irish sex worker, m'kay?

An Irish sex worker who turned out to be kind of perfect. For Flip, at least.

No need to include me in that equation.

Sex on the brain turned out to be a moment at the clinic a couple of days ago when I went for a routine scan. I couldn't look the poor tech in the eye after she whipped out the probe thingy, my mind bending to the previous night, when I'd used my wand and I'd tried not to think about Matt. Inevitably, my brain had gone there anyway, and seeing him there, in the room, watching me as I lay on that bed in that totally unsexual and sterile setting, still made me feel all shivery.

Maybe I'm just a pervert. Or maybe it was those eyes, the intensity in that green-gold gaze.

When the tech produced a bottle of lube, I had to bite my lip to keep from announcing I was so turned on, that wouldn't be necessary. I began to giggle at the ridiculous thought, embarrassed and, yes, still kind of turned on. I snort-laughed and almost peed myself, Matt's attention turning from intense to bemused. When he asked later what had made me laugh, I couldn't think of an answer that was anything other than *your cock.*

Truly. Your cock. And I almost said that.

Pregnancy hormones are *insane*.

I'm trying to shake off the recurring cringe as my bare feet pad across the warm wooden floor on the way to my desk when my phone vibrates with a text.

"Who can that be?" I say to Flip. "My money's on Daddy."

Did I say that a little smuttily? A girl can dream. *And she does. Often.*

MATT: I have a dinner this evening, so I won't be home for long.

I frown down at my phone, my mood dipping along with my head. I was looking forward to hanging out with Matt tonight. I'd had a good day and was feeling kind of peppy.

Not anymore.

ME: Okay. Well, you have fun!

MATT: It's nothing special. Just dinner with the guys from Maven and their better halves.

My heart gives a little wobble. I should've met them all by now, but I've been so caught up in my own head. And now I feel like it's just too late. I mean, I will meet them. I'll have to, because Matt has already spoken about asking them to be godparents—*padrinos* and *madrinas*, so he says.

He asked if I had anyone in mind, but I just shrugged and said he could choose because it meant more to him than me. Who would I ask, anyway?

ME: I hope you have a good time. You deserve to let your hair down.

He rarely goes out—barely drinks around me.

MATT: They'd all love to meet you, if you're up for it.

But they're married. And we're not together. Don't you think it's a little strange?
Though I begin to type this out, I delete it all while ignoring the chicken that has begun to cluck in my head.

ME: I will meet them but not tonight. I'm beat.

MATT: The offer's there if you change your mind.

ME: Thanks, but I won't, but you have fun. And don't do anything I wouldn't do!

MATT: Oh, the possibilities.

ME: Of fun?

MATT: Of the kinds of things you wouldn't do. Given the kinds of things I know you've already done . . .

His text seems to arrive with a taunting inflection and that velvety tone of his. Is he flirting, or am I imagining things?

ME: That's an origin story we won't EVER reveal to Flip.

MATT: It would certainly make the "where do babies come from" conversation very awkward.

ME: Agreed!

MATT: A child will always be too young to hear how he was conceived, especially when the tale includes pseudo sex workers, green lingerie, and the kind of mind-blowing sex that ruins you for all other encounters.

I type Matt, please.
"Please more" or "please stop"? Conflicted, I delete the text again.

MATT: Just so we're straight, I mean me. The best night of my life was playing whore for you.

I press my palm to my cheek, my skin suddenly feeling as though it's been pricked by a million hot pins. *Oh, Matt. This isn't allowed.*

MATT: So what do you say?

I say he's not alone in that. For me, there will never be another man like him.

MATT: You should come with me. Then you could make sure I won't get up to no good . . .

"Oh." My hand drops, my stomach along with it. Does he mean what I think he means, what it sounds like? That he has plans of . . . hooking up?

No. My denials are almost instant. Not Matt. No way. I know he hasn't . . . not since I moved in. *Unless there's a stash of condoms at work and his hookups are between office hours.*

"A man is a man is a man. Not one of them can be trusted." My mother's voice whips me back to the past. One of those evenings

she was drunk and sad and looking for validation. *"If they're smilin' and treatin' you nice, it's because they're hiding somethin'."*

But those are her experiences. And, okay, they're also mine, in the past. But Matt isn't Pete, and that's not what's happening here—it's not what his text meant because that's not who Matt is. I know this as clearly as I know my own name.

Yet my chest still aches, my stomach knotty and tense. I put my phone down on the desk and make my way to the nearest bathroom, where I splash a little cold water on my face.

"We're not together," I tell my reflection. "But he still wouldn't disrespect me like that."

But my eyes fill with tears anyway as I realize why I feel so sad.

It won't be tonight, but the time will come when I'll lose Matt to someone else.

Chapter 35
MATT

I straighten the collar of my shirt in the mirror, my expression tense. I've been home for an hour, and Ryan is nowhere to be seen. I knocked on her door, but there was no answer. I know she's in there—I heard her shower going. Which, if I'm honest, feels like a cheap excuse not to deal with this.

Long story short? I'm getting the silent treatment because of a little teasing. Or pushing. But fuck it, I really wanted her to be there tonight. By my side. I fucking hate being the fifth wheel.

It's great that my friends are all loved up, but I could do without having my face rubbed in their happiness when I feel like I'm getting nowhere with Ryan. It's time. Time for her to get off the fence. To take a fucking risk—on me.

I pull on the drawer and pick up my Cartier cuff links, then drop them immediately in favor of the Graff knots. Love knots, supposedly. They could be a lucky talisman. They were once before. *I got so lucky that night.*

It's not like I've been putting pressure on her to meet my friends—I love living in our bubble for two. I just wish there was more of that. More days. More nights. More intimacy that isn't swept under the rug the next morning.

I just want this so badly—I want her more than anything—and I'll be damned if I become the one before the man she eventually falls for.

Enough, I think, stabbing the cuff link through the hole in my double cuff, flicking the foot of it open. My shoulders feel tight as I repeat the action, then whack on my jacket and jab my hand through my hair. I grab my wallet and phone, and after taking one more look at my resolute expression, I leave my room and thunder down the stairs.

As I reach the hallway, I notice the door to the formal lounge is open as muted light spills across the floor.

What the . . . The only people regularly in that room are the cleaners. It still looks like it did the day the interior designer fluffed her last throw pillow before handing me an eye-watering bill.

"Ryan?" I call out stridently, the soles of my shoes loud against the tiles. I'm still fucked off. Annoyed. With myself, with her. I'm done with this bullshit.

"In here."

I press the flat of my hand to the door. "We need to talk," I begin, my words spilling hard yet honestly before the door is fully open. "I take your rent. I give you your space. I eat my fucking dinner alone like some feudal lord, but for the love of God, Ryan, it's time to meet me half . . ." My words draw off, the rest echoing in my head: *halfway and just come to dinner with me.*

"I changed my mind." Her voice is small and her words tentative as she stands on the far side of the room, framed by the art deco cocktail cabinet of burl wood. "I hope that's okay."

Dazed, I open my mouth, but the words aren't immediately available. I shake my head, rattling the jammed cogs of my brain. "Yeah, of course." And so much for righting my brain's workings, as my gaze slides over her like that of an old letch. Only, she doesn't seem to take offense.

"You might want to cover Flip's ears."

Her mouth curls, her answer amused. "Because?"

"Because fuck me, you look beautiful."

Her dress is a deep forest green, a shade so dark it's almost black. Perilously thin straps hold at her shoulders, the neckline kind of swagging over her chest. *A bit like the ribbon on her cardigan that tormented me, all allure and suggestion.* The fabric is silky looking, and it clings to all those curves like water, accentuating our compact little bump. *And her magnificent tits.*

She's a modern-day Aphrodite, the goddess of fertility. Decadent, lush, and sumptuous, and all the superlatives I can think of.

"Stunning," I kind of stutter, just in case I haven't made that clear enough.

"Thank you," she murmurs, leaning back on her elbow. Maybe her back hurts—if I'm lucky. Or maybe it's more a case that she knows exactly what I'm thinking.

Breasts. Best thing in the world.

Then I remember I have feet, so I move them, crossing the room in long strides as she watches. Her gaze, it feels good. The way she's looking at me makes me want to curl myself around her.

"So it's okay? I can come?"

I nod because I don't dare open my mouth, the words on my tongue not fit for this moment. *Yes, you can. Multiple times, if I have anything to do with it. On my fingers and tongue and all over my Gaston-like chin. And my cock. So many times on my cock, please. Let's make up for lost time, darlin'.*

"What made you change your mind?" Before I know what I'm doing, I reach out and touch a lock of her dark, silky hair. I'm not sure that was the original plan, as in my mind's eye, I slide that thin strap from her shoulder and press my lips there. *Oops. Let's stay in instead.*

As her chest expands with a deep inhale, I remember I asked her a question. *What was it again?*

"I guess it's just time."

Right. Yes. Agreed. It's time for things to change.

◆ ◆ ◆

Dave, our driver for tonight, texts me when he arrives. In one of the company Bentley SUVs.

"Car's here," I say, sliding my phone away.

I'm not one to use a driver usually. That's more Oliver's, and sometimes Fin's, style. They like to be ferried about and profess to work as the driver drives. Me, I consider driving my thinking time. Tonight, I won't be driving, but I'll be thinking plenty. I'll be trying to work out the reason she's by my side tonight. Because it's surely something less vague than it just being time she met my friends.

Time. I worry it's been working against us. I've been desperate to fix things between us and concerned that, if I don't fix them before the baby arrives—if I don't get Ryan to see what she means to me, and how good we could be—I'll blow my chance at happiness. Because when he's here, our babe, the variables will change. It'll be a whole new wonderful and frightening game where he'll be our focus, as it should be.

I can't wait to see love shining from her as she holds our babe in her arms. But children change a person, they shift priorities. Realities. They bring love, yeah, but they also expose you to new fears. They take up so much time and space in your house and your car and your brain. And I just want to see a flicker of that love in her eyes for me. *Before the whirlwind arrives and we get lost in it.*

In my heart and in my soul, I need this. I long to spend my life complaining about her being a bed hog, and teasing that she steals all the blankets during her crocodilian death rolls. I want to see her lift her eyes from her screen at the end of the day, all shy smiles as she realizes I've been watching her. I want our clothes hanging in the same closet, her lotions and potions littering the bathroom vanity. I want to complain about the shoes she leaves everywhere and have the right to tease her eternally for owning a million hair ties while never being able to find a single one.

Love fills my heart—it pumps through my veins and is embedded in my tissues. *In muscle, in sinew, in bone.* I want our baby. I want our life together. I want her love.

She already has mine.

"I'll get my coat." Ryan makes to move before pausing. She glances down to where my fingers have looped her wrist.

I want to tell her. Say the words, *I love you, Ryan. Do you think you could love me?* "You've got a bit of . . ."

She inhales a tiny, shaking breath as my hand rises, as I press my finger to her bared collarbone. She's all dark eyes and fluttering lashes as I draw it across that delicate wing.

"Something sparkly, see?" I pull that finger away, holding it up for her to examine. Maybe because I'm a chickenshit. Or maybe that wasn't the point—maybe it was a test administered without my full consciousness. The proof in her shaking breaths that something has turned.

◆ ◆ ◆

Where the hell are they taking us?

Dave drops us off at the address Fin supplied, along with the advice that Evie had planned the night. Fin, as our company cruise director, has been just about everywhere that's fun. It's literally his job to know all the hot spots, the places to entertain billionaires from every nation. *Cruise director, director of client relations. Same same.*

In other words, feck knows what we're in for if he's not in charge.

"Through here, apparently." I push open an ancient-looking gate that leads to a courtyard of ancient cobblestone.

"It's kind of atmospheric," Ryan murmurs, her eyes shining in the moonlight.

"If by *atmospheric* you mean as spooky as shit, yeah."

"Oh!"

"Careful." I catch her as she wobbles, heels and cobblestones not being the best combination. "Can I?" I don't really wait as I settle my arm around her back. My heart stills, lifting in its cavity as she slides me a soft smile and leans into me.

In that instant, I see us forty years from now. My arms still around her for practicality. For safety. For love. And always because of her tempting curves.

"Was that your stomach?" she asks, half laughing.

"It was singing to you." Her expression is so feckin' cute. "And I'm starvin'."

"You're always hungry."

Hungry for you. "Yeah, but right now, I'm so hungry I'd eat the arse off a low-flying seagull."

A door opens as we approach, and music pours out. Soft jazz and a song about love and dancing cheek to cheek.

As we enter, I can't help but smile. "I can see Evie booked this."

"That's Oliver's wife, right?"

"Yeah." *Don't look so nervous, darlin'. They're gonna love you because I do.* "She's a vet," I say. "Animal mad. That's probably how she ended up with him, come to think of it."

"Because he's an animal?" Her expression turns doubtful.

"As wily as a wolf. You'll like him."

"And Fin? What's he like."

"Ah, well, you'll like him more. He's like a golden retriever. Maybe a handsome Lab? Once upon a time, pre-Mila, he'd probably have had a go at humping your leg."

"The reformed playboy," she asserts, amusement filling her tone. "The wolf and the pooch. What does that make you?"

I give a shrug. "A horny toad?"

With a soft laugh, she slides her arm through mine. "Does that mean I need to kiss you to get my prince?"

"Stick with the toad that's really a lizard."

"Oh, yeah?"

"Much sexier, I think. Especially with all that tongue action."

"Don't even think about it." Her words are heavy with warning.

"What, this?" I make a lewd gesture. Gene Simmons has nothing on me.

God, I want this too. A lifetime of her telling me no and laughing anyway. Of course that would be the moment the hostess appears. Blond hair pulled back in a sparkly scarf, slacks, a white shirt, and spats, of all things, on her feet. I'm sensing a theme.

"Sorry to keep you waiting," she murmurs, pretending to have missed my oral air sex.

Sucks to be her.

"Table for Maven," I say with a give-no-fucks assurance and a mile-wide grin.

"Of course," she assents. "May I take your coat?" She directs this toward Ryan, who currently looks like she'd prefer to pull it over her head.

"Allow me," I put in. Ryan turns, and I help slip it from her shoulders, which means it's too late for this wave of . . . second thoughts, probably caveman-style. But I can see right down the front of her dress, which means most other people will be able to see down it too. I suddenly want to cover her back up, then pick her up, before carrying her out of this place. Keep all this loveliness for myself.

But I can't do that *and* share with them how much she means to me. Not in one sitting, anyway. So we follow the hostess. Or rather, Ryan does. Meanwhile, I follow *mi mujer*, my woman, and the hypnotic sway of her hips. *I'd follow this woman anywhere.*

"Here they are!" Fin stands first as we approach the table, all smiles and welcome and well-bred bonhomie. Oliver next, his manners and suit impeccable. Introductions are made, Evie and Mila doling out hugs and effusive greetings.

"Oh, my gosh, you are stunning!" Evie grabs Ryan's hand, sending an accusing look my way. "You didn't tell me you were punching, Matt."

"Hush, don't tell her. She might leave." I lower my voice as though sharing a secret. "I got my claws into her at a low moment, just the way Oliver taught me."

"Charming," Oliver murmurs, amused or unimpressed. It's hard to tell.

"It's okay, baby," Evie says, chucking his chin. "I love you anyway."

"And Matt likes his women pregnant," Fin says as I press my hand to the small of Ryan's back, guiding her into her seat.

"Like a fetish?" Ryan asks with a chuckle before turning those baby blues my way. "Am I not the first?"

"You're like . . ." I pretend to count on my fingers. "At least my twelfth. But my fetish isn't for pregnant women. It's for christening cake. Who found this place?" I ask, glancing around the restaurant. We've been given a private room that's not technically closed off from the main space, so still part of the general atmosphere.

"Mila did," Evie offers up. "Or one of her projects did. It's great, right? I keep expecting a young Evelyn Waugh to walk in."

"Who's she?" My mouth curls, and Evie sends me an unimpressed look. But I get what she means. The place is . . . of an era, I suppose. Sophisticated and sexy, thanks to a moody color scheme full of tactile furnishings and lamps made from ostrich plumage. It's a distinctly 1930s kind of vibe without being overly kitsch.

"Har-*har*," Evie says, overstressing. "Well, I think this place is like the Bloomsbury set and Jay Gatsby had a restaurant baby."

"It was Abena who told me about it," Mila offers up. "She was the interior designer who planned your home office?"

"Ryan's home office," I say, glancing fondly her way. "She's in there beavering away most days."

"Matt says you're investing for him," Mila says, turning her way.

"A little." Ryan nods. "Just keeping my hand in."

"As the vicar said to the actress."

"Oh, my God!" Evie exclaims. "My husband made a funny!"

"Maybe we should ask Abena to design the nursery," I murmur low in Ryan's ear. Although where that will be is anyone's idea. Upstairs? Downstairs? I'm not even sure what we need. I know Letty and Ryan went shopping, but my sister said they bought very little. She said Ryan seemed overwhelmed, but that there's still plenty of time. But is there really? Aren't pregnant women supposed to nest at some point? Not like pigeons or anything. "What do you think?" I ask when she doesn't answer.

"Maybe," she hedges, her gaze slipping away.

My expression flickers, ice dropping into my evening warmth. We are turning a corner, aren't we? *Don't expect too much too fast,* I remind myself as I slide my hand to the small of her back, finding the muscles tense there.

"I'll send her a message if you like?" Mila offers.

Ryan adjusts her position in her seat. "That's okay. I have her number."

"You okay?" I whisper as the conversation moves on.

She gives a quick nod and an even quicker smile.

"Thanks for coming tonight," I say. "It means a lot to me."

"Of course." Her next smile is genuine, and it holds. Even in the low light I see the color in her cheeks.

"Have I told you I love how you blush?"

"I don't blush."

"Course not," I murmur, biting back a grin. And pressing the meat of my palm to her lower back. "Nice?"

Ryan bites her lip, her expression part pleasured, part pained. But then she slides me a look that seems to say, *I know your game*.

"I think it's nice."

"Stop with the tone," she half whispers, half warns.

"And stop this?" I ask, pressing harder now.

She bites back a groan, and my grin breaks free.

"Don't be too pleased with yourself," she protests. "It's a symptom of this pregnancy. Pink cheeks too."

"Nothing to do with my magic hands?"

"It's hormonal fluctuations and increased blood flow."

I make a low noise. Part inquiry, part *tell me more*.

"Stop that!" Her blush deepens as her eyes dart away. Though her smile is so wide it's as if I just reached out and tickled her.

"Maybe I should be the one blushing, because you say the *sexiest* things."

"Hogwash!"

"Stop," I purr. "You're giving me increased blood flow myself!"

"Ohmygod." She slides a lock of hair behind her ear, her words running together as she ducks her head. "You are the worst."

She might be right.

The worst kind of fool for her.

◆ ◆ ◆

The food is grand and the whiskey even better. I order a steak, and Ryan has pasta, though we end up sharing our plates. The evening passes in a blur of friendship and laughter. Which, of course, includes embarrassing stories.

"No, no, no," Mila says, waving her hand as she laughs. "It isn't Stockholm syndrome. Is it?" Glancing her husband's way, she takes his face in her hand.

Fin bends to meet her lips with his. "I mean, we were both stuck on an island."

"And high on shrooms," Evie puts in. "Maybe what should be worrying you is how he practically stalked you when you got back to London."

"No," Fin says, all seriousness. "I didn't stalk her. It was more like a little friendly . . . blackmail. Technically, if you want to blame anyone, blame him," Fin says, throwing the accusation my way.

"Thank me, more like."

"What did you do?" Ryan asks, glancing up at me.

"He told me to read *Bridgerton*," Fin answers for me.

"Bollocks!" I scoff. "Get back to the topic of blackmail."

"No," Fin retorts. "Love deserves a sacrifice—that's what I learned from romance books. That or a diabolical plan."

"Diabolical?" Evie sends a sly glance Oliver's way. His answer is to take her hand and press a kiss to the back of it.

"Come on, Evie." Mila giggles. "Don't be mad. The man did buy you a menagerie."

"That's true." Evie gives a considering nod. "And bitches do love a menagerie," she says, glancing Ryan's way. "And lions and tigers and labradoodles."

"Those guys are too cute." This from Mila as she rests in the crook of Fin's arm. "Do you know what you're having yet?" Her eyes dip with warmth to a bump called Flip.

"According to Clo, a guinea pig," I say, reaching for my glass.

"Clodagh is such a hoot," Mila says. "Matt's family's great, aren't they?"

"Ah, yeah," Ryan begins hesitantly. "They've been really welcoming."

I stroke my thumb across her back. *No need to feel awkward, teacup.*

"Then, of course, Matt is pretty great too." Ryan tilts her head my way, and her smile just gets me. *Like an arrow to the heart.*

Chapter 36
RYAN

The house is warm and welcoming, the lamps lit and the hallway smelling of beeswax polish, and of the gardenias. Mary picked them in the garden yesterday while collecting herbs, then popped the pretty display in the silver urn.

We've had such a wonderful evening. Fantastic food and wonderful company. Lots of laughter and even a dance or two. I'm so glad I've met Matt's friends, and also a little sorry I put it off for so long. *Especially as they'll be part of our child's life.* But then again, maybe it's for the best I didn't build those relationships. *Less to leave behind.*

Matt closes the door behind me, and I feel his hands at my shoulder, helping me off with my coat.

"Stay with me tonight." His voice is all husk and want as he captures my hand and turns me to face him.

The thing we've been dancing around all night. I wonder if Matt thinks we've turned a corner. Who knows, maybe we have. But it's not happiness I see lurking just beyond. *For me, at least.* Because I will lose him. There can be no other conclusion to *us*.

I can't commit myself to him because love doesn't harbor secrets. Not when they eat you from the inside.

It's been a sobering realization that, one day, he'll meet someone, and I'll lose him. *Sobering and a little heartbreaking.* But there's no man on this earth finer than Matt Romero, and he deserves the world. Not my twisted love.

I wish I were stronger. I'm not. So tonight is mine. The ultimate act of selfishness as I tip onto my toes, my hand pressed to his lapel.

Please forgive me, I silently intone. *I'll remember everything.* The fine fabric beneath my fingers and the soft press of his breath as he lowers his head to meet me halfway. Our mouths meet with a tenderness, all soft lips and halting, aching breaths. But we kiss intentionally, freely, as for the first time since that night in October, I allow myself to think of him as mine.

My love is mine and I am his . . .

But only for tonight.

◆ ◆ ◆

Matt's bedroom, like the rest of the house, is stylish and sleek. His bed is huge, of course, the nightstands housing banker-style lamps, stacked with books. *A photography book, one on Victorian engineering, another about Greek mythology.* Those are placed at the side of the bed he doesn't sleep on, I know.

Many a morning I have visited his room after he's left for work. I've curled in his messy sheets and inhaled the scent of him from his pillows. And I've flicked through the pages of the only book he seems to have recently read. *Our baby bible.*

My footsteps echo against the wooden parquet flooring as I meander slowly around the edge of the room. Taking it all in, as though this is my first time in here.

"It's nice," I say, glancing over my shoulder. "I like what you've done with the place."

Matt stands in the doorway, hands slung low into his pockets as he plays along with my white lie. We both know the door to the left leads to an en suite bathroom large enough to party in and that beyond the door to the right is a closet fit for a king.

At the far side of the room, flanking the original fireplace, two leather chairs stand empty but for throw pillows and fur-like blankets. Wooden shutters keep out the night, a huge tribal rug underfoot muffling my steps now. Art hangs from the dark-hued walls, some modern, some abstract, and a brass-studded ottoman is placed at the end of the bed. Every piece of furniture, both new and old, seems to have been selected with thought for its position within the space.

The room is unique and eclectic and very him.

At the sound of the door quietly closing, I angle my head over my shoulder. "Get the light?" I hate how that sounds like both a request and a come-on.

Ignoring my request, he cants his head, coming closer still. He slides my hair over my shoulder, and I give a little gasp as his lips find my neck.

Though my panties are tiny, green and lacy, and not unfamiliar to him, I'm not wearing the matching bra tonight because it no longer fits. *Thank goodness for the concealed support of my dress.* I want darkness because I don't look the same as I did. My body is so changed, and I'm afraid I'll look ridiculous—like a hippo in a tiny strip of La Perla.

"Please, Matt, I'm—"

"Beautiful." His lips coast down my neck as his fingers tug the zipper at my side. "I can't wait to see you, Ryan."

Those bedroom tones and the straps of my dress slipping from my shoulders. I close my eyes as the fabric tantalizes my skin, sliding over the tips of my breasts. Pooling on the floor.

"Because you're so fucking beautiful."

I push out a breath, suddenly all sensation, every inch of my skin aware of every inch of him. The brush of his pants against my naked thighs, his chest as it grazes my back. The press of his lips against my neck. The feel of his strong arms as they band around me, and the subsequent hot press of his cock.

"You'll stay." The tenderness in his tone breaks my heart into a million pieces.

"You know I have to steal away like a thief during the night."

"Then I'll just have to keep you busy till morning," he murmurs, taking my breasts in his hands. "My little teacup." His words are shaped against my skin.

Is it called a pet name because it makes me want to curl into him?

"So delicate and curved."

"Matt." I make a moan of his name as his thumbs glide over my hardened nipples. A soft tug, and I gasp, my body jolting from his.

"And look how you fill my hands."

"I feel like I'd fill a barrow," I half scoff.

"Hush," he whispers, pressing a kiss to my neck. "How I feel when I look at you is fucking primal. I just want to pounce on you because you're so fucking sexy. I'm sure I lose a little piece of my mind every time I so much as glance your way."

"You're crazy."

"Crazy for you. Turn around, darlin'." His hands find my hips. "Turn around and let me see what I've been dreaming of. *Fuck me.*" His midnight gaze sweeps over me, bold, possessive, hungry.

"Well, now that we're here . . ." My words hold a confidence I don't really feel as I push away a glimpse of tomorrow. Of my regret.

"You can fuck me any day of the week, teacup." His lips tip. "And twice on Sundays, if I'm good."

"*If* you're good?" I reach for the buttons of his shirt, pulling it from the waist to hide how my hands shake.

"Oh, I'll be good," he says, reaching between his shoulder blades to pull it up and over his head. "I'll be so good, you'll weep."

I know, I think as his lips brush a light tease across my own. I swallow his groan—eat it up—as my fingertips find their objective. Warm skin and muscle, his abs rippling in response to my touch. My fingers moving lower and pressing over the bulge in his pants.

"God, I want you, Ryan." He gives a tiny sucking pull to my bottom lip. "I want you so much, I can barely see straight."

"Yes, let's . . ." I feel myself growing wet, my body aching for this. *My heart aching for him.*

Like the moves have been choregraphed, like I'm not the size of a hippo in La Perla panties and heels, Matt moves us across the room to the bed. Before I have the chance to sit, his body folds gracefully before me, his hands pressing to my bump as though in benediction.

A kiss to the center, so sweet, before his fingers loop my right ankle. One shoe. Two. My hands falling to his shoulders for balance. He sets them to the side and then hooks his thumbs into the elastic of my panties and slips them down my legs. I keep my hands where they are, my equilibrium still rocking.

Down on the bed, things moving faster now. My hands in his hair, his tongue hot and clever as it licks into my mouth. "Please, I need you."

"I know, darlin'. God, I know."

He parts my knees, the air on my pulsing clit almost too much. Too much and not enough as his attentions move to my breasts, and he engulfs my nipple with a soft groan.

"Oh, God!" I arch against him, moaning loudly as he licks and laves, as he uses his fingers to echo that tight pull.

"God, you're so fucking lovely. And the sounds you make."

"Touch me, please," I beg, widening the space between my legs.

"Soon, teacup," he whispers, canting his head to watch my reactions before he draws the pebbled bud back into his mouth. His gaze holds mine over the curve of my breast as he grazes gently with his teeth.

"That feels . . ." Immense. The wet velvet of his tongue, the threat of his teeth, and the teasing brush of his stubble make my nerve endings sing, makes me almost—

"Do you think you could come like this?"

—*burst*.

"I don't . . ." I gasp as my insides throb. "I don't want to find out."

Matt gives a dark chuckle, and I cry out, my hips surging as he swipes his thumb between my legs. "Maybe not this time." His words like pure appreciation. "Fuck, you are a feast for the senses."

I open my eyes to find him watching where he teases. Where he plays. His thumb dipping lower, gathering my wetness to paint it across my clit.

"Dios." His eyes burn bright as he brings it to his mouth and sucks on it. *"Me encanta el sabor de tu coño.* And I do love the taste of your pussy, teacup," he whispers as he leans across me, dragging a pillow from the top of the bed to support the arch of my back. "Lie back now and let me taste a little more."

"You're so sweet," I whisper.

"And you taste like hot honey," he says, pressing the rasp of his dark stubble to my inner thigh.

"Oh!" A bite, then a lick to soothe.

"Darlin'," he says, pressing my legs wider. "I wish you could see how ready you are. How wet you are and how you pulse for me."

I begin to twist under him, the thrill of his words, and the truth in them, when he circles my clit.

"Oh, Lord!" I almost levitate from the bed but for his fingers driving inside me, holding me there. My body offers him no resistance, my hips undulating to meet those slow thrusts as his tongue lavishes me as though I'm a taste to be savored. My fingers twist in those thick dark strands, anchoring him there as though I could keep him for good. Or at least until . . .

Forever. I'd like to keep him forever, I think as a tear darts from the corner of my eyelid.

◆ ◆ ◆

MATT

My beating heart and staccato breaths. The rustling of bedding as she pushes up onto one elbow, watching me strip. Her eyes fall to the curve of my bicep and the ladder of my abdominals as I run my fingers over them. And lower, over the dark trail of hair.

Down, down—she watches me take my jutting cock in my hand, and the thrill that runs through me feels almost seismic as she pushes my hand away.

"Let me." Her fingers are cool on my scalding skin.

Take my cock. Take my hand. Let's do this for the rest of our lives.

I never claimed to be a poet, but Christ, I can't stop my body from shaking.

Does she notice, can she see what her touch does to me?

I can barely believe we're here. Finally. *Finally.* This woman is everything to me.

"I love your hands on me," I rasp, staring at the neutral polish on her nails as she presses her hand to my taut thigh. She draws it upward, inward, cupping my balls.

Oh, fuck. Marry me. Spend your life torturing and toying with me.

Keep it together, fucknut. Take the blow job and call it a win.

Only if I can keep her forever. Only if I can . . .

Her tongue darts out to lick, and my body bows at the contact.

I growl her name as I slide my hand into her hair, moving it aside to better see. The gentle lap of her tongue against the thick ruddiness of my cock seems almost obscene. Not that I'm not straining, begging for more.

And more she grants when she suddenly sucks me down. Briefly, her mouth and my cock part ways with an audible *pop*. "Did you have a question?" she asks, her eyes all fake innocence.

"Teacup," I growl, using her nickname now as I press my hand to her head, encouraging her back to . . .

"I guess not," she whispers, taking me back into her mouth.

"Yes." My affirmation is a stuttering sigh. "Yeah, suck me."

She makes a noise of agreement, of pleasure, one that dials my own gratification sky fucking high. Her head begins to bob, her mouth sliding messily, wetly.

Fuck. Just fuck.

"You look so good with my cock in your pretty, pretty mouth," I whisper, beginning to move tentatively with her, my hand at the back of her head. "But you're gonna make me come."

"Mmmm." Her blue eyes lift to mine, and I almost lose it there, my pulse pounding in my ears as my legs threaten to give.

"You wicked, wicked woman." My words sound more Irish than ever—happier than ever as I pull back and exchange one appendage for another, pressing her back against the bed to kiss the fuck right out of her. "And by God, I love you for it," I admit without thought—without thought for her reaction. For the rules I'm breaking. The consequences. "It's true," I whisper, my hand on her cheek. "I'm in love with you. I think I have been from the start."

Chapter 37
RYAN

Light spills in through the window as my eyelids reluctantly flicker, not quite ready to join the day. I straighten my legs, the stretch of muscle and bone so delicious, it feels almost as though I spent the night having the best kind of—

"Sex." My head slices right to find Matt on his side staring down at me. His arm is bent and his head is propped against one hand, his dark hair an adorable mess.

"Already?" He quirks one highly provocative brow. "You're keen."

My heart thunders—the shock of finding myself still here, the echoing pulse of it thrumming between my legs. Or maybe it's the way he's looking at me that makes my heart pound. *Like I'm his world.*

"Wow." I clear my throat when it becomes clear it's my turn to speak. "So much for stealing away like a thief."

"I'm so glad you didn't." His finger sweeps tenderly down the slope of my nose. "And full disclosure? I intend on keeping you here."

"What, forever?" My attempt at a joke, or more like panicked mutterings.

"I like the sound of that." He lifts his hand to my round belly. I resist the urge, the instinct, to push it away. It's not that I want to but more like I feel that I should, despite what passed between us.

"I'm in love with you. I think I have been from the start." Those words. His words. So tempting and enough to make me giddy and foolish. *"Tell me something. It doesn't have to be that."*

But I said it—told him I loved him back. The words escaping. My heart breaking.

My mind is a mess, filled with fragmented moments, and snapshots of last night. The passion, the rightness of it all. The way he looked at me and the things he said made me feel utterly adored.

And earlier in the evening, with his friends. The love he has for them was so clear, as was their love for him. I shouldn't have let my emotions rule my head, allowed my jealousy of some faceless future woman to blind me to reason. Because one day I will wake to the reality that I've lost him.

Because this can't be. I can't live with a lie, and I can't tell him the truth.

That I don't deserve him.

The one good man in Manhattan, in London. I found home in his arms and in his passion and his promises. But he's worth more than me.

Oblivious to my truths, he lowers to press his lips to my swollen belly. I quickly wipe away a tear. *I'll save him for you, little one. This man will always be your daddy.*

"Buenos días, mi dulce niño." His honeyed whisper coasts over my skin. "Morning, my sweet child. I hope Mommy and Daddy didn't keep you awake last night." His eyes are shining as he pulls away again. "Forever," he whispers. "You know, I think that might not be long enough."

"Matt." I watch his smile stall, and my heart begins to thrash against my ribs. *Not yet,* something whispers inside.

"What is it?" He reaches for my hand as though he can already feel me pulling away.

Just a little longer. Ignore the sunshine because the night isn't done.

"I feel kind of cheated," I say, plucking the words out of thin air. I intertwine my fingers with his.

His features relax as he presses his mouth to my knuckles, his tone playful as he asks, "Cheated how?"

"If only I'd known you look like a pirate in the morning . . ." I take advantage of his closeness to press my hand to the dark shadow accentuating the hollows of his cheeks and lips.

"A pirate?" he purrs in question. "Just say the word, and I'll plunder your booty."

A chuckle stutters from my chest. *God, I'll miss his terrible jokes.*

"Fine," he says, snuggling closer. "I'll settle for a cuddle."

A cuddle sounds like a heavenly kind of torture. But I say nothing else as his arm loops around me, hauling me closer. I become the small spoon to his big one. Or *ladle* would be a more accurate description.

"This is nice." I sigh deeply, sinking into the feeling of his body and the comfort of his hand pressed to my bump. Touch is a human need. That's what Ava, my old neighbor, said. And I've been starving myself. *But not for no purpose* whispers in my head.

The night isn't over. Go away, sunshine. I close my eyes tight, allowing myself to hang on to this moment for a little longer. But the tears still well and fall, making tiny puddles on the pillow.

You can hurt for the ones you love—that's what this experience has taught me. My heart isn't breaking for nothing. It's breaking for him. *I'm just sorry I'll have to hurt you,* I whisper silently, tightening my arm over his. *So, so sorry.*

"Nice doesn't cover it," he murmurs, unaware of my sudden torrent of turmoil as he gathers my hair to one side, brushing his lips lightly across my nape. "It's perfect. This is a perfect moment in time. Because you're here. And you're perfect for me."

My heart suddenly feels as though it's bleeding, blood and hurt spilling from it unseen and soaking into the sheets. I'm the opposite of perfect—the antithesis to it. My lies aren't spoken but ones of omission. If he knew what I've done in the name of hate, he wouldn't want me anywhere near him—anywhere near our child.

My imperfections are many, and—my heart plummets. Oh, my God! My selfish heart! I crossed a line last night, the one I swore I wouldn't. This little one isn't even here, and I'm already breaking my promises to her.

What kind of mother will I make? A mother like mine, one who'll cause a lifetime of pain.

"You're the biggest mistake I ever made."

"No fucking good."

"You couldn't even make your daddy stay."

I begin to push Matt's arm away. I swore I'd never be like her, like my mother. But maybe the apple didn't really fall far from the tree.

"Stop." Matt presses the reprimand to my cheek, his hold on me tightening. "Whatever's going on in that head of yours needs to stop, because I'm not letting you go."

I say his name. It sounds like a plea as my fingers tighten on his arm, as though I could transfer my thoughts and fears, make him understand by touch. "You don't know me."

"Yeah, I do."

"You only see what you want to see, because you're too good."

"Good. Nice." There's an edge to his words as his teeth graze my earlobe. "I thought I would've convinced you otherwise last night. Convinced you *thoroughly*. I wasn't being nice, and I wasn't being gentlemanly, when I pushed you to your knees. Or when I painted my adoration over these." He palms my breasts, rolling the hardened buds of my nipples between his fingertips.

This time, his name is all sigh and no protest, the pleasured pain of his touch drowning everything else out.

"It's possession, Ryan. I want you. Want to keep you. And I will, because the truth of it is, I already own a part of you. Just as you own a part of me." His hand slips between my legs, pleasure coiling instantly at the connection, my mind going hazy around the edges.

"If you think we're going back to how things were, you're wrong. I know you're worried, that you're scared, but just be with me. Time will work out the rest."

My traitorous clit gives a needy pulse as his fingers find it, my body convulsing with his slippery pinch.

"You're in my life and in my head, darlin'. Don't try to tell me I'm alone in that."

I reach up behind me, pulling his mouth to my neck, the brush of his stubble setting me aflame. I want this. I want him. Now and always. But I'll settle for what I can steal right now.

Go away, sunshine. Bring back the night.

"I do love you," I whisper, rocking into his touch. *Please don't hate me later.*

"Fuck the rest, teacup. Just be here with me. Tell me what you need."

You, my heart bleeds.

You, my pulse pounds.

But not a sound do I allow from my mouth.

"This is what I think about when you're not around." His words are a lick of heat. "Nights alone with my cock in my hand, I think of this pussy, warm and wet, waiting for me."

Everything pulls tight at the confession, the husky quality of his admission.

"This body."

I inhale sharply as he hooks my leg.

"This face."

I'm so slick and ready for this, the satin glide of him making us both moan.

"This . . ."

I cry out as he anchors us together with his first thrust.

". . . heart."

My hand still hooked around his neck, I pull him close so he can't see my tears.

"*Te sientes jodidamente bien*. You feel so fucking good," he groans in my ear. "So tight. *Te amo con locura*. Ryan, I fucking love you." His lips lay claim to my neck as his words break my heart.

He cups my breast, his other hand sinking lower to swipe tight circles around my clit. The undulation of his hips, our bodies locked and rocking together. My fingers twisting in the sheets.

"I won't let you go."

Go away, sunshine. Let him lie to me a little more.

"Tell me that you hear me."

"Yes." A whisper as a sweet agony ripples through my insides.

"Yes," he echoes, feeling it too. "I've got you, darlin'. You're not alone anymore. You can let go."

Chapter 38
MATT

My stomach rumbles, hunger clawing at my insides. I stretch out along the bed, the sensation flooding my arms, legs, and chest with those feel-good endorphins. I feel grand—kind of amazing, actually. Until the mattress gives under the weight of my falling hand. Instead of finding Ryan, it only finds space.

No. I swallow over the unspoken word. *Not again . . .*

The sheets rustle as I sit, the lack of noise the first thing I notice. I throw my legs out of bed and slip on last night's pants, extra careful with the zipper. No need to worry. My pocket-rocket workaholic is probably in the office.

She was more excited about decorating the office than a nursery, my brain unhelpfully supplies as I make my way into the hallway. It doesn't mean anything. Anything other than she's been in the world alone for so long her leaps of faith are just hard earned.

But that's behind us now. She loves me. And with my body, heart, and soul, I'll always be hers.

There's no sign of her in her office, so I make my way downstairs. And down again.

Relief I didn't think I needed floods my nervous system as I find her in the kitchen. And my barefoot approach means I get to watch her for a moment without her noticing. Her back to me, she hardly looks pregnant. Hair piled haphazardly on top of her head, slim shoulders, and that heart-shaped arse. She's wearing my shirt from last night—best realization of the morning—plus a pair of pale leggings. Bent at the waist, she appears to be poring over the book Letty gifted her.

Baby's First Year.

I wonder idly if she's not used to receiving gifts or if it's more the nature of this gift that seems to mean so much. The fact that it's for our baby.

I'm gonna spoil her so much. The thought gives me such a kick. No more Tube journeys for her. I'm gonna get her a fancy car. A driver if she wants. Holidays. Jewelry . . . except she doesn't wear it. Fuck it, I'm gonna buy it anyway.

I can't wait to see what life has in store for us.

"Morning. Afternoon? Haven't checked my phone yet." Fuck knows what time it is as I wrap my arms around her and press a kiss to her head. Before my noisy stomach makes my feet move in the direction of the fridge.

"You hungry?" I throw over my shoulder as I pull the door wide. "I feel like bacon and eggs. Fancy bacon and eggs?"

"I'm not hungry."

"Have you already eaten?" I rub an itch on my sternum, then begin to rifle through the shelves. "I'm starved." As usual. "I could eat the hand of God," I mutter, ducking to better see the lower shelves.

"Matt."

"Hmm?" *Where's the feckin' bacon? Cheese. Brie? Nah. Red Leicester. A bacon-egg-and-cheese sandwich with lashings of brown sauce. Yes, sounds like just the thing.* My guts rumble again.

"Matt," she calls, a little stronger now. "We need to talk."

My shoulders stiffen, and the block of cheese hits the glass shelf with a little thud. Nothing good ever came from hearing that sentence.

Fuck, no. We are not having this conversation. We are *not* in this place. Not after last night. This morning? *It's just a misunderstanding,* my brain supplies as I shove the bacon back.

A trick of the memory, of the past. It's got to be. Until I turn and get a look at her.

My heart sinks. She's been crying, her eyes red and her skin blotchy. But the most telling fact of all is how she can't look me in the face.

Bottles and jars rattle as the fridge door slams closed behind me, my feet moving me across the kitchen as though on wheels.

"What is it?" I say, rounding the stupid island, my hands finding her shoulders tense. "What's going on?" What the fuck did I miss?

"Your mother sent me a gift." She sniffs. "A care package, I guess you'd call it." Her hand lifts as though by invisible puppet strings as she points to the couch.

"Right?" But this is far from right. It doesn't make any sense. What the hell did she send?

"It arrived this morning. She included a tin of tea. Tea leaves. And I hate tea, by the way."

"Then . . . why are you always drinking the stuff?"

"And a tiny knitted cardigan she said she made herself. A *matinee coat,* she called it."

"Yeah, she knits." What the fuck did I say that for?

"It's so beautiful." Her eyes turn all watery.

"Okay." Is the idea of family freaking her out?

"And there was a cake."

"She likes to bake. And feed people."

"And pictures of you and Letty and your brothers when you were all small. In green fields and gardens, all wrapped up in sweaters and scarves. And others where you're all as brown as berries and on the beach."

"We had a good childhood." *And I'm so sorry you didn't get the same.*

"She said they'd help me see family likenesses, when the time comes. Does Flip have your nose or Hugo's? Does she have your cheekbones? My eyes? My father's smile?"

Ah, fuck.

"Not that I'd know."

"Doesn't matter," I say quickly as I rub her arms. "Doesn't matter who he looks like. As long as he doesn't look like Hugo," I add flippantly. "Because that fucker got some nose on him."

"Some of these things she sent she must've kept since your birth. Mementos she's held on to for thirty-eight years." She wipes the back of her hand under her nose. "Can you imagine that?"

"She's got an attic full of memories, darlin'. She's just that kind of person."

"I think the word you're looking for is *loving*. A perfect mom."

"Ah, love. There isn't any such thing." I stroke my thumb across her cheek. "You'll make mistakes—we both will. And Ma will be the first to tell you she has too."

"Do you know what my mother gave me when I left?"

I give a quick shake of my head. Because I don't think I want to know. As unfair as that seems.

"A *good riddance*. A *fuck you*. And in the place of a farewell, I got '*I didn't want you anyway.*'"

"Ah, darlin'. I'm sorry." The hurt in her eyes pulls at my insides, twisting them into knots. Because what in the name of actual fuck? She said she'd had a bad childhood, but this has narcissism written all over it. What kind of... well, those aren't the words of anyone who deserves the title of *mother*.

But I get it—I think. Get why this is coming up now. My mother being her usual mothering self has dredged up a nasty piece of Ryan's history—just like in the wine bar, when she broke the news of her pregnancy and assumed I'd walk away. *Just as her own father did.*

We got through that, so we can get through whatever fear has been dredged up this morning.

"Honestly?" I say, taking her sad but lovely face in my hands. "She sounds like a piece of work, and I'm glad she's not around to hurt you anymore. You didn't deserve that. Not as a kid. Not as a human."

"I'm glad she's dead too." There's a vehemence in her tone, an absolute sincerity on her face.

"Thanks for telling me, darlin'. Whatever you have to say, whatever you tell me. I promise to shoulder it."

"Matt." Her gaze slides away. "You don't know what you're saying."

"I do. I'm here for it all. And I'm sorry if the stuff Ma sent is making you feel like this." That it's triggering somehow.

"It's not the package," she says kind of manically. "It's this—this fuckup I'm responsible for." Her fierce blue eyes fill with tears, her words turning wobbly as she tears away from me, putting the kitchen island between us like a barrier. "I can't stay here with you."

Concrete fills my guts, a cold, heavy sensation seeping through me. "What do you mean you can't? I love you—we're having a fuckin' baby!"

"It's not fair to you, and it's not fair to the baby. I know I said I'd stay, but I think it's better we do this now before things get too complicated."

"Too complicated?" I almost bellow, the concrete falling away to leave cold, hard rage. "No." *Just . . . fuck that.* "You said you'd stay so I could be a part of this. You're supposed to stay now because you want to be with me. Because we're about to become a fucking family!"

Sunshine streams through the window, the summer day a stark contrast to the winter she's created in my heart. Until I notice how frozen she is, framed by the window and a verdant garden backdrop. Ryan is a Madonna in stained glass, whose trauma responses deserve to be handled better.

"I'm sorry. I didn't mean to shout. You're just . . . spooked." Hyperindependence is a trauma response, right? I'm sure I read that somewhere. And by God, she's suffered some trauma. A father who didn't want to be part of her life. A mother who didn't deserve to be in it. "I get it," I begin, not sure where I'm going with this. "We're all products of our experiences. But you're so strong. You made a life for yourself, pushing through all that toxic family and career bullshit. And then you met a man who you thought you could trust. Before he reminded you that the human race sucks." I want to take her in my arms and promise to take her pain away. "You think you can't rely on anyone, but you can, Ryan. You can rely on me."

"Matt, please," she says softly, her eyes begging me for something I won't give.

"You can trust in me." I want to go to her, but I don't trust myself. Not as something seems to come over her. A calmness or detachment, maybe.

"I love you," I say as a realization sets in. She hasn't once in this exchange said the same. "Last night, you said you loved me."

"That's the problem with people like you," she begins. "People who say what they mean. They think other people mean what they say too."

"Bullshit." My retort is a bullet I know she'll dodge. Grief has seven stages, but I wonder how many stages trauma has. And what they are. Denial? Bargaining? Anger? Sounds right about where we are now. How many more stages before we reach healing?

"Mama might've been an evil whore, but she taught me some things."

"Words of wisdom?" I say, folding my arms. Even my stance is combative.

"Sure." She gives a spiky shrug. "The truth. You can't trust what someone says on New Year's Eve, on their deathbed, or when they're fucking you."

"And who was fucking who last night?" I demand as blood boils like lava in my veins. I don't know what this is I'm feeling. Is it pity? Is it rage? Hurt. And pain. It feels like she's punched her hand through my chest to twist my heart.

All these months I've trodden lightly, followed her cues, withstood her dismissals, and refused to shrink from her denials. But cruelty. What am I supposed to do with that?

"I think we were fucking each other," she says, unconsciously reaching to protect her stomach. *Our child.*

"So that's it?" I demand flatly. "I'm just supposed to let you walk away?"

"Yes." A whisper. An almost imperceptible nod.

"And what about the baby? It wasn't New Year's, I wasn't dying, and we weren't fucking when you said I could be a part of his life."

"I won't take fatherhood from you."

I shake my head. Disbelief. Distrust. My head is a mess, and this is just so fucked up.

Her gaze drops. "I'm sorry. But we were just a fantasy I lived for a little while."

Chapter 39
RYAN

I hate the look on his face. The hesitation and the pain as I make him doubt my love. I hate what I'm doing to him, but I don't do it lightly. And I do it for him. *What's best for him.*

"Fuck this bullshit," he says, stalking across the room. "Last night, this fucking morning, I was there—I was inside you. You can't fake those kinds of emotions."

"Maybe you can't," I whisper, turning to the window.

"You're just frightened," he says, coming to stand behind me. In the reflection, I watch his hand rise. But he lowers it again without reaching for me. *Maybe he's learning.*

"You're right." Confessing a little of the truth won't hurt me. "I'm frightened all the goddamn time. I'm frightened of being on my own, and of not being able to cope. I worry about baby brain and a shift in my focus and losing my edge. I worry that I won't be able to do my job—I worry that I won't get a job. Here. Back home. But worst of all," I say, as my voice breaks, "I'm so very afraid that I'll turn into my mom."

"That's not gonna happen." In our reflection, Matt swipes a hand through his hair. "You're not that person. You're kind and loving—"

I give a laugh that sounds like a sob.

"It's fucking true."

"You don't know," I say, my attention slicing over my shoulder. "After all, she was my only role model."

"You're your own role model, Ryan. And you love this baby." His arm comes around me to touch me, but I spin away.

"But will this baby love me back, or will she learn to hate me?"

"What are you talking about?" he demands, catching my arm and stilling me. "You'll be an amazing mum—look at all you've done for him so far."

"Drinking tea I don't like and staying away from wine and not shoving coke up my nose is a pretty low bar."

"You moved in with me. That was some leap of faith, and you didn't do it for you."

His words strike me true. I accepted his proposal for so many reasons, but at the heart of each was that one constant. Our child. I said yes for safety, for security. And it was a leap of faith, and he was our soft landing. And I did it so Matt could be a father and so our child wouldn't be fatherless. But that's not enough to keep me here.

"All that other shit? Those obstacles? You'll overcome every one of them. You've seen some stuff, suffered I don't know what. But you've survived. Look at yourself, Ryan. You've fucking thrived."

"Impending motherhood has made me soft. Made me delusional." *Made me think for a little while that I could keep you.* "What happens when I turn back into the real me?"

"I love the real you," he says with such adamancy, my words dialing up his rage. "Don't you dare tell me I don't know her."

"I'm not worthy of your love," I retort, pulling from his hold. "Aren't you listening? You don't know, Matt. You just don't know. Last night, in bed, lying across your chest, I wanted to rip out all your fucking tenderness."

"I would've let you—let you tear open my chest if it meant I could show you my love. To prove it to you."

"Do you know why I stayed?" I demand as I pivot. Bodily. Tactically. "Because I needed a roof over my head. And I needed someone to keep me accountable."

"Fucking bullshit!" he yells, full of rage. "This was never about what was good for you."

"You don't know me," I repeat, turning for the door to my apartment. I need to leave. Go. I can't be here anymore. "You don't know the things that I've done."

"You're the first woman I have ever loved. The only one."

My heart aches to hear that. But he'll find someone else. Who couldn't love him?

"You shouldn't hang your hopes on me," I say, almost at the door when I turn to face him. "I'm not a good person. You shouldn't trust me."

"Don't leave."

He looks so hurt. *I hate that I have to do this.*

"You'll find someone else. Someone like Mila or Evie. A woman with goodness inside her."

"Fuck that."

"Evie and her animals. Mila and her social causes. Ryan and her . . . m-mercenary ways." I catch myself just in time.

"Fuck all your excuses," he retorts angrily. "I don't want Mila, I don't want Evie, or anyone like them. I love you! The Ryan I know isn't a quitter. She's fearless and, yes"—he gives a huff of a laugh—"oh so fucking independent. You don't have to leave. You've just been conditioned to think the worst of yourself. Of everything. Can't you see that?"

"I know who I am." I bring my fingers to my chest. "And I above all people know what I'm capable of."

"And what about me?" He takes a step toward me, but I hold up my hand. *Stop. Don't. Let's not do this again.* "You think I deserve better? That I'm worth more than you? You don't know a fucking thing," he says, coming closer anyway. "The night back in October when I left you in the foyer. It wasn't for condoms." In front of me now, he tips my chin as he says so softly, "It was so I could go and beat some sense into that fuckhead. One of them, anyway."

I feel my brow furrow.

"Brandon," he spits. "I wanted to smash in his face, but I was careful. I didn't want you to cop trouble. Not at work," he adds like a taunt.

Something blooms hot in my chest—a realization. After that night, the asshole pretty much left me alone. I thought he'd gotten the message finally. And he had. I just hadn't realized the mode of delivery. "Why would you do that?"

"Because he deserved it. Because I hate bullies. Now ask me what I did to the other fucker."

"To Pete?" I'd know if he . . .

"Best not say his name around me, teacup. Not when I'm feeling this charged."

"You wouldn't—"

"Hurt you? Never." His thumb strokes my cheek. "Can't say the same for anyone else, though."

"What did you do, Matt?"

"Just . . . systematically destroyed your ex. His livelihood. And the company you used to work for."

"But you said—"

"I know what I said. I also know what I've done. And the two aren't the same." He gives a casual flick of his wrist. "You didn't want to. Said you'd prefer to leave it all in the past. But . . ." He pulls away and shoves his hands into his pockets, almost rocking on his heels. "There are always consequences, Ryan. Without them, how do we learn?"

"No."

"I punished that fucker in the bathroom for making you feel powerless. And maybe the fact that he didn't get away with it means next time he'll think twice. Next time, he won't push it further—impose his will in much worse ways. Same goes for Pete, though on a much grander scale."

My heart sinks, but not for what he's done. For what I might've driven him to.

"Consequences," he adds. "There should always be consequences. For breaking the law, breaking promises, bending rules. Or what's the point?"

"You're not—" *Judge and jury*, I was about to say.

"Would you like to see him do to his wife what he did to you?"

"It's not my place to police him." And she's not my responsibility.

"It's not my place either. But don't confuse my motives. I'm no knight in shining armor. It was pure ego. I wanted to hurt him, and so I have. Ruined him for what he did to you. See?" He holds out his hands. "Not so perfect after all."

"This changes nothing, Matt. In fact, it makes my point. I did this, didn't I? I'm the catalyst for all this ugliness."

The look he sends me is pure disgust. "You want to play the martyr, you go on ahead. Because fuck you for doing this. For leaving me. You'll always be the missing part of my life."

"Maybe you should fight me."

Consternation flickers on his brow. Confusion, maybe.

"Not fight *for* me. Fight to protect our child," I say, pressing my hands to my stomach. My heart beats out of my chest as the things he's said and done begin to swirl through my head. Without me, he wouldn't have been pushed to this. This is not who he is.

"What are you talking about?"

The ugliness bubbles up inside, my admission. My confession. Am I really going to tell—share the secret I have held inside me all these years? Reveal my black soul and admit to the act of retribution there is no repenting for?

"I don't deserve all this . . . goodness." I press my hands to my belly as my eyes fill with tears and my heart with shame. "I don't deserve to be happy, and I don't deserve to be a mother. Not when I killed my own."

Chapter 40
MATT

In front of me, Ryan begins to shake, the tremors running through her body almost seismic.

"Oh, God." Her hand moves in slow motion, rising to her face. "I've never said that out loud before." She presses her fingers to her lips as though she might be sick.

Immobile, I can't make sense of what she just said.

Was it a birth thing?

She grew up with her mother—she said she left. Which means . . .

No. She's no killer.

Killer. The word rebounds from the walls of my brain as I recall her heated reaction in October when I playfully called her that—and when those fucknuts from Dreyland called her the same.

Killer queen. Dynamite and—

Ryan staggers to the sink, reaching it just in time. She begins to retch, her distress this time spurring me into action.

Three long strides, and I'm holding her hair, rubbing her back, making soothing noises as she contorts herself. Her belly and height make the job a difficult one, the meager contents of her stomach not helping much either.

"It's okay," I say, over and over. As she retches. As she sobs. "Here." I grab a towel and press it into her hands. She puts it to her face, her shoulders still shaking.

My heart aches for her, but my fucking ego wants to make her feel worse. And my poor fucking head feels like it's gonna burst. She's not a killer, but whatever this is has her tied in knots.

She makes no attempt to stop me as I bend and swoop her up. I carry her to the sectional and lower us to it, holding her in my lap like a child. Breath after tortured breath, her tears soak the towel until there's nothing left for her to give.

"Hey," I whisper.

Her eyes lift briefly to mine before she gives a long breath, her gaze sliding to the garden.

"My mother didn't want me." Next comes a deep swallow. She repurposes the towel, twisting it in between her fingers. "I was just an attempt to keep a man. It didn't work." Her gaze darts my way, and I push a deep breath from my lungs.

"That's not what's happening here." *Unless we're talking about some sick reversal.* I hook my finger around the hair stuck to her cheek. Pulling it free, I smooth it over her shoulder. "I'm here when you're ready. You can tell me anything."

"Anything to send you away? Because it will."

I don't answer. I can't imagine my life without her. And I can't see her as a killer.

"As a child I lived in a constant state of uncertainty, not that I knew it back then. I had questions. Lots of them, always. Would I go to school that day? Would I find food in the fridge? What kind of mood would I find her in? Would she be drunk and mean or drunk and newly in love? And then there were the men." A shiver of revulsion runs through her, and the concrete returns to my stomach.

"So many, I don't remember all their faces as they drifted in and out of our lives. New daddies, uncles, and others who'd barely acknowledge me. And then when they'd leave, and they would leave, she'd start on me again.

"'Look at you, you scrawny no-good thing. You weren't even enough to make your goddamn daddy stay.' She said it so often I thought it was my fault for the longest time. Do you know what that does to a child?"

"I can't imagine," I whisper, pressing my hand to her back.

"Well, it was nothing good. God, I hated her," she adds, her tone low and mean. "And I hated how she demeaned herself for them. How she demeaned me."

My stomach turns over. I want to ask her what that means. Did she suffer at the hands of men as a child? But I won't push. All in her own time.

"I look like her, you know?" Her head turns my way, the light in her eyes dead. "Every now and again, I pass a mirror or a store window and catch a glimpse. Not of myself, but of her. And I'm reminded all over again who I am. Where I came from. Underneath all this—the clothes, the hair, the bravado. Even the job. It's still Ryan, her daughter. I'm part of her, and she's part of me. And it terrifies me."

"You're not her. No way. You're amazing, and I love you," I choke out, my heart twisting for her.

Her smile is a tiny, fragile thing as she touches my cheek fleetingly.

"I left home as soon as I could. Left her in that no-good town. I put myself through community college, and I transferred my final year to somewhere less . . ." She sighs, her shoulders rising and falling with the memory. With the weight of all that she's carrying. "Less me."

I put my hand over hers and clasp her fingers tight.

"I got a decent job, in time. Made some money. Got smart. Avoided the usual pitfalls." Men, I intuit as she glances my way. The unsuitable ones, I hope she means. "I never went home once. But I called. She was the only person I had in the world. 'You think you're so much better than me, don't you?' That's what she'd say if I caught her on a bad day. And God forbid if I told her anything about my life. A boyfriend, and it'd be 'Look at you, falling in the same traps. You with your smarts and your big ideas.' She'd delight in that, like she wanted me to fail. To be miserable. But I guess she was miserable her whole life, and that was my fault."

"Babies are born innocent." I tug on her hand. "You hear me? You got dealt a shit hand, but none of it was your fault."

And you didn't murder her, I know.

God, her expression is heartbreaking. "Maybe not. But later. That's on me."

"You don't have to tell me, not if you don't want to." *Maybe it's better I don't know.*

Fuck that. There isn't anything she can't tell me.

"I have to tell you. See, you have to take this baby from me," she whispers, pressing her hands to her distended abdomen. "I don't deserve her, and she doesn't deserve to be like me." Big fat tears hit the round of her belly, spreading like inkblots on my shirt.

"You're wrong." I know it.

"I'd send her money," she whispers. "And there's a part of me that hates that I helped her when she did so little for me. But I didn't give her money to help. I did it because I knew she'd drink herself to death." Her head turns my way. "And she did. And I have to live with that every day."

Chapter 41
MATT

Ryan cries herself to sleep in my arms, tears she must've kept inside for years.

And my heart aches for her and longs for her. Fuck her admission, because nothing will change the way I feel.

She's not a killer. She's just a human put in a shitty situation. A child traumatized. An adult scarred. Mothering is meant to protect you from harm. But in her life, it was the cause.

I love her, but she says she's still leaving.

I love her even when she promises to hand over our child.

She says my love will be enough. That she can't trust herself, that I should feel the same.

She says she's a monster, but in the grand scheme of the evils in this world, she's no murderer. She's also beyond listening, though what am I supposed to do, to say? I'm not sure it'll help, admitting that I don't see her actions quite the same way. Or that I don't give a fuck what she's done. If she's a monster, then she's my monster.

"Because you are mine," I whisper, curling her hair around her tiny shell-like ear. "You're mine and I'm yours, and you'd better get used to it, for better or worse. And yes, I said what I said, teacup."

I'm pressing a kiss to her head when she almost breaks my nose with her head as she comes awake with a surge, her hands clutching her belly and her face a rictus of pain.

"Oh. The baby—I think she's coming."

And I think she might be right, according to the damp warmth spreading across my lap.

Chapter 42
MATT

"Get out of the fucking way!" I lean on the horn as I try to squeeze the Range Rover through a space more suited to a MINI.

"Wanker!" A courier whips his bicycle around the front of us, accompanying the insult with the matching universal hand signal. And I don't mean the signal for turning left.

"We're having a baby here!" I yell, hanging my head out the window.

Shit. I've become one of *those* people. The soft-arse *We're pregnant!* idiots. I'm not having a baby; Ryan is. Soon, judging by the noises she keeps making.

"Please stop shouting," she says.

I pull my head back inside, immediately regretful. Shit scared and panicking. And very glad I'm not suffering through this, as another contraction hits and she makes that unearthly sound again. *Part alien, part ancient plea.* I've heard men say they wish they could've shared their partner's labor pains, but I call bullshit because it looks like some seriously heavy pain.

"I'm sorry, darlin'." I reach out across the center console, taking her hand in mine. *At least, when it looks safe to do so.* "I'm sorry for yelling and for the stupid feckin' rush hour traffic. But most of all, I'm sorry I can't take away your pain."

"You're forgiven," she says, her words barely a whisper, her forehead beaded with perspiration. "Tell me something?"

Why do her words sound so bittersweet?

"I love you. I can't wait to meet our baby."

"You're gonna be such a good father. She'll be so, so lucky."

"She will. On both parental fronts, because you are amazing, my love."

"Promise me you'll choose her."

"What?" Fear lances through me as a tear slides down her cheek. She doesn't speak for a beat, her eyes closing as though in prayer.

"It's too early," she whispers. Her gaze doesn't hold.

"I know," I say, my eyes as wide as saucers as though full of reassurance. "But you heard what Dr. T. had to say on the phone. Thirty-five is the new forty."

"Something isn't right, Matt. I know it."

"It's just been a rough day." I give her hand a tiny, reassuring squeeze. "Emotions running high and all that."

"Promise me," she demands, her grip suddenly piercing.

I lick my lips, not sure what I'm supposed to say. Do I lie? Play along? Keep repeating that it's all gonna be okay?

"Matt." Her voice cracks on my name, and now *my* eyes fill with tears.

"No." I set my jaw, forcing the waterworks back. *She's scared. Of course she's scared. I myself am fucking terrified.* "I don't promise."

Her hand tightens this time, almost crushing my fingers.

"Please do this for me." Her words ache, and my heart bleeds that she feels this way.

"Stop it." Reassurance, not demand. "Everything is going to be *fine*." *Please, Lord. It has to be.*

"I've been so happy," she whispers. "But I can't do this."

"I don't know how to break it to you," I half mumble. "I hear there's no way out of this situation but through."

"I want you to take her, Matt. Love her enough for the both of us."

"No. I'll love her enough for one. No more, no less. You'll have to pick up the rest. Don't be a lazy fecker, now."

My version of tough love, but Jesus God, does she know something I don't? Is this some kind of intuition I can't tune in to? "Fucking move!" I yell, pushing my palm on the horn again.

In my side mirror, blue lights begin to flash. And as the police car pulls alongside me, I want to weep with joy. I have never been so pleased to see one of London's finest. I'll make the biggest donation they've ever seen if they only help us get to the fuckin' hospital.

◆ ◆ ◆

And they do, God bless those boys in blue.

At the hospital, I abandon the car, leaving the keys inside it. Let someone steal it. I don't give a flying fuck.

"Excuse me," a voice calls as I carry my darling over the threshold. "Excuse me!" the voice calls again, a little more strident the second time.

I swing around, and Ryan's slipper shoots off the end of her foot. Her arm around my neck, she presses her worried face into my shirt.

"Yes?" I answer tersely, piercing the security guard with a look. *What the fuck do you want? Can't you see we're a bit busy here?* He's gonna tell me I can't park there, I know it. And I'm gonna reply: *Congratulations, you just won a 150 grand's worth of car!*

"That's against health and safety regulations," the fella says.

Just what we need. A fucking jobsworth. "Do I look like I give a fuck?" I demand. "Show me the way to the birthing suite!"

"Matt," Ryan whispers. "Please," I add in a mutter.

"You have to get checked in first," the security guard says. "And look." Like a game show hostess, he indicates the wheelchair by his side.

"Fine," I say, crossing to it. That minor setback put to rights, we're on our way again.

I dip my head to Ryan's ear, pushing the wheelchair like I drove my car. *Like a man on the edge.* "How far are the contractions apart now, my love?"

"Three minutes," she whispers, gripping my phone tighter as that wave of pain hits again. "It hurts," she admits a few moments later, her hand smoothing over her taut bump.

"I'm sorry. Would it make you feel any better if I let you punch me in the face?"

"Choose the balls," a comedian, or nurse, says as we reach the check-in desk.

Once we've registered, all systems are go. The wheelchair driving is taken out of my hands, leaving me trotting alongside as Ryan is rolled into a birthing suite. And it isn't long before Dr. Travers enters the room like the lead actor striding onto a stage. Honestly, it's the first time I've set eyes on him and been relieved to see the fella. That air of hubris is very fucking welcome right now.

"How're we doing?"

"Fine," I say.

He shoots me an unimpressed look.

"But Ryan is in a lot of pain," I add, wincing as she squeezes my hand, riding out another contraction.

"So it's game on." He sounds completely unconcerned as he watches the nurse hook Ryan up to a monitor. "We'll have a wee look, then, shall we?" he says, turning to the sink.

"Please." Ryan grabs for the back of the doctor's scrubs. "Please, don't risk my baby."

"I have no intentions of that, hen." He gives a reassuring pat to the back of her hand.

"I mean it. You have to put her first."

"I know this is overwhelming for you right now, but you're in safe hands." He holds them out as though ready to catch a ball. *Catching wasn't mentioned in the baby bible, was it?*

"If there has to be a choice," she says, raising her voice for all to hear. "The baby comes first. Those are my wishes."

"Now, Ryan," the doc begins again.

"The baby," she reiterates, louder. And more Ryan-like. "That's all that matters. She comes first or he'll sue your ass. Tell them," she demands. "Promise me, Matt."

"Ryan, please."

She puts her hand to her stomach one last time, her gaze finding mine. "I love you," she whispers. And then, right before my eyes, she just . . . fades.

"She's bradying." A nurse—midwife—takes Ryan's wrist in her fingers.

"She's hemorrhaging," says someone else.

Everything seems to speed up, actions and reactions seeming to happen in fragments. The top of the bed is lowered, equipment appearing from nowhere as something akin to controlled pandemonium hits the room.

"You have to leave." The wrist-holding nurse, I think, begins to push me bodily toward the door.

"No. Tell me she's okay," I demand. "What's going on? What's happening, please?"

"Someone will be with you shortly to explain. But right now, we need to get Ryan into surgery."

The bed and medics whip by me in a blur, the woman at the center of my world small, unresponsive, and unreachable in the eye of that storm.

Chapter 43
MATT

Dear Baby Maeve,
I want to tell you about how you came into this world. Longed for but early.

You were supposed to be a July baby, but you were in a bit of a hurry . . .

When you read this letter and learn of those precarious first days, I hope you'll know that whatever else life has in store for you, you can face it. Because you're tenacious. A fighter. Just like your mother. And so damned beautiful like her too.

You were born a little early, nearly thirty-five weeks, and you came into the world at five fifteen in the afternoon due to something called a placental abruption. My heart feels heavy just writing that because I couldn't protect you. Or your mother.

You needed to be resuscitated. You both did. And I wasn't there when this happened, rushed out of the room by the medics because the stakes were too high. I thank God for it now because I don't think I could've stood to watch you both suffer.

Instead, I waited and waited for news of you both, wearing holes in the hospital floor. And I swore to all that is holy that, once I had you both in my arms, I'd hold you so tight and never let either of you go. It was the longest two hours of my life and the most terrifying thing I have ever faced. I felt alone for the first time ever, and it was the saddest place in the world.

When they told me what had happened, I cried. Oh, fuck, how I cried. Sorry for the cursing. (I know you'll fleece me out of cash as soon as you're old enough for your cousin Clodagh to teach you her ways).

Let me tell you about your mother. Her love for you knew no bounds while you were inside her. She nourished you with her body. Protected you with her heart. And made the medical team promise they would put your life first. She made me promise, too, but how could I choose between the two of you?

In the end, I'm glad I didn't have to.

Your mother is amazing. She's my hero. And maybe she'll be yours too.

I can't wait until this afternoon when I get to commit myself to her forever, and call her my wife.

Maevy-wavy, you and your mother are what I live for.

Love always,
Daddy.

P.S. While your amazing mom fills your baby book with the prettiest photographs of you, I'm collecting the stinkers and saving them for your twenty-first birthday party. I'm gonna have them all enlarged and wallpaper the walls with them! *Cue dastardly laughter here*

Epilogue
RYAN

"Have you seen this?" A curious-looking smile plays on Letty's mouth as she holds out her phone.

We're standing on the terrace of Matt's—of *our*—vacation home, situated close to one of the most charming *pueblos blancos*, or white villages, in southern Spain. Set among olive and citrus groves with views of mountain ranges and undulating valleys, the house—or rather, estate—is so beautiful. Full of ancient Moorish accents and vibrant bougainvillea tumbling down sun-drenched walls, it's become our haven.

The sky is azure, the sun so bright, and the air is fragrant with the smell of bitter orange blossoms. It's a perfect day to get married.

It's been nine busy months since my world imploded. Nine months since fear made me pull the pin on self-destruct. At least until Mother Earth stepped in to finish me off.

Or rather show me I was worth fighting for.

And I did fight. I fought for my life, and my body fought for Maeve's. And when we both came out on the other side, I learned to fight for Matt's love in place of fighting against it.

As harrowing as my birth experience was, it was also humbling. *Get over yourself,* the world seemed to say. *Rest. Get well. You're needed here.* And from thinking I deserved to be alone, I was suddenly surrounded by love. And stuck in a hospital bed, unable to run away from it!

Matt never left my side, and his loved ones rallied too. They brought words of hope and joined us in our silent prayers for Maeve, fingers pressed to the windows of the NICU.

What I'd felt before her birth, my insecurities, self-loathing, and hurt—they weren't cured by those days. But the sense of perspective I felt when we were allowed to take her home certainly helped. Everything else seemed so unimportant, so inconsequential, after I'd bargained with God and offered my life for hers. I'd do that again in a heartbeat—and it was that love that made me set my baggage down.

Have I forgiven myself for my part in my mother's death? Not entirely. But I have reached the point where I recognize I might've been the knife, but I wasn't the hand.

I look forward now, not back, trusting that life is made in the living of it, through both the good and the bad. And that love is made in the doing of it. And if Matt's love has taught me anything, it's that you don't love someone for their perfection. You love them in spite of everything they're not.

It's a lesson that's been hard to learn, and I guess I'm still learning it. There are moments when old patterns creep back in. Sometimes when we argue—and we do argue, because we're not perfect—I can feel myself closing off. Drawing away. But then I remember it's just a moment. An experience. It doesn't mean it's the end of us. That I have to go it alone.

And when he tells me he loves me, I remind myself I'm worth his love.

"You gonna read that or what?"

"What? Oh, yeah." I glance down at Letty's phone. *And the online edition of a newspaper?* A gossip column, judging from the byline.

A Little Bird Told Us . . .

Gather round, little cluckers. Let us bow our heads and reflect.

Stop all texts and close down email,

Silence the notifications on your phone.

Our time, our opportunities, have passed.

Bring out the mourners, for he is gone . . .

From the market, at least.

"What the . . ." I glance up. Letty is smiling a real smile now. "What is this? Reads like really bad funeral poetry. Who died?"

"Read the rest." She puts her fingers to her mouth as though to suppress the chuckle that makes the flowers in her hair tremble anyway. "It's hilarious, I promise."

So eyes down, I scroll.

It's a sad day indeed for London's single gals, as the last of the Maven Inc. bachelors is no more.

"No more . . ." I murmur, lifting my head to scan the crowd below.

"Don't worry—they're all there. Present and accounted for." Letty sounds so amused right now. "None of them have fallen off the terrace and suffered a terrible death on the rocks below. At least, I haven't pushed them," she adds, all wide-eyed innocence.

"Let's try to keep it that way. I'd like to keep your brother around for the next fifty years or so." A subtle thrill shimmers through me.

"Read the rest," Letty demands.

So I glance back and read a little more.

The dark-haired and mysterious Matías Romero is to be married this morning, so we've heard.

"What in tarnation?" I say unironically as I hand back her phone. "Is this for real?"

"I knew he wouldn't have mentioned it! I'd like to say he's a dark horse, but personally, I think he's more like a donkey."

"Flattering!" I laugh a little. I mean, he does have that ass.

"There's no accounting for taste, no offense," she adds with a grin. "But the thirsty ladies of London are really into him. You should read some of the comments—they're a hoot!"

"He has a fan club?"

"Yeah, but he's last on the list of three. Which, to my mind, makes him the equivalent of the weird-looking, slightly bruised melon left in the produce aisle."

"Not nice, Letty," I playfully chastise. This family's love language is torturing each other. And I am here for it!

"Weird how they think he's a catch."

I've opened my mouth to respond—to defend my man's honor—when the sound of his voice makes us both turn.

"I am a catch."

I get a little excited hitch in my chest when our eyes meet. *Hello there, handsome.*

He stands, framed by the terrace doors, so suave in his wedding suit of pale, lightweight linen. A matching vest skims his trim waist, and his white shirt is open at the neck, his face tan and his hair a little long. *The perfect length for fastening my fingers in.*

His boutonniere is in honor of our daughter. *Maeve, the queen of roses.* And in his hand, he's holding . . . a folded newspaper?

"You, a catch?" Letty's dismissive snort breaks the spell between us. For some reason, she mimes reeling in an invisible fishing rod. "Like an auld boot when you're expecting a rainbow trout."

"I feel like I'm missing something," he says, sounding mildly confused.

"I was just showing Ryan your fan club news. We haven't gotten to the comments yet."

"What?"

"That stupid column—the one that's been chasing you Maven boys."

"Not me," he scoffs. "They were only ever interested in the posh two."

"Like you haven't been stopped in the street for a selfie!" she says as she moves toward the doors.

"Did that really happen?" I ask, delighted by the exchange—and the reveal. *Because our love language also might include a little teasing.* Aside from the teasing that goes on in the bedroom. Though technically, that might be edging.

"That happened once," he mutters, his brows pulling down. And the blades of his cheekbones turning a tiny bit pink. *I love it!*

"Yeah, yeah," Letty retorts. "I'll see you downstairs?" she adds, sliding me a look over her shoulder.

I nod, and she presses a quick kiss to her brother's cheek. Then she's gone.

"Who knew I was marrying a celebrity?" I purr, absolutely ready to get some mileage out of this.

"I think you'll find it's the other way around," Matt says as he comes closer, unfolding a copy of *The Financial Times*, unmistakable due to its pink pages.

"Where did you get that?" And more to the point, what's this about?

"Oliver. He and Evie thought you might like to read it." They both flew in this morning.

"I'm not sure today is the day for . . ." That's as far as I get as he widens the pages to a picture—of me. My corporate headshot. "Did you know about this?" But Matt is already shaking his head. And smiling, so I guess it must be good news. "*New Kid on the Block*," I say, reading the headline aloud. "Might've been worse. They might've said *girl*."

"Try *powerhouse*," he says, a playful smile tugging at his lips.

"I'm not sure about that." But the compliment still feels like a warm hug. I quickly scan the rest of the article and read out the good parts. "*Socially responsible private equity fund has bumper start.*"

"And so it has. Thanks to you."

"To us," I whisper.

Because in the cutthroat world of investing, Maven Inc. is diversifying. While the fund recently began to channel some of its energies into investments with social causes (thanks to Evie and Mila's good influence), they now have a new division to do that for them. Headed up by yours truly.

It's been a learning curve, but it turns out that my instincts are transferrable. Instead of looking to investment purely on potential profit margin, I now examine what good that investment will also bring to the world. We have a new era of investors too. Those whose motives are impact-driven wealth, individuals looking to aid substantial social and environmental change. While also getting rich off the back of those changes.

"Did you read the quote from the director of investment solutions?" Matt asks, his next smile huge and proud. "In case you've forgotten, that would be you."

"I'm never gonna forget that." Because my role is perfect. It feels like it was made for me. I guess it was. *It fits me like a glove.*

"And you know what they say, behind every great woman . . ."

"Is a man reminding her she's left her phone on the breakfast table?" Because I have been affected by the dreaded baby brain. It's been a small price to pay as, between us, we strive to support each other, striking a near-perfect work-life balance.

Matt and I work together. We live together. We take care of our child together. And we thrive together. I can't wait to see what the next fifty years have in store for us. *Together.*

"Inky fingers!" I give a little squeal as I slap Matt's hands away. He drops the paper and moves toward me. "You'll ruin my dress before we even make it to the altar."

"Not if you take it off," he purrs oh so suggestively.

"Do you know how long it took Letty to fasten me into this thing? See these," I say, turning around to flash the row of tiny silk-covered buttons at him. I give a sharp intake of breath as his lips find my shoulder and his hands my breasts. My dress is light and flowing and fit for a princess, though fitted at the bodice a little like a serving wench's dress. *So I can't really blame him . . .*

"I won't have the patience to unfasten them all tonight." His voice is low and velvety, his mouth at my ear. "I might just need to *rip* the fabric."

"The silk," I whisper as his mouth lays claim to my neck. "Maybe I won't have the patience to wait until tonight."

"Fuck it," he says, bending me forward over the ornate railing.

"We can't," I say—laugh—as I twist my head over my shoulder. "Not when everyone is waiting for us."

"Let them wait." His gaze flicks to the garden, and his expression changes from simmering lust to love.

I glance around myself, my heart warm as I see our friends and family assembling on either side of an aisle bordered with flowers. Matt's brothers and sisters move to take their seats; Catherine, my wonderful mother-in-law-to-be, already in hers. Maeve sits on her lap as Antonio, her lelo (Clo said she's happy to share him), makes our darling giggle by hiding and peeking from behind his hands. It's so wild how much Matt looks like him.

"Look at her." His whisper is a soft puff of air against my neck, his arms tightening around my middle. "She's so perfect. I know it sounds silly, maybe," he says with an emotional swallow. "But thank you."

Such sincerity. Such love.

But from her blue eyes to her easy temperament, Maeve is all Romero. It's funny how, my whole pregnancy, I said I was carrying a daughter, and Matt maintained our bump was a boy.

Somehow, the universe manifested both of our plans. And so much more.

Five things I can see.

I'm not stressed or overwhelmed but rejoicing.

I see mountains and lakes. Our home from home. Our family and their love as I watch them down below.

Four things I can hear.

The chink of champagne glasses ready to toast. Matt's brothers' teasing jeers. Our daughter's infectious giggle and the sound of Matt's soft puff of laughter in my ear.

Three things I can touch.

The iron rail beneath my fingers, old and strong. How our love will be at the end of our journey. Matt's strong arms around me and, always, his love.

Two things I can smell.

My man's cologne and the hint of whiskey on his breath as I turn.

One thing to taste.

Now and for always, my lips on his.

"There's no need for thanks," I say, pulling away from our kiss. Touching him. Loving him. "You saved me." When he opens his mouth to protest, I press my finger there. "Come on, it's time."

"Yeah?" One elegant eyebrow lifts.

"Yeah. I have a date with the best thing to ever come out of Manhattan."

"Zeppole?" he asks with a quirk to his head.

"With my darling white knight."

And he was worth every penny.

ACKNOWLEDGEMENTS

First and foremost, I'd like to thank anyone who has ever taken a chance on one of my books. Years in, it still blows my mind that there are people on the other side. Readers, no less! My kind of people. Thanks for making my days, my weeks, my months, and my years with your reviews and your kind words. I'm humbled and so very grateful for your support.

I'd like to thank Lindsey Faber, Sammia Hamer, Annie S., and Anna B. for helping make this book what it is. Lindsey, I appreciate your deft touch, and I've never loved the editing process quite so much! And my thanks to Annie and Anna for their eagle eyes and perfect suggestions.

My thanks always to my little crew. To Lisa, Elizabeth, and Michelle, you're all amazing. And to the Lambs, thanks for being there.

And to Tee, the best author bestie.

And finally, thanks to my family for putting up with my vague looks and (at times) monosyllabic answers. To my amazing kids, thanks for letting me steal all your good lines (cue dastardly laughter here), and to M for the endless cups of tea, for putting up with the writing ogre, and for your love.

Turn the page to see a preview of Donna Alam's book *The Gamble*!

I bet he's a really good kisser . . .

Of course he's a good kisser. With a mouth like that, how could he be anything else? Not that I've had that pleasure, and not that I think a kiss is the reason he's brought me into this room.

I wish I had lips like his, full and soft looking. I imagine kissing him would be just like kissing a girl. Better even, because that one time I kissed Jenny Sullivan at camp didn't exactly rock my world.

"I tried to explain, Lavender, but it's like he wasn't listening."

I sway a little to the muted sound of the music playing in the other room. I ordinarily hate house parties, but this house is in Chelsea, and they're serving champagne, not warm beer in disposable cups. The guests are dressed like it's a debutante ball, in fancy frocks and evening suits. And the party pills on offer are being passed around on silver trays. *Not that party pills are my thing.*

Anyway, Tod asked me to come with him tonight, and he's pretty good at talking me into things I don't want to do. But if nothing else, it's a networking experience. Rich people enjoy investing in art, and I enjoy selling it to them.

"Then he said it wasn't his problem," he continues, throwing up his hands in a gesture of futility.

"Really?" I tilt my head as though engrossed. I suppose I am, but more with the shapes his mouth makes than the sounds. *His voice can be a bit whiny.* He makes shapes with his hands as he talks too. I've never found a man's fingers so intriguing. They're kind of stubby, I suppose, but those calloused tips make me shiver with the slightest brush.

Or they would if he ever touched me.

I don't even mind the paint that collects under his fingernails. *Much.* And dirty fingernails usually give me the biggest ick.

"Please tell me you understand." He makes puppy dog eyes at me, which is annoying, given he's not a Labrador. "There wasn't anything else I could do."

One of these days, I'm going to get that mouth to kiss me and those hands to touch me, and then—

"Say something. Please."

"Of course." I place my champagne flute back on the table, my spiked heels echoing as I take a couple of hip-swaying steps closer. "Of course I understand."

One day, he'll notice the silken swish of my dress and the toned length of my thigh through the long slit.

"Oh, thank God." The words rush out, and when he smiles, it warms my insides like a mouthful of good booze. "You're just the best, Ned."

I almost grimace. It's not the cutest of pet names, but I suppose it's cuter than Lav. I hate it when my brothers call me that. It's so undignified being referred to as a toilet.

"So you'll go speak with him?"

"Absolutely." I dust my hands across Tod's shoulders, and when he lifts his chin, I adjust the angle of his dickey bow.

"I don't mind telling you, I've never met anyone as frightening as him. Well," he adds as his eyes dart down, "apart from you."

"I'm not frightening," I murmur.

"Lavender, you're my best friend, but you're fucking terrifying. Or at least, I used to think so."

"Silly." His boyish smile curves into my palm as I cup his cheek. *Friends.* Ours will be a love born of this friendship. I just know that Tod will one day glance across the breakfast table, and like a bolt of lightning, he'll realize I'm the only woman he needs in his life. Then we'll sail off into the sunset, like some real-life Barbie and her Ken.

"I meant it as a compliment."

I make a noise. Such high praise.

"But you'll need to be scary because I told him you were good for it."

"Oh, I'm up for it. I mean, good for it."

"Great!" He claps one hand on my shoulder, as though the solid action might fortify me. Meanwhile, I get a little lost staring into his lovely eyes. "Ned?"

No, I *do not* like being referred to as one-half of a pantomime donkey.

"Are you listening?"

"Sorry." I give myself an internal shake. "Who do I need to frighten again?"

"Deveraux." His expression falters. "Raif Deveraux?"

The corners of my mouth twitch. "Sounds like something out of a movie. The name's Deveraux. Raif Deveraux," I intone deeply, borrowing from the 007 movies. "That's not a real name."

"That really is his name."

"Yeah, and mine's Felicity Tugwell," I splutter, coming up with my Bond girl alter ego on the fly. God, I crack myself up sometimes.

"You mean you've never heard of him?"

"Should I have?" I eye Tod critically. "Have you been helping yourself to the party pills?"

He makes an exasperated noise. "Everyone knows about Deveraux. He owns most of the clubs in London, plus a bunch of hotels. And remember when I went to Ibiza last year and told you about that club with the two-thousand-euro table service? Well, that club is his. He owns half the island, people say. And a chunk of Marbella!"

I shrug. How would I know any of that, let alone be interested? My party days are well behind me.

"I thought everyone knew about him."

"Obviously not."

"The man is as rich as Midas and has more intrigue than . . . Machiavelli!"

"Then he has a very unfortunate name. It doesn't sound the least bit threatening."

"Not threaten—were you even listening to me?"

"Of course I was. I'm just saying his name is more suited to a hero in a historical romance. He doesn't sound like someone you should be terrified of."

"Well, I am." With a groan, Tod swings away and rakes his hands through his hair, dramatic soul that he is. I take myself back to the champagne and tip a little more from the bottle into my glass.

"Come on, Tod. You know what I mean. Some luscious-locked dark-haired Fabio type, all rippling muscles and loincloth." I take a quick sip, warming to my theme. "Or even better, buckskins and shiny leather hessian boots."

This is the perfect intro for Tod to tease me about my reading choices. But he doesn't. Instead, when I turn around, he seems to be genuinely distressed.

"He's going to kill me. He'll probably use my head to serve overpriced cocktails in."

"Don't be ridiculous."

"Ned, I owe him big."

"Big what?"

His shoulders slump. "Money. I owe him money. While you were networking, I got into a game of poker."

"But you don't gamble."

"I know!"

"More to the point, you don't have any money *to* gamble."

He pulls a face as though I've rubbed a sore point. Poker? I thought he'd left me to schmooze while he'd snuck off to fumble in a dark corner with some silly girl.

"Start from the beginning." My tone sounds weary as I perch my bum on the edge of a leather Chesterfield sofa.

"When I left you talking to that finance bro, I wandered into a back room where a game was going on. Deveraux was there, and I found myself staring at him because, well, because I've never seen him in real life. And never without a gorgeous girl hanging off his arm."

I fake gag. "Another Eurotrash playboy. Just what the world needs."

"I don't know where he's from. He's got a weird accent. Anyway, he asked if I wanted to buy in, and because I didn't want to look like a total weirdo, standing there staring at him, I said yes."

"You've only been gone an hour. How bad can it be?"

"Very bad." His lids flutter, and he swallows audibly. "I bet everything."

I resist the urge to shrug. Everything when you have nothing probably seems like a lot. Tod currently lives with me—he's a roommate who doesn't pay rent, rather than the one you split your utilities with. He uses my hot water, eats my fridge contents, and drinks my wine, and has done little else since he wandered into Whit & With, my art gallery, and charmed me into showing some of his work. I'm always loaning him money, which he says he'll pay back with his next commission, though he never does.

He thinks he's doing me a huge favor by doing a few shifts as a gallery assistant each week rather than the other way around, because I do actually pay him.

I ignore the unhappy poking sensation at my temple. If the gallery doesn't break even soon, I think my brother Leif might cut his losses. Leif, or Whit, as he prefers, is my not-so-silent partner. Without him, I wouldn't have a business. But he's a banker, not a charity.

Maybe I should've asked Whit to give Tod money lessons, because he's hopeless with the stuff. He's also hopeless with appointments. And the passing of time. The unloading of the dishwasher and adulting in general. It's his artistic temperament, I suppose. When his muse strikes him, everything else in his life seems to gray out.

"I suppose I can loan you what you need," I say, sighing resignedly.

"No, you can't."

"It's not like it would be the first time." Ignoring his frown, I carry on. "Come on. How much are we talking about? A few hundred?" Tod says nothing. "A thousand. A few thousand?" I suppose I can manage that much. *If I pull out my emergency credit card.*

But Tod shakes his head.

"More?" Damn. I'll need to ask one of my brothers. Obviously not Whit. My eldest brother has more money than God, but he's not one to part with it willy-nilly. Not that I blame him, I suppose.

"Worse than that," Tod says, morose. Jesus, is he about to cry?

"Not more than five figures. Tod?"

"That's what I've been trying to tell you. I didn't think I'd gotten in so deep. I almost passed out when I realized I had, but then, I had this amazing hand—a winning hand. The only problem was, I had nothing left to play with. But then I told him about you. And I said . . ."

"You said what?" I demand.

"That you were good for it."

"I hope you didn't say it that way." My words take on a warning tone.

"What? Oh. No."

"Because *that* would be less than flattering," I add, not ready to release my frown. "And while I know nothing about poker, I do know we wouldn't be having this conversation if your hand was *that* amazing."

"I had four of a kind, but Raif—"

"So you lost."

"Had a straight flush . . ." he finishes, his voice small. "I've got to pay up. I told him I'd come and find you. And he said, 'Good.'"

"Good?"

"Because I thought I would find you, and we could leave before he realized."

"You thought we could leave because you can't pay him?"

"Yes. Sort of. But he sent his thugs with me and they're standing outside the door."

"Tod, is this some kind of joke?"

"It's bad. Really bad—"

"You're telling me!"

"—because he doesn't want your money. He wants you."

ABOUT THE AUTHOR

Donna Alam is a #7 Amazon Kindle Store and *USA Today* bestselling author. A writer of love stories with heart, humor, and heat, she aspires to sprinkle a little joy into the lives of her readers. When not bashing away at her keyboard, Alam can often be found hiding from her responsibilities with a book in her hand and a mop of a dog at her feet.

Follow the Author on Amazon

If you enjoyed this book, follow Donna Alam on Amazon to be notified when the author releases a new book!
To do this, please follow these instructions:

Desktop:

1) Search for the author's name on Amazon or in the Amazon App.
2) Click on the author's name to arrive on their Amazon page.
3) Click the 'Follow' button.

Mobile and Tablet:

1) Search for the author's name on Amazon or in the Amazon App.
2) Click on one of the author's books.
3) Click on the author's name to arrive on the their Amazon page.

Kindle eReader und Kindle App:

If you enjoyed this book on a Kindle eReader or in the Kindle App, you will find the author 'Follow' button after the last page.